Praise for
King's Ransom

"For those who love stories of faith and courage, *King's Ransom* is a must-read. In a time when our world suffers under the blight of unreasoning hatred, this little known chapter in history yields unforgettable lessons."
— OLIVER L. NORTH, LtCol USMC (Ret.), best-selling author
of *Mission Compromised* and *Jericho Sanction*

"Like a rich tapestry done in vivid colors, *King's Ransom* weaves twentieth-century history and heart-stopping intrigue into an intricate pattern that delights the eye and engages the imagination. The authors guide us through the Bulgarian culture and countryside with deft hands, never allowing historical detail to overshadow the powerful story or the carefully drawn characters, who truly come alive on the page. A masterful work!"
— LIZ CURTIS HIGGS, best-selling author of *Thorn in My Heart*

"Steeped in historical accuracy, *King's Ransom* rivets our hearts with true stories of previously unsung heroes. Their song has found our own time and place, thanks to the keen research of Jan Beazely and Thom Lemmons. A mesmeric read about a period in history when the lines between evil and good blurred, this story shows how honor and love triumphed in this forgotten kingdom of hidden heroes."
— ANNE DE GRAAF, Christy Award–winning author
of *Into the Nevernight*

"*King's Ransom* is, in a word, wonderful. It's well written, rich with historical detail, populated with vibrant characters, and deft in illustrating the struggles of both the Bulgarian Jews during World War II and the gentiles who helped them. Highly recommended!"
— SYLVIA BAMBOLA, author of *Refiner's Fire, Tears in a Bottle,*
and *Waters of Marah*

A NOVEL BASED ON A TRUE STORY

KING'S RANSOM

JAN BEAZELY & THOM LEMMONS

WATERBROOK
PRESS

KING'S RANSOM
PUBLISHED BY WATERBROOK PRESS
2375 Telstar Drive, Suite 160
Colorado Springs, Colorado 80920
A division of Random House, Inc.

ISBN 1-57856-778-5

Library of Congress Cataloging-in-Publication Data
Beazely, Jan.
    King's ransom / Jan Beazely and Thom Lemmons.— 1st ed.
        p. cm.
    ISBN 1-57856-778-5
    1. Boris III, Czar of Bulgaria, 1894–1943—Fiction. 2. Holocaust, Jewish (1939–1945)—Bulgaria—Fiction. 3. World War, 1939–1945—Bulgaria—Fiction. 4. Bulgaria—History—1878–1944—Fiction. 5. Jews—Bulgaria—Fiction. I. Lemmons, Thom. II. Title.
    PS3602.E264K56 2004
    813'.6—dc22

                                2004011474

Printed in the United States of America
2004—First Edition

10 9 8 7 6 5 4 3 2 1

To my children,
Heather, Jessica, and Austin,
with the prayer that they might live in a world
where hatred is an endangered species

—Thom

PREFACE

Though based on historical events, this is a work of fiction. Except for certain recognizable historical characters, any similarity to persons living or dead is purely coincidental.

ACKNOWLEDGMENTS

We could not have completed this work without the gracious assistance of Stephane Groueff and Radka Groueva, who personally lived through the times and witnessed many of the events depicted in this story. Their personal reminiscences of their father, Pavel Grouev, were of immeasurable value.

Dr. Bozhin Pandurov—"Doc" to those of us who know and love him—was our guide, translator, and consultant *extraordinaire* on historical matters pertaining to Bulgaria.

Additionally, the histories of Stephane Groueff (*Crown of Thorns* [Lanham, MD: Madison, 1987]) and Michael Bar-Zohar (*Beyond Hitler's Grasp* [Avon, MA: Adams Media, 1998]) became our bible as we sought to reconstruct the troubled era covered in this novel. For the reader interested in more of the historical detail surrounding the events of Tsar Boris's reign and the rescue of the Bulgarian Jews, these two books are essential reading.

Any errors or inaccuracies in this novel are the authors' own and are in no way the fault of any person or resource listed above.

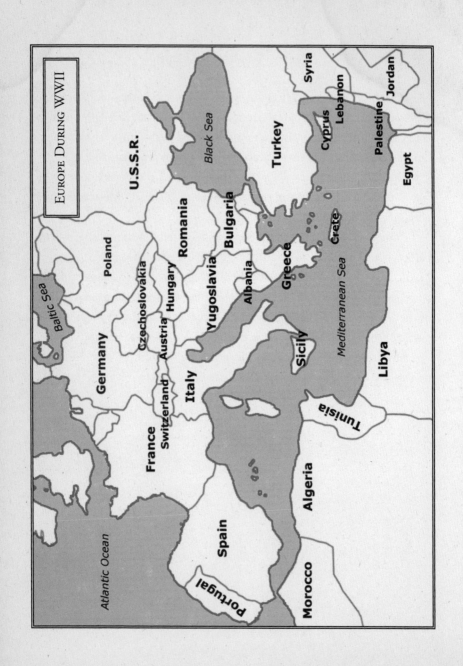

Europe During WWII

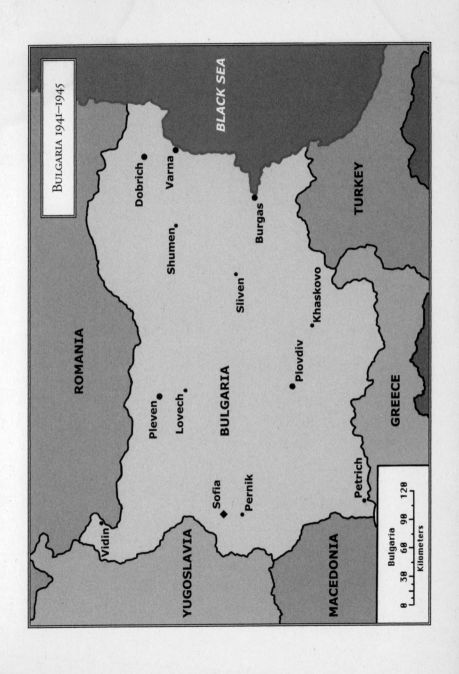

BULGARIA 1941–1945

BLACK SEA

ROMANIA

Vidin

Pleven

Lovech

Sofia

Pernik

BULGARIA

Dobrich

Varna

Shumen

Burgas

Sliven

Plovdiv

Khaskovo

Petrich

TURKEY

GREECE

YUGOSLAVIA

MACEDONIA

Bulgaria

Kilometers

0   30   60   90   120

Prologue: Sofia, May 1996

Dobri thought maybe the crush of the crowd would kill him. *What a thing that would be: to live through everything I've witnessed, only to be trampled to death.*

Someone touched his arm, a youngish fellow wearing a dark blue Italian suit and no tie. He was pointing toward the gilt domes of Alexander Nevsky Cathedral. "When his plane lands, they'll radio ahead, and the bells will start ringing to announce him."

The young man's hair was mussed, and Dobri was pretty sure he could smell *rakia* on his breath. He had probably used Simeon's imminent arrival as an excuse for an all-day party.

"What if someone tries to stop him?" Dobri said.

"What do you mean?"

Poor young man. You could never guess, could you? "The secret police. You don't think they want him here, do you?"

The young man laughed. "Look around you, *dyado*. Even Communists aren't crazy enough to try anything today. Simeon is bulletproof."

"Don't call me 'grandfather.' And don't talk to me like I'm Bai Ganio. I may be from a village, but I know how the world works."

The young man shrugged, held up his hands in surrender, grinned at Dobri, and sifted back into the crowd.

Dobri had never seen such a solid mass of humanity. Alexander Battenberg Square was an unbroken sea of people from the monument all the way to the Presidential Palace. The plaza around the cathedral was packed shoulder to shoulder. The buildings rose up like reefs out of the human tide, and every window was crammed with faces. Everyone waving, everyone shouting. All of them waiting.

Dobri wasn't sure whether they were waiting for the beginning of something or the end of something. He had lived too long, seen too many good things end before their time and too many bad things begin. In his home village, beginnings and endings were easier to know. The sun came up, and you knew it was time to drive the sheep out for grazing. The mornings got warmer, and it was time to start thinking about the spring shearing. The faces were always people you knew; the greetings and farewells marked the familiar boundaries of the days. Life made sense.

But here in Sofia's tangled streets there was nothing to see but the faces of strangers everywhere, and the tall buildings blocked out the comforting signposts of mountain, tree, and sky. Dobri hated crowds; they made him edgy and shy footed, like a herd of goats when the weather was changing. They reminded him of the old days, the weight of his responsibilities. A crowd could hide trouble from watchful eyes until it was too late. Dobri hoped Simeon had good men around him. He'd need them today.

Dobri wished he could find a way out of this dense uproar. He closed his eyes and imagined he was listening to the breeze sift through the *zdravetz* blossoming on the hillsides above his village. He clutched the staff he had carved from a good, straight bough of beech. He leaned on it, trying to take some of the strain off his back. It was a long walk, all the way from Bailovo. He wished he could sit somewhere and rest. But in this mob, he might as well be wishing for dew from the moon. *Ah, Lord, I'm too old for this. Couldn't I have just sent someone? I'm a fool, coming all the way here to give Simeon something he probably doesn't want, surely doesn't need. How can I ever get close enough to see him, let alone give him the staff or say anything to him? Dobri Dimitrov, you are a crazy old man, and that's the whole of it.*

But no. It wouldn't do, and he knew it. Whether this was an ending or a beginning, he had a part to play, and he had to see it through. There was nothing else to be done.

A man near Dobri had a picture of Simeon. He had fastened it to a long pole so he could carry the portrait above the crowd. Dobri had seen the pictures in the newspapers, of course. But still he was struck by the way Simeon reminded him of Tsar Boris. It wasn't so much his appearance; Simeon's features were more like his mother's. It was something about the expression in his eyes, maybe; the way Simeon seemed to look out and see the duty before him. Even in exile, Dobri guessed, Simeon could never forget his country.

When the widowed queen had left with her two young children, Simeon had been barely nine years old. Dobri's last memory of him framed the frightened face of a child hurrying into the darkness with his mother and sister toward the car that would drive them from Vrana to the station, to the train that would carry them in secrecy out of the country, out of the grasp of the Communists. Looking at the portrait on the pole, Dobri could still see the tender eyes of the child. The years had added layers of complexity; that was certain. But he thought he could still trace the outlines of the child within the man.

An old woman pushed through the crowd toward the portrait on the pole. In one hand she grasped a bunch of roses, and she began brushing them across the image of Simeon, as if in blessing. In a creaky, high voice she sang the first few words of the "Mnogoya Leta": "Grant, O Lord, many years to Thy servant, the king…" An impromptu choir formed, people with their arms across each other's shoulders, swaying and singing. Dobri wanted to sing, but instead he scanned the crowd for signs of the Communist secret police. Things were supposed to be different since 1989, but…

Or maybe the young man in the Italian suit was right. Maybe today was a day for joy, not suspicion. Everywhere around Dobri, people were smiling. Not far away, a father had his daughter on his shoulders, bouncing her up and down. The little girl, who looked to be no more than eight or so, held on to her father's head and screamed with laughter. People were waving bottles of wine, toasting each other and Simeon—and spilling a good deal in the process. It looked like the Feast of Kyril and Methodie in Bailovo, only much bigger. How could that be? These city people couldn't possibly know each other. But maybe today, because of their anticipation, they thought they did. They knew this one thing they shared, maybe, and that was enough for today.

Under the entrance portico of the Royal Palace—National Art Museum, Dobri corrected himself—there was a man with a worried look. As Dobri watched, the man put a hand to his ear and started speaking, apparently to no one. Nobody around the man seemed to notice, but Dobri knew. He took another, more careful look at his surroundings. There—in the circular drive in front of the National Bank. And there—on the pediment of one of the monuments in the park across the square. More worried men talking to themselves. Quickly Dobri scanned the rooftops around him. No sign of activity.

Maybe it's nothing. I was trained to see threats before they exist; maybe they won't come to pass—today, at least. Lord God, may it be so… Dobri crossed himself. Besides, what could he do? He was an old man with long white hair and a beard to match, wearing the homespun cloak and rough breeches of a peasant. He carried nothing but a hand-carved staff. Who was going to listen to him?

Ah, Daria, my dear one. How I wish you could have seen this day with me.

The bells of Alexander Nevsky clanged, and the noise of the crowd, loud before, now grew deafening. In between the huge peals of Nevsky, Dobri could hear the other churches joining in the chorus: Sveta Nedelia, to the east, and the Russian Church, closer to where he stood. And over it all, the cavernous booming of Nevsky. Dobri looked at the church, piled huge and white in the bright day like a confection fashioned by God himself, the gold domes gleaming like crowns in the sunlight. *So. Simeon has returned to his native soil at last. But will Bulgaria recognize the gifts he brings? Or will his nation use him up as it did his father?*

The group around the portrait on the pole had begun again the "Mnogoya Leta," redoubled in volume. This time, Dobri crossed himself and joined in.

"Grant, O Lord, many years to Thy servant, the king…"

2

Sofia: September 1940

King Boris waved to the cheering crowds. He backed slowly off the palace balcony, still waving and smiling, and nodded to the guards on either side, who closed the French doors. He turned and strode toward the main stairway.

"I had no idea so many of the people knew the words to the 'Mnogoya Leta,'" he said to Pavel Grouev, walking beside him. "Those who weren't singing 'Shoomi Maritza' were belting out that old hymn at the top of their lungs."

"This is a great day, Your Majesty," said the portly Grouev. "You have brought the Dobrudja back to Bulgaria. Surely you can understand their enthusiasm."

"Well, a pact with the devil ought to be good for something."

The older man's eyes whisked around at those accompanying them.

"Don't worry, Pavel," the king said. "The German diplomats left by train this morning. They're probably already across the Yugoslav border, tossing down schnapps in their club car and celebrating this latest propaganda coup for the Fuehrer."

"There are other ears, Your Majesty."

Boris smiled at his chief of cabinet. "Always looking over your shoulder on my behalf, aren't you, Bacho Pavlé? At any rate, this little land gift from Berlin ought to pacify our prime minister and interior minister for a while."

"To have the farms and grazing lands of the Dobrudja as part of Bulgaria again will help the economy," Grouev said, "and good news on the economic front is long overdue. Still, Filov and Gabrovski will not be content until you sign a formal treaty."

The king said nothing more until the two of them had entered Grouev's bottom-floor office and closed the door. When he faced Grouev, the king's smile was gone. "We walk a tightrope, Pavel, with Hitler and Stalin holding the ends. Anger either of them, and…" He gave a sad chuckle and ran a hand across his bald scalp. "Isn't it ironic? My wife is pro-Italian, my army and ministers are pro-German, and the majority of my people are pro-Russian. I think perhaps only I am pro-Bulgarian."

"These are complicated times, Your Majesty."

Boris scooped a folder off Grouev's desk and began leafing through it. "What have we heard from the British lately?"

"The same as always; they urge caution in your dealings with Berlin and insist Hitler cannot win, in the long run."

"I'm interested in surviving the short run."

"Earle came to see me again yesterday."

"Anything new from Roosevelt?"

Grouev shook his head. "They keep on saying they will never allow Great Britain to fall. They want to use our ports on the Black Sea."

"Easy for them to ask. They have an ocean between themselves and Hitler."

"They aren't at war, Your Majesty."

"And how long do you think that can last?"

Grouev shrugged. "You should probably consult with the Ministry of War as to when our troops should begin occupation of the Dobrudja—"

"Don't try to change the subject. Chernov will send our boys east whenever we tell him. What do you think the Americans will do?"

Grouev puffed out his cheeks. He peered up at the plaster ceiling for several seconds and then looked directly at Boris. "They will not play the go-between, Your Majesty. Ultimately, I don't believe they intend to negotiate with Hitler. I believe they intend to fight him."

Boris looked away. "Then Europe will be engulfed. And what will become of our poor little country? When giants wrestle, everything around them gets smashed."

The young man's body was absurdly light in his arms. When the life has gone out, not much is left, *he thought. But the blood still dripped everywhere, draining in sticky, thickening rivulets from the bullet-riddled corpse. He had the vague notion that it was wrong to bring such a mess into his father's rooms, but he knew it was necessary. Surely even Le Monarque would understand, once he saw…*

"What are you doing?" his father shouted. He was sitting on his Louis XIV couch, polishing his medals. He looked enraged. "Why have you brought this into my house?"

"This is one of our brave young men, Your Majesty," Boris replied. "He died fighting for Bulgaria, on your orders. He was killed by the French, coming up from Salonika."

"What does that have to do with me?" King Ferdinand said. "He was a soldier. Dying is what soldiers do."

"But Your Majesty… Father…"

"Get out of here, you weakling! You aren't fit to be king! You aren't even fit to be Bulgarian!"

Boris began weeping. He had to leave, but his feet were suddenly as heavy as blocks of cement. He was afraid to look down at the body, because he knew what he would see.

Boris's eyes snapped open. He saw the gilded moldings on the ceiling of his chamber and heard a bird singing outside his window. He took a deep breath and willed the dream images to fade from his mind. He sat up and pulled back the bedclothes. He needed to clear his head. He needed to take a drive.

He put on a dressing gown and stepped into his slippers on the way to the door. Opening the door slightly, he said, "Have the garage get the Packard ready to drive. And please find out if the queen is going to Vrana today."

"Yes, Your Majesty." The guard's footsteps clicked away down the marble corridor.

Boris put on a plain woolen touring outfit and grabbed his favorite gray fedora. He ate a light breakfast of white cheese, toast, and fruit. On his way past the winter garden, he was pleased to see the children already up, dressed, and at their studies. As soon as Simeon saw him, he dashed into his father's arms. Maria-Louisa followed more slowly, as usual, playing the disciplined older sister.

"Papa, where you go? Take me!" the three-year-old Simeon said.

"Now, Son. You have your lessons. Is Mother taking you to Vrana when she goes today, do you know?"

"Yes, she said so," Maria-Louisa answered. "She told us we were leaving after our lessons were finished this afternoon."

"Well then. You must do as your mother says. And I'll see you both there this evening." He hugged the children, then stood and gave the teacher a smile.

When he arrived at the garage, he turned to the guard who had followed him from the palace. "Um, Dimitrov, isn't it? Dobri Dimitrov?"

"Yes, Your Majesty. At your service."

"Thank you, Dobri. But today I think I'll go by myself. I'd just like some time alone with my thoughts."

The guard's expression wavered. "Your Majesty, I—"

"I understand, Corporal Dimitrov, and I appreciate your concern. But today...I'm afraid I must insist."

The guard hesitated, then snapped to attention. "As you wish, Your Majesty."

"Thank you, Dobri. Please inform the queen that I'll join her at Vrana early this evening, won't you?"

"Yes, Your Majesty."

Boris acknowledged the guard's salute, smiled and nodded at the garage attendant who held the open door of the Packard, and got in behind the wheel.

He drove south, over the west flank of Mount Vitosha, toward Dupnitza. But instead of stopping in the town, he drove on, finally turning off the highway on the small road that led into the mountains above the village of Rila. Maybe he would walk in the quiet colonnades of the monastery or, better yet, in the natural cathedral of the surrounding wooded hillsides. He needed to hear the rushing of the Struma River. He needed to smell the damp leaves on the forest floor.

October was near; the trees at the higher elevations would be starting to drop their foliage. Boris loved to watch the yellow and orange leaves fluttering to the ground. They put him in mind of butterflies performing some exquisite funeral dance: spinning toward the ground in one final, beautiful spiral.

He wanted to listen to the quiet voice of his land, let it slowly drown out the clashing demands of politicians and generals. Just for a while, he wanted to imagine he was only a man, not a king. He wanted to purchase the illusion of solitude, to surround himself with something real and immense. He wanted to be in a place that welcomed him without requiring him.

The final ascent to the monastery was a stretch of road curving gently through an arbor of stately beeches. It was like entering a portico in God's own house. Was the grove a way into the monastery, or was it the other way around? Boris could never decide. On his left, the columns of beech marched up the slope, and to his right dropped the steep, wooded gorge where the Struma ran, low and quiet from summer's long spending of the Rila snow mass. In the spring it would be a rowdy froth. And the canopy would cast a tender, greening light on the forest floor beneath, unlike the quiet stretch of gold and ochre that now draped the drowsy land. Boris preferred the autumn for some reason. Perhaps it better matched his mood.

As the stone walls of the monastery loomed nearer, the only other vehicle in view was a donkey cart; the tethered beast had its nose in a patch of late clover.

Boris paused in the entry and allowed his hand to rest on one of the old stones framing the archway. He tried to imagine Saint Ivan of Rila standing in this same spot a thousand years before, drawing on a strength that ran as deep as the bones of the mountains all around.

He went into the courtyard. A few monks moved along the porticoed walkways. Boris crossed to the cathedral. At the doorway he took off his hat, made the sign of the cross, then went inside. The smell of the incense settled over him like a comfortable old sweater. He took a five-leva note out of his wallet and put it in the tray beside the stacked beeswax tapers. He picked up two tapers and went to the nearest altar. He lit one taper and placed it in the lower tray in memory of his departed mother. The other candle was for the tray above. He had intended this second one for his father, but as he began to light it, he realized he was thinking not of *Le Monarque,* serving an indignant exile in his house at Saxe-Coburg, but of the peasant whose donkey was tethered outside the front gate of the monastery.

This faceless Bulgarian had driven up the road, maybe from Rila, maybe from Boboshevo, maybe from someplace too small to have a name. It was not an easy journey, along rutted mountain roads. He would have had to allow a whole day to get here and another to return, most likely. He would have brought some small gift for the monks, to show proper respect—a piece of lace his wife had tatted, a pail of apples he had gathered. He might seek a blessing for an ailing parent or ask a priest's advice about some personal matter. Maybe he would sit for a while in the sun of the courtyard or get a drink from the monastery fountain, its water still cold from the snows in the peaks. Then he would walk back out to the cart, untie the donkey, and point toward home.

What did such a man know of treaties and statecraft? Was there anything in his days to remind him of the existence of places like Berlin or London or Tokyo? Why should the doings of potentates in countries halfway around the world be of any concern to him?

And yet, as Boris held the wick of his taper to the flame, then pressed its base into the wet sand of the upper tray, he found himself praying for this Bulgarian whose name he didn't know, begging the Almighty to save him from the conflagration gathering on the horizon.

"Don't you want your change, Your Majesty?"

Boris turned around and saw the old, stooped priest holding the five-leva bill he had put in the tray.

"Father Ilarion! I hoped I might see you today."

He kissed the hand of the black-robed monk and acknowledged his bow.

"Five leva is a lot, even for candles as fine as ours," Ilarion said.

"I thought you might take the difference and buy yourself some teeth."

"What for? I've already outlived my taste buds. One mush is pretty much like another. What do you hear from young Stefan?"

"His Eminence is as incorrigible as ever. On Saturday he's singing in the cafés, and on Sunday he's preaching them all into hell."

Ilarion shook his head. "How he ever got to be metropolitan…"

"Best we don't know, Father. And besides, the people love him."

"Who wouldn't? Stefan is a one-man show." The old monk turned to put the five-leva note back in the collection box. He half turned his face toward Boris. "He writes me of disturbing developments in the Sobranje, Your Majesty."

Boris clenched his jaw and studied the floor at his feet. "I see Metropolitan Stefan has been making free with his billets-doux again." He tried a chuckle, but it wasn't too successful. "I thought, here at least, worldly problems were kept out."

"The problems of the world are the problems of God's children. Our mission is to care for all the sheep of his pasture. Especially in this place."

"What can I do, Father? Right now, every Bulgarian is praising Germany as our benefactor, the Great Power that helped us get back the Dobrudja. Towns are naming streets after Hitler and Mussolini."

"Still, Your Majesty, that alone does not justify everything Germany would have us do."

"I know!" Boris's voice rang through the vaults of the church. He looked up at the frescoed central dome and passed a hand over his eyes. "I know, Father," he said in a quieter voice. "But I'm in no position…at least not now."

"Can you get the votes in the Sobranje to block it?"

"I don't know. Punev and some of the other journalists have caught the scent and are pillorying Gabrovski and Filov in the newspapers. I'm sure the Holy Synod will do what it can to mobilize the people. And Tzankov is trying to form a voting bloc with some of the opposition deputies. But"—he shook his head—"Gabrovski and his Germanophiles have a strong hand right now. And with Uncle Ivan leaning on our northern border, nobody wants to look like a Communist lover." He peered at the old monk. "Do you know what Lenin did to the churches when the Bolsheviks took power?"

"The Bulgarian Communists are hardly as—"

"Things happen in wartime, Father." Boris pulled in a deep breath; his shoulders sagged. "Things no one could ever imagine."

Ilarion laid a hand on the king's arm. "Come outside, my son. Let's walk awhile."

The day was bright, the sky such a solid blue it seemed to Boris he could dig his fingers into it. But from the angle of the shadows across the stone pavement, he knew he couldn't stay much longer. "I'm sorry, Father Ilarion. I shouldn't burden you with matters of state."

"People come here to talk, my son. I hear many things, all day long— things people think they can't say to anyone else."

"My lips to God's ears, then?"

"Exactly."

"I wish you'd speak to your sovereign. Put in a good word for me."

The monk's eyes twinkled at him. "Why don't you speak for yourself?"

Boris stood beside the Packard with his hands on his hips. He looked at the decrepit bridge and cursed under his breath. He should have known better than to allow himself some side errand after leaving the monastery. And he had promised Giovanna he would be home this evening.

Balan had told him about the little valley with the stand of odd-looking junipers—possibly a new subspecies. He had wasted all this time finding the place, and now he couldn't even get to it.

"That old bridge will never hold your car, sonny."

Boris turned around. An old woman had come along the road—more a rutted path, really—he had followed from the Rila highway to this dead end. She was using a mulberry stick for a staff, and a lop-eared dog trotted at her heels.

"Good afternoon, *babo*. It looks as if I can go no farther this way. I wonder, can you tell me the quickest way back to the Rila road?"

"For a ride home, I'd be glad to guide you."

Boris smiled and gave her a small bow. He opened the passenger door and motioned her inside.

The old woman turned to her dog. "Go home, Leto. You don't need to ride in this gentleman's nice car." To Boris's amusement, the dog wheeled and trotted off to the northeast. Its form was soon lost behind a plum thicket.

"Which way?" Boris asked when he had closed the driver's door. "Or should I just follow Leto?"

The old woman chuckled. "Turn around and go that way, just to the left of that big beech. The Rila road is about two miles farther on."

They reached the road and, soon after, the outskirts of Rila village. "There is my house, on the right, where the checkered cloth hangs from the arbor."

Boris pulled to the side of the road in front of the old woman's cottage. She opened her door, then turned back to him. "Please, come in. I should at least offer you some bread in exchange for driving me."

Boris resisted the urge to glance at his wrist watch. He smiled and nodded, setting the Packard's parking brake.

"I am Anna Serenkova," the old woman said as she tugged open the weather-beaten door of her home. "I've lived here all my life. Where are your people from?"

Boris removed his hat and stooped beneath the low doorframe. "I am… from Sofia."

"Well, Mr. Sofia, sit down. I'll get us a bite to eat."

Boris sat at the small, stained pine table. The table and its two chairs were the only furniture in the room. The walls had been whitewashed at some time, and here and there photographs were tacked into the plaster. Beside the front door was an icon, a reproduction printed on cardboard of the Blessed Virgin of Pazardjik. Another low door presumably led to a sleeping room.

Anna Serenkova clumped a heavy plate and a saltcellar onto the table. The plate contained half a loaf of white bread.

"All I can offer you to drink is water," she said.

"That's quite all right." Boris tore a hunk of bread from the loaf and sprinkled it with a little salt. Just then, the door opened. Boris turned to see a young man in the uniform of the Bulgarian army removing his hat and coat as he closed the door behind him.

"Hello, Mother. Sorry to be late, but I—Holy Saint Ivan!"

The young man stiffened to attention and snapped off a regulation salute. "Permission to remain, Your Majesty!"

Boris stood and returned the salute. "Permission granted, ah, Private Serenkov. Please, this is your mother's house. Come and sit down."

Anna Serenkova gasped and fell to her knees, crossing herself over and over. "Oh, Tsar Boris! Please forgive me! I didn't recognize you. I am a silly old woman to speak to you as if you were no more than some—"

"My dear woman. You must believe that no offense was taken. After all, you guided me safely back to the road. Please, seat yourself."

As soon as he decently could, Boris excused himself from the company of Anna Serenkova and her son. He drove away from the house, waving at his hosts. They stood at the side of the road, returning his wave until the descending curve into Rila hid them from sight.

3

Daria hated evenings when King Boris was late; while Queen Giovanna struggled to control her nerves, Daria was the one who became frazzled. The queen could maintain her cool, composed exterior with everyone else—even the children—but Daria saw the twitch in her fingers, the smile reined in just a bit too tightly, and she knew. Sometimes the pressure of helping the queen perpetrate the facade was almost too much. After all these years, she had no illusions about her mistress. Queen Giovanna was royal, but she was also Italian, after all. How much restraint was really healthy for the soul?

The evening was cool; Daria wished she had thrown on a sweater before going out to the guard post. She clasped her elbows and found herself wondering if Corporal Dimitrov would be on duty at Vrana tonight. Hoping, really, if she was honest with herself.

Daria, you have no business thinking like that, you postema ragazza. Why would you want to love a soldier just when the whole world is getting ready for war? Besides, how do you know he doesn't already have a sweetheart? And maybe he doesn't like Jewish girls.

Daria thought about Paolo. Every girl at the orphanage had made calf eyes at the dark-haired, laughing boy who brought fresh milk to the kitchen door of the *nonni* every morning. Every one of them worshiped at the dark altar of his charms. And Paolo knew—oh yes, he knew. He flirted, he blew kisses, and then with the casual cruelty of an invincible boy, he drove away in his little goat cart without so much as a backward glance, leaving them all sighing for his return the next day.

One day, not too long before Princess Giovanna's governess had taken Daria away to the great house in Tuscany where she would enter the service of the royal family, Daria had convinced herself it was time to say something to Paolo. It was her week to work in the kitchen—Friday of that week. She had spent the first five days in an agony of trepidation, and today's sunset brought the Sabbath. The next time Paolo was here another girl would have taken her place, and it was now or never. She heard the tinkling bells on his goats' collars and the taut clatter of the full tin jugs. She heard the clear reach of his voice, still not deepened to a man's, singing out in the lane: *"Latte, signori! Latte fresca!"*

The old cook was reaching for the door latch. "I'll go, Nonna Samuela," Daria said, rushing at the latch before the cook could object. She went outside, watching as Paolo lifted a jug from his cart down to the ground.

He turned and looked at her, and the words she had prepared so carefully were now completely forgotten. His lips opened in a grin, and Daria was melted by the splendor of his lovely mouth, his strong, even teeth. He tossed a lock of hair out of his eyes, and she forgot to breathe.

Now, stupida! Before he leaves!

With her heart loping like a colt, she walked over to the jug. She took hold of the handles, then looked full in Paolo's face.

"I can sew, Paolo. I'll make you a cap, if you like."

There. Her shameless proposition was out in the light of day.

Paolo gave her a surprised look, and his smile widened. Daria thought she was going to die from ecstasy. *He likes me! Paolo likes me, and he will let me make him a cap.*

"What? You think I want a stinking skullcap like the kike boys wear?" And he laughed at her as he turned away to mount his cart. He was still laughing as he drove away.

It was her first heartbreak. After she had been in the royal family's service for five years or so, she learned, while accompanying Princess Giovanna and her mother on a visit to the orphanage, that one of the girls there had had a baby by Paolo. An old man and his wife now brought the orphanage its milk, the *nonni* told them.

Daria knocked on the door of the guards' hut. It opened a handbreadth, and a man's face was there.

"The queen wants to know if you've heard from His Majesty."

"No, nothing yet."

Oh, Your Majesty—

The guard started to shut the door.

"Wait. Who was the last to see him before he left this morning?"

The man's face turned away from the door. She could hear the intonation of his question, but not its exact words.

"Corporal Dimitrov says he drove the Packard away from the garage at about eight thirty."

"Alone?"

"Yes, Miss Richetti. The corporal says he went alone. It was his wish."

Of course. Why on earth, especially after that ambush in the Araba-Konak Pass all those years ago, does he still insist on going out by himself?

"May I please speak directly to Corporal Dimitrov?"

The guard pulled a face. "Miss Richetti, we're very busy—"

"And Her Majesty is very worried."

She heard the rattle of a phone. The guard's face disappeared. There was murmuring inside the guardhouse. The soldier was back.

"It's all right, Miss Richetti. That was the detail at the front gate. His Majesty just turned off the highway. He'll be here in a minute."

Daria closed her eyes and drew a deep breath. A few seconds later the edges of the guardhouse yellowed in the oncoming headlights. She heard the low rumbling of the Packard sedan's engine. The men in the guardhouse scrambled outside and formed a rank, saluting their sovereign as he drove past. She watched the taillights until they were out of sight around a curve in the driveway. Breathing a prayer of thanks, she began walking back toward the house.

"Aren't you cold, Miss Richetti?"

She turned around. Corporal Dimitrov was looking at her. In the light leaking through the guardhouse's open door it was hard to tell, but Daria thought the lower lip visible below the full, brushy mustache was turned up in a slight smile.

"I'm…fine, Corporal Dimitrov. Thank you. Just fine. I'll…be going now…Corporal Dimitrov."

"Yes, Miss Richetti." His face was a light-colored blur in the darkness; his eyes were pools of shadow. Was he secretly laughing at her? "Please give my warmest greetings to Her Majesty," he said. "And tell her I'm sorry for her worry."

"Yes, Corporal Dimitrov, I will."

Why do I keep saying his entire name?

"Well, good night, then," he said. He went into the guardhouse, then turned back toward her in the doorway. "Next time you come to visit, you might bring a jacket."

She couldn't think of anything to say, so she shrugged.

He nodded toward her as he closed the door.

Daria's feet crunched on the gravel of the driveway as she walked away. *"Postema ragazza,"* she chanted with every step. *"Postema ragazza, postema ragazza, postema ragazza…"*

Liliana Panitza felt cold inside, and she knew the feeling had nothing to do with the fall breezes sifting down onto Sofia through the Balkan passes. She looked again at the pages Alexander had given her to transcribe: twelve sheets of plain paper, covered front and back with neat columns of his handwriting—columns of names.

Jewish names.

Alexander was different since this summer, since returning from Berlin. Lily could tell it in the way he spoke to the other workers in the office. She could tell it by his increasing impatience with people who didn't agree with him. And most of all she could tell it in the way he held her at night—or didn't, as was more and more the case these days.

Lily had vague misgivings about the way she was living. Each Sunday during her childhood, her mother took her to Mass at the little church near their house in Varna. She listened to the sermons; she lit candles to the saints and dutifully said the prayers the priests taught them to say. And at first, after she moved to the excitement and bustle of Sofia, she still kept the old ways. She went to church at Sveta Nedelia or Alexander Nevsky and repeated her prayers. She tried to listen to the sermons.

But something started to change. The churches in Sofia were bigger— maybe that was it. The icons of the saints, so splendid with gold and silver, were farther away. The Bible lessons frescoed on the walls and domed ceilings were higher, more distant from her eyes. The people around her at Mass were not old Bunin, the broom maker, nor Baba Radkova, who swept the steps of the city hall and taught old songs to neighborhood children. No, the people around her now were strangers. They didn't know her name or the names of her relatives. What did they care what she did or where she went?

And then she met Alexander Belev.

She could hardly believe her good fortune, getting a job as a typist in one of the government offices in the center of the city. And then, about a week after beginning her employment there, the dashing Undersecretary Belev had handed her a sheaf of notes to transcribe. Their eyes had met, and for the next three days Lily Panitza could scarcely think of anything else. A few days later he asked her to join him for dinner. Two weeks later Lily moved into his apartment.

But lately Alexander had become increasingly distracted. Even when they were alone at night, he could scarcely talk about anything but work. Sometimes when he was making love to her, Lily could swear he was composing memos in his head.

These were great days, he said. A New Europe was taking shape, and Bulgaria had to be on the forefront of developments, he said. The modern state had to be concerned with the integrity of its populace; undesirable elements had to be closely controlled—or neutralized. The principles of scientific development had to be brought to bear on Bulgarian society in order for the nation to take its place in the New Europe. Bulgaria was like a farmer's field: to remain healthy, it had to be carefully tended and constantly weeded.

The girl at the desk across the room—Damonova, wasn't it? Simone Damonova?—was staring at Lily. From the corner of her eye, Lily could see her gawking. Lily kept her eyes on the list Alexander had given her. She reached for a pencil and pretended to make notations here and there.

Why didn't the hussy mind her own business? Or had someone asked her to keep an eye on Lily? Was a dossier being compiled? *10:15 a.m.: Subject spent a long time staring into space after A. Belev handed her a document. Seemed to be anxious...* That was how it sometimes worked, Alexander had told her. A whisper here, a rumor there, and funding appeared or evaporated. Careers waxed and waned; players circled each other cautiously, waiting for a false move or a miscalculation. Secretariats fell out of favor. Ministries changed hands, all based on the shifting sands of political favor and temporary advantage.

Lily didn't understand politics. It all sounded so important and inevitable when Alexander explained it. And Lily couldn't deny that Interior Minister Gabrovski certainly seemed to take an interest in Alexander's work; since Alexander's return from Berlin, the two men had conferred nearly every day.

Lily had typed large parts of the initial drafts of the legislation Gabrovski had presented to the Sobranje last month. Much of it she didn't begin to comprehend. But those things she understood troubled her greatly: Jews had to go to local government offices and register themselves and their property; Bulgarians could no longer adopt Jewish orphans; Jews could not vote or run for office; they were henceforth barred from military duty; the number of Jews allowed to attend colleges and professional schools was to be limited; Jews could not intermarry with non-Jews...

And now this list of names. Clearly something sinister was taking place within the Ministry of the Interior, and Alexander was deeply involved.

Damonova got up from her desk and flounced across the room, taking care to walk her hip-swinging walk past Alexander's open doorway. Had she tossed a smirk at Lily, just before turning down the hallway toward the rest room? Lily hated her.

Lily thought about the Jewish people she knew. Simon Levi certainly didn't seem like a danger to Bulgaria. He went to work each day at his law office and went home each night to his family. Dr. Benaroya, her gynecologist, was one of the kindest and most professional men she had ever known. Was his name somewhere on this list she was supposed to type?

She needed to talk to someone—but who? She had to be careful. Even in her short time here, Lily had seen how quickly circumstances could change for those who found themselves stranded by a political ebb tide. No one would think twice about ridding the office of a typist who stirred up trouble. Even Alexander would be unable to save her—if indeed he would want to.

How Lily wished she had a friend, someone with whom she could unburden herself, someone who could listen, keep her secrets, and, above all, help her think through the puzzle of what to do. Not for the first time, she felt a pang of regret that she had met Alexander so soon after moving here. He took up all the space in her life that could have been used for other things.

Damonova was coming back, straightening her skirt. Lily stared at Alexander's list as if it were the most fascinating thing ever put on paper, as if it contained the secret to her health and happiness. She picked up another stray piece of paper from her desk and laid it alongside the list, peering from one to the other as if making a painstaking comparison between the two. Damonova was coming closer. She stood in front of Lily's desk. What on earth could the stupid girl want? Lily let her shift from one foot to another for a few seconds, then looked up.

"Sorry, I didn't know you were standing there."

Damonova had her hands on her hips, like some trollop from a Preslav hay farm.

"Lily, I just wondered if you wanted to go to lunch with me. We could go by that new dress shop on the way—"

"Oh, thank you, no. I brought a sandwich to eat at my desk. I've just got so much to do."

Damonova gave a sly glance over her shoulder, toward Alexander's doorway. "Yes, I see. Well, maybe another time." She pranced back to her desk. Lily wished she would trip and fall on her face.

Lily reached into her desk drawer and took out two sheets of clean paper. She wound them onto the platen on her typewriter and settled Alexander's list in front of her. She started to type. And then she had an idea. There was someone, maybe, someone she could entrust with part of her burden at least. Someone who might even be in a position to do something. Yes…

The typed columns crawled down her paper, but Lily was forming a plan.

"The vegetables at this stall look better than those, Anna. And be sure to get a basket of the kale, especially. Her Majesty specifically requested it."

"Yes, Miss Richetti."

"And tell Liudmil to bring the car down to the other end of the park. We'll load everything from there."

Anna nodded and walked away between the food stalls. Daria looked at her lists one more time. There wouldn't be many more opportunities for the fresh market this late in the fall. They could have whatever they wanted whenever they wanted it, of course, if Tsar Boris weren't so careful about ostentation. "I am the king of a poor country. Why should I have oranges flown in from Africa in January when my people are eating nothing but bread and cheese?" He was a good man, and Daria loved him, of course. But his stands on principle could come at rather inconvenient times.

Daria heard a voice behind her—a man speaking German. He wore a diplomatic badge, and Daria realized he was one of the entourage Tsar Boris had received at dinner in the palace the night before. He stood at one of the stalls that displayed carvings and other folk crafts, and he was haggling—good-naturedly, it appeared—with the proprietor, an old man bearing a scar across his face that half closed one eye. The German was holding a set of nesting dolls. Probably for a daughter back in Berlin. He pointed and gestured, holding out three fingers, and the old man smiled and shook his head, holding up four. The age-old debate between buyer and seller. They were speaking the same language, whether they realized it or not.

Since September there had been German emissaries in the palace almost nonstop. Queen Giovanna had told Daria that the Fuehrer was hoping the goodwill generated by the return of the Dobrudja would persuade King Boris that Bulgaria's fate lay with Germany. Even Mussolini was in on the act, the queen said, issuing veiled invitations for Bulgaria to aid his stalled offensive in Greece and hinting that Thrace and Macedonia might be available for restoration to Bulgaria in exchange for military cooperation. "As if Thrace and Macedonia were his to give," she said. Queen Giovanna's voice took on an ugly edge when she talked about the Italian dictator. Instead of Il Duce, she sometimes called him *Il Danno*—"Danger"—or even *Il Diabolico*.

Daria felt uneasy around the Germans. Though the Third Reich gave out the public impression of civilized gentility, other bits of information were sometimes heard: dark, disturbing reports of things that had happened since *Kristallnacht,* almost two years ago now. It was clear that Hitler's regime was openly, officially hostile toward Jews. Daria had heard rumors that some Bulgarian Jews were trying to hire a ship to take them out of Europe altogether—to make aliyah to Palestine, in fact. It was hard to believe that Bulgarian citizens, some from families who had lived here since the time of the Caesars, would feel so unsafe in their own land. But if Germany prevailed…

It was odd when she thought about it; until the rise of the Nazi Party, Daria had hardly given her Jewishness a thought. Naturally, at the orphanage they had classes in Hebrew, and attendance at the Sabbath services was obligatory. But since joining the royal household at the age of thirteen, she had lived in a world that was largely gentile. The king and his family certainly never disrespected her heritage—they rarely took note of it. Sometimes she went with Princess Giovanna to church services in their private chapel at the house near Assisi. On Sundays when the weather was fine, she accompanied the princess or her mother on the pleasant stroll to the Basilica di San Francesco. Once or twice through the years, King Victor Emmanuel had asked Daria if she cared to attend temple on Yom Kippur or one of the other high days, but she had been largely indifferent.

Over these last few years, though, to be a European Jew was to live under a lengthening shadow. Her ancestry lay like a forgotten dream within her, but Nazi cruelties had brought it, fluttering and wary, to the forefront of her mind. In all the years since leaving the orphanage, she had grown unaccustomed to thinking much about being Jewish. But these days she could hardly think of herself any other way. As far as she knew, no one outside the palace had any idea of her ethnicity or any reason to wonder about it. But with pogroms springing up across the German sphere of influence, she was beginning to feel vulnerable.

"Daria! Daria Richetti!"

A young woman waved and hurried toward her. She was blond, attractive, and compactly built. She had her hands in her coat pockets and her face turned toward the ground, as if she felt the need to see where her feet were going. As she got nearer, Daria remembered where they had met: at the dedication of one of the queen's clinics for children, some officials of the Interior Ministry had been invited. This woman, Liliana Panitza, was there with one of the department heads. The Panitza girl was friendly and bright and also the only woman at the affair close to Daria's age. They had chatted amicably during the reception following the speeches.

"Hello, Liliana. What brings you to the market on such a cool day?"

"I was hoping to find you. I have to talk to you, Daria. You have to help."

"What do you mean?"

Liliana's eyes shifted back and forth, and Daria had the chilling impression she was afraid of being followed.

"Is there somewhere close where we can talk without being overheard?"

"What in God's name—"

"There. That bench, behind the apple seller."

The bench was under an old elm, about fifteen feet from Pirotska Street. The minaret of the Banya Bashi Mosque rose behind them. People were walking past on the sidewalk, but no one seemed to notice the two women as they settled themselves on the stone bench.

"Daria, things are happening in the Interior Ministry, and you have to warn His Majesty."

"What? I—"

"Let me finish. I don't know exactly what's being planned, but just after the Sobranje began debating the Law for the Defense of the Nation, my boss started having me type some things…"

4

November 1940

Metropolitan Stefan wadded the newspaper and flung it against the wall.

"Damned Fascists!"

"Language, Your Eminence…"

"No, I'm speaking in the biblical sense. They are damned—every one of them—for what they're doing to this country!"

"Normally one defers to God on such matters."

"It's not funny, Georgi. They'll pass that stupid law, no matter what the Holy Synod or anyone else says, and it'll be *Kristallnacht* all over again, only in Bulgaria this time."

"The newspapers seem to be taking up the cry."

"Yes, the intelligentsia can smell a rat, all right. And the unions. But that academic prig Filov won't even return my phone calls. And Gabrovski—he thinks his armpits don't sweat, he and his Ratnik hoodlums."

The churchman paced his study, hands on hips.

"Ah, Georgi, I don't know what to do. I need a drink."

Stefan poured a tumbler half-full of *slivovitza* and questioned his companion with a raised eyebrow. Getting a nod, he reached for another tumbler.

"Not so full, Your Eminence, please! I have to drive home this evening. So, Prime Minister Filov thinks he can safely ignore even the chief prelate of the Bulgarian Orthodox Church."

Stefan slumped into an armchair and propped his feet on an ottoman. He shrugged, then took a large swig from the tumbler. The plum brandy felt good sliding down his throat like cool fire.

"As long as they're marching in lockstep with Berlin, they think they're invincible," Stefan said. "Why should they listen to the church?"

"How long will our country be able to remain neutral?"

"Who knows? Germany and Russia are both plying Boris with assurances, like two men in a bar buying drinks for the same woman."

"Is that illustration going in your next sermon?"

"Depends on who's listening." Stefan took another drink. "But this business with the Jews—it frightens me, Georgi. Bulgarians ought to know better. What are there—maybe fifty thousand Jews in the whole country? And they're mostly small shop owners, subsistence farmers, artisans. They sweated out life under the Turks, just like the rest of us, all those centuries. They're our neighbors, Georgi, our friends! And now, just because Hitler thinks it's a good idea, we're supposed to make them criminals? I'm to believe that Dyado Simonov from his hole-in-the-wall cobbler shop somewhere in Yutch Bonar is plotting with the Bolsheviks to overthrow the governments of the Western world?" He shook his head and took another drink.

"Surely there won't be pogroms here. This isn't Germany, after all—"

"Don't you understand? They're making them register, Georgi! And that's just the first step: isolate them and get their names on a list. Then they'll find a reason to take away their property—national security or some such claptrap. And after that, internment camps, forced labor… I don't know. It makes me sick to think about it."

The three-engined Junkers transport lumbered to a halt near the hangar. Boris peered out the window.

"It's Ribbentrop with him this time. Give me the Order of Kyril and Methodie, Balan, and the Civil Engineers Badge. Here, help me pin them on before they open the doors."

Stanislav Balan took the requested medals from the velvet-lined case and squinted as he helped the king don the insignia of Bulgaria's two highest nonmilitary honors. The last time he had met with high-ranking German officials, the party had included the flamboyant Goering, supreme commander of the *Luftwaffe,* so Boris had worn his Air Medal. It helped break the ice.

Snow was piled beside the tarmac. Boris could see his breath feathering white in front of his face as they walked toward Hitler and his foreign minister. The Fuehrer was smiling and nodding.

"Welcome to Salzburg, Your Majesty," said the short man with the now-famous toothbrush mustache. "Thank you for coming."

"How could I refuse a ride in such a fine aircraft, Your Excellency?"

"Ah, you liked the Junkers?"

"I should say. But I was surprised that the craft was equipped with gasoline engines. I should have thought diesel would deliver more power, especially at high altitudes."

"Ah, Your Majesty, you know very well I'm not as astute a mechanical engineer as yourself. I leave all that to my designers."

Boris introduced Popov, the foreign minister, and Balan, Handjiev, and Bardarov, his aides.

"Where is Prime Minister Filov?" Ribbentrop said.

"Unfortunately, the prime minister sends his regrets. A pressing legislative matter claimed him at the last minute."

Boris thought he detected the flicker of a scowl on Hitler's face at this news, but it was quickly masked.

"Well, come along, gentlemen," Hitler said. "The cars are waiting to take us to Berchtesgaden. With a little luck, we'll be there in time for tea."

A fire was roaring up the flue of the spacious living room at Berchtesgaden. A tea service was ready, and Hitler was every bit the gracious host, plying the Bulgarians with hot tea and sweetbreads and conversing eagerly. Soon he had Popov and Balan bellowing with laughter over some anecdote involving a mule, an army private, and a farmer's daughter. Boris watched the German leader with a mixture of admiration and suspicion. Clearly, the man was both charismatic and brilliant. How else could the son of a minor bureaucrat have risen to the leadership of arguably the strongest nation on earth?

And yet there was another side to this man who had focused the attention of the world on the German nation. When surrounded by his own functionaries, Hitler could become strident, more than a little demagogic. He was less likely to charm, more likely to demand and pontificate. One heard unpleasant things about those who had disappointed this little man with the unruly lock of hair. Or more likely, one began hearing nothing at all.

Hitler came over to Boris and extended a hand toward one of the ornate doorways. "Will Your Majesty favor me with some time in private? There is much to tell and much to hear."

Here we go. Keep a tight tongue and a clear eye, my lad. "Of course, Your Excellency. It will be my pleasure."

The room they entered was cozy, but its vaulted ceiling still lent an impression of scale. A large window gave out upon a magnificent mountainscape, and the stone walls were hung with oils of rich, vibrant color. Some were European masters, and others Boris didn't recognize—several scenes from Teutonic mythology. A fire was already laid in the hearth. Hitler gestured toward a brocaded armchair on one side of the fireplace, and he seated himself across from Boris in a matching chair.

"Will there be anything else, *mein* Fuehrer?"

"No, Sergeant. Please see that we aren't disturbed."

The SS sergeant saluted, backed through the doorway, and closed the doors softly after him.

"Thank you again for coming, Your Majesty. As the leader of a great nation—and a nation that has traditionally been a great friend of the German people—you have a right to know about events that may affect you and, also important, events that are shaping the New Europe."

"I'm grateful for your consideration, Your Excellency. Indeed, the people of Bulgaria have long been friends of Germany, both in victory and defeat."

"Yes. And Germany has never forgotten that, I can assure you. But the days of defeat are behind us, Your Majesty. Our victory is inevitable. The brightest days for both our peoples are just ahead."

Hitler spent much of the next two hours detailing the successes of his armed forces. The Wehrmacht had rolled up Poland in much less than the time expected, he said. So quickly, in fact, that Britain and France were still blinking their eyes like overfed cats when the Tenth Army rolled into Warsaw. He had hoped France and England knew enough to stay out of the situation, he said, since the resolution of "the Polish question" had laid the groundwork for a lasting peace in eastern Europe, but regrettably they had declared war on Germany, and subsequent events had proved the inadvisability of such policies. The Low Countries had fallen to the blitzkrieg unleashed by his army, he said, and France and England had proved no match for the better-equipped Wehrmacht and *Luftwaffe*. "Even now, our air forces are pounding the British homeland, and our submarines are interdicting their supplies. France is neutralized, and Great Britain cannot last much longer." "Fortress Europe" would soon be a reality, he said, and peace would ensue, a peace built on the irresistible strength of Germany and its allies.

"How does Russia feel about all this?" Boris said.

Hitler looked at him strangely. For a moment Boris thought he was going to laugh. "We have agreements with Russia," he said finally. "We believe they understand it is in their best interest not to trouble us."

So. The rumors have some truth. But how long can such an unnatural alliance hold?

"I'm glad to hear that," Boris said. "As you know, Bulgaria has a great historical affinity with the Russian people."

"The people, yes. But…their leaders…"

"We keep a careful watch on Communists in Bulgaria."

"Prudent. Very prudent."

But all was not well with the military campaign, Hitler said. Mussolini's incursion into Greece was undertaken without adequate consultation, and the Italian army's lackluster performance there could not be permitted to create an opening on Germany's southern flank. "Our armies must go to his aid, Your Majesty. And to do that, we have to cross Bulgaria."

Boris said nothing for a long time. He maintained what he hoped was a calm, interested expression. Hitler seemed content to wait for his response. A coal popped softly in the fireplace. Somewhere, in another part of the house, Boris could hear the rattle of dishes.

"Some would consider our complicity an act of war," he finally said.

"All the more reason Bulgaria should declare herself openly as an ally of Germany, Italy, and Japan. With such friends, your enemies would be less inclined to be adventurous at your expense."

"Your Italian counterpart has implied that our help with Greece could improve our longstanding claims on Thrace and Macedonia."

Hitler's eyes widened. Apparently, Il Duce had not cleared the offer with his German friends.

"But I must confess, Your Excellency, geography does not favor your intentions. Surely Yugoslavia presents a more direct route to Greece for your eastern forces?"

"Yugoslavia has agreements with Greece. I don't want to have to fight my way through them to come to Mussolini's aid."

"What about Turkey? They also have an understanding with Greece, and they are on our eastern border."

"They wouldn't dream of bothering you if you signed a treaty with us."

"Possibly. Forgive me, Your Excellency, for throwing up so many objections, but Bulgaria does not have anything approaching your Wehrmacht to enforce its sovereignty. I must do my best to think of every alternative before committing to anything so dreadfully important."

He paused, but Hitler motioned for him to continue.

"Even if Bulgaria is your best path to Greece, wouldn't it be better to wait until spring? A winter campaign in the Balkans would present untold logistical difficulties, even in the most favorable circumstances. And besides, if our farmers have to worry about rationing and all the problems that arise in wartime, it could hamper our ability to provide the food supplies that could be so important to an operation in Greece. Truly, Your Excellency, while I'm most flattered by the importance you place on our support, a healthy, neutral Bulgaria is really in your best interest. We can provide at once a cushion between you and any belligerents and also a steady supply of matériel and foodstuffs."

Hitler sat very still for several seconds. Boris could see him weighing the arguments, tracing ramifications in his mind. Finally he looked up at Boris and gave him a cold little smile.

"Well of course, Your Majesty, you must do what you believe is in the best interests of your people. Germany wants to be your friend, please believe me. And also understand this." He leaned forward on the edge of his chair, and his face became very straight, very direct. "We must go to Greece in the spring at the latest. We have every desire to cross your territory peacefully. But cross it we must."

The diplomatic counteroffensive had started even before they got home; a cable was waiting for them at Vrazhdebna Airport as soon as the Junkers touched down.

"It's from the Kremlin telegraph office," Balan said. "Sent by our Russian envoy, Your Majesty."

Boris leaned back in the car seat and closed his eyes. "Read it to me."

"'Molotov urgently requests you reconsider USSR offer.' Stop. 'USSR guarantees our security upon signing mutual assistance pact.' Stop. 'Territorial claims and economic assistance a possibility.' Stop. 'Strenuous objection to German involvement.' Stop. 'Never forget historical friendship of our two countries.' It's signed by Stamenov."

"The Russians most likely knew about the Berchtesgaden meeting before our airplane was off the ground," Boris said. "Uncle Ivan is nervous. He doesn't like us getting cozy with Berlin. Odd, considering Stalin's understanding with Hitler, don't you think?"

Balan snorted. "That'll never hold. The wolf and the bear don't hunt together."

"Sobolev is probably already in Sofia," Boris said. "He's probably sitting in Filov's office, twisting his arm. Still, it's a good thing I insisted Filov stay here. If he'd been at Berchtesgaden, I doubt Hitler would have let us out of there without getting our signatures on a treaty."

Boris had the beginning twinges of a headache: a flat, intractable pain that felt like a bruise just inside his skull above the eyebrows. He closed his eyes, massaging the bridge of his nose between his thumb and index finger. He would get the palace surgeon to mix him some powders as soon as they arrived.

Spring. The Germans will be across our borders. "We want to come as friends," *Hitler had said. Half a million uniforms is a lot of friends. Too many. But what can I do? What can Bulgaria do? God, help me. Help my country.*

"Let's go, Stanislav. To the palace."

He heard Balan give the order. The car swerved and lurched as the driver merged into the traffic going west into the center of the city.

Buko Lazarov held the dried tobacco leaf to his nose. He closed his eyes and inhaled deeply.

"Ah, yes. This is good, even for Doulovo leaf. When did this arrive?"

"In yesterday's shipment."

"Where's it going?"

"Mostly to the cigarette plant in Plovdiv."

Lazarov nodded. "The last few years have been pretty good. Less trouble with fungus, especially up north." He held the leaf up to the light, then carefully rubbed it between his thumb and forefinger. "Yes, this is good. Be sure and tell Bardjiev in Plovdiv to watch the humidity levels—this leaf feels a little on the dry side. And tell him I said if he's going to blend it with Burley, make certain the Burley is completely cured. Some of those guys around Yambol get in a hurry now and then."

The other man nodded and made some notes on his clipboard. "Anything else?"

Buko shook his head. "No, I think that covers it." He looked at his watch. "I have to go, Kyril. We're having friends over tonight, and if I don't get home, my wife…" He made a face and wagged his hand. The other man laughed.

Buko walked down the steps of the Fernandes tobacco warehouse. He heard a train whistle and glanced at the depot, across the ravine and close to the top of the adjacent hillside. He looked at his watch again. Either the five fifteen was early, or he was in peril of Anka's wrath. What was his grandfather's Ladino expression? *Mujer arravyada, maldisyon de el syelo*—"an angry woman is the curse of heaven." Buko picked up the pace.

Buko Lazarov loved his job. He loved the smell of curing tobacco and the texture of the broad leaves. He loved the aroma of the leaf when it came out of the hogsheads after aging. He loved going to the fields during the growing season and talking to the farmers. He liked to debate the relative merits of different varieties, to speculate on the optimal blends. Everyone in the company recognized him as a buyer who knew his commodity from top to bottom, from seedbed to curing barn.

But mostly, Buko Lazarov loved the thick pungency of tobacco smoke and the low, lazy talk that so often accompanied it. Buko was fond of saying that he judged a country's level of civilization by the degree of its appreciation for fine tobacco. He loved nothing better than smoking with friends, maybe sitting in someone's backyard on a summer evening, usually with a bottle of wine or brandy close at hand. When the air was still and the smoke hovered above their heads like a blue blanket of contemplation, that was as good as life could get. He could stay that way for hours—until the bottle and the humidor were empty or the dawn began swallowing the starlight, whichever came first.

Of course, if this new law passed that everyone was talking about, evenings like that would be a thing of the past. Some fellow from the Jewish Central Consistory in Sofia had come out to Kyustendil and talked to the men's meeting at Buko's synagogue. He'd said the Law for the Defense of the Nation would impose a nine o'clock curfew on Jews and might even prohibit gatherings, except for religious services. It was crazy. Did they really think the Jews were enemies of the state? Hadn't Buko's father been decorated for bravery by the king, both in the First Balkan War and the Great War? There had been Lazarovs living in Kyustendil for as long as anyone could remember. Buko knew everyone; one of the local delegates to the Sobranje was an acquaintance, and the other was a childhood friend.

It was the Germans, of course. The government was bending over backward to keep Hitler happy. Not that Buko blamed them—up to a point. Getting the Dobrudja back was a major coup for Tsar Boris. And Germany was buying a huge proportion of the Bulgarian tobacco crop—Buko knew that firsthand. But was it worth it? That was the question at the back of many minds, especially Jewish minds. Buko's grandfather used to say, "When you're dancing with an ugly woman, the best part is when the music stops." But the way things were going, Buko wasn't sure Bulgaria had much choice of partners anymore.

He looked at his watch. He might make it in time to preserve himself in Anka's good graces after all. He was looking forward to the evening; he'd been saving back a special bottle of *rakia* for the occasion. His street was coming into view now. He walked a little faster.

5

Dobri Dimitrov was worried. Even by the standards of the last few months, the meeting was going badly. From his station in front of the large double doors, he could easily hear the raised voices, the angry tones. Something crucial was clearly afoot; the chief ministers had been closeted with Tsar Boris since six o'clock this evening. Just a short while ago the large clock on the second-floor landing had sounded midnight. And still, from the sound of things inside, any sort of agreement was distant.

Only four of them—Interior Minister Gabrovski, Defense Minister Daskalov, Foreign Minister Popov, and Prime Minister Filov—were with the king. During the course of his long duty tonight, Dobri had learned the tones of each man's voice: Popov generally subdued and soft-spoken, Filov droning and professorial. Daskalov seemed to be taking his cues from Filov, and Gabrovski, though prone to excited outbursts, was most often playing the accompaniment to the prime minister's theme—whatever that was.

What alarmed Dobri most were the eruptions he had heard from Tsar Boris. Twice he heard the king swear loudly, most uncommon in a meeting of state, no matter how informal. And once he was alarmed to hear, ringing above the hubbub, "I'd sooner abdicate!"

What could be dire enough to cause the king to despair of his duty to his country? Tsar Boris *was* Bulgaria. If he abandoned her, what hope could remain for any of them?

Soft footsteps brushed the marble floor. Without leaving the posture of attention, he shifted his eyes toward the sound. A figure approached down the dim hallway. He prepared to challenge the intruder, but then she spoke.

It was Daria Richetti, the queen's personal aide.

"Corporal Dimitrov, please excuse me. I know you're on duty, but the queen asked me to inquire if His Majesty is still meeting with the ministers."

She had been about to retire before being sent on her errand, he guessed; her hair had been pinned up either in haste or without much attention to detail. Wisps of chestnut brown strayed down her shoulders and framed her round, lovely face. Dobri felt an urge to reach out and brush the hair from her cheeks. How would it feel, teased gently between his fingers? *Watch out, Dobri. You're on duty.*

His eyes slid up and down the hallway. He really shouldn't violate protocol. But the tsaritza had sent her to find out, hadn't she? The poor girl needed an answer. Dobri gave her a quick nod.

"He is? Still in there?" She pointed at the closed doors.

What else do you think I meant, girl? He nodded again. If any of the boys in the squad could see him now, he'd never hear the end of it.

"I see. Well…thank you, Corporal Dimitrov." She was hugging herself in the unheated hallway. It was January, after all. For a moment she seemed about to add something but then turned and shuffled back the way she had come.

Dobri watched her go. Then he heard himself say, "You really ought to start bringing a jacket when you come to visit."

She turned her head, and forever after he would swear he could actually feel the smile she sent toward him. Then she was gone.

Fool! Are you trying to get yourself tossed in the brig?

But he realized he was smiling too.

" 'Do not mistreat an alien or oppress him, for you were aliens in Egypt.… Do not follow the crowd in doing wrong.… Have nothing to do with a false charge.… Do not oppress an alien; you yourselves know how it feels to be aliens, because you were aliens in Egypt.' Here ends the reading. In the name of the Father and the Son and the Holy Ghost, amen."

Metropolitan Stefan made the sign of the cross over the open Bible on the lectern. He closed his eyes for a moment, then looked out over the congregation gathered below him.

"My dear children, if the Holy God of Israel so commanded his people that they should consider the plight of the foreigners among them, how much more should we, his children through the blood of his Son, Jesus Christ, consider the plight of those who are our own fellow countrymen?"

Their faces upturned, they waited quietly for the next words he would speak. Stefan wondered how long it would take for a report of today's homily to reach the desk of the interior minister. Or had someone already been sent? Was one of the congregants standing below him an agent of Gabrovski? When he went back to his rooms after today's service, would men be waiting for him?

I guess I might as well give them something to work with.

"If the church of Jesus Christ stands by and merely watches the persecution of other human beings, if in this nation we allow ourselves to stomach the passage and enforcement of unjust laws, then, my children, we have become something else, and God will have to look elsewhere for a people."

Stefan watched them. He watched for frowns and averted eyes. He watched to see who might stalk out of Alexander Nevsky Cathedral and away beneath the cold skies, among the piles of soot-darkened snow shoved to the sides of the streets.

"We live in a time of choice, my beloved. We can say, 'It isn't my problem. I don't want to get involved. It's too risky.' Or, like some, we can even say, 'They've got it coming.'

"But in your heart of hearts, my dear children, you can hear the voice of God at Sinai, commanding his people to look after the welfare of the fatherless, the widow, and the foreigner. And you can choose, if you will, to listen. To help. They are not foreigners—you know this. They are your neighbors. They are your friends. They are Bulgarians, just like you, and in your heart you know what's being done to them is unjust, ungodly, and immoral."

His eyes roved the walls of the cathedral; the saints looked back at him from their icons. How patient they appeared, forever frozen in holy contemplation on the walls of the church—placid with the inevitability of their assured destinies. Whatever struggles they had faced were forgotten by the serene faces memorialized on the walls and ceiling of Nevsky. Whatever weaknesses, whatever fears had prowled their hearts in the night watches—none of them were visible in the icons. Only calm was left. Only peace.

And when the worshipers looked up at Stefan himself, standing in this gleaming marble pulpit, draped in his vestments, what did they see? Did they suspect that beneath the miter, the stole, and the sticharion was a man who struggled with the knowledge of his own inadequacies? Did they dream that the fellow standing above them would rather be somewhere else right now?

Stefan saw a figure near the edge of the nave, as close as possible to the door to still be able to hear. A short man with a wispy beard, he had thrust his hands into the pockets of a black coat. He had a round, wide-brimmed black hat pulled down low on his head. And it seemed he was hanging on every word of the sermon. Stefan didn't recognize him. Was he from the secret police? He had to force his eyes away from the man in the black coat and back to the congregation.

In his mind he heard again the concussion of the bomb in the Sveta Nedelia dome, smelled the choking dust, heard the screams of those crushed beneath the wreckage of the cathedral. It was one thing to risk injury and death for himself, but what about those who might be around him? The Bolsheviks had shown years ago how little they cared for human life. Why should the pro-German faction be any different now?

No. I must continue to speak. God, protect these innocent ones from violence. But protect me from the temptation to keep silent.

"You may ask, 'Father, how can you say these things? It's the law. It's the government.' But I say to you, my dear children: any law that unjustly takes the bread from a man's mouth and the roof from over his head is no law, but a crime. And those who pass such a law are not a government—they are brigands."

Just as he began to sing the dismissal, he noticed the short, black-clad man walking out of the cathedral. He moved quickly, like someone who had just made an important decision.

Well, I'm in the thick of it now, Lord. I hope you're satisfied.

The American seated across the desk had the bearing of a soldier and the demeanor of a statesman. William J. Donovan had his arm draped casually over the back of the leather chair in front of Boris's desk, but Boris could tell his eyes missed nothing. Why exactly was President Roosevelt's special intelligence officer in Sofia at just this moment?

"Your foreign minister painted a rather pessimistic picture for me yesterday," Donovan said. "I assured him of the ultimate victory of the Allies and reminded him of the key position Bulgaria holds in the Balkan region, and all he could say was that sometimes keys could not lock doors tightly enough."

Boris smiled. "Popov is a very cautious man. That's why I put him over foreign affairs. When you have rowdy neighbors, it's best to speak softly."

"We had a president a few years back who said something like that. He also believed in carrying a big stick."

"Ah, yes. Well, I'm afraid your Treaty of Neuilly rather shortened Bulgaria's stick."

"And Germany's. But our friend in Berlin doesn't seem to feel too obligated by treaties he doesn't like."

"Some would say that an unjust treaty ought to be abrogated."

"And some would say that invading Poland was the act of a tyrant."

"Yes. Well, I suppose you should put such questions to someone qualified to speak on Germany's behalf."

Donovan's eyes narrowed. "I may just do that, given the opportunity. But right now, with your permission, I'd like to speak about the disadvantages of becoming Germany's ally."

Boris met the American's eyes steadily and waited out the silence.

Donovan cleared his throat. "I know you're in a difficult position, Your Majesty. Your country is only now starting to dig out of the difficult economic situation following the last war."

"Thanks largely to the generous trade policies of Berlin," Boris said.

"Granted. But you must understand, sir, that Germany will not prevail in this war. We will not permit Great Britain to be defeated, nor will we permit Fascism to retain its hold upon Greece. And then where will Bulgaria be?"

"Where is Bulgaria now, Colonel? I'll tell you. She sits anxiously, with Turkish divisions massing on her eastern border and, at last report, more than six hundred thousand German troops on her northern frontier, just across the Danube in Romania. Bulgaria is watching carefully as Berlin negotiates with Yugoslavia, her neighbor to the west. Do you know how badly Yugoslavia would like to get the advantage of us, Colonel? Bulgaria listens with great respect to Russian warnings and British warnings and American warnings, yet from Germany she receives aid and friendship—real help. In 1937, when the League of Nations at last approved our long overdue requests to replace our obsolete armaments, only Germany was willing to deal with us. Neither France nor Britain showed any interest. Yes, Colonel Donovan, I'm afraid Bulgaria is indeed in a dangerous place; above all, she is fearful of being alone and surrounded by hostile nations with no expectation of aid from any quarter.

"Frankly, Colonel, I had hoped that the American government might act as mediator, to avert as much bloodshed as possible. I've been doing my best, as the leader of a small, poor nation, to play for time, hoping against hope that peace would somehow prevail. But now it seems your country is rushing to war as well. I'm afraid civilization cannot survive the coming conflict."

"The only danger to civilization is Hitler's victory," Donovan said. "He's a despot, and my government will not negotiate with him. He must be defeated. That's the only way civilization can survive."

Boris held up his hands. "I respect your opinions, Colonel. I only hope my country can endure them."

Donovan looked at him for a long time. "Correct me if I'm wrong, Your Majesty. While you won't willingly join Germany as an aggressor, you might very well acquiesce to having German troops cross your territory. You are likely to continue to provide them with matériel. You will delay as long as possible any open declaration of alliance with Germany, yet if you could—or were forced to—enter into an agreement that allowed you to be a passive, nonbelligerent collaborator, you might do so, believing such an agreement was in the best interests of your country." He tilted his face downward for a moment, then looked back at Boris. "Is that about right?"

Boris gave the American a tiny smile but said nothing for a long time. When Donovan made as if to rise, Boris cleared his throat. Donovan eased back down.

"Colonel Donovan, I have seen war. I have been in the trenches, heard the screaming of gassed men, smelled the burnt gunpowder and the stench of septic wounds. I have written more letters to bereaved parents, wives, and children than I care to remember. I have pinned medals on men whose minds died before their bodies. And I tell you this: the blood of a single Bulgarian soldier is more precious to me than the goodwill of the most powerful nation on earth—whoever that may be."

Donovan studied him for maybe ten seconds.

"I see." He nodded, more to himself than to Boris. "Well, I suppose there's not much more to be said. Thank you for seeing me, Your Majesty."

Boris stood and extended his hand. "It was my pleasure, Colonel. Please give my warmest greetings to your president." He held on to the American's hand a trifle longer, until Donovan's eyes again met his. "And please help him understand: we have no easy options here. We have only choices that are bad and those that are worse."

She was on the spiral staircase leading from the children's rooms to the third-floor passage when she felt the fear curling cold inside her chest. As often as the sensation overtook her these days, she thought she might master it, but so far, each time the darkness rose in her, it was as if she were feeling it for the first time. This dread had a sinuous quality about it; it charmed her in some perverse way, as a snake charms the bird it means to devour.

At first she thought telling Queen Giovanna would help; her royal mistress would become her ally. The burden of the fear, once shared, would become lighter.

But she had come to realize that fear was capable of rooting itself uniquely, insidiously, in each heart where it was sown. Fear crept into you, unerringly seeking the softened places, the unfenced borders.

She had listened that day in the open-air market as Lily told about her duties in the Interior Ministry: how she had typed most of the initial drafts of the Law for the Defense of the Nation from the handwritten notes of her boss, Alexander Belev. She told Daria of his trips to Berlin and the determination he seemed to draw from these junkets, the subtle ways he was changed upon his return to Sofia. Daria guessed from Lily's tone and expression that her relationship with Belev might go beyond the professional.

Lily had spoken of the frequent meetings between Belev and Gabrovski, the Germanophile minister of the interior. And she had told Daria about the lists.

Daria had listened to it all, growing colder by the moment as the horrible logic unfolded. There were many in Bulgaria who thought everything Germany did was good. Especially in these days, with the German army's seeming invincibility—not to mention the return of the Dobrudja—it was easy to find those who were more than willing to emulate all things German.

Daria had watched the queen's face as she repeated Lily Panitza's warning: "Something terrible is being planned in the Interior Ministry, something directed at the Jews." And in Queen Giovanna's eyes Daria saw the reflection of her own anxiety. This was no prattle from a silly girl trying to seize a moment of celebrity. This was a warning of dangers to come—dangers that, to judge from the queen's blanched face, her clenched jaw, might be beyond the reach of even royal intervention. The queen's reaction confirmed Daria's deepest dread.

And that dread had held Daria in its grip for at least some portion of every day since. The sinking of the decrepit *Salvador,* on its way to carry desperate Bulgarian Jews to Palestine, had only darkened her mood. And the pleasant interlude of her unintended rendezvous with Corporal Dimitrov was no more than a fleeting distraction.

Daria had never known her Jewish mother; she had died, still a child herself, during the delivery of the infant conceived in her by a son of Tuscan nobility. And now the blood of this stranger made Daria the target of anyone who believed the Nazi propaganda. Although she had served Queen Giovanna since coming of age, she was an enemy of Bulgaria—of the New Europe— because of her lineage. It was the law.

Maybe no one outside the royal family knew she was Jewish. Maybe she could simply hide from the whole thing; even Liliana Panitza had no idea, as far as Daria knew, that she was Jewish. She had come to Daria only because of her connections to the royal family.

But what if somewhere, in some ledger or on some list typed by Panitza or one of her co-workers, what if Belev was already thinking of her, planning the best way to remove her from the palace's protection? She had the urge to shut herself in some unused place, maybe at the top of the hidden staircase in the palace attic. Maybe there was a corner where she could hide out of sight of anyone who might discover her ancestry.

But no. Crown Prince Simeon and Princess Maria-Louisa were downstairs, waiting impatiently for Daria to fetch one of the old albums of their mother's family, the faded daguerreotypes and photographs of Princess Giovanna's childhood in the Italian royal court. It was a favorite game of theirs, to look at the old pictures and guess the names of their forebears. Sometimes they would make up stories about the people in the pictures. Actually, it was a favorite game of Princess Maria-Louisa's; she could usually persuade or bully her younger brother into going along. The children were waiting for her, and Daria couldn't let this chilling dread cause her to disappoint them.

She went to the closet where the dusty books were kept. She collected one of the albums covered in dark leather with the coat of arms of the Italian royal family tooled into the front. Then, just for a change, she pulled down another album from the section devoted to King Boris and his family.

She struggled down the twisting stairs, cradling the heavy albums in the crook of one arm and holding on to the rail with her other hand. She reached the bottom floor and leaned against the door camouflaged in a wall panel on the outside. She crossed the large foyer at the foot of the marble staircase, guarded by ornamental iron balustrades, that provided the public access to the second and third floors of the royal family's wing. Her heels made a crisp clicking sound on the marble parquet, laid in alternating ocher and white tiles. She went into the winter garden, where the crown prince and his sister were riding tricycles in mad races across the stone floor. Maria-Louisa, more daring than her brother, swerved in and out between the huge clay pots holding the miniature palms and other tropical plants that made this room a refuge during the cold season. Daria had to smile. The princess's legs were almost too long for the tricycle; her knees barely missed the handlebars as she pedaled.

"Your Royal Highnesses! I have the picture books!"

The children converged on her, and for an instant Daria thought she would be run down. But the tricycles skidded to a halt, and the two children were soon bouncing in front of her, holding out their hands. "Me first! Me first!"

She herded them to a corner near the fountain and a group of wicker chairs with cushions and footstools. The crown prince grabbed one of the stools and dragged it near the chair where Daria had seated herself and arranged the albums in her lap. Princess Maria-Louisa slid onto the arm of Daria's chair, leaning into her and reaching for the cover of the Italian album.

"No, Your Highness. This one first, all right?"

Daria opened the album of Tsar Boris's family. The first picture was of Boris's father, King Ferdinand. But it was a pose Daria had not seen: King Ferdinand was sitting with one knee crossed over another, on a veranda or perhaps a balcony. He was wearing a summer suit and a Panama hat. His smartly groomed beard and mustache were dark, rather than the speckled gray Daria remembered, and he hadn't yet gained the heaviness his later years had brought him. He sat in a wicker chair surrounded by overhanging palm fronds—apparently someplace in a warm climate. Seated across from him was a woman about his same age—not Eleonore, the German noblewoman he had married after the death of his first wife. No, this had to be Maria-Louisa of Parma, the woman who had borne Ferdinand his four children. Standing behind the couple, her hand resting on the back of Maria-Louisa's chair, was Clémentine d'Orléans, Ferdinand's mother—a she-dragon, from what Daria had heard.

"Is that my grandmother—my real one?" Princess Maria-Louisa said.

"Yes, Your Highness. She was your father's mother. You're named for her." Maria-Louisa nodded. "Was she pretty?"

"Well, you can see her. What do you think?"

"I think she is."

"I think so too. And do you know who this man is?"

"*Le Monarque,*" Prince Simeon said, putting a chubby finger on the seated figure. "'The Ruler,' Papa said."

"Very good, Your Highness. And this older woman?"

"Is she a maid?"

Daria laughed. "Oh no, Your Highness. And from what I've heard of her, she'd be more than a little put out to hear herself called such. No, that's your great-grandmother, Princess Clémentine d'Orléans."

"Her father was the king of France?"

"Yes, Princess. The last one."

"Why don't they have a king in France anymore?"

"Well…a lot of people thought they could decide things better for themselves than the king. So…they changed the rules, and they didn't need a king anymore."

"What happened to him?"

"He moved to England, I think."

"Just like our grandfather moved back to Germany," Princess Maria-Louisa said.

"Yes."

"Mother told me once that some people were angry at Grandfather, and that's why he had to leave, why he had to let Father become king."

"Yes, Princess. That's the way I understand it."

"They were angry at Grandfather because of the war."

"The war was very terrible. Many Bulgarians died."

"Are we going to have another war, Mademoiselle Daria?"

What shall I tell her? What are these children able to hear?

"Your father is working very hard to keep Bulgaria out of the war, Your Highness. He is a very clever man. I...I think everything will be all right." Daria swallowed hard, willing herself not to allow her sudden panic to show on her face.

Crown Prince Simeon was studying the picture of his grandfather. For a child not yet four years old, he had the most serious expression Daria had ever seen. He looked up at her.

"Grandpa have to go?"

"Yes, Your Highness."

"Great-grandma's papa have to go?"

Daria nodded.

Simeon's eyes suddenly shimmered with tears. "Papa have to go?"

Daria pulled the little boy into her lap. "Oh no, my dear. Your father is a very good king, and his people love him very much. He is staying. I know he is."

The three of them stayed that way, holding each other, for a long time.

6

March 1941

There was a knock on the door. Boris looked up. "Yes?"

Dobri Dimitrov stood at attention in the doorway. "Your Majesty, the prime minister is here to see you."

"Yes, Corporal. Please send him in at once."

Bogdan Filov hurried into the room, removing his hat. He bowed. "Your Majesty."

"Your Excellency. Please sit down."

Filov was graying but still vigorous. His mustache was dark and luxuriant, framing thick, deeply pigmented lips. Though at first glance he appeared rotund, Filov was solidly built, and his years outdoors on various archaeological digs had left him with a ruddy complexion that persisted, even when his career began to take him more often to the lecture hall than the field. His hands, though perfectly manicured, were square and scarred; they might almost have belonged to a village tradesman. But Bogdan Filov was a man of great erudition; he spoke several modern languages and could read a few ancient ones.

Boris found the prime minister an interesting study. He had no political experience and admitted no such aspirations prior to being appointed minister of education under the previous prime minister, Kiosseivanov. But he was shrewd and a quick learner, and when Kiosseivanov overstepped his bounds one time too many, the king decided to require his resignation in favor of the increasingly adept academician, Filov.

"The signing went very well, Your Majesty," Filov said as he removed his gloves and stuffed them in the pocket of his gray overcoat. "The Fuehrer expressed deep satisfaction at Bulgaria's joining. If I may be permitted to say, Your Majesty's hesitancy about the pact does not appear to have harmed our interests." He chuckled. "He was in such a good mood, he took seconds of dessert at the dinner following the signing."

"I'm glad to hear it, Your Excellency. And our stipulation about the non-involvement of our troops?"

"Ribbentrop gave me assurances."

"Yugoslavia?"

"That was interesting. First of all, Ribbentrop seems confident that Prince Paul will soon sign the pact. Then, at dinner that evening, Hitler told me that if Yugoslavia made a false move, he would crush it without mercy. It seemed an odd thing to say about a prospective ally, but perhaps he has knowledge I don't possess. Then he said that any eventual revision of borders should be settled to Bulgaria's advantage. He even suggested resurfacing our claims regarding Macedonia."

"Did he?"

Filov nodded. "And in any case, now that we've signed before Belgrade, I don't think we have to worry any longer about them driving a wedge between us and Berlin."

"True enough, I suppose."

"Hitler said Germany's industrial base had an insurmountable lead on Britain, and even if the Americans become involved, he believes it will be at least three years before their production can reach significant levels. By then, he says, it won't matter."

Boris stroked his mustache. *So he has already written off the Americans. I question—*

"And Ribbentrop gave me this."

Boris watched as Filov reached into the inside pocket of his overcoat and withdrew a long, white envelope. The prime minister unfolded a document from the envelope and laid it—a little ceremoniously—on the king's desk. Boris gave him a quizzical look, then picked up the letter and began reading. He had scanned about half the first page before he looked up in surprise.

"They will recognize Bulgaria's claim to an Aegean outlet when postwar boundaries are settled?"

Filov nodded, smiling. "At last. We'll have access to both the Black and

Aegean seas. But Ribbentrop stressed this must be kept silent until after the war."

"I should say. And the war is far from won, whatever the Fuehrer may think."

"Not that again! Your Majesty, with all due respect, Foreign Minister Popov's pessimism about a German victory is quite—"

"I am capable of making up my own mind, Mr. Filov. However, we are now signatories to a treaty with Germany and its allies, so such prognostications are moot, at least at the moment." *Especially since Field Marshal List's divisions have already crossed the Danube and will reach Sofia tomorrow.*

Filov had a chastened expression. "I'm sorry, Your Majesty. I intended no disrespect. I thought after our last meeting that you were convinced of the advantages of this alliance."

"Of its unavoidability, perhaps, Your Excellency. Whether history will prove it ultimately advantageous…only God knows."

Dobri shook his head in disbelief. He handed the newspaper back to Yevtich. "Incredible. In less than two weeks, the German army has reduced Yugoslavia to rubble."

"Looks like Hitler didn't take too kindly to Simovitch declining Berlin's invitation."

"He should've gone along, like Prince Paul."

"Some people can't take a joke, I guess. But it looks like Tsar Boris backed the right horse."

Dobri looked at Yevtich. "Tsar Boris kept us out of Hitler's gun sights, Yevtich. That's what he set out to do, and that's what he did. If General Simovitch had cared as much about the Yugoslav people as Tsar Boris does about Bulgaria, he would've never rejected the treaty already signed by his own regent."

Yevtich took a drag on his cigarette. "I don't know, Corporal. Sometimes you have to fight. I don't like these Jewish laws the Sobranje is cramming down our throats, and everybody knows it's all because of the Germans. The price of not having Hitler's tanks in our streets is turning over our Jews to him. I've got Jewish friends, and they're scared."

"If we had fought, Yevtich, you and I and most likely every Jew in Bulgaria would already be dead. Sofia would look like Belgrade—nothing left standing higher than ground level. Would we be better off?"

Yevtich shrugged. "Maybe not, Corporal. But I still don't trust these Germans."

A courier stepped inside the duty room and saluted.

"Corporal Dimitrov, you're to report to the palace immediately. To the War Chancery office. See Captain Kalayev."

"Of the private guard?"

"Yes, Corporal."

Dobri shrugged and pulled a questioning face at Yevtich. He buttoned his uniform and grabbed his hat. "All right, I'm coming."

He arrived in the office to find Kalayev waiting for him in the vestibule. Dobri saluted.

"Ah, Dimitrov. Congratulations."

"May I be permitted to ask, sir, what I'm being congratulated for?"

"Why, for your promotion, Dimitrov. We have a rather sudden vacancy in the household guard, and you've been recommended to fill it. You'll be accompanying Tsar Boris on his trips abroad. That means you must have the rank of sergeant of the guard." He handed Dobri an envelope stamped with the king's seal.

"Thank you, sir. This is a very great honor. May I be permitted to ask, sir, what is the nature of the vacancy that I am being promoted to fill?"

The captain looked at Dobri, an amused smile toying with the corners of his lips. "You mean to tell me you're the only one in the palace who hasn't heard about Bojilov and his big mouth?"

Dobri's eyes widened. "Ah, yes, sir, maybe I heard a few rumors…"

"Well, they're true. And I'd advise you, Sergeant, if you want to retain this billet, to keep your political opinions to yourself and follow the orders you're given. His Majesty is a tolerant man, but some people think that means they can say whatever they please."

"Yes, sir. I'll remember that."

"I'm sure you will. And by the way, His Majesty shares my confidence in you, it seems. He personally recommended your promotion to this duty."

"I'll do my best to be worthy of his trust—and yours, sir."

"Fine. Here's your paperwork, already signed by His Majesty. Your pay goes up twenty leva per month. And you need to go pack; you leave with His Majesty in the morning."

"May I be permitted to ask our destination, sir?"

"Of course. You're going to Vienna; the Fuehrer's plane will be waiting at Vrazhdebna. Any other questions, Sergeant?"

"No, sir."

"Very well. His Majesty goes to the airport at eight o'clock sharp. Don't be late. Dismissed."

Dobri saluted, executed a smart about-face, and left.

It was the beginning of a dizzying time for the newly appointed sergeant of the guard. Tsar Boris went to Vienna to discuss the Bulgarian historical claims to Macedonia, but he came home with a mandate from Hitler for Bulgaria to occupy and administer the disputed territories. Since Yugoslavia's status was now that of an occupied country, rather than an ally, it seemed Hitler was intent upon dismantling the nation and parceling its territories out to its neighbors. Tsar Boris seemed satisfied with the results of the closed-door meetings with the German leadership. As soon as news of the Macedonian occupation was publicized in Sofia, huge throngs flooded the streets around the palace, chanting, *"Tsar Obedinitel"*—"King Unifier"—and singing "Shoomi Maritza" until their throats were raw. And soon after the king's return from the Vienna meetings, word came to the palace that Germany was requesting Bulgarian occupation of Thrace also. If the crowds were happy before, they were delirious now. Even the Russian sympathizers in the government were smiling when they came to the palace for meetings. With the return of the Dobrudja the previous autumn and now the occupation of Macedonia and Thrace, Tsar Boris had, without shedding a single drop of Bulgarian blood, realized the longstanding national dream of re-creating Great Bulgaria.

For Dobri it was not all celebration, however. As a squad leader of the king's personal guards, he often accompanied Tsar Boris on tours of the newly occupied lands. Though their entourage was most often met with cheering crowds waving red and white *martenitsa* tassels, Dobri couldn't get out of his mind the way the last war had begun—with a bullet from the pistol of a single Serbian zealot. Dobri knew that not everyone in Thrace and Macedonia was happy about the polite Bulgarian troops occupying their checkpoints and crossroads and the ethnic Bulgarian Macedonians being installed in their government offices. The Internal Macedonian Revolutionary Organization was strong in these parts; it took only one desperate partisan to subject Tsar Boris, during a visit in, say, Skopje, to the same fate as Archduke Ferdinand in Sarajevo twenty-seven years before. When Tsar Boris was standing in his car, smiling and waving, Dobri's eyes never rested; his hand stayed close to his holster. He couldn't truly relax until they were back in the palace or at Vrana.

In mid-May Dobri was informed he would be accompanying the king on a three-week junket across Europe. The itinerary called first for a stop at Obersalzburg and a diplomatic call on Hitler. Then they were to go to Rome for meetings with Mussolini and his foreign minister, Ciano. Just before returning to Sofia, the king had scheduled a visit with his father, the deposed King Ferdinand, at his ancestral home in northern Bavaria.

Dobri knew Tsar Boris was not looking forward to seeing his father. Relations between them had never been easy; by all accounts the old king was a harsh taskmaster, especially where Boris, the crown prince, was concerned. But since Ferdinand's forced abdication in favor of Boris, just after the disastrous events of 1918, Ferdinand had grown increasingly demanding and critical of his older son. While providing security for the king, Dobri had heard him talk with his advisors about the bilious letters he received from his father. It was clear to Dobri that, though Tsar Boris would never permit himself to be less than a dutiful, respectful son, he would have much preferred to skip the Bavarian leg of the trip.

The royal party arrived at the Berghof, Hitler's sprawling private compound near Obersalzburg, in the company of a dazzling array of German generals, ambassadors, and functionaries. Dobri enjoyed meeting his counterparts in the Fuehrer's security corps; he learned things just by watching them. One of them, Sergeant Franzen, motioned to Dobri soon after the party reached the Berghof.

Franzen pointed discreetly toward Hitler. The diplomats and leaders

were congregating on the other side of the large split-level living room, near
the immense picture window overlooking Berchtesgaden, Untersberg, and
Salzburg.

Dobri wasn't certain what Franzen was hinting at, but as he watched the
way Hitler interacted with Tsar Boris, he began to notice something surpris-
ing: with his gestures and expressions, the German leader appeared very
respectful, almost to the point of being deferential, to the king of Bulgaria.

Dobri peered a question at Franzen, who gave him a conspiratorial wink
and a quick nod.

"Der Obergefreiter und der Koenig."

Dobri searched through his rudimentary German and came up with the
translation: "The corporal and the king." He smiled at Franzen and nodded.
It was true: Hitler acted almost like an awed schoolboy in Tsar Boris's presence. Though he was the commander in chief of the strongest armed forces
in Europe, this commoner from northern Austria was a bit intimidated by
Tsar Boris, a scion of the house of Saxe-Coburg-Gotha. Dobri remembered
where he was, though, and did his best not to let his pride in his monarch be
too obvious.

The trip to Rome was inconclusive. Though Tsar Boris hoped to come
to an understanding with Mussolini on some disputed mines and towns in
Albania currently occupied by the Italian army, Dobri gathered that Mussolini proved evasive.

At last they could avoid it no longer: in Rome, they boarded a train for
Bavaria. It was time to go see King Ferdinand.

The old king had recently celebrated his eightieth birthday, and according to Tsar Boris, he was quite put out that none of his children had come to
see him. Never mind that the date fell smack in the middle of the negotiations surrounding the treaty with Germany. "He'll never forgive me for not
being there," Dobri heard Tsar Boris say. "He will demand to be allowed to
return to Bulgaria, and of course I can't agree to that—it's politically impossible, especially now."

When they arrived at the villa outside Coburg, King Ferdinand was waiting for them at the ornate entrance. He was in full uniform, sporting a chest
glittering with medals. He had on a black shako draped with gold chains and

satin cords, complete with an enormous gold plume jutting into the air above his head. He cut an imposing figure. When Tsar Boris approached, Ferdinand gave him a smart salute. Boris bowed to him—a little stiffly, Dobri thought—and the old king invited them all into his house.

One afternoon, when they had been there just less than a week, Dobri was attending Tsar Boris as he sat with his father on a veranda overlooking the park that sloped from the rear of the house toward a fine old forest, maybe half a kilometer away. As was usual when the two of them were by themselves, there were long silences in the conversation. Boris had been speaking, in very general terms, of the progress of the alliance with Germany, when the old king made an impatient sound and struck the stone pavement with his walking stick.

"So! They're calling you King Unifier now, I hear."

Tsar Boris waited, his eyes turned slightly away from his father.

"Hitler hands you the territories on a silver platter, and for that the people are ready to put a shrine to you in Nevsky. Never mind that I sweated blood in 1908 and again in 1916, trying to return my country to its former glory. And for my trouble I'm forgotten—even by my own children."

"Father, you mustn't say that—"

"Sitting here on my birthday, the biblical fourscore, alone, lonely, abandoned by the nation I built. I have not forgotten Bulgaria, mind you," he said, wagging a finger in his son's face. "No, even in my exile, I have worked tirelessly for her. And for what? By now I should have been back there, among the people whom I served with my heart and soul all those years."

Tsar Boris was massaging the bridge of his nose. He was getting one of his headaches. He would probably eat little or nothing at dinner tonight, Dobri guessed.

"Father, you know that is impossible—"

"Impossible? For the man who won back the Dobrudja, Macedonia, and Thrace without firing a single shot? How, impossible? For such a diplomat, such a consummate politician, I should think negotiating the return of your father to his rightful homeland would be child's play."

"I'm sorry, Father."

"But who notices? Who cares? Not even the newspapers. Perhaps they spent five or six lines, somewhere in the back pages, noting the eightieth birthday of the king who brought Bulgaria into the modern age. An insult! Worse than nothing!"

Dobri caught himself wishing Tsar Boris would remind his father of the misery of the years following the Great War: the hopeless poverty of a land that had been at war almost constantly since 1908; the anxiety of waiting on the deliberations of the victorious Allies, then the shame of the punitive Treaty of Neuilly that gutted Bulgaria's army and stripped her of her hard-won territorial gains. Why didn't His Majesty recall to his father's mind the fact that it was King Ferdinand's disastrous policies that had made Bulgaria a stench to the Allies and provoked an angry populace to demand his abdication?

But no. Tsar Boris listened patiently to the spite, the complaints; he let his father spew it all out. And then he answered softly, deferentially. Dobri didn't understand how such patience was possible.

They arrived back in Sofia on June 20, and two days later Dobri admitted a constant stream of worried officials and generals to the king's offices in the palace chancery. Soon all Sofia was aghast at the news: Germany had invaded Russia.

Dobri was apprehensive, but he wasn't surprised. Rumors had been circulating for weeks around the War Office about German divisions massing on the Russian border. No one had really believed the alliance between Hitler and Stalin could hold. But now it was no longer a matter for speculation. Bulgaria's military and political ally was at war with Bulgaria's historical and cultural patron. What would Germany require of Bulgaria now?

"Darling, please sit down. You're making me nervous with all this pacing."

Lily might as well not have spoken. Alexander was ignoring her—maybe he didn't even hear her. She hated times like this. There was nothing she could do or say that would soothe him. He'd hardly touched the dinner she'd prepared. She'd made his favorite foods. To start, Lily had a *shopska* salad of fresh cucumbers, black olives, tomatoes, onions, and peppers, liberally sprinkled with grated *sirene* cheese and seasoned with vinaigrette. That was followed by *shishke* bought fresh at the butcher's and pan-fried to sizzling perfection, served with roasted peppers stuffed with egg and cheese. And to top it all off, she had stopped by the patisserie on Tsar Simeon Avenue and bought a rich, caramel-coated crème brûlée.

But he had barely noticed. All he could think about right now was the bad meeting with the new German ambassador.

"In front of Gabrovski, Lily—think of it! This Beckerle chewed me out in front of my boss as if I were some schoolboy who hadn't done his lessons. As if I haven't worked night and day to get the Jewish situation under control."

He stopped pacing and held out his hands to her.

"We started with nothing, Lily, nothing! Beckerle doesn't understand the obstacles we face here."

He was directing his words toward her, but Lily knew from experience that he wasn't talking to her. She was a convenient backstop for his thoughts, nothing more. After a while, he would get tired, and then one of two things would happen: either he would reach for her, use her the way some men used a bottle of *rakia,* or he would flop down on the secondhand horsehair sofa and fall asleep reading one of the dog-eared pulp magazines he kept stacked in at least one corner of every room in the apartment, leaving her to sleep alone. Lily wasn't sure which alternative she preferred.

"Surely it wasn't as bad as you think, *lyubimi.* After all, you said he complimented the amount of revenue generated by the new taxes."

"Yes, well, I suppose that part went pretty well. But why did he have to pick on the work brigades? It's not like the Jews are really in the army. They can't carry weapons or serve as support personnel in the field. They don't do anything but build roads and bridges or work on flood-control projects. They aren't real soldiers at all. But Beckerle threw a fit because they were still wearing Bulgarian uniforms, still organized in squads and platoons."

"That's easily changed, isn't it?"

"I suppose." He stopped pacing and ran a hand through his hair. "But I can't think of everything. I can't read the Germans' minds."

"No, and surely Minister Gabrovski doesn't expect you to. Come, *mili moy.* Sit down for a while. You're upsetting yourself. In a week or two everything Beckerle complained about will be taken care of, and everyone will be happy again, you'll see."

He looked at her and finally gave her a grudging smile. "Of course, Lily, you're right. You're always right, aren't you?" He came to her, knelt on the floor by her chair, and put his head in her lap. Lily stroked the hair over his temples and kneaded the tense muscles at the base of his neck and in his shoulders.

"There, now. There. You have to learn to look beyond a single day's work, Alexander. You have to learn to be patient, take the long view."

"Um-hmm."

Lily looked down at him. For the thousandth time, she tried to understand the place in her heart that was open to him, would always be open to him. He was bad for her. As often as not, he gave her about as much notice as the furniture. She couldn't remember more than a few times he had asked her opinion of anything. He was a bottomless vat into which she was always pouring herself.

And maybe that was it: Alexander's occasional desire for her was as close as Lily could come to imagining love. Maybe she thought she could change him. Maybe she was trying to save him. Maybe that was how she was trying to save herself.

From what? She wasn't sure. She thought about her conversations with Daria Richetti. What commerce was there between the Lily Panitza who could not stomach the persecution of the Jews and the Lily Panitza who loved the man most directly responsible for it? Was it possible Lily was trying, with her subterfuge, to redeem Alexander from the deepest evil of his own ambitions? Was she trying in some indirect fashion to prevent him from committing a sin so horrible that it could never be forgiven?

She ran her fingers through his dark, curly hair and tried to stop her mind. Maybe he would love her tonight. Maybe, for just a little while, she would forget everything except the way she felt when he touched her. Maybe she could convince herself for a little while that even this meager love was worth something. Tomorrow would come soon enough.

7

August 1941

Metropolitan Stefan dabbed his face and the back of his neck with a handkerchief as he entered the main foyer of the palace. He hated August. By this time of year he was dreadfully tired of summer, but the persistent heat only seemed to bear down harder, stubbornly resisting the coming cool of autumn. In other years he might have planned a holiday in Borovitz or maybe even the Swiss Alps, but with the country going to hell all around him, he couldn't leave Sofia. It gave him another reason to rail against the Fascists in the Sobranje; they had robbed him of some well-deserved relaxation in a cooler climate.

People bowed to him on the stairway. He felt like a big, lumbering, sweating bear in his black cassock and chimney-pot hat. Stefan would have much preferred to call on the palace wearing a nice light-colored linen suit with a clean white shirt and a tie knotted at his throat. But the present crisis demanded all the reinforcement he could squeeze from the gravity of his ecclesiastical office. He wore the robes because he knew they made his presence more imposing, not because they reflected his sartorial preferences. *A black cassock in August! What ever made me want to be a priest?*

The secretary in the anteroom looked up as Stefan approached. "Your Eminence, the chief of cabinet is expecting you." The young man got up and opened the tall double doors into the salon. Stefan nodded at him and went in.

Pavel Grouev stood in the center of the large salon, talking with a petite, blond, blue-eyed young woman. After a moment Stefan recognized Radka Groueva, the daughter and youngest child of the king's senior advisor. She looked at him as he came in.

"Good afternoon, Your Eminence. My goodness, aren't you terribly hot under all that black wool?"

"Radka!" Pavel Grouev wore a mortified expression.

"It's all right, Mr. Grouev. Actually, I'm delighted that someone cares enough about a man of the church these days to inquire after his comfort. And yes, Miss Groueva, I am approximately as hot as a bread oven under all this black wool. Frankly, I'd much rather be in my shirt sleeves, sipping a nice glass of lemonade."

"Then why don't you go do that? You wouldn't mind, would you, Father?" she said, giving Pavel Grouev a wide-eyed look. Stefan liked Radka; she reminded him of himself many years ago. He especially enjoyed the discomfort on her father's face. Grouev was always so serious, so circumspect. Having a daughter like Radka was probably good for him.

"Actually, Miss Groueva, your father didn't call me here. I came to see him."

"Yes, and it's probably time you were leaving, my dear," Grouev said, taking his daughter's elbow and steering her toward the door. "Tell Mama I shouldn't be too late tonight."

"Good-bye, then, Your Eminence. Are you sure you wouldn't like for me to bring you a glass of lemonade?"

Stefan smiled at her. "Thank you, no, Miss Groueva. It was very nice to see you."

She kissed her father lightly on the cheek and went out. He closed the door behind her, looking a little relieved, and turned to face the metropolitan.

"Mr. Grouev, is His Majesty here?"

Pavel Grouev walked over to a window and pulled back one of the heavy velvet curtains. He peered up and to the side, toward the flagpole above the main entrance.

"I see His Majesty's standard is flying," Grouev said, dropping the curtain and turning back toward the cleric. "So I suppose he is here."

"As if you didn't talk face to face with him ten times between breakfast and lunch."

Grouev smiled and shrugged.

"Well, never mind. Mr. Grouev, someone has to talk sense into him. The Holy Synod has, in no uncertain terms, condemned the Law for the Defense of the Nation. The king knows this. He, and he alone, can put a stop to this unconscionable treatment of the Jews."

"I think you overestimate what His Majesty can do on his own recognizance. He must function within the constraints of policy and expediency—"

"Expediency! Don't talk to me about expediency. That's the excuse people have always used when they wanted to do something contemptible without taking the blame for it—or when they're afraid to stand up for what they know is right."

"Your Eminence, these are complicated times."

"And getting more complicated by the hour. But that doesn't justify theft of property in the name of taxation or punitive curfews that make people as good as prisoners in their own homes. And radios! Why can't Jewish citizens keep their radios, for heaven's sake?"

"The Ministry of the Interior—"

"Is headed by an idiot. I wouldn't spit on Gabrovski if he were on fire in the middle of town."

"Your Eminence, we are in a delicate position with our German allies."

Stefan nodded. "Yes, I can see that. You've gotten in bed with the devil, and you're afraid he's going to roll over on you."

"Would you have us embrace the Bolsheviks?"

"I would have us embrace justice, Mr. Grouev! Why do we need the permission of one or another of the great powers to do what is right for our own people?"

The chief of cabinet locked his hands behind his back and turned away.

"Of course you're correct, Your Eminence. And I wish I could tell you that tomorrow all the Jewish measures could be retracted and life could go back to normal." He turned and met Stefan's eyes. "But you and I know we are not living in normal days. It is a time of hard choices, some of which will surely appear wrong to those who do not appreciate all the factors involved."

"What are you trying to say, Mr. Grouev?"

Pavel Grouev looked at him for several seconds, then turned away again. "Only what I have already said, Your Eminence."

"I will tell you something, Mr. Grouev," Stefan said in a low voice. He took a step toward the other man. "If I have to drag Jews into my church and forcibly dunk them in the baptistery, if I have to fill the place with Jews from wall to wall and lock the doors against Gabrovski and his Ratnik ruffians, I will do it. I will not add my inaction to the criminal mistreatment of fellow Bulgarians, be they Jew, Christian, Muslim, or—or Druid! If they want the Jews, they'll have to burn down Alexander Nevsky Cathedral with me in it!"

Grouev nodded slowly, his face toward the floor.

"I believe you, Your Eminence. And…I applaud you. But I cannot do any more to help you. At least, not just now. I'm very sorry."

Stefan flung up his arms and stalked out of the salon.

Pavel Grouev watched the metropolitan leave. When the doors closed behind him, Pavel's eye was drawn to a small mark on the wall, beside the doorway, about a foot from the floor. It was a faint black smudge, the mark of a shoe scuffing against the wall.

Grouev remembered the occasion of that mark. It was the morning after the midnight coup of May 19, 1934—the night that changed Tsar Boris forever. That was the night the young king lost what was left of his innocence.

Up until then, Boris had trusted the best motives of those around him. He was a true believer in democracy, firmly opposed to authoritarian rule— indeed, he could hardly bring himself to sign the death decrees of convicted criminals and insurgents. Politicians maneuvered around him, cabinets came and went, and he held himself above the details, ever believing that taken together, their actions were those of patriots, people who were loyal to Bulgaria in their heart of hearts.

But the coup of 1934 changed all that. When even his beloved army betrayed him—the force in which he had served at the risk of his own life in the trenches of the Great War—when even the generals treated the constitution and the nation with contempt in service of their own interests, Boris changed.

Though there was nothing he could do to prevent the completion of the coup, he correctly counted on his tremendous personal popularity to insulate him from harm. Even if the leaders didn't respect him, they needed him. They needed the appearance of legitimacy the king's continued presence would give them. And so Boris watched and waited. He knew the coalition that had carried out the government takeover would eventually begin to fall apart of its own weight—and that he could even subtly hasten the process. In those days he often signed his personal notes as Tarpeniev—"Mr. Patience." During that time he sometimes seemed to Pavel to truly have the patience of the spider. It was as close as Tsar Boris ever came to emulating the cunning of his father, and it was chilling to watch.

On the morning after the coup, Kimon Gheorgiev, the man who was to be prime minister of the new government, was leaving a meeting with the king in which Tsar Boris had bargained for the most favorable terms he could. Gheorgiev slipped on his way out of this very salon, kicking the wall beside the door. A black scuff mark now marred the silk moiré wallpaper. One of the palace staff got a cloth to clean the wall, but Tsar Boris stopped him.

"I want a souvenir of this night," the king said. "Leave the wall as it is."

Less than a year later both the Gheorgiev government and its successor had failed, and Tsar Boris had firmly taken the reins of power. Matters had remained so ever since. And the saddest part of it all, Grouev thought, was that at no time since did Tsar Boris seem to enjoy the exercise of authority. His attitude reminded Pavel of the time his own father had forced him to choose between shooting his favorite dog or watching it die slowly and painfully. Bulgaria had compelled Boris to this role; he would not have accepted it otherwise.

Pavel thought about what Metropolitan Stefan had said just now. He thought about the priest's righteous indignation. He wished he could tell Stefan something that would comfort him. He wished he could assure him that the king was aware of matters and was guiding them to a favorable conclusion. But such assurances were beyond his power, beyond even Tsar Boris's power. The world was tearing itself apart around them, and all tiny Bulgaria could do was wait and watch. It was Tarpeniev's time again. The king's patience had served the country well thus far. Pavel prayed it would do so once more.

Boris had no warning of the attack until he felt the icy slush slam into the back of his neck. Then he heard Maria-Louisa screaming with laughter. He wheeled around, scooping a handful of snow as he turned. The princess was trying to run away, but her feet tangled, and she fell into a drift. Boris charged her with a roar, brandishing his arm for the throw.

She waved her hands in front of her face, giggling helplessly as he continued to threaten her. He could hear Giovanna laughing from her observation point in the safety of the terrace's neutral zone. He wheeled about and made as if to launch the missile at his wife.

A miniature assailant grabbed him about the knees.

"Not Mama!" Simeon said, trying to wrestle his father to the ground.

"Betrayed! By my own forces!" Boris fell into the drift beside Maria-Louisa with Simeon tumbling on top of him.

"That's quite enough!" Giovanna said. "Children, release your father at once!"

Boris stood with a child wriggling under either arm. The three of them were covered with snow; they looked like living pastries dusted with powdered sugar.

"I claim victory!" he said.

"I claim a hot bath for the three of you, and the sooner the better," Giovanna said.

"And then hot chocolate with peppermint?"

"Yes, Maria-Louisa. Go tell Mademoiselle Daria."

The children shouted their approval.

Boris set them down at the edge of the terrace and brushed the snow from their clothes. They scampered toward the house as he stamped the snow off his pants and shoes and dusted the front of his coat. He collapsed into the wicker chair beside his wife's.

He smiled at her and held out his hand. She took it, and together they sat quite still, appreciating this view of the countryside surrounding their villa. The foothills of the Rhodope Mountains fell away in white folds toward the Maritza valley and Plovdiv, on the northeast horizon. The air was so still Boris wished he didn't have to breathe. The sky was heavy with clouds, but no snow was falling. It was a moment as tranquil and flawless as the blue heart of a diamond.

Someone behind them cleared his throat. Boris turned around, and Sergeant Dimitrov was there. And he was holding a telegram.

"Yes, Sergeant?"

"Your Majesty, I beg your pardon, but this just came up from the telegraph office in Kritchim, and it's marked 'Urgent.'"

Boris closed his eyes for an instant, then rose from his chair and faced Dimitrov. "Very well." He held out his hand and received the cable. He tore it open, and his eyes scanned it for a few seconds. He sighed.

"Sergeant Dimitrov, I'm afraid this means I'll have to return to Sofia immediately. You come with me and bring one more of your men. Leave the rest of the detail here with the queen."

For an instant, Boris saw something—disappointment?—flicker across Dimitrov's face, but the soldier quickly masked it.

"Yes, Your Majesty. When will it be Your Majesty's pleasure to leave?"

Boris looked down at his wife. He laid a hand on her shoulder. "Never, Sergeant. But I expect we'd better be ready to go in half an hour."

Dimitrov saluted and left.

Giovanna stood and came beside him, putting an arm around his waist. "Is it bad?"

He gave her a sad smile. "Nothing we haven't faced before, my love. Just business."

Her eyes searched his face. Then she managed a brave little smile and a nod. "Then go. We'll be along before Sunday, as we planned."

"Yes. Let the children enjoy their holiday." He turned to go.

"I love you."

He turned back toward her. *Dear God in heaven, what did I ever do that was worthy of receiving the gift of such a woman?*

"I love you, too, my dear. With every heartbeat."

"You did what?"

Popov and Filov eyed each other nervously.

"We agreed," Filov said. "But Your Majesty, Herr Beckerle was most insistent. Article 3 of the pact requires us—"

"I don't care if that village constable Beckerle was marching around the room waving a pistol in the air! You had no business agreeing to his demands in my absence!"

"But…technically, Your Majesty, the United States' declaration of war on Japan makes them the aggressor—"

"Don't be stupid, Minister Popov! The attack on Pearl Harbor was a clear provocation!"

"The Japanese don't see it that way, and they are our allies, not the United States."

"Oh, really? And will Hirohito be here to protect us when the American B-17s are dumping bombs on our heads?"

Boris whirled away from his two cowed ministers and stomped across the room.

"Your Majesty, please try to understand. Berlin would not take no for an answer! Besides, with the United States and Britain so far away, our little co-declaration is purely symbolic, at best."

Boris whirled on them. "Do you know what you remind me of, Mr. Filov? You're like the village strumpet who yells 'rape' when it's too late. You could have at least played a bit coy, don't you think? You could have asked for a little time. But no, you jumped right in the haystack and let them have their way with you!"

The stocky prime minister's face reddened, and his knuckles were clenched white in his lap, but Boris didn't care. Bulgaria had declared war on the United States! It was ludicrous! They'd be lucky if a single building in Sofia was left standing.

"Your Majesty, the German armies—"

"The German armies are fighting a two-front war now, Mr. Popov, and pretty soon they'll have more than Britain to worry about on the west. They can bellow all they like about their latest triumphs on the Russian front; the Wehrmacht is stalled for the winter, and who knows what will happen in the spring."

Boris rubbed a hand across his bald scalp and stared at the floor. "When does this go to the Sobranje?"

"Tomorrow," Filov said.

Boris smacked a fist into his palm. "Absurd! There's no time to do anything!" He looked up at the two men, seated in front of his desk. "You may go. You've done quite enough for one day, I think."

The Sobranje was a storm of angry voices, a riot of shouting faces and waving arms. But for all the noisy protesting from the opposition deputies, the die was already cast. Filov had the votes, and everyone knew it. The declaration of war was ratified on the basis of "Bulgaria's legal obligations as a signatory to the Tripartite Pact." Boris watched as much of it as he could stand, then left.

When the bodyguards found him, long after sundown, he was in a darkened corner of Alexander Nevsky Cathedral. The king was on his knees, praying.

Buko Lazarov was stunned. And Milcho wouldn't look at him—that was the worst part. He just sat slumped behind his desk and watched the floor beside Buko's feet.

"I'm sorry, Buko. I... It's out of my hands, really. The bigwigs in the Sofia office..." Milcho's voice drifted into silence.

"But, Milcho, I've worked for this company over twenty years! I'm the one who recommended you for hiring. I thought we were friends."

"That's not it, Buko. It's got nothing to do with that."

"Well, what then? You call me in here with no warning and tell me my job's been eliminated, and you give me no reason, and I'm not supposed to take it personally? Milcho, this is crazy! You and I both know I'm the best tobacco buyer you've got in the Kyustendil district—maybe in the whole southern region. I've worked hard for this company. I've made a difference. When I came here in 1920, you were shipping maybe a thousand barrels per season, and now—"

Milcho Gerdjikov slapped the top of his desk and jerked himself upright. "Don't you get it, Buko? It's the law! All the big companies in this country are feeling the pressure. The way things are right now, no one who wants to stay in business can afford to look like a—"

Buko waited. "A what, Milcho?"

Milcho closed his eyes. His shoulders drooped again. "A Jew lover."

Buko felt the blood roaring in his ears. The room seemed to collapse inward, the ugly reality of this moment surging over him until he was half choked by it.

Without looking at him, Milcho slid an envelope across the desk.

"Here, Buko. It's your last month's paycheck. I pulled a few strings and got it processed early."

Buko knew there had to be some words for a time like this. But his mind groped and came up empty. Or maybe the words were too big to fit inside the constricted reach of his shocked consciousness. He leaned over and took the envelope. He stared at the top of Milcho's head for a few seconds, then turned around and walked out of his office. He didn't close the door behind him.

He walked down the stairs and through the entryway toward the front door. He was barely aware of people passing him, brushing past him. It was almost as if he were a shade, what his Sephardic grandmother used to call a *fantasma*. He passed through these people, his co-workers—former co-workers, he reminded himself—but made no impression on them. Unseeing and unseen. When had he disappeared? When had they?

He walked out the front door and down the steps. He looked back at the buildings. The Fernandes tobacco warehouse was three and a half stories tall. It could easily store two or three thousand of the largest hogsheads. For the last twenty or so years, much of Buko's life was stored here. He turned away and began the walk toward home. Over his shoulder he heard the clank of empty freight cars at the railway station. It sounded to him like the empty rattle of his own future.

What would they do? Just two or three days ago Anka had shown him the notice from the Ministry of the Interior: the new tax on their house alone, calculated from the valuation they had been required to send in several months previously, came to over sixty thousand leva, nearly a fourth of its value. Not to mention the personal property they had also been required to declare. The notice said half the tax was due and payable immediately; the other half was required within six months. If not, the paper said, the property would be confiscated and sold at auction. And now Buko's job was gone.

"Up in smoke," he said aloud, and a laugh came out of him that sounded more like someone choking.

When the decree came down requiring Jews to turn in their radios, Buko's friend Moise Tomasov had carried his set out into the backyard and taken an ax to it. He said he'd rather destroy it himself than turn it over to the Fascists. He gathered the pieces into a sack and drove to the Struma Bridge, outside of town, where he threw them into the river. Buko wondered if Tomasov wasn't onto something. Wouldn't it be better to decide one's own fate, even if that fate was destruction, than to meekly hand the decision to someone else? But maybe it was best not to wander too far down that path. Not yet anyway.

In the end, he guessed, they would do what Jews had done for centuries: they would pray, they would hope, and they would stick together. If they had to, he and Anka could move in with her mother, who rented an apartment above a dry-goods store in the center of Kyustendil. Her Christian landlord didn't have to pay the Jewish tax, and he had shown no inclination to turn Baba Marika into the street. Let them take his house, his little vegetable plot on the outskirts of town, his rattletrap Peugeot. He and Anka and Baba Marika would still have each other. And surely God would not abandon them.

8

By late March 1942 spring was starting to make an appearance in Vienna. As the motorcade began its drive from the airport up to Obersalzburg, Boris looked out at the pink clusters of dogwood and alpine rose, the flowering of the goat willows. Out of habit, he catalogued them by their scientific names as he saw them: *Cornus florida, Rhododendron ferrugineum, Salix caprea.*

But the air at Obersalzburg's higher altitude still held winter's chill. Boris was glad to see the fire in the hearth of the Great Room at the Berghof. He went straight to it and warmed his hands while the rest of the entourage sorted itself out.

A woman was in the room when Boris entered, but she gave him a quick smile and left without speaking. He wondered if she was Eva Braun, the Fuehrer's rumored mistress. Maybe she was and that was why she kept herself out of sight when official guests were about. At least he had never seen her before.

In the car on the drive from the airport, Ribbentrop had come directly to the point, as usual: "Bulgaria must immediately break off diplomatic relations with the Soviet Union. Their legation is less than a stone's throw from your palace, and the place is no doubt crawling with spies who are reporting the movements of our troops through your country. The Fuehrer has been more than lenient with you; he hasn't asked you for a single platoon of Bulgarian troops for the struggle on the eastern front. The least you can do is cease friendly relations with the enemies of the pact."

Boris had listened carefully to the foreign minister. Afterward he allowed a long, thoughtful pause to precede his reply.

"We are most grateful that the Fuehrer has not required the involvement of our troops against Russia, considering my country's long history of friendship toward the Russian people. Of course, our army is still poorly equipped for modern warfare. With Germany's generosity, we are finally approaching some state of readiness, but we still have far to go.

"I wonder if you have considered, Herr Reichsminister, the advantages of having the Bulgarian army where it presently is? We are relieving the heavily tasked Wehrmacht of the necessity of occupying Macedonia and Thrace; we are able to keep a careful watch on the border with Turkey.

"Besides, Minister Ribbentrop, have you thought about the likely consequences of our breaking off relations with Moscow? Think about the vulnerability of our Black Sea coast. Why should Stalin not view our severing of ties as a provocation? No, I submit that any sudden diplomatic changes of that sort would be better preceded by a buildup of German naval forces in the Black Sea, to forestall the opening of a new Soviet front on our seacoast. Think how valuable our ports of Varna and Bourgas would become if you were ever in a position to land a force in the Ukraine. Why risk that?"

Ribbentrop pinched his lips together and drew a long breath, in and out through his nose. But he offered no rebuttal, and Boris decided to press ahead.

"Turkey's neutrality is fragile, Your Excellency. I don't think I need to remind you how troublesome their belligerence could be, both to Bulgaria and to Germany. And as for the activity in the Soviet legation—I assure Your Excellency that we are keeping a most careful watch on them. We don't need our own Communist underground getting any encouragement from their Russian colleagues."

He kept his voice low, his tone even. The Nazi foreign minister listened, and it was clear that his words were having some effect. Boris expected this topic would resurface in his forthcoming meeting with Hitler, but at least he had presented his case.

"Perhaps we can discuss this further, Your Excellency? This is too important for a single conversation, don't you think?"

He rubbed his hands together and pressed his palms toward the fire. He wondered if Ribbentrop had been speaking on orders from Hitler. Would the Fuehrer push for Bulgarian troops at the Russian front? If he did, would Boris's delaying tactic satisfy him?

His room for maneuver was growing more and more constricted. Even within Boris's own government, pressure was building for a greater commitment to the Tripartite Pact. "If we want to participate in the spoils, we need to play a bigger role in the victory" the reasoning ran. Sometimes, after conferences with a roomful of ministers all prodding him to do more in support of the German cause, Boris's jaw muscles were cramped from gritting his teeth.

And the dreams were getting worse. Just last night he had again felt the familiar terror as he stood in his father's room, holding the bloody corpse of the faceless soldier. He knew the words *Le Monarque* would say, even before he said them. He felt scalded with shame but powerless to resist Ferdinand's tirade. And every blow struck home: Yes, he was worthless; yes, he was weak and indecisive. No, he had no business being king—he wished he could abdicate, let Bulgarians decide their own fate.

Boris remembered the last words his mother had said to him as he stood at her bedside, a confused and frightened five-year-old crown prince whose life was carried out largely in an official atmosphere of parades, ceremonies, and rituals. His twenty-nine-year-old mother, dying from the exhaustion of giving birth to Boris's younger sister, Princess Nadejda, had called each of her children to her side when she felt the end coming. Boris, as the oldest, was last. His beautiful mother turned her face to him and said, "Be kind, my son. Always be kind."

The few tender, private moments Boris could recall from his early years were those he had spent in his mother's presence. And after she was gone, the four of them—Boris, Kyril, Evdokia, and Nadejda—became each other's playmates, confidants, friends, and allies. They sheltered each other from the aloofness and severity of *Le Monarque*. In the years since, Boris had decided his mother was too gentle to tolerate life with the haughty and demanding Ferdinand, too kind to survive the prospect of her children's conversions into extensions of their father's image of himself.

But maybe she had underestimated the power of her own deathbed prayer. Boris could never escape the knowledge that he was the son of Ferdinand of Saxe-Coburg-Gotha, but more and more he also knew himself to be the son of Maria-Louisa of Parma. Though he had only known her for the first five years of his life, her presence was still strong enough within him to oppose the pride and authoritarianism his father had tried to instill in his royal heir. Sometimes Boris was able to appreciate the wisdom her gentleness lent him. Other times, he wondered if it wasn't preferable to be wholly one way or the other. For as long as he could remember, he had felt himself stretched between his duty to Bulgaria and his instinctive love of individual Bulgarians.

"Ah! Your Majesty!"

Boris turned. Hitler was striding up to him, holding out his hand in greeting. Boris returned the Fuehrer's firm grip.

"Your Excellency. Thank you for inviting me."

"Of course, of course! Well, then, shall we?" Hitler gestured to the chairs near the fireplace.

They sat in dark leather armchairs, facing each other across a small, round table. Boris winced inwardly when Hitler opened with a polite inquiry about the availability of "a few companies" of Bulgarian troops for "support roles" at or near the eastern front. Boris, as delicately as he could, restated his reasons for remaining neutral toward the Soviet Union and keeping Bulgarian troops away from the conflict between Germany and Russia.

"The Bulgarian soldier fights best on his own soil," Boris said, "not in a conflict involving matters he can't readily understand. I truly believe we can best serve the interests of the Reich by ensuring the stability of Macedonia and Thrace and balancing the potential threat posed by Turkey."

Hitler nodded. He sat quite still for a few seconds, then nodded again. "Yes. Well, I can certainly understand Your Majesty's point of view. Though, naturally, the Russian campaign has been difficult. The winter was harsh, and the number of supply trains we could get through to our troops was less than a tenth of what they really needed. Fortunately, we've been able to supply some of them by air.

"In fact, some of the general staff made trouble," Hitler said. "They wanted to withdraw for the winter, but I was adamant. I had to replace Field Marshal von Brauchitsch and assume much of the direct command myself, but I was not about to repeat the mistakes of Napoleon. One would think my generals hadn't read their history." Hitler gave a scoffing laugh and shook his head.

The man never held a rank higher than lance corporal. Boris hoped his disdain was camouflaged. He reminded himself of what this particular lance corporal had been able to accomplish—and what he might yet be capable of.

Hitler told Boris he planned to bring up four million reserve troops very soon, when the spring thaw was well under way, and strike through the Caucasus toward the Persian Gulf, there to unite with Japanese forces. Then, no doubt, matters at the eastern front would take a much more favorable turn.

After about three hours, Hitler suggested they have lunch, and Boris readily agreed. They walked through the vaulted entrance corridor into the dining room, and Hitler, as usual, went to the center of the long table, facing the windows with their view of the Untersberg. Boris took a seat on Hitler's right. To his chagrin, Reichsminister von Ribbentrop came in and seated himself on Boris's right. It didn't bode well for Boris's digestion that he would spend most of the meal turning his head as if he were watching a tennis match, attending to Hitler and his foreign minister.

The bright light of the mountain spring day glowed in the burled larch paneling of the dining room. As the white-jacketed, gloved waiters brought in the food and drink, Hitler launched into a rhapsody on the view.

"Best thing in the world for the digestion, that view," he said. "You know, of course, Your Majesty, the legend that places Charlemagne's burial place there, in the Untersberg."

Boris gave a polite nod as he sipped at the straw-colored Piesporter a waiter had just poured for him. "It is said that one day Charlemagne will arise from his tomb under the mountain and restore the Holy Roman Empire to its former glory."

Hitler nodded, gazing with a strange expression at the mountain. "Yes. I find that prophecy very comforting. I think perhaps it is no coincidence that destiny led me to this place."

"Tell me, Your Majesty, of the measures you're taking to control the Bolshevik underground in your country," Ribbentrop said.

Boris turned toward Ribbentrop and gave him a polite smile. He turned back toward Hitler. "Herr von Ribbentrop and I were speaking about this matter earlier, Your Excellency. I was assuring him that we are just as anxious as anyone else that our Communists remain well in hand."

Ribbentrop leaned around Boris. "Yes, *mein* Fuehrer, and His Majesty assured me we would continue the conversation."

Hitler stared at Boris, then at Ribbentrop. Boris felt his pulse quickening. He took deep breaths and did his best to appear unperturbed. He turned again toward Ribbentrop.

"Herr Reichsminister, my law enforcement officials have extensive dossiers on all known or potential insurgents. These people do not enjoy the support of the general population, I can promise you—"

"And the Bulgarians are great friends of Russia, as you mentioned," Ribbentrop said.

Boris again turned toward Hitler. "Herr Ribbentrop is, of course, referring to the historical and cultural ties many Bulgarians feel. After all, it was the Russian tsar who forced the Ottoman Empire to take its foot off Bulgaria's neck in 1878."

"Yes, the history is quite interesting," Ribbentrop said, "but the Reich is very much concerned with the present safety of its troops while they are in your country."

Boris turned sharply to face Ribbentrop. "Frankly, Herr Reichsminister, I am not as concerned with any supposed Communist insurgency as I am with the increasingly troublesome meddling of certain German elements in Bulgaria's internal political affairs."

Ribbentrop's eyes widened. The words had come out sharper than Boris intended, but he decided to let them stand.

"What's this?" Hitler said, leaning forward to give his foreign minister a sharp look.

"I beg your pardon, Your Excellency, if my words sounded impertinent," Boris said to Hitler. "But it has become known to me, from indisputable sources, that some of your diplomatic and press corps in Sofia are lending encouragement to our National Legions and other right-wing troublemakers." He turned again to Ribbentrop. "I would think, Herr Reichsminister, that you would appreciate knowing who is executing diplomatic policy in my country, since that falls within your area of responsibility?"

"I knew nothing of this," Ribbentrop said, glancing from Boris to Hitler.

"I remind you, Herr Reichsminister, that Bulgaria's enthusiastic allegiance to the Tripartite Pact is due in part to the deliberate pace with which I am implementing the, ah, unfolding of our participation in the war effort. If General Loukov and others within the National Legions had their way, Bulgarian boys would be shipped out tomorrow, with no preparation of public opinion, no explanation of the necessity or even the advisability of such drastic measures. I'm afraid the high regard presently enjoyed by the Reich among my people would suffer as a result."

"Herr von Ribbentrop, we must not allow this any longer," Hitler said, waving his knife to emphasize his words. "If there is some connection between our people and these groups His Majesty has mentioned, it must be immediately severed."

"Yes, *mein* Fuehrer. I will see to it."

"I appreciate that, Herr Reichsminister," Boris said. "You might find it interesting that one of our arms-procurement engineers has friends in your Air Ministry. He has been known to carry letters from Sofia to Reichsmarshall Goering."

Boris could tell from the flush in Ribbentrop's cheeks that he had hit a nerve. The rivalry between the foreign minister and the flamboyant Goering was becoming well known in diplomatic circles. Ribbentrop chewed on this information and said nothing else to Boris during the meal, which suited the king perfectly.

During the flight home, Boris found himself thinking of his favorite Saxe-Coburg uncle, Albert, who had been crowned Albert I, king of Belgium. Uncle Albert had been dead, what, just over eight years now, was it? He had been climbing a steep, rocky escarpment in his beloved Ardennes. *He leaned against a block of stone at the summit,* the official communiqué had read. *The block fell away, carrying His Majesty with it.*

The death of the brave king who had personally led his troops in the horrendous trench warfare of the Great War was lamented around the world. It was odd: though Belgium had fought against the Axis powers—with which Bulgaria was allied—Boris had never been able to think of Uncle Albert as an enemy. Nor had he ever quite believed that the experienced climber and mountain hiker hadn't known the rock on which he leaned would move.

What had Albert seen from that final summit? In his darkest moments, Boris envied Albert his clean, quick end.

Boris stared at the terrain crawling past below the aircraft and wondered how much longer it would be before they landed at Vrazhdebna. He needed to see his children.

As they moved through the crowd of dignitaries and officials, Daria kept her head down. She stayed as close to Queen Giovanna as she dared, trying to be little more than a piece of human furniture. The less notice she attracted, the better.

Daria couldn't understand why the queen had insisted she accompany Her Majesty to this particular exhibition. To be sure, it was hosted by the Italian legation, and its theme, "The Fight Against Malaria," was consistent with the tsaritza's interest in hospitals and public health. But why was she so intent on Daria coming with her? Daria's fear had grown so that she could barely manage the weekly trips to the market. And now, in this glittering throng of the powerful, she was very likely surrounded by Nazis and official anti-Semites of every stripe. She could hardly draw a breath.

Queen Giovanna moved among them with her customary calm and grace, greeting most of the diplomats in their own languages. She had stopped in the center of one of the smaller salons in the exhibition hall to exchange a few words with a Frenchman when she fastened on someone in the southwest corner of the room. She extricated herself from the conversation so smoothly that the French dignitary was already bowing before she moved away from him.

With Daria in her wake, Queen Giovanna bore straight for a small, round man wearing a pair of old-fashioned pince-nez spectacles as he leaned over to peer at one of the exhibits. It was the Italian ambassador, Count Magistrati.

"*Buon giorno,* Count Magistrati. How good to see you again!"

The man raised himself and turned. He smiled and took the queen's proffered hand. With a practiced motion, he bowed and brushed his lips across the backs of her fingers.

"*Maestà,* the pleasure is surely mine."

"What do you hear these days from your brother-in-law?"

Magistrati gave a shrug and a polite smile. "I'm afraid the war keeps Galeazzo very busy. I haven't spoken to him or had correspondence in nearly a month."

"What a shame. Count Ciano was always one of my favorites back home in Italy."

"I know he would be most pleased with the knowledge, *Maestà.*"

"I'm sorry, I interrupted your study of this exhibit. What is it? May I look with you?" Giovanna took the count's elbow, and together they leaned over the vitrine case. But they had no sooner done so than Daria heard the queen murmur to Magistrati, "I need a favor, Massimo. I need it done quietly and as soon as possible."

The count cast a quizzical glance toward the tsaritza, but she gestured pointedly toward the display, and his eyes returned to their perusal.

"I need Italian passports for some friends who must leave Bulgaria as soon as possible."

"Why must they leave so suddenly and secretly, may I ask?"

"They're Jewish."

"Ah, *Maestà.* You know the prohibition against—"

"I give you my personal guarantee, Massimo; they will not remain in Italy. They will go to Argentina. I need ten passports with transit visas."

A photographer approached, and Queen Giovanna laughed and nodded at Magistrati as if he had just said something witty. She redirected her attention to the display case. The camera flashed, the photographer moved on, and she leaned toward him again.

"Please, Massimo, for the sake of our families' long friendship, I ask this."

"I…I will see what may be done."

"Good. I'll send my aide around tomorrow. *Mille grazie,* Massimo."

The count didn't look nearly so pleased when Queen Giovanna left him as he had when she first greeted him. He managed a courtly bow.

They left the exhibition soon after. Queen Giovanna made enough stops at other displays and carried on enough brief conversations for them to seem in no particular hurry, but Daria realized the conversation with Magistrati was the purpose of the queen's attendance here.

When they were in the car on the way back to the palace, Queen Giovanna turned to Daria. "Tomorrow afternoon I want you to go to the Italian embassy. Count Magistrati will be expecting you."

"Your Majesty, I…I'm afraid. I don't know if I can do this."

The queen looked at Daria. Her expression was stern but not unkind. She laid a hand on her arm. "Your fear is not without reason, *cara mia*. But you must do this. It would never do for me to be seen calling on Magistrati—too many questions. And there isn't anyone else in the palace I trust to do this errand. You will be safe, Daria. I give you my word."

Daria took a deep breath and nodded.

"Do this: try not to think of yourself," Queen Giovanna said. "Instead, think of the ten people—three young children among them—who will be delivered from their fears because you faced yours."

"I understand, Your Majesty. I will do my best."

"Yes, you will. That is the way of the good who must live in evil times; they take the path of service, though it is lined with dangers on either side."

Daria looked at her. "Yes, Your Majesty. I understand."

9

Metropolitan Stefan watched as the neat ranks passed the reviewing stand in front of the Tsar Osvoboditel Monument. Each grade had its own formation. Each class of schoolchildren was led by the boy and girl with the highest marks. The leading boy and girl of each class proudly held aloft garlanded icons of Saint Kyril and his brother, Saint Methodie, who had invented the Slavic alphabet and taught it first to the Bulgarians—as everyone knew, if they had any sense.

Stefan loved Kyril and Methodie Day. He loved the honeyed May sunlight. He loved living in a country that revered learning. He loved the faces of the children, the sound of their voices when they sang.

His black-coated companion was here today, Stefan noticed. He had seen the short, bearded man with the wide black hat at the edges of the throng gathered along the street to watch the parade. Stefan had almost gotten used to the sight of him: at the doorway of the cathedral during a Sunday service, a face in a crowd at a civic ceremony, walking past a café where Stefan was eating lunch. Always at a distance, never in the same place for very long. He never approached Stefan, never made any demands or threats. But he was there.

The metropolitan had plenty of enemies these days; the black-coated man could be working for any of them. Ratnik, the right-wing Fighters, as they styled themselves, had published numerous articles in the press, calling Stefan an agitator and demanding his indictment as an antigovernment conspirator. And the Brannik Fascist youth organization, the Defenders, had printed threatening fliers and distributed them in the streets of Sofia. Sometimes they heckled his speeches. Once a handful of Brannik toughs had waited outside Alexander Nevsky, harassing churchgoers for listening to "a Bolshevik-loving, antipatriotic lunatic who masquerades as a man of God." Stefan found himself impressed; he had no idea any of the beardless Fascist delinquents had the wit to string together so many epithets.

The parade was finishing; it was time to stroll with the crowd of onlookers to the National Library for the rest of the festivities. As they left the reviewing stand, Stefan fell in beside Dimitar Stoyanov, "Ellin Pellin" as his pseudonymous works named him, who was one of the honorary chairmen of this year's celebration.

"How are things in Bailovo, old friend?" Stefan asked the writer.

Stoyanov smiled and shook his head. "Ah, Your Eminence. Sadly, I haven't been to the village of my birth in a good six months now. You probably know more about what's going on there than I do."

"Dimitar! I'm shocked. You, of all people, should know the importance of remembering who you are and where you come from."

"I do remember—and so do many of the good people of Bailovo, and that's why I stay away."

Stefan laughed.

"It was a good ceremony this year," Stoyanov said.

"Yes, it was. I think the children become more beautiful every spring."

"Even in ugly times, beauty finds a way to survive."

"That sounds like a line from one of your books."

"Maybe so." Stoyanov stroked his long white mustache. "Maybe my next one."

"Write it soon, Dimitar. I think our country is forgetting about beauty, about truth, about common decency. I never thought I would see Bulgaria aping the mindless cruelty that passes for public policy in Berlin."

They walked several paces without saying anything.

"I see your name in the papers pretty often these days," Stoyanov said.

"Reading the gossip columns again, are you?"

The writer chuckled. "Well, now that you mention it, the quality of the editorial pages has rather deteriorated lately." He looked at the metropolitan. "I sometimes worry about you, Your Eminence."

"Too late for that. I'm certifiably mad."

"I worry about your safety."

Stefan looked at his friend, then away. "Too late for that, too. We're in a war, Dimitar. My battlefield is a different one, but the risks are much the same. It's my duty."

"I thought you might say something like that."

"I thank you for your concern."

"No need."

"The initial draft of the Law for the Defense of the Nation was an important step, but only a first step. My latest trip to Berlin has taught me this; there is more to be done."

Alexander leaned over the conference table as he spoke, making firm eye contact with Interior Minister Gabrovski, who was nodding thoughtfully. Lily tried to keep her eyes on her notepad, to get down everything that was said, as Alexander had insisted, but she couldn't help watching the face of Alexander's boss. This meeting was so important to Alexander. It was all he had been able to talk about, to think about, for the past month. Everything depended upon it, he had said.

"It isn't enough to restrict the enemies of our country," Alexander said, punching the air with his index finger. "We have to impose a radical solution. A final solution."

Gabrovski leaned his elbows on the table and made a tent of his fingertips. "A final solution. What do you suggest?"

"While I was in Berlin, there was a meeting of the Reich state security office. They've come up with a plan."

As Lily took notes, she felt a cold place in the center of her chest, felt it blooming and spreading like a flower of ice. Even as she copied down the words that came from Alexander's mouth, she couldn't believe what she was hearing—what her own hands were writing.

Large camps in the eastern regions of the Reich…railroad spurs directly onto the compound…utmost security and secrecy…planning for sufficient capacity…Belzec…Sobibor…Treblinka…Maidanek… Auschwitz…

"And Berlin is willing to allow Bulgaria to utilize these…facilities? What will it cost?" Gabrovski said.

"We can pay for everything with confiscated property," Alexander said.

"I've done some calculations. Here." He slid a folder across the table to the interior minister.

Gabrovski flipped through the papers in the folder. "Hmm. Railroad cars…assembly points in public buildings…census estimates by district… extra security details…" Gabrovski raised his eyebrows in admiration. "I think you've thought of everything, Mr. Belev. Impressive thoroughness."

"Thank you, sir."

"But it won't be easy. The Sobranje—"

"I've thought about that too. If we can convince the prime minister of the urgency of this matter, a resolution could be brought to the Sobranje, giving plenary powers for state security measures to the Council of Ministers. The Sobranje needn't know any unnecessary details."

"And this new bureau you've proposed…" Gabrovski consulted the folder. "This Commissariat for Jewish Questions will administer the council's decisions?"

"That's the plan, sir."

Gabrovski nodded. He pushed himself up from the table and paced slowly to the other end of the room, then back, his hands in his pockets. Alexander's eyes never left Gabrovski's face. His anxious eagerness tugged at Lily's heart.

"I see only one difficulty," Gabrovski said finally. With his chin, he pointed out the window, across Alexander Battenberg Square—toward the Royal Palace.

There were a quiet few seconds.

"His Majesty is a good man, a kind man," Gabrovski said. "Too kind. His humanitarianism sometimes leads him astray from what must be done for the good of the nation." Gabrovski put his palms on the table and leaned toward Alexander. "And he has friends in the Jewish community. This is well known."

"And yet, even His Majesty is not above the will of the people," Alexander said. "With all the territorial gains for Bulgaria made possible by the goodwill of the Reich, it would be…unwise for him to place that goodwill in jeopardy, no?"

Gabrovski nodded thoughtfully, staring out the window toward the palace. "True enough. It becomes even more important that we maintain and even increase our propaganda efforts in the public press."

"We should also keep encouraging our friends in the National Legions," Alexander said.

"Yes. So, Alexander, here is what you must do. Say nothing about these plans for now. I'll speak with the prime minister. If he reacts as favorably as I think he will, we'll decide on a legislative strategy, as you've suggested. In the meantime, continue to refine your logistics. When the moment is right, we must be ready to move without hesitation."

Alexander nodded. Though he maintained a professional demeanor, Lily could see the flush of pleasure in his cheeks.

Gabrovski gathered the files Alexander had presented. He put them in his portfolio, tucked it under his arm, and extended a hand across the conference table. Alexander stood and took the minister's hand in a firm grip.

"Good work, Alexander. My confidence in you continues to be justified."

"Thank you, sir."

Gabrovski nodded a farewell in Lily's direction, then turned and left the room.

Alexander allowed a smile to broaden on his face. He looked at Lily.

"Did you get it? All of it?"

She looked at her notes, then at Alexander. She forced a smile. "Yes, Alexander. Everything."

The cart was almost full. And a good thing, Buko thought—the daylight was fading almost as fast as his strength. He dumped in the armload of wood and leaned against the cart to catch his breath.

"Five loads today, Lazarov—not bad."

Buko nodded. "Thank you again, Sotir, for letting me help you."

Sotir Podorov shrugged. "I needed the help. Since my son joined the army, I'm always needing another pair of hands."

"How much do you think you'll clear today?"

Sotir peered at the sky as he calculated. "I guess maybe…ten leva. Twelve, if this last load weighs out well. Eight or nine, after I pay you."

Enough to buy bread—and maybe a piece of meat. Thank you, Sotir.

Sotir tossed the ax into the cart, just behind the seat, and went to get the donkey, tethered under some nearby birches. Buko pressed his hands into the small of his back, wincing as he stretched his sore muscles. He wasn't yet accustomed to this kind of work. His hands had finally toughened up and weren't bleeding so much anymore, but his back and legs still complained every morning when he got out of bed.

Buko watched Sotir fetching the donkey. The old peddler and handyman cupped the beast's snout in his hands. He talked to it, smiled, and laughed as if sharing a joke with a friend across a café table. He reminded Buko of some of the day laborers on the tobacco plantations around Pleven. Eight months ago Buko might have stood talking to a farm manager about the crop and weather conditions while men like Sotir Podorov worked in the field, bent over the tobacco stalks. Now Podorov was Buko's employer.

At least he was still at home with Anka and Baba Marika. Most of the younger Jewish men had already been rounded up and sent to one of the labor camps in the countryside. From the few letters smuggled back to families in Kyustendil, it sounded as though their treatment depended a lot on the disposition of the camp commander. Some treated the men fairly and saw that they got rest and decent rations. But other commanders were rabidly anti-Semitic, working the men cruelly and making them sleep in leaky sheds not even fit for animals—feeding them moldy bread and cheese or gruel as thin as dishwater.

Last night Anka told him that the Foreign Ministry had issued a proclamation: Bulgarian Jews living abroad were to be considered the same as the Jews of whatever country they were in. A Jew from Sofia who found himself picked up by the SS in Kraków might as well have been born and raised in Poland. His Bulgarian citizenship made no difference to the Reich, according to the new regulation. The story was in one of the newspapers someone had smuggled into the Kyustendil synagogue.

And darker rumors had begun trickling into Bulgaria: the Nazis had established concentration camps, it was said. Hitler meant to imprison every Jew within his reach, some said. And after that…no one wanted to guess.

So far, at least, there was no talk of such a fate for Bulgarian Jews. Some of the labor camps were bad, but not as bad as what was rumored to be happening in Poland and elsewhere in the Reich. Bulgarian Jews might be losing their homes and savings, and they ran the risk of being roughed up by Ratnik gangs, but they weren't being herded into ghettos. It was still better for Bulgarian Jews than most other places in Europe, from what Buko could tell.

Sotir backed the donkey into the traces. "There, now, Juliana. Be a good girl and let Daddy hitch his cart, yes?"

"You think this brake will hold all the way down the mountain?" Buko fingered the ancient mechanism, giving Sotir a doubtful look.

"It will hold, Buko. It has to. I will pray to the Blessed Virgin and the saints, and we'll be safe. You'll see."

"All the same, I'd just as soon walk. Less work for Juliana."

Sotir laughed. "You hear that, Juliana? This good man is thinking of you. Or maybe he trusts his two legs more than your four. What do you say to that?"

The donkey shook her ears and swished her tail. The bit jangled in her mouth as she chewed the last bit of clover she had cropped beneath the birches.

It was fully dark by the time they reached the outskirts of Kyustendil. Sotir went into his singsong cry: "Firewood! Already chopped to fit your stove! Ten stotinki the half rick! Firewood…" They would drive up and down the streets until the cart was empty or Sotir's voice gave out, whichever came first. But Sotir's voice never gave out.

They had just left a house that had bought four large armloads of wood. The cart was nearly empty, Sotir's pocket bulged with coin, and he was not in such a hurry to sell as when they had first gotten to town. Juliana ambled along, and Sotir was content to let the reins dangle across her flanks.

"Why do you think Hitler hates your people so?" Sotir said.

"No one knows for sure. Some say he was treated badly by a Jewish employer or teacher during his youth. I tried to read his book once, but it was so full of nonsense and drivel, I couldn't wade through it. Somehow he seems to have gotten the idea that all Jews are Bolsheviks, trying to gain control of the world. It's crazy. He's a sick man."

"I knew an old woman once who was convinced the clouds were going to freeze into chunks of ice and fall on her head," Sotir said. "She went around all the time wearing a bucket. If anybody tried to talk to her, tried to ask her why she had a bucket on her head, she wouldn't answer. She wouldn't even look at you.

"One day I decided to play a little joke. I saw her coming down the lane of the village, and I ran inside and got my mother's bucket. I put it on my head and walked out to meet the old woman." Sotir chuckled at the memory. "You'd have thought she was seeing her long-lost child. She ran up to me and threw her arms around me. She started talking about all the crazy people in our village who were going to die when the clouds started freezing, but she was so glad there would be at least one other person left alive for her to talk to."

A woman waved at them from her doorway. Sotir tugged on the reins and stopped Juliana. Buko got down and gathered an armload of wood, collected the ten stotinki, and handed the coins to Sotir before climbing back onto the seat. Sotir clicked his tongue, and Juliana leaned into the traces.

"Anyway, as I was saying. To that old woman, anyone who didn't wear a bucket was crazy. The madman looks at the rest of the world and sees only madness. And when the madman controls the strongest army in Europe…"

Juliana clopped along a few paces.

"What about you, then, Sotir? Aren't you afraid, associating with a Jew? Aren't you afraid of someone labeling you a Bolshevik or a Jew lover or an enemy of the state? What if they start sending everybody to labor camps who talks to a Jew, who treats a Jew like a human being?"

There was a thoughtful silence.

"I don't know, Buko. I've lived in Kyustendil for a long time. I'm nobody much, if you think about it, just a peddler and an odd-job man. I don't know about things like politics and war and treaties. I don't think I could tell you the difference between a Bolshevik and a Nazi. I don't understand about enemies of the state. I don't even know the difference between good tobacco and rabbit-weed, to tell you the truth. I haven't studied much of anything. All I know is this: I couldn't have gathered enough wood to sell today without your help. And you needed something to do to make a little money. So it seems to me the right thing to do is for you and me to help each other. I think that's how people ought to get along, Buko. I leave all that other stuff to the kings and generals and people who've been away to school. And if you go to church on Saturday instead of Sunday, or if you listen to a rabbi instead of a priest, or if you pray straight to God instead of going through his only begotten Son, I don't see how that makes a difference in the amount of wood we can gather in a day's time."

For some unaccountable reason, Buko remembered some lines from the scriptures he had read over forty years ago at his bar mitzvah. The rabbi, an old man named Alazar, had called Buko up to do his Haftarah. And the section allotted to Buko was from the scroll of the prophet Isaiah:

> You have been a refuge for the poor,
>   a refuge for the needy in his distress,
> a shelter from the storm
>   and a shade from the heat.
> For the breath of the ruthless
>   is like a storm driving against a wall
>   and like the heat of the desert.
> You silence the uproar of foreigners;
>   as heat is reduced by the shadow of a cloud,
>   so the song of the ruthless is stilled.

Buko had been wearing the suit his mother had sewn for the occasion. He had on the stiff brown shoes that he had saved his own money to buy. His yarmulke kept trying to slip off the back of his head, and his prayer shawl wouldn't lie correctly on his shoulders.

Anka was at temple that day; her older brother was in Buko's midrash class. When Buko saw her in her white linen dress with the organdy lace at the neck and hem, he knew he wanted to marry her someday. He was only thirteen; it was his first bout of prescience.

Buko remembered everything about that day: the sweet taste of the orange-almond cake, topped with *dulci di fruta,* the relief he felt when he had finished singing his portion of the Haftarah, the way the new shoes rubbed a blister on his heel.

But tonight, for the first time, he had learned the meaning of the words he had chanted so many years ago.

He reached out his hand in the darkness and gripped Sotir Podorov's shoulder.

10

August 1942

Pavel Grouev read the document and shook his head. He dropped it on the desk and stared above Boris's head, out the window that overlooked Alexander Battenberg Square. He got up and paced the small room with his hands shoved into his pockets. He gave Boris a quick look but instantly turned back to the window.

"Go ahead, Bacho Pavlé. Say it."

Grouev motioned toward the draft on the king's desk. He opened his mouth to speak but just shook his head.

Boris waited, his hands folded in front of him.

"The prime minister is making himself the virtual king of Bulgaria, where the Jews are concerned," Pavel said finally. "This says he doesn't even have to consult the Sobranje! It's an abrogation of the constitution! It's…" Grouev stuffed his hands in his pockets. "I'm sorry, Your Majesty. I'm saying too much."

Boris looked at his advisor and tried to imagine everything that was going through his mind. As mild as his comments had been, Boris knew that the habitually reticent Grouev must be seething inside to say as much as he had.

"The Holy Synod will rant and rave, won't they?" Boris said.

Pavel gave a grudging nod.

"Metropolitan Stefan, notwithstanding our friendship, will accuse me of selling out the Bulgarian Jews."

Again Pavel nodded.

"And history? History will say that Bulgaria, a nation founded on tolerance and whose constitution guarantees civil liberties to every citizen, regardless of creed or religion, turned her back on her principles. Is that something you're afraid of, my friend?"

Pavel's eyes again met the king's for a second, then he looked away with another nod, like a man admitting he had some dread disease.

"Bacho Pavlé, think for a moment. Think what's at stake here. Don't just think about the fifty thousand Jews in Bulgaria; think of the hundreds of thousands of Bulgarians who will live or die, depending on what we say or do during the next few years, the next few months.

"I didn't want this burden. You, of all people, know this. I'm a democrat at heart; I think all the pomp and folderol is so much foolishness. But through some combination of divine providence or fate, I am in this place at this time, and I must be king of all the Bulgarians—"

"The bad, as well as the good," Pavel said, finishing Boris's familiar formula.

"That's right. You must surely know what a narrow path we walk with Berlin. One false step—"

There was a knock on the door.

"Your Majesty, the prime minister is here."

"Thank you, Sergeant Dimitrov. Please show him in."

Bogdan Filov bustled in. "Thank you, Your Majesty. I'm sorry to disturb you, but a matter of some urgency has arisen."

The prime minister nodded toward Grouev, but the chief of cabinet managed to be looking somewhere else at that moment. Boris bowed his head slightly, brushed his forehead with his fingertips, and sighed.

"Please, Your Excellency. What is it?"

"Your Majesty, I must have your signature on these Extraordinary Orders for the immediate relocation of certain persons from the capital."

Boris looked at the document the prime minister handed across his desk. He read for a moment, then looked up at Filov.

"I see no reason for my signature on this document."

"But, Your Majesty, the Special Measures just passed by the Council of Ministers—"

"Are a matter for you to look to yourself, Mr. Prime Minister. If you truly think it needful to send Jewish families out of Sofia into the countryside, you should take it up with the constabulary or the minister of the interior. But the sovereign of this country need not concern himself with these details, and he certainly need not sign documents that can be perfectly well enforced by those to whom the law has entrusted such activities. Do I make myself clear?"

"Well…Your Majesty, I—"

"I mean, you might as well ask me to do personal inspections of the cemeteries to be sure the graves are being dug according to regulations. Do you have no officers capable of carrying out the resolutions you pass in the Council of Ministers?"

"I'm sorry, Your Majesty. I thought, given the current climate, that—"

"Was there anything else, Mr. Filov?"

Filov's face flushed. His jaw muscles worked for a few seconds, but he kept his teeth firmly clamped against whatever was inside. He made a stiff bow and went out.

As soon as the door closed behind the prime minister, Boris slapped the desktop with both hands.

"Do you see what they do to me, Pavel? They pass these horrible laws and then expect me to lend my influence to their implementation! It's ridiculous! How dare Filov come to me and ask for my signature! The idiot! Can you believe it?"

Grouev shook his head. "I'm sorry, Your Majesty. It's truly a shame."

"And then, of course, the Holy Synod paints me as a villain, no better than Ratnik. 'The king must intervene,' they say. 'The king must do something!'"

Pavel grunted in sympathy.

"What in God's name do they want me to do? We have nothing to bargain with. Don't they see that? If this were a chess game, Bulgaria would have a few pawns and maybe a rook to stand against the other side's queen, its bishops, and its knights! Of course I'm inconsistent, Pavel. Of course I make a nod to this side and then a gesture the other way. Of course I allow the Fascists their exercise of power, because the fate of this country hangs by a thread, and all we need is for someone to whisper in Beckerle's ear over at the German embassy, to suggest to him that the king of Bulgaria is wavering in his support for the Reich. Have the Holy Synod already forgotten what they did to Yugoslavia? What makes them think Bulgaria's fate would be any different? Is that what they want? Who will protect their precious Jews if that happens?"

Boris could feel himself losing control, could feel his emotions taking over. It was as if *Le Monarque* had suddenly come into the room, staring at Boris in that haughty way he had.

You're too weak to be a king…too weak to be Bulgarian…

Boris held his head in his hands. "What can I do, Pavel? I don't think Hitler can win! Haven't I said it a hundred times? And even if he could, how can I allow what he would do to my Jewish citizens?"

"*Oui,* Your Majesty. It's an impossible predicament."

Boris stared blindly at the opposite wall.

"I have nothing, Pavel. No leverage, no bargaining power—nothing. Only a poor nation filled with a few million people whose lives I want to save.

"Do you know what happened the other day, Pavel? I was at Tsarska-Bistritza, at the mountain retreat. It was a beautiful day. Balan and I had just left the lodge for a hike up to the Rila lakes. I was in better spirits than I had been in weeks." Boris smiled and shook his head at the memory. "No politicians, no Germans, no generals—just me, Balan, the mountains, and the sky. A perfect day.

"I could tell something was on Stanislav's mind, but with these young men, who knows? Maybe a girl, maybe he lost a wager… I paid it no heed.

"We had just climbed above the tree line. I turned to make some remark to Stanislav, but he spoke first. 'Your Majesty, forgive me. I have to ask a favor of you.' He wanted me to pardon Traytcho Kostov."

"The insurgent?"

"Yes. A Communist, a convicted conspirator. 'I've known him since primary school,' Balan said. 'He always helped the poorer students, gave up his own time, and his sister is a friend of mine. She pleaded most urgently.'"

"I told Balan that even Kostov didn't contest his guilt, that he was found guilty of subversion by the tribunal, and that there really wasn't anything I could do. We hiked on a bit more, but of course now the mood was spoiled. I stopped and asked Balan to tell me more. I listened, even though I didn't want to.

"And do you know what I did? The next day I commuted Kostov's sentence to life imprisonment. In that office"—Boris pointed at the wall, to the next suite of rooms—"I told Balan that his friend's brother would be spared. The other six were hanged a few days later. But not Traytcho Kostov."

He turned to face Grouev. "My father is right, Pavel. I'm weak. I rule with my heart. I can't even sign a death warrant for a convicted Bolshevik insurgent. I'm pitiful. I should abdicate and be done with it."

Grouev stood very still, averting his eyes.

"Other heads of state look at the world and see strategies, opportunities, dangers, possibilities. Do you know what I see, Pavel? I see faces."

Pavel Grouev was looking at him now with that mixture of apprehension and sympathy that told Boris he had ranted long enough. He was in danger of becoming pathetic.

"All I can ask is this: when the decisive moment comes—whatever form it takes—they must trust me to act properly. But until that moment comes, they must trust me to act cautiously. That's all I know; it's the only way I can manage."

Dobri had never carried such an odd request to the king; he shook his head as he watched the foreign minister's liaison officer going down the front steps of the palace. Still not quite sure he had heard correctly, he turned toward the royal family's wing. It was nearly 5:00 p.m., and the tsar and tsaritza would be in the private drawing room, enjoying time with their children before dinner.

Dobri knocked on the door. A pleasant flush came over him when it opened and he saw Daria Richetti standing there.

"Good evening, Miss Richetti. I have a message from the Foreign Ministry for His Majesty, and the liaison officer said it should be delivered as soon as possible. May I come in?"

"You're always welcome, Sergeant Dimitrov." She smiled at him in that beautiful way she had. Dobri thought everyone in the room might hear the pulse hammering in his ears.

She closed the door behind him and went to the large armchairs where Tsar Boris and Tsaritza Giovanna sat, listening raptly as Crown Prince Simeon methodically repeated the addition tables he had learned that day.

Watching her lean over to speak to Tsar Boris, Dobri thought about what a strange, heady time it was for him. He was in daily contact with the most admired and respected man in Bulgaria. He had important work to do, and he took great pleasure in doing it well. He genuinely loved the royal family. And…there was Daria.

He dreamed about her. He had rehearsed a thousand times in his mind the words he would say to her if ever the moment seemed right. He could close his eyes in his quarters at night and see the way she walked, the way she moved her arm to open a door, the way the light had played across her face the last time he saw her. He had memorized every nuance and timbre of her voice. He knew her smell. He spent large stretches of time imagining the taste and feel of her lips.

And he dared to hope his attentions might not be entirely unpleasant to her. The way she had smiled at him just now, the way her eyes held his an instant longer than they needed to—surely she could tell what was happening to him, and surely she wouldn't be cruel enough to encourage him, in the hundreds of delightfully vague ways she did, if she didn't have some feelings for him in return.

Still, he shouldn't kid himself; he was the son of peasants from Bailovo. If it hadn't been for Ellin Pellin, who would have even heard of Bailovo? Daria Richetti was a lady, the confidante of a queen, raised among the powerful, the wealthy, the wise. How could he be foolish enough to think such a woman could entertain serious thoughts about some hayseed playing soldier?

Then again, it was wartime. When the tides of history shifted, sometimes people sought harbor in places they wouldn't have otherwise considered.

Dobri thought about what he had heard a few days ago, standing outside Chancellor Grouev's office. Tsar Boris sounded like someone at the edge of a chasm, trying to think of reasons not to jump. How could a man so simply good, so loyal to his people, bear up under the conflicting demands of politics and statecraft? It saddened Dobri. It made him wish he and Daria Richetti could go away somewhere, to a cabin on the top of an inaccessible mountain range, and close their door and shut out the cruelties of a world that could inflict such undeserved hurt on a fine, true man like Tsar Boris.

The king was coming toward him. Dobri stiffened to attention.

"Stand at ease, Sergeant Dimitrov. What's the message from the Foreign Ministry?"

"Well, Your Majesty, it's unusual. I hope I have this sorted out. The

Foreign Ministry received a communication from some of the Japanese general staff who are attending the maneuvers the day after tomorrow in the Rhodope Mountains. It seems they have heard of your reputation as an amateur botanist and… I'm sorry, Your Majesty. I've forgotten the word the liaison officer used. It has something to do with bugs…"

"Entomologist," Tsar Boris said, smiling. "Go on, Sergeant."

"Yes, entomologist. At any rate, these generals have requested that Your Majesty organize a field trip in the mountains. They want to collect some specimens of a certain butterfly? One that is…named for Your Majesty? They say that Emperor Hirohito is also an…entomologist of some skill, and…" Dobri fell silent, sure that he had botched the message beyond salvage.

Tsar Boris threw back his head and laughed. The others looked at him and Dobri. The sergeant was wishing he could simply disappear.

"Forgive me, Sergeant Dimitrov. I'm not laughing at you. Your message makes perfect sense."

"What is it?" the queen asked, coming to her husband. "Let the rest of us in on the joke."

"It's just that when the sergeant gave me the message from the Foreign Ministry liaison, I instantly received a picture in my mind of these somber Japanese generals leaping about some meadow in the Rhodope Mountains, trying to gather *Lepidoptera borisii* in their nets."

The queen started to smile, then covered her mouth with her hand. "Yes, as whole troops of Bulgarian infantry look on," she said, her shoulders starting to shake, "trying not to laugh out loud and create a diplomatic incident."

Soon the three of them were doubled over with mirth. Daria Richetti was still standing by the armchairs, near the children, not sure what to make of the sudden outburst. Dobri laughed as much from relief as anything else.

"Ah, Sergeant Dimitrov, I haven't laughed like that in a good month," Tsar Boris said finally, bracing himself with a grip on Dobri's shoulder. The king wiped his eyes with the heel of his hand. "Please, I insist that you stay and have dinner with us."

Dobri's jaw dropped. "May it please Your Majesty, I hardly think I should intrude—"

"Nonsense. Miss Richetti," the king said, turning toward Daria, "please tell the staff to set another place at the table. Sergeant Dimitrov will be join-ing us." He turned to Dobri. "I hope you won't make me resort to issuing an order, Sergeant."

"No, Your Majesty, I...I'd be deeply honored."

Dobri spent the next hour enmeshed in a thin gauze of rapture, it seemed. They could have served him oatmeal instead of the fresh trout and garden vegetables the stewards brought on the steaming plates, and Dobri would not have noticed the difference.

He sat next to Daria Richetti, across the table from the tsaritza and Princess Maria-Louisa. Tsar Boris was at the head of the table to his right, on the other side of Daria, and Crown Prince Simeon was immediately to his left.

The little boy was a delight, one of Dobri's favorite parts of duty in the palace. Dobri liked nothing better than the expression on Simeon's chubby face when he, or another of the soldiers in the palace guard, snapped to atten-tion upon seeing the crown prince. Simeon would immediately halt whatever he was doing and return the salute with the most businesslike expression on his face that any drill instructor could ask for. The five-year-old was the dar-ling of any regiment that might be favored with a visit; Dobri had seen the pictures in King Boris's official annuals of the crown prince in his miniature uniform, posed in front of a bivouac tent somewhere in the Rila Mountains, surrounded by ranks of smiling soldiers. As a boy, Dobri remembered seeing a similar picture in one of old King Ferdinand's annuals: a small Crown Prince Boris posing with a regiment on maneuvers.

During the meal, the crown prince peppered Dobri with questions and commentary: "What does that patch on your sleeve mean?" "That one over your pocket is an artillery badge, isn't it, Sergeant?" "One of my regiments is the Forty-first Heavy Artillery. Do you know it?" "My godfather, General Nikolaev, says I have the makings of an artillery commander." "Have you fought in any battles?" "Have you ever seen Chancellor Hitler?" "I want to fly in a bomber someday..."

Dobri found it easiest to simply nod and maintain eye contact with the crown prince. But never for an instant did he lose the awareness of Daria Richetti at his right shoulder. Her presence so near made it seem to Dobri that he was sharing the room with a beautiful portrait come to life. Once or twice their elbows brushed, and Dobri would have given a month's pay to know if her touch was intentional.

During a lull in the crown prince's monologue, Tsar Boris looked at Dobri. "Sergeant, I seem to remember that you're from Bailovo. Is that correct?"

"Yes, Your Majesty. I was born and raised there."

"Wonderful! Bailovo is the home of my dear friend Dimitar Ivanov Stoyanov. He goes by the pen name of Ellin Pellin. You must know that, of course."

"Yes, Your Majesty. He's by far the most famous person ever to come from our village."

"But maybe not the most handsome," the tsaritza said, her eyes flicking between Dobri and Daria. "What do you think, Mademoiselle Daria?"

Dobri thought he might die; the pink creeping up his neck would probably have been visible in the dark. And the longer Miss Richetti paused before answering, the more he wished for the sudden gift of invisibility.

"Perhaps not," Daria said finally, "though I have always found older men striking—in a distinguished, patriarchal kind of way. His Majesty, for instance."

"Oh, ho! Now you've graduated into the ranks of the politicians, Mademoiselle Daria," Tsar Boris said, grinning widely. "And that's not necessarily a promotion, I might add."

After dessert the king said, "I have enjoyed this dinner as much as any I've had in a long time. Sergeant Dimitrov, we may have to invite you again."

"Your Majesty, I would be most pleased."

"And now, my dears, I must be going. Regrettably, there are some ministers in another room who will be growing impatient if I don't attend them." He stood from his place, took his wife's hand, and gave her fingers a courtly kiss. "Miss Richetti, would you be so kind as to show Sergeant Dimitrov out?"

"It would be my pleasure."

"Very well then. Adieu."

Dobri stood to attention and gave the king a farewell salute. When Tsar Boris had gone, Daria laid a hand on Dobri's arm.

"Thank you for joining us, Sergeant Dimitrov. I'll see you out now."

When they had taken a few paces toward the door, Dobri turned to her.

"Miss Richetti, if I may be so bold… Would you do me the favor of calling me simply Dobri?"

She smiled, but more, he thought, to herself than to him. "I would—Dobri—if you will do me the return favor of calling me Daria."

"Nothing would give me greater pleasure."

They were at the door. She faced him.

"Or me. Well. Good night then…Dobri."

"Good night, Daria."

Only the strictest discipline kept the sergeant of the guard from skipping down the marble hallway on the way back to his duty station.

Radka Groueva stood beneath the Tsar Osvoboditel Monument, scanning the street impatiently for any sign of her friends. Why were Betty and Zizi always late? True, Radka lived closer to the meeting place than the others, but many mornings, by the time her friends got here, the three of them had to walk so fast to avoid tardiness that they arrived at school out of breath and just in time for the first bell. Radka didn't like to be so rushed, especially in case Todor Pazardjiev was lounging in front of the school gate with some of his buddies. Surely it couldn't make much of a favorable impression on him, seeing her all red faced and puffing.

Finally she saw them: two black-clad figures ducking in and out among the morning pedestrian traffic in Alexander Battenberg Square.

"Betty! Zizi! Hurry up for once!"

But when they reached her, Radka could tell from their expressions something was amiss. And in a moment she saw what it was: a thumbnail-sized yellow star pinned to the lapel of Zizi's uniform. Against the black of her school jacket, it stood out like an accusation.

"Zizi, what's this?"

"It's the yellow star, stupid," Betty said. "She has to wear it because of the new laws."

Zizi wore a stricken expression. She stared at the pavement in front of her.

"But, Zizi, I didn't even know you were Jewish."

Zizi managed a shrug. "If…if you and Betty don't want to walk with me, it's all right. I'll understand."

Radka and Betty stared at each other.

"What are you talking about?" Radka said finally. "You're our friend. You were our friend yesterday, and you're our friend today. Right, Betty?"

Betty nodded.

"What difference does this stupid star make, anyway? Now, come on. We're going to be late to school."

Radka put her arm around Zizi's shoulders, and the three friends crossed Alexander Battenberg Square into the park beside the Sobranje, headed toward school.

11

Lily watched from the second-floor window of her office as Alexander got out of the black limousine, flanked by the Ratnik toughs he called his bodyguards. Lily hated Ratnik; they were arrogant, intolerant, and eager for any kind of fight. And they were also the people Alexander spent most of his time with these days.

Since the passage of the latest measures, Alexander was busier than ever. With the large allocation the Council of Ministers gave him, he rented a whole building on Alexander Dondukov Boulevard, not far from the Presidential Palace. He hired a staff of more than one hundred people and set them to gathering information on Jewish citizens throughout the country. He organized his newly created Commissariat for Jewish Questions into four departments: Public and Professional Activities, Treasury, Agency Activities, and Administration.

And he closeted himself in his work even more. Lily remembered a time when Alexander's office door was always open. He treated visitors—even Jews—politely if not pleasantly. Now he would see no one without an appointment, except of course Gabrovski, Filov, or the German envoy, Beckerle. Lily was charged with controlling the access into his inner sanctum. He had become despotic, impatient—even with her. The way he treated her at work was no different from the way he treated anyone else. Sometimes, in the evenings, there were still moments…

Why did she stay? Lily asked herself this maybe a hundred times a day. She told herself again and again that this couldn't end well. She had never felt good about the way their relationship had begun, and Alexander's work was pulling him deeper and deeper. She could hardly tell where the work ended and he began.

And such work. Somewhere out there, a dark judgment was building. Lily didn't know if it would find them soon or late. But it was coming; she sensed it in her deepest parts. For those who failed to show mercy, no mercy would be shown. This was the near-constant dread of her days.

She heard Alexander's footsteps on the stairs. She went to her desk and readied the sheet with his appointments for the day. He had meetings with the heads of departments, which could easily last all morning. This afternoon he was scheduled for a conference with some commissariat district officers—mostly from the coastal areas around Varna and Bourgas. She looked at the name of the Varna commissioner—Stevrolov, Ivan Stevrolov. She remembered a boy named Stevrolov who went to her school. Was it the same person? He was good in math; he always seemed to come in first or second in the math bees. He had been in her class through the fourth grade, then his family had moved to the other side of town, and she had lost track of him.

We've both come a long way from those days, haven't we, Ivan? Our biggest problem used to be whether our mamas had packed the sweets we liked for our lunches.

Alexander bustled in, snatching the appointment sheet from her outstretched hand as he passed. "Come in, Miss Panitza," he said, walking through his door. "I need you to take a few notes before my first appointment."

Lily got her pad and pen. As she stood to follow Alexander into his office, she saw Simone Damonova looking at her in that way she had. Why had Alexander insisted on bringing her into the commissariat? Lily was sure Damonova would do anything to ingratiate herself with Alexander—or maybe, just to alienate him from Lily. Simone was that kind of woman. Lily did her best to allow her eyes to slide over Damonova's face without stopping, as if she didn't notice the tramp staring at her like some cheeky gypsy. Lily went into Alexander's office and closed the door.

"The people on this list have agreed to monitor Jewish activity on behalf of the commissariat," Alexander announced, handing her a piece of paper. "Each of them should receive a pamphlet with our guidelines and the list of procedures to follow in reporting suspicious activities. Please be sure these get sent out today by courier. Bagriov will be expecting the packets from you this afternoon."

Lily grimaced. Bagriov was one of the worst Ratnik bullies.

"By the end of the day, I want to know the progress of the signage details."

Soon after moving to the building on Dondukov, Alexander had ordered the Administrative and Agency divisions to develop a joint plan for posting signs in front of every Jewish business and house, starting in Sofia and continuing throughout every city with more than ten thousand inhabitants. By this time the Jewish neighborhood of Yutch Bonar was almost covered over with the placards. Lily nodded as she wrote down her boss's request.

"And I still haven't heard from Christev about the badges."

The commissariat had ordered that Bulgarian Jews had to begin wearing the yellow star. True, due to concerns about public opinion, the celluloid buttons were smaller in Bulgaria than anywhere else in Europe—a little less than the size of a stotinka coin—but it was still a form of public isolation for Jews. Lily had already heard about Ratnik and Brannik gangs roaming the streets, tearing the Jews' badges from their clothing, then beating them for violating the law.

But the badges weren't arriving fast enough. For reasons no one could spell out, the plants that were supposed to be turning out the badges had been unable to achieve sufficient capacity. Lily had heard Alexander ranting on the phone in his office, demanding to know why the badges couldn't be manufactured more quickly. The chairman of the Subcommittee on Implementation, Damian Christev, had been charged with the responsibility of finding out where the bottleneck was and clearing it. She made a note to send him another memo.

"That's all for now. When the department heads arrive, show them in," he said.

"Alexander, I just remembered. A letter came for you yesterday, from the Royal Palace. It looks like it was sent from the office of the chief of the king's cabinet."

"What does Grouev want now?"

"I don't know. I didn't open it, of course."

"Why didn't you tell me about it before?"

"It only came late yesterday. You had already left."

He shook his head, smirking. "You slept in the same place I did."

Lily stared at her knuckles. "You know I don't like to talk about work—after hours."

"Yes, yes, whatever. Well, bring it in, then you can get started with the things I've given you."

She retrieved the letter from her in-basket and placed it on the corner of his desk. Then she left, closing the door behind her. She had just wound a sheet of paper into her typewriter for the memo to Christev when Alexander shouted, "What! This is an outrage!"

Lily heard some thrashing, then quick footsteps. Alexander's door flung open. He was striding out and pulling on his coat. The letter from the palace was crumpled in his fist.

"Cancel my appointments for the morning! I'll be at Gabrovski's."

"When will he return?"

Pavel Grouev smiled at the interior minister, seated across the desk. "Mr. Gabrovski, Tsar Boris did not file his itinerary with me when he left for Borovitz. He simply left, saying he wished not to be disturbed. I'm sorry, but it's impossible for me to tell you when the next appointment with him will be available."

Gabrovski leaned forward on the desk. "But it is a matter of some urgency, Mr. Grouev."

"Yes, so you said."

"The exemptions His Majesty is asking us to make in the new regulations will create a difficult enforcement situation."

Grouev put his elbows on the desk and laced his fingers. He gave Gabrovski what he hoped looked like a patient, attentive expression.

"The new law specifically defines Jewishness according to ancestry, not religion. If we exempt christened Jews from wearing the star, as His Majesty requests, there will be no end to the confusion. Not to mention the charade of Jews getting themselves dunked in the churches just to circumvent the law. Herr Beckerle is already incensed at the pitiful size of our Jewish stars. I cannot imagine that Berlin will take His Majesty's requests in a favorable light."

"Excuse me, Mr. Gabrovski, one small correction: I don't believe His Majesty couched the alterations as a request."

Gabrovski fumed for a few seconds. Pavel was enjoying this. The interior minister's black mustache was fairly bristling. Pavel could see the beads of sweat on his bald head.

"Be that as it may, Mr. Grouev, we mustn't forget our German allies. His Majesty caused quite another stir with them when he sent the telegram of thanks for the birthday wishes from the Jewish community leaders. They published it in their newspaper, for heaven's sake! And again when he permitted the rabbi to come to the palace and have an audience with him about the pending legislation."

"In the first place, Mr. Gabrovski, Tsar Boris was well within his rights to express appreciation for their good wishes on the crown prince's birthday, especially since those wishes came from Bulgarian citizens. In the second place, Mr. Filov has already conveyed to the king Herr Beckerle's protest over the rabbi's visit, and you can ask the prime minister how the matter was received, if you care to know. And in the third place…" Pavel paused to take a slow breath; he wanted to keep his voice level, and he could feel his emotions gathering steam. "In the third place, Tsar Boris is the sovereign of this country. I, for one, will continue to trust him to do what is best in his own eyes for the greater good of Bulgaria. I believe most Bulgarians feel the same way."

Pavel watched Gabrovski chew on this. After a moment the interior minister took a deep breath and managed a weak smile that never reached his eyes.

"It appears this interview has reached its logical conclusion, Mr. Grouev." Gabrovski stood up. "Please convey my best wishes to His Majesty the next time you speak to him—whenever that may be—and let him know of my request for an appointment."

"Of course, Mr. Gabrovski."

Gabrovski gave a little bow and left the office.

Grouev permitted himself a small grin. It felt good to release a bit of his pent-up frustration over the Jewish matter, even if he had done it rather delicately, and with the king as a sort of proxy for his own sentiments.

Still, Pavel was astute enough to realize that behind Gabrovski's irritation lay always the ticklish matter of how far one could press the Germans. The constant communications between the right-wing Ratnik and National Legion factions and the German diplomatic corps had been curtailed somewhat since last March, when Tsar Boris had spoken so bluntly to the Fuehrer. But the communication was still taking place. It was no secret to anyone that General Loukov, for one, would welcome a Fascist coup and the chance to throw Bulgaria more vigorously into the war on the side of Germany. And there was always the matter of the six hundred thousand or so German troops in and around Bulgaria.

How long could Tsar Boris continue to delay? If the situation on the Russian front didn't improve, Berlin would likely press more urgently for Bulgarian involvement. And the Jewish problem… Pavel feared Bulgaria had yet to see the worst.

The Queen Eleanora Orphanage was coming into view. The escort car ahead of Queen Giovanna's sedan turned into the driveway, and the rest of the three-car motorcade followed suit. The guards in the lead car got out and formed an honor cordon for the queen. Daria helped her make a final adjustment to her hat, then followed her out of the black Packard and into the gray three-story building.

And when they were inside, Daria saw the faces of the children. On these visits with the queen, Daria nearly always found the eyes of a young girl who made her think she was seeing a version of herself many years ago. The mixture of sadness, resignation, and hope worked over time to mold the faces of the children into a neutral mask that would do for almost any occasion. Diversions were always welcomed but generally not to be counted on for anything long-term. The children looked at them as they walked in; their eyes widened slightly at the uniforms of the guards, and the few older ones who recognized the queen whispered to each other as they bowed or curtsied, but Daria could tell most of them were guarding against expectations that could cause pain later. In an orphanage you learned early that the most reliable bulwark against disappointment was a carefully maintained wall of detachment.

Then there were the smells: the wild musk of growing children, the institutional overtones of bleach and lye soap, the pervasive aroma of cabbage and boiling beans.

As many visits as Queen Giovanna made to Bulgaria's orphanages, Daria had become accustomed to these involuntary excursions into her past. The first few times the intensity of the flood of recollection surprised her, overwhelmed her. But in these last few years, she had almost become inured; she could walk out without weeping for the children she had to leave behind.

And then she saw them. On all the children, pinned to the orphanage workers—tiny yellow stars. Queen Eleanora was a Jewish orphanage. All of them had to wear the mark. Without thinking, Daria touched her fingertips to her lapel. No badge. Of course not. She was in the royal household; no one could force her to wear the damning yellow star except Tsar Boris or his queen. Daria's secret was safe.

And yet the stars winked at her from the clothing of the children like tiny, accusing yellow eyes. Like her own private constellation, the stars followed Daria, but not to guide or comfort. No, they pointed to her, marked her as a circling of rooks marks a carcass. *See! Here's one you missed. Let her join us. Let her take her place among the marked ones.*

As she waited with the queen in the auditorium, Daria consciously thought about keeping her feet perfectly still. She willed herself to take deep, deliberate breaths. She clenched her teeth against the wail of fear that crouched somewhere near her breastbone.

The matron of the Queen Eleanora Orphanage was a woman everyone called Madame Beraha. She stood beside the queen as the soldiers brought in the hundred bolts of woolen cloth donated to the orphanage by the palace. Madame Beraha was a stout woman with iron gray hair done up in a severe bun. She wore the star on her right lapel, and Daria noticed she had made a slight modification: in the center of her badge she had glued a tiny portrait of the queen.

The supervisors brought as many of the children as they could into the auditorium to witness the gift from the palace and to listen to Madame Beraha's speech of gratitude. The matron told them how many pairs of trousers and how many shifts would be made from the donated material. The children themselves would do the sewing, she said, and with the work of their own hands they would fashion Her Majesty's generosity into sturdy garments that would directly benefit the orphanage for years to come.

When Madame Beraha finished, the tsaritza said a few words about the gift, intended to bring comfort to the children "in these hard times." Led by their supervisors, the children applauded the queen's remarks. A little girl came forward with a double fistful of *zdravetz*. She thrust the bouquet toward Giovanna and dashed into the safe anonymity of the audience as soon as she could. Daria watched her go, wishing she could follow.

In the car on the way back to the palace, Queen Giovanna handed the *zdravetz* bouquet to Daria. "Please put these in some water when we get back. I'll give them to Sonia, in the kitchen. She loves the smell of *zdravetz*."

As Daria took the flowers, the queen peered closely at her. Daria quickly averted her face, looking out the window.

"What's wrong, Daria? Something's troubling you."

"No, Your Majesty. I'm fine."

"I don't think so. Was it something at the orphanage?"

"I suppose so."

Daria didn't look at her, but she knew Queen Giovanna was studying her and would not stop until she knew the source of Daria's unease. They rode awhile in silence.

"The stars. All the children had them," Daria said finally.

"Yes. I find it hateful. As if those poor orphans had somewhere to hide."

"I wish my motives were that noble. I wish I were upset on someone else's behalf."

"Oh, Daria. The fear again?"

Daria nodded, staring at the flowers she held in her lap.

"You know, of course, that the king and I will do everything in our power to protect you."

"Yes, and I'm grateful, Your Majesty. But somehow…the threat seems larger. I mean no disrespect, but it seems larger even than Bulgaria. As if it covers the whole world."

At certain times Queen Giovanna's eyes had a steely hardness about them that was frightening. And at other times, like now, she could look at Daria with so much tenderness and concern that she wanted to weep for the sheer joy of knowing such compassion. Daria felt the tears welling up, burning the corners of her eyes, spilling onto her cheeks.

"It is as if I am the only Jew in the world, and all the hatred is aimed at me."

Queen Giovanna pressed a kerchief into Daria's hands. "That is one of the most pernicious things about fear. Fear lies to you, tells you that you are utterly alone and helpless." She touched Daria's cheek with her hand. "That is rarely so. And certainly not with you, dear Daria."

"Thank you, Your Majesty. Please forgive me."

"For what? Being human?"

"For burdening you with my problems, when you have so much else to think of."

The queen gave a dismissive wave. *"Non è niente."*

When they had gone perhaps half a block, the queen turned toward Daria again. "Do you remember the boy who used to sell those bracelets of dried grasses in the piazza of the Basilica di San Francesco?"

"Only vaguely, Your Majesty. Why do you ask?"

Queen Giovanna was looking out her window. "I don't know, exactly. But I was just thinking of Sundays there, in Assisi. The times we used to walk to the church. And in my mind he is always there: his rusty pail with a few coins scattered in the bottom, holding out his little plaited grass trinkets to anyone who passed him. He used to say something over and over again. Do you remember?"

"*'I braccialetti di benedizione... Sono fatti dalle erbe di—'*"

"*'Terra tuscan buona,'* yes, that's it, isn't it? *'Dalla terra di Dio, le erbe dalla terra di Dio.'* Thank you, Daria. I've been trying and trying, but I couldn't remember it exactly."

"Blessing bracelets," Daria said quietly. "From the good Tuscan earth— from God's earth, grasses from God's earth. It's a bit like a poem, isn't it? I didn't even know I remembered it, Your Majesty."

Queen Giovanna smiled, still gazing out her window at Pirotska Street rolling past.

"Yes, I often find it to be that way. We don't remember all we know. Until we need to." She put her hand a little way out of the partially opened window and cupped the moving air in her palm. "It was that way for me the very first time I saw Boris, did you know that?"

Daria rarely heard Giovanna refer to the king by his Christian name. She felt odd—as if she were eavesdropping on a conversation too intimate for comfort. "No, Your Majesty. I didn't know."

Queen Giovanna nodded. "Yes. When he called on my father the first time, back in the summer of '27. Oh, at first I thought he was a little old— a man of thirty, after all!" She chuckled quietly. "But the way he talked to my father… His French was, of course, perfect. But so was his Italian. He was so serious, so well informed. And then, his eyes…"

"Yes, I remember you told me he spoke very well."

The queen's eyes twinkled at Daria. "But there were other things I didn't tell you—even you, my dearest Daria. The way his eyes changed with the light: blue in the sunshine and a deep sea green by candlelight."

Daria looked away. Queen Giovanna laughed softly, a sound like the low fluting of a dove. She touched Daria's arm.

"Am I embarrassing you, Daria? I'm sorry. You must be wondering why, after all these years, I'm bringing up all these personal details."

Daria shrugged. She wasn't quite sure she wanted to hear the answer.

"I'm afraid I don't know," Queen Giovanna said. "The heart has its own reasons, they say. Maybe it's that way with the mind, too. Maybe it sorts the past, stores it away in some deep place against a time of need.

"The newspapers had already paired us, you know. I sometimes wonder if Boris got the idea of proposing from *Le Figaro* or *Die Welt*."

"Yes, Your Majesty, I remember hearing about the rumors."

"But when I saw him, talked to him…I didn't care about the newspapers anymore. I didn't care about anything.

"Oh, I couldn't let him know that, naturally. I was the *Principessa di Savoia,* after all, the daughter of the king and queen. But inside…"

"How did he find out?" Daria felt her cheeks burning, but the question had burst its bonds, and it was too late for more restraint.

Queen Giovanna's eyes widened, then she smiled broadly. "Ah. You have an…interest in someone, I gather?"

Daria nodded helplessly. *Postema ragazza… Postema ragazza… Postema ragazza…*

"Someone with a very full, handsome mustache? Someone who looks very dashing in his uniform? Someone, maybe, who has recently eaten dinner at the private table?"

"Please, Your Majesty, don't think me foolish. I know he's only a sergeant, but..."

Daria felt the queen's arm encircling her shoulders.

"Oh, Daria, *cara mia*. I don't think you're foolish. Never. But I do think maybe you're falling in love."

12

Metropolitan Stefan lifted the cup to his lips. He took some of the cherry red wine into his mouth and swirled it with his tongue for a few seconds, then swallowed it slowly. He allowed the taste to rest on his palate for some moments.

"Ah, yes, Madame Karavelova, this is maybe the finest Merlot I've tasted this season. You say it's from Haskovo?"

The stately woman, seated across from him in a tapestry-covered Regency fauteuil, smiled and nodded. "Stambolovo, to be more precise. I'm glad you like it. You're one of the few connoisseurs I know who shares my taste for the heartier tones."

"I'm honored to be in such elite company, my dear lady."

She laughed. "Better than the company you keep when you travel, one hears."

Stefan put his hand over his heart. "My detractors do me wrong, Madame Karavelova. As a shepherd of the flock, it's my solemn duty to seek the straying sheep."

"But to fall into the mire with them?"

"Only the Good Shepherd has feet that never slip." Stefan gave her a sideways, slightly guilty look. "I guess it's a consequence of my taste for the heartier tones."

"No doubt, Your Eminence. But you should watch yourself, especially in these times."

"You're right, of course, Madame Karavelova. Your dear departed husband was always giving me similar warnings. A man of such wisdom."

"He liked you a great deal, Stefan. As do I. He often said to me that if the Sobranje had a handful of men as unafraid to speak their minds as you, twice the laws would get passed in half the time."

"He was a great leader."

She inclined her head in a little bow of thanks.

"What can I do about the problems you mentioned?" she said.

"Say something to the king, Madame Karavelova. He respects you, as does everyone in Bulgaria. We must force the police to put an end to the Brannik and Ratnik gangs' harassment of the Jews. If Bulgaria's most respected citizens register the full measure of their disapproval, the government cannot continue turning a blind eye to these abuses."

Madame Karavelova toyed with the stem of her wineglass. "Your preaching on this topic has earned you the attention of the government censors."

"I could not possibly care less for their opinion," Stefan said. "I care far more what my Lord thinks of me."

"An admirable conviction, Stefan, and I'm not surprised by it. A Bolshevik bomb at Sveta Nedelia didn't slow you down. I don't see why a few Fascists should."

The metropolitan looked into his wine as he swirled it in his glass. "I've thought about that day a lot. I still don't know why God chose to spare me or why he let so many innocents die. I was reading from the gospel of John over General Georghiev's coffin when the explosion sent the central cupola crashing down into the nave. The noise, the dust, the screaming, the mangled bodies…" He took a quick gulp of wine and shook his head as he swallowed. "I've heard my grandfather talk about what it was like in the old days, fighting the Turks. But at least they bombed military installations. To destroy women and children in a church…"

"Perhaps God knew you would be needed for other days."

He looked at her. "Perhaps. This much I know: since the day I was born, the one thing I have never been able to abide is the sight of the strong taking advantage of the weak. I am the grandson of a revolutionary, the son of an Orthodox priest who was also a revolutionary. By the time I was twenty-three, I had already made myself the enemy of the tax bullies in my village.

"I cannot look on and allow the repression of my fellow citizens. And I believe most Bulgarians feel the same way. For five hundred years we endured the Ottoman yoke together, Jews as well as Christians. We must not allow the Nazis to cause us to forget all we have suffered together. Madame Karavelova, will you help me?"

"But I have no pulpit, Your Eminence."

"Ah yes, you have. You have the pulpit of respect. You have the pulpit of the esteem in which the king holds you. You have the pulpit of your revered husband's memory." He leaned forward, his eyes fixed on her. "Use them! Help me as I help Bulgaria save its soul."

Gabrovski looked nervous as he prepared to deliver his speech. Pavel Grouev watched as the interior minister carefully straightened his manuscript for the third time, his eyes flickering over the chamber where the pro-government majority of the Sobranje sat quietly, waiting for him to begin. He took a handkerchief from his pocket and dabbed at his lips, then wiped his bald head. He cleared his throat. He straightened his tie.

And then, just before he launched into his address, his eyes swept the balcony and caught Grouev's. Pavel was seated in the exact center of the first row, and he returned Gabrovski's look with a calm, patient expression.

"Deputies of the people of Bulgaria, it takes no wise man to perceive that we live in perilous times. All around us, we see a world at war. The destiny of Europe hangs in the balance, and we are justified in feeling fear and uncertainty.

"But I submit to you, dear colleagues, that we also live in a time of great opportunity. For those who are prepared to accept the risks, these are days when great things may be accomplished. And as I look at Bulgaria today, I see a number of important and encouraging signs."

He went on to talk about the expansion of Bulgaria's borders, thanks to "the important friends of our country" who sponsored and made possible the annexation of the Dobrudja and the administration of Macedonia and Thrace. He spoke of the modernization and improvement of the army. He talked about the increasing opportunities in trade and commerce, how industry in Bulgaria was enjoying a strength not known since the early days of the century, and perhaps even surpassing those times. And then he came to the part Pavel was most interested in, the part he was here to witness on behalf of the palace.

"Some detractors point to a few incidents and say Bulgaria is mindlessly copying Berlin," Gabrovski said. "Some who fail to grasp the complexities of national security in such difficult times have said that the Law for the Defense of the Nation is an unjust law. They have taken the complaints of a few Jewish and Communist malcontents as the symptom of some great, dark conspiracy of evil.

"I think it is time for the Jewish question to take a backseat to more important matters. Yes, we have passed laws for the regulation of our Jews. Let us apply these laws fairly and humanely and get on with the more serious business of readying Bulgaria to take her place in the New Europe. To those who suspect some ulterior motive, I say, 'Where is the proof?' Those of us in this room are not criminals, nor are we barbarians. We want to protect our motherland, but we must do it in a moral, sensible, and lawful way."

Grouev nodded his approval. The interior minister had followed the script reasonably well—with one or two departures. His comments would be useful in encouraging the state police to rein in the right-wing extremists Madame Karavelova and others were so upset about. As Pavel looked about the chamber, he could see several members of the Sobranje nodding their heads. Apparently, the Holy Synod and Madame Karavelova weren't the only ones needing some reassurance about the interior minister's intentions.

Pavel got up and excused himself past the people seated in his row. He went down the stairs toward the Battenberg Square doors, thinking that His Majesty would be pleased to know the gentle persuasion had produced fruit—for now, at least.

Daria liked mornings at the Kritchim villa better than almost anything. In the winter, the vast stillness of the Rhodope Mountains wrapped the place in a down blanket of serenity. And in the summer, the birdsong that started so quietly, just before dawn, gathered throughout the broadening of sunrise into a glad, unruly chorus that made it almost impossible to greet the day with anything less than contentment.

She smiled as she arranged the fresh flowers in Queen Giovanna's favorite Limoges vase. This would be the perfect centerpiece for today's breakfast table. The wildflowers were her favorites—the asters and cornflowers and *zdravetz*. It would have been much easier, of course, to order up armloads of roses from the market in Kritchim village or even from Stamboliski; it was the height of the season. And Daria did love driving through the Valley of Roses this time of year; the road from Karlovo to Sliven was an amazement to the eyes and the nose, with fields on either side of the highway ablaze in fragrant blooms. But there was something quiet and perfect about these demure Bulgarian blossoms gathered from the sloping meadows round about the royal estate. They seemed more personal to Daria somehow, more intimate.

Everyone else in the house was still asleep. The motorcade hadn't gotten away from Vrana until nearly eight o'clock yesterday evening. Daria had waited with Giovanna and the children at the royal estate, trying to calm the growing impatience of the crown prince and his sister. One after another, last-minute matters queued up to keep Tsar Boris at the palace far past the time he had promised they would leave for the country house.

At last his car swept up the long driveway of the house at Vrana. There was a flurry of activity as trunks and valises were loaded and final instructions were given to the Vrana staff. Pavel Grouev was there to see them off, and Tsar Boris gave him a few extra directives about some important diplomatic visitors the king was expecting at Kritchim during his stay—Daria didn't hear exactly who the guests were.

And then, just as they were getting in the cars, Queen Giovanna pulled Daria aside. "You need to ride in that car," she said, pointing to one of the dark vehicles that would follow the Packard driven by the king.

"But I always ride with you and the children—"

"Not this time. Just get in."

Confused, Daria went toward the waiting car. Tsar Boris was watching, his eyes going back and forth between his wife and Daria. "My dear? I thought Mademoiselle Richetti—"

The queen gave him a slight shake of the head, then nodded for Daria to get into the other car. Daria shrugged and reached for the rear door handle.

"No, Miss Richetti. Why don't you sit up front?"

Daria looked up at the man who had spoken, who was about to get in the driver's seat. It was Dobri Dimitrov.

She slid into the front passenger seat just as he was getting behind the wheel. She looked at him and smiled.

"I'm Daria. Remember?"

He nodded. "I won't make that mistake again."

They talked all the way from Vrana as the last of the summer twilight faded into darkness along the western skyline behind them. Dobri's voice was quiet and resonant against the humming of the tires on the road. The taillights of the king's Packard winked in and out in front of them. But the image Daria remembered best during the drive from Sofia to Kritchim was the sight of Dobri's hands on the steering wheel, softly lit by the car's instrument panel. Now and then his right hand would move to the shift lever, as the slowing of the motorcade necessitated downshifting. His fingers would wrap around the shaft of the lever and maneuver it into place, then return to the steering wheel. His hands moved quietly and surely; they knew where they needed to be. They held the machine in control, but carefully. There was no hesitation, no extra movement. Daria caught herself thinking about how his hands would feel, smoothed against her cheek or stroking her shoulder. They would be solid, she thought, and a little hard—the hands of a man accustomed to work. But they would also be warm and very gentle.

Dobri told her about his native village of Bailovo, how the foothills of the Rhodope Mountains cupped it like a father's hands on the face of a beloved child. "My mother told me," he said, "that on the day I was born a stork began building a nest on the roof of the church. She said it was a good sign." He told about the festivals, when everybody in Bailovo would gather in the town market to eat and laugh and dance the *horo* to the skirling of the *kaval* and the thump-and-click of the *tapan*. "I swiped more than my share of hot *shishke* when nobody was looking," he said. "I'm afraid I was a bit of a rowdy."

Daria asked him why he left Bailovo. "Did they finally put a price on your head for all the sausages you stole?"

Dobri laughed, and in the dim light of the car's dashboard Daria could see the hollow of his throat pulsing with the laughter. She fought the urge to place a fingertip there.

"No, I wasn't exiled exactly. I was the youngest of five children, you see, and the army was the best opportunity for me."

"You were the baby?"

He gave her a sideways look. "That's what my mother called it. I was always the baby to her."

"Isn't she still living?"

He shook his head. "My parents died within a month of each other. One winter, my mother took a chill and died with a fever, and my father lost interest in living soon after. My oldest brother, Ilya, takes care of the sheep and the land these days."

"I'm sorry. You must miss them."

Dobri shrugged and nodded. He looked at her.

"What about you? Have you lived all your life with the tsaritza?"

Daria sat in the long silence that followed, realizing she was trapped. To speak of her past was to betray her vulnerability; to remain silent was to betray the trust she felt growing between herself and Dobri.

"What's the matter?" he said, glancing at her. "Aren't you going to tell me? And after I confessed my life as a sausage thief."

She tried to smile. "It's just that…I…" She took a deep breath and stared straight ahead. "I'm Jewish, Dobri."

He said nothing for a long time, and with each second that passed, Daria felt despair edging closer and closer.

"I think I knew you were Jewish, but I'm not sure how," he said finally. "I guess I heard it somewhere around the palace."

Dobri eased the car through a series of sharp curves. Daria kept her eyes forward, watching the taillights of the king's car as it swerved back and forth in front of them. What was Dobri thinking about her now? In her mind, she heard Paolo's taunting: *You think I want a stinking skullcap like the kike boys wear?*

"Isn't there more? Have I said something wrong?" he said.

She shook her head and stared at her hands, folded in her lap.

"No, I…I just didn't know you knew about…"

"I have said something wrong after all."

"No, really you haven't. It's just that it's not a good time to be Jewish in Europe."

After another while he said, "Daria, you know that Tsar Boris won't let anything happen to you."

It wasn't precisely the reassurance she had hoped for, but it was better than nothing.

Daria heard footsteps on the stairs in the foyer behind her. She turned to see the king and queen coming toward the dining room. Queen Giovanna's hand was on King Boris's arm. The two of them were smiling quietly at each other. Daria felt the urge to look away; it seemed impertinent, somehow, to be witnessing their intimate satisfaction. Queen Giovanna saw her, though, and gave her a smile in greeting, followed by a tilted, appraising look. Daria returned the queen's glance as frankly as she could but soon felt the blush working its way up her neck.

"So, Mademoiselle Daria, how did you find the drive last night?" Tsar Boris said, giving her a broad wink. "I hope Sergeant Dimitrov's war talk didn't bore you?"

"No, I'd say the campaign is going well," Queen Giovanna said. "I'm sure Daria found it all quite fascinating."

"Really, both of you. How cruel to make sport of a poor Tuscan girl," Daria said. "And now, if you'll excuse me, I'll notify the staff to serve breakfast." She gave her best imitation of an indignant toss of her head and strode toward the kitchen. The king's and queen's laughter rang behind her.

"Shall I go and rouse the children?" Daria said when the three of them were seated at the table.

One of the kitchen staff set a large crockery pitcher of milk in front of Tsar Boris, and he poured a tumbler full for Queen Giovanna, then one for Daria, before helping himself. "Oh no, let them sleep. This is a holiday, after all. As late as we were in getting away from Sofia, they'll probably sleep till noon."

"When does our guest arrive?" the queen asked her husband.

"The day after tomorrow. He's flying in to Sofia tomorrow night, then Pavel will have him driven over. I hope we can find some fallow deer. He says he's anxious to try his hand at our Bulgarian game."

"Who is it?" Daria asked. "Someone from one of our foreign embassies?"

"No, it's Reichsmarshall Goering. I promised him some shooting last March when I was in Berlin, and this is the time he's chosen to claim his chance."

Daria felt a cold place in the center of her chest. One of Hitler's closest aides—here in Kritchim. There would be no way to avoid him. How would she manage?

"Will he be here for very many days?"

The king gave her an odd look. "No, only two or three. Is something the matter?"

"No, of course not, Your Majesty. I was just…reviewing the arrangements for the staff. He'll need linens, and the menu will have to allow for another person. That's all."

Boris looked at her a moment longer, then nodded. "Yes, well, I'm sure you'll see to everything in your usual splendid fashion, Mademoiselle Daria."

Queen Giovanna gave her a worried look, then a little half smile. "I hope the Reichsmarshall's palate won't be offended by some fresh *shopska* salad. The vegetables are so lovely this summer, it would be a shame not to use them."

"Yes, Your Majesty. I'll see to it. I'll tell the staff."

Hermann Goering was a fleshy, broad-shouldered man with a head of wavy blond hair. Dobri recognized him easily from his many pictures in the newspapers. His taste for flashy clothing was well known, and on the day he arrived at Kritchim, he wore a tan-colored tweed touring jacket over a bright red vest. The dark green lederhosen and jaunty feathered cap completed the spectacle. Goering flashed a mouthful of perfect white teeth as he saluted Tsar Boris.

"Your Majesty, the Bulgarian countryside is every bit as lovely as you said. It is surpassed in beauty only by this breathtaking woman at your side."

Queen Giovanna smiled and extended her hand, which the Reichsmarshall kissed.

"I hope the shooting lives up to your expectations," Tsar Boris said as they walked toward the front steps.

"Oh, I'm sure it will, Your Majesty. I've found nothing disappointing in Bulgaria so far, and I trust that will continue."

Boris gave Goering a little smile. "Well. Here we are. Sergeant Dimitrov will show you to your quarters, and we'll have the staff bring the rest of your luggage."

That evening the cooks prepared *jaegerschnitzel* and noodles in honor of their important guest. Dobri would have much preferred a simple bowl of *bob chorba,* with maybe some bread and cheese and a glass of beer to wash it down, but the Reichsmarshall likely had different tastes. The saving grace, though, was the *shopska* salad Queen Giovanna ordered. Dobri was polishing off a large bowl of it in the kitchen when Daria came in from the dining room. He smiled at her, then realized her face was ashen and her hands were shaking.

He stood. "What is it, Daria? What's the matter?"

She had her eyes closed and was taking deep breaths, trying to calm herself. She looked at him.

"I'm sorry, Dobri. I had to get out of there, just for a few minutes."

He gave her a wordless, questioning look.

"It's the Reichsmarshall. Several times during the meal I've noticed him looking at me. He…he makes me afraid."

"Now, now." He glanced at the doors to the dining room. Hesitantly, like a man about to hold an infant for the first time, he put his hands on her shoulders. "Shh…you mustn't. You're in the royal household. Not even Hermann Goering would be foolish enough to try anything."

She gave him the flicker of a smile.

"There, now, you see?"

"Thank you, Dobri. But it's not really that—not that I'm afraid he'll do me any harm. It's… Oh, I don't know how to say it. He reminds me of the danger. For all of us…all Jews. I've heard he was very involved in the anti-Jewish measures in Germany. And when he looks at me, it's as if he can see…what I am."

"Oh, I have no doubt of that. Anybody who looks at you can see what you are—one of the most beautiful women in Bulgaria. Even a German can't fail to notice that."

His hands had slipped down near her elbows. She leaned into him, and after a moment his arms encircled her, pressing her to his chest. Her hair was in his face, and he breathed her in as a surfacing diver takes in his first lungful of air. He felt her arms go around his waist.

After a time she released him and stood away. She looked at him, and he thought he might drown in the darkness of her eyes.

She studied him the way he had seen old people study one of the holy icons in a church. She measured him, paced the length and breadth of him with her gaze. He waited.

Slowly she raised a hand to his face, then brushed her fingertips against the hollow of his neck.

He wanted to take her hand and press it to his lips, but he wanted to feel her touch on his skin forever. It was like watching a bird and wanting to hold it in your hand. The one pleasure spoils the other, and he didn't know which to choose.

She stepped back from him. "I can go back now. The queen will want the children seen to bed."

Dobri nodded at her. "Take heart, Daria."

She gave him an odd look and nodded. Then she turned and was gone.

13

September 1942

The drive from Kritchim to Assenovgrad was one of Simeon's favorites. His father enjoyed maneuvering the car along the narrow road that wound through the Rhodope Mountains, and Simeon enjoyed sitting in the front seat beside his father. His father always seemed happy and relaxed when driving, so Simeon could ask him one question after another, and he didn't seem to mind. That Sergeant Dimitrov was in the backseat made the trip even better; the crown prince liked Sergeant Dimitrov very much. Unlike many of the adults around the palace, Sergeant Dimitrov seemed to really listen to Simeon, not just wait politely until he could get on with his business. Simeon liked the way Sergeant Dimitrov explained things. He used words Simeon could understand, but not in a way that reminded Simeon he was only five years old. And besides that, Sergeant Dimitrov always carried a gun. What could be better?

When they reached the fortress, Simeon's father parked the car at the base of the long stone-paved path that wound to the crest of the cliff. He got out of the car and squatted so Simeon could climb onto his shoulders and ride to the top.

"No, Papa. Today I want to climb by myself."

His father looked surprised. "Are you sure, Simeon? It's a long way up. I always carry you."

"Yes, Pa—Your Majesty, I know. But I'm five years old. I'm the crown prince. I should walk up to the fortress myself now."

His father gave a strange look at Sergeant Dimitrov: something that was a smile, but not quite. Sergeant Dimitrov looked at Simeon as if he had just said something very good—as if he were one of the adults making the important talk and not just a child, listening.

The muscles in Simeon's legs were getting sore by the time they reached the final flight of steps, rough-carved from the living stone of the mountain-side, that led to the high plateau where the fortress stood. But Simeon just gritted his teeth and kept climbing. He didn't want to seem tired in front of Papa and Sergeant Dimitrov. He wanted to be strong. He wanted to make it there on his own.

The Assenov Fortress lay before him; the late summer sun splashed across its stonework, giving it the color of a lion's hide. The arched doorways and windows reminded him of the pictures he had seen of the Roman aqueducts near Mama's home in Italy. The rounded, windowed turret at the very top and center of the building was like the central vault of the chapel at Bachkovo Monastery.

But the watchtower was the part of the fortress that always drew Simeon like a magnet. He could travel in his mind back to the days of Tsar Ivan Assen II, standing like the king of the whole world in this high, safe place. The view from the watchtower of Assenov Fortress made Simeon feel as if he could fly.

He could hear his father and Sergeant Dimitrov coming up the steps behind him. He didn't want to turn around, didn't want to take his eyes away from the view spreading beneath his feet. He felt Papa's hand on his shoulder. They stood that way for a long time, both of them just looking.

"Papa, why do you think Tsar Ivan Assen II built this tower?"

"Well, I would say because this mountaintop commands a view of such a wide area. It would be hard for an enemy to sneak up on anyone stationed here."

"I don't think so, Papa."

"Really? Why, then?"

"I think the king built this tower so he could come up here and remember how beautiful his country was."

Pavel Grouev sighed deeply and looked at the clock on his desk. It was a Junghans table clock in a polished walnut case so ornate it almost looked like a shrine. A remnant of King Ferdinand's obsession for unusual timepieces, it had been given to Pavel by the old king upon the occasion of his promotion from the Foreign Ministry Office to the palace chancellery. Pavel liked the clock; its tiny chimes had a pure sound that reminded him of crystal goblets tapped together.

It was past seven o'clock. This speech didn't have to be finished tonight, after all; Tsar Boris wouldn't need it for another week or so. Stanislav Balan had left more than an hour ago. Pavel decided to call it a night and go home.

Walking in the autumn darkness, he contemplated the speech he was drafting for Tsar Boris. Pavel was so lost in his study that he almost stumbled over his daughter sitting on the front steps of their building.

"Radka! What are you doing out here, my dear? It's completely dark outside."

"I was waiting for you, Papi."

Something in her tone alerted him. "What's the matter, *draga?*"

A tear leaked from the corner of her eye. "It's Zizi, Papi. Today she came here for a while, after school, to help me study for a literature test tomorrow. You know me, Papi; I say things sometimes. Well, while we were studying, I threw down the book and said I couldn't stand reading any more of it. A story about a man turning into a cockroach, Papi, after all! I said the man had a sick mind and trying to understand him was like trying to pick up ants with tweezers."

"Hmm. Sounds like Kafka."

"Franz Kafka, yes, that was it. And when I said that, Zizi got all offended at me and said I didn't like Kafka just because he was Jewish. Papi, I didn't even know Kafka was Jewish, but before I knew it, I was trying to apologize to Zizi for something I didn't even know I'd done."

"I'm sorry, my dear. It must have been very hard to have your friend angry with you."

Her face was still angled down. Pavel looked at her a few seconds more. "Is there something else, Radka?"

She looked at him, and fresh tears bulged in her eyes.

"Papi, is something bad going to happen to Zizi? She's my friend. She was my friend long before she was Jewish."

Pavel smiled at his daughter. He pulled her to him and wrapped her close.

"Now, my darling. You must try not to worry. Everything possible is being done to make sure nothing terrible happens to Zizi or anybody else."

"Really, Papi?"

"Really. Now, go tell Mama I'm home. And if you don't mind, get me a cup of tea."

As he watched his daughter go inside, Pavel prayed he had told her the right thing.

Looking over her shoulder a final time as she stepped from the lee of the Levski Monument, Lily Panitza crossed the plaza and went in the leftmost of the three side doors on the west end of Alexander Nevsky Cathedral. She paused to allow her eyes to adjust to the semidarkness; it was a bright autumn day outside. There were quite a few visitors inside, though, and that was good; Lily wanted the shelter of crowds as much as possible.

She looked at her watch. She hoped Daria Richetti was punctual; Lily needed time to pass her information and get something to eat from the sidewalk café on Moskovska Street, her cover for a lunch-hour excursion in this direction. Still a bit winded from the quick walk over, Lily began moving toward the agreed rendezvous beneath the Saint Sofia icon in the main nave.

To Lily's relief, Daria was there ahead of her. She looked nervous, which in turn ratcheted up Lily's anxiety. Was Daria followed? It wouldn't be at all far-fetched to think agents were assigned to members of the royal household and its servants. Lily shielded herself behind a column, scanning the rotunda for anything or anyone who made her suspicious. Finally she decided to risk an approach.

She walked up beside Daria, keeping her eyes always on the icon.

"I'm glad you could come," she said quietly.

"Your note indicated you needed to tell me something." Daria kept her body angled away from Lily, allowing her face only a half-turn in Lily's direction. "Please tell me quickly; I'd like to leave as soon as possible."

"Do you think you were followed?"

"No, I don't think so. I sometimes take walks in the vicinity of the palace. I made this look like one of those."

"Something is getting ready to happen at the Commissariat for Jewish

Questions. I think someone from Berlin is coming to meet with Alex—with Commissar Belev and maybe Interior Minister Gabrovski. There have been several coded cables, lots of requests for background information, status of programs, procedures, that kind of thing. Someone wants to know as much as possible about what our office has been doing for the last year or so."

"When?"

"I don't know yet. But the commissar has been shut in with every one of his directors, and he's had lots of meetings with Gabrovski—maybe the prime minister, too. I thought His Majesty should know."

"He may know already, but I'll make sure—somehow. Is that all?"

"Yes."

Daria drifted toward the front doors. Lily stayed by the icon a few minutes longer, then went to the front foyer and bought a taper. She went to an altar just inside the main doors and lit her candle. She placed it in the upper tray, intending to say a quick prayer for her mother. But to her surprise, the only words that would form in her mind were from a hymn for the Easter Vigil:

> He has brought down rulers....
> He has helped his servant Israel....

"Herr Beckerle said that he has been directed by Berlin to request plans be put in motion here for the deportations to Poland. He said they were requesting 250 reichsmark for each transportee, to be paid in consideration of the costs of the, ah, operation."

Boris propped his elbows on the desk and bridged his fingertips. "I see, Mr. Filov. And you told him—"

"As you and I discussed, I pointed out to Herr Beckerle that our manpower needs were critical. With the continuing administration and occupation of Macedonia and Thrace, along with other wartime needs, our armed forces are stretched to the limit. We simply cannot allow the Jewish men to leave the country, I said, and still have adequate work crews for our road- and bridge-building needs."

"And how did the German ambassador receive this assessment?"

"He seemed to understand, Your Majesty. I told him we certainly appreciated the generous offer of the Reich. He also mentioned the possibility of Berlin sending us an advisor on Jewish questions."

"An advisor? How interesting. All in all, then, Mr. Filov, you would say you left Herr Beckerle with a sympathetic understanding of our particular problems?"

"I believe so, Your Majesty. I assured him that Bulgaria would do its duty, and that while a partial deportation might be possible before too long, we could under no circumstances agree to a total relocation of our Jews until certain objectives were accomplished. I was most clear on that, Your Majesty."

"Yes, thank you, Mr. Filov; I appreciate your attention to that detail. It's very important that the work on our roads and bridges not be compromised. Did he, by any chance, ask to speak to you again on this matter?"

"Not directly, Your Majesty. He only said that some follow-up meetings might be in order after he had communicated with Berlin."

"Yes, well… If he requests such a meeting, you will, of course, inform me?"

"Absolutely, Your Majesty."

"Good. Very well, Mr. Filov. I appreciate your thoroughness in all this."

Filov stood and gathered his coat, muffler, and hat. "Will Your Majesty be attending the opening of *Il Trovatore* this evening? Mrs. Filov and I are most anxious to hear this new soprano everyone is raving about."

"I don't know, Mr. Filov. Mr. Grouev was just asking me the same thing, and I told him—"

There was a knock on the door, and Boris opened it.

"Excuse me, Your Majesty. The veterans are ready for you," Dobri Dimitrov said.

"Thank you, Sergeant." Boris turned back to the prime minister. "Well, Mr. Filov, I really must be going now. I have a little ceremony to attend."

"Of course, Your Majesty. I was just leaving."

Boris ushered Filov out of the office. He crossed the room and knocked on a door in the panel of the side wall. Pavel Grouev opened it.

"Did he say to Beckerle what you suggested?" Pavel asked.

"Apparently. Come, Pavel. The Veterans League awaits us in the ballroom."

As they walked together down the hall, Pavel said, "Did the Germans accept our objections?"

"For now, Bacho Pavlé. For now."

"...and the rooster said to the farmer, 'Quiet, you fool! I'm trying for the buzzards!' "

Buko Lazarov and the other men burst into laughter, but Anka and the women shushed them.

"Buko, do you want the police to come see what all this noise is?" she said, shaking a finger at him. She went to the heavy curtains and pulled them together for about the hundredth time in the past two hours.

Buko took another swig of *rakia* and a pull on his cigar. He grimaced.

"Whoever cured this tobacco should be shot."

"Sorry, Buko. It was all I could afford."

"Never mind, Simcho. I shouldn't be so fussy. I'm just glad to have something to smoke for a change." He looked around at the other men in the small apartment. "And I'm glad to be with my friends. This *Chanukh* is one I'll never forget."

"I still can't believe they sent us home from the camps," another man said. "I thought I'd be freezing all winter in that cattle shed we called a barracks, and instead I'm home in time for *Chanukh*."

"When I get back to Skopje, Uncle Buko, I'll tell them how fat the living is here in the north."

Buko grinned at his nephew and took a playful swipe at his head. "Yes, you do that, Dimo. You tell my sister that her son learned something in the time he spent in the camps of Bulgaria."

"Yeah," said Simcho, "how to eat stale bread and burned beans and call it beef and potatoes."

The men laughed again. From the women's corner, Anka looked at Buko again and shook her head, but she didn't scold this time.

"It was bad luck to be visiting your uncle when the press gangs came through," one of the men said to Dimo. "May the new year bring better things."

"For us all," someone said. All the men nodded.

"Well, as long as I can spend it in Skopje, that'll be all I ask," Dimo said. "No offense, Uncle Buko, but I've seen all I want of Bulgaria for a while."

"Soon as the war's over, if Tsar Boris has his way, you'll be living in Bulgaria again," Simcho said. "I hear the Fuehrer is already having the maps redrawn; Macedonia's coming back to Bulgaria."

"If the Fuehrer is drawing the maps, we won't be on it anywhere," Buko said.

"Oh, come on, Uncle Buko, don't be so pessimistic," said Dimo. "It could be a lot worse. And, look, they just turned us loose and sent us home from the work brigades. Maybe Hitler's gotten bored with the Jews. Maybe it's somebody else's turn in the camps for a while."

Buko shook his head.

"Well, it's time to get going," Simcho said, standing up and scratching his belly. "It takes longer to get home when you're sneaking along the back ways." He looked over to the corner where the women were gathered. "Sonia! It's time."

Over the next forty-five minutes, the other guests left in ones and twos, slipping quietly down the stairs to the alley behind the dry-goods store and into the night. The party was technically in violation of the Jewish curfew, but these last few months, enforcement hadn't been so strict. As long as the guests didn't draw attention to themselves, they could be reasonably confident of arriving home unmolested. Finally the only ones left were Buko, Anka, and Dimo. Baba Marika had given up on the party early in the evening; she was in her bed in the apartment's other tiny room.

"Well, Dimo, you can put down your bedroll in that corner, unless you'll reconsider and take the couch."

"No, Uncle. I already owe you for finding me a ride south. I wouldn't dream of putting you and Aunt Anka out of your bed."

Anka handed Dimo a package wrapped in brown paper. "Here, Dimo. Take this to your mother from me. It's just a few odds and ends I found that belonged to Buko's mother. Your sister's getting to be of an age that she might like some of this."

Dimo unwrapped the package. He held up a small charm bracelet made of gold chain. The bracelet had a single charm: a white lacquered disk set with a Magen David of sky blue sapphire.

"These are pretty, Aunt Anka. And you're right; Elena will love them, especially if they belonged to Baba Ioanna. I'll make sure Mother gets them."

"Well, it's late. If you're going to be at Mikhail Dobrovetski's house at six tomorrow morning, we'd all better get some sleep," Buko said.

Anka slipped quietly into the other room to change into her nightgown. Buko blew out the kerosene lamps, then he and Dimo undressed in the dark. The cold December air seeped slowly into the still room, making it seem even quieter, more motionless.

"Uncle Buko, I really want to thank you. I didn't like to think about walking all the way to Skopje. And I really wanted to go home."

"Of course, Dimo. It's the least we could do. After all, if it weren't for me, you probably wouldn't have been in that camp in the first place."

Anka came back in, and Buko scooted over, making a place for her beside him on the couch. They settled the layers of blankets over them, and the room quieted again.

"Uncle Buko, do you really think Hitler's going to win?"

Buko felt Anka stiffen. She hated talk about the war; she wouldn't let Buko speak of the things he heard from the other men in Kyustendil, the day- or week-old headlines he glimpsed on the newspapers he scrounged from the trash bins. "If it's going to get worse," she said, "I'd just as soon not see it coming, since I can't do anything about it anyway." Anka believed in the power of silent suffering; she had learned it from her mother.

Buko sighed. "I don't know, Dimo. It's hard to tell. The best thing to do is wait and watch...and hope for the best."

Daria opened the door, and Monsignor Roncalli came in, smiling and bowing to the queen. Giovanna rose to meet him, also smiling, and took his hand in both of hers. She kissed his ring and motioned him toward a chair.

"*Buon giorno, Maestà.* I bring you Christmas greetings from His Holiness, the pope."

"Thank you, Monsignor. May the new year bring peace at last."

The archbishop sighed. "Yes, *Maestà,* may God grant it so. But he will have to knock some sense into some very thick heads to accomplish it, I fear."

"I hear rumors His Holiness is thinking of posting you as nuncio to Paris."

Roncalli shook his head and gave the queen a little smile. "Well, *Maestà,* that's what some of them are saying. And I do not deny that for a farm boy from Sotto il Monte, the City of Lights has a certain attraction. But in a way that's what worries me."

"What do you mean?"

"Well, it's like this. As papal nuncio, I always get invited to these diplomatic soirees: you know, where everyone comes into a huge, glittering room, surrounded by glittering people. As soon as you can, you grab a tiny plate of decorative food so your hands will have something to do, and you stand around, trying to think of things to say to these people whom everyone knows but no one knows. Then—wouldn't you know it?—in walks a beautiful woman in a low-cut dress, and everyone turns and stares…at me!"

Queen Giovanna laughed.

"You see how it is? I will be in the most glamorous city in the world—aside from *La bella Roma,* of course—but with everyone watching me all the time, I might as well be back home in Lombardia, eating chickpea soup and drinking well water!"

Queen Giovanna shook her head. "Oh, Monsignor, I think you will do very well in Paris, indeed! But whatever will we do without you in Sofia?"

Roncalli made a dismissive gesture. Daria offered him a small glass of claret, which he took with a quick smile of thanks.

"How are my father and mother?" Queen Giovanna asked.

"They're well. They send you their affection."

"How are things in Rome?"

The archbishop shrugged. "Depends on whom you ask. Mussolini keeps a tight leash on the papers, so the headlines are all about the inevitable triumph of the Axis. But when you get people away from the cameras and microphones, you get a different story."

Queen Giovanna nodded. "I thought as much." She took a sip of her claret, then set the glass back on the small round table beside her chair. "Has the Holy Father done anything further to protect Italy's Jews?"

Roncalli had an uncomfortable look. "*Maestà,* His Holiness is in a most delicate position. He does what he can to oppose the Charter of Race's most odious provisions and has had some successes. But as long as the Fascist government controls the army and police, the Holy Father's influence is very much limited to the spiritual and moral spheres."

"It has long been my opinion, Monsignor, that we should never underestimate the power of the spiritual and moral spheres."

He smiled and saluted her with his glass. "Well said, *Maestà.*"

"And you, Monsignor? What do you make of the Nazi doctrine of race?"

He swirled the remnants of his wine and stared into his glass for several seconds. "It is very disturbing to me," he said without looking up. "If taken to its logical conclusion…I fear, when all is known, that we may be living through one of the greatest horrors of all time." He met her eyes. "One day history will judge those who perpetrated this hatred, as well as those who watched and did nothing. And those of us who have chosen to intervene will judge ourselves, grieved that we didn't do more."

A moment of silence passed. The archbishop began patting his coat pockets. His hand encountered the thing he sought, and his face brightened.

"I almost forgot. I brought something for the princess. Is she available?"

Queen Giovanna motioned to Daria, who went to the winter garden, where she had left Princess Maria-Louisa and Crown Prince Simeon playing. She brought the princess into the salon. Princess Maria-Louisa made a very pretty curtsy to Archbishop Roncalli, and he stood and gave her a courtly bow.

"*Principessa,* I believe you have a birthday coming very soon, yes?"

Princess Maria-Louisa smiled and gave a shy nod.

"Well, dear? You can speak, after all," the queen said. "Tell Monsignor Roncalli how old you'll be."

"Ten, if you please, sir," she said in passable Italian, her finger straying near her mouth before her mother's look scared it back to its place at her side.

"Ten! My heavens! How is that possible? Well, here is something for your tenth birthday, my child. I hope you like it."

The archbishop took from his pocket a small bag of navy blue velvet, tied at the top with a gold-colored drawstring. He leaned over and held it out to the princess, who approached, curtsied again, and took it.

"Thank you, sir."

"You're very welcome, *Principessa*. Please, open it."

Princess Maria-Louisa tugged at the drawstring and gave an excited gasp. She held up for everyone's inspection a small, delicate ballerina fashioned of crystal, wearing exquisitely small shoes of silver.

"Oh, Monsignor! It's very beautiful."

"I'm so glad you like it, Your Royal Highness."

Clutching the prize to her chest, Princess Maria-Louisa dashed from the room.

"Such a pity we couldn't have made a Catholic of her," the archbishop said, smiling after the princess.

Queen Giovanna clucked her tongue. "Now, let's not have that again. I fail to see the humor in it frankly. The Holy Father was fit to be tied."

"Yes, but he is a reasonable man. In his heart of hearts, he understood your husband had no other choice."

"Besides, I take her to Mass with me each week in our private chapel."

Roncalli shrugged. "Of course. One hand washes the other. One day when Orthodox and Roman Catholics are in heaven together, we'll all have a good laugh about it." The archbishop looked at the queen. "And now, *Maestà*, I must be going. The train to Istanbul leaves in an hour, and I have one or two more calls to make along the way."

Queen Giovanna stood and allowed Roncalli to kiss her hand. "It was so good to see you again, Monsignor. You're always welcome."

"As are you, my child. And anyone else from your delightful country. And I mean that most sincerely."

"I believe you." She stepped close to him and said in a lower voice, "I have a few more, ah, friends whom I hope to send to you in the next few weeks. You'll be able to help them?"

He nodded. "Of course. To South America?"

"No, to Palestine this time. If it can be done."

"I will see. Just have them come to the usual place."

"I understand."

The archbishop gave her a final bow, then nodded politely at Daria. "*Arrivederci,* then. Until next time."

"*Arrivederci,* Monsignor."

> Christ is born! Glorify Him!
> Christ descends from the heavens; welcome Him!
> Christ is now on earth, O be jubilant!
> Sing to the Lord, the whole earth,
> And sing praises to Him with joy, O ye people,
> For He has been exalted!

Boris listened to the hymn. He watched Metropolitan Stefan performing his holy offices, and he thought about the world waiting for him just outside the doors of Alexander Nevsky.

The choir sang of jubilation, of the coming of the Prince of Peace. Metropolitan Stefan intoned the liturgy that exhorted mankind to be glad and joyful, for God had at last come to dwell with his people. In here, a different world was announced; a realm of peace was celebrated. Inside Alexander Nevsky, with the sound of the choir soaring and echoing through the architecture, and the saints bearing witness from their icons, and the incense wafting through the nave like fragrant prayer, and the low, rolling voice of the metropolitan underscoring everything with the gravity of eternal truth, it was just barely possible to believe that God's peace truly rested on those who found favor with him.

But as soon as he returned from the Mass with his family, Boris knew that a different reality would reassert itself. This reality had little to do with peace, little to do with God's favor. It niggled at Boris's mind all day and encircled his bed at night—waiting with the patience of death for his waking. It stalked the horizon of his consciousness like a squall line, moving always toward him, always nearer. It demanded answers: When? How many? Why not? It pressed him always harder, more insistently, backing him into a corner partly inevitable, partly of his own making.

What had the one world to do with the other? Boris wondered. How did the reality in here make connection with the reality out there? What did the good news of Christ's advent have to do with the bodies piling up on the eastern front? How did the jubilation of Christmas square with the steadily increasing pressure on him to order Bulgarian boys to take their place in the siege lines at Stalingrad? Could the Star of Bethlehem withstand the dark, billowing hatred that threatened to swallow Europe's Jews?

And even if the Nazis were defeated, the darkness might still overtake them all. Boris looked at Metropolitan Stefan, so majestic in his robes of office, and tried to imagine him in one of Stalin's gulags. With no Wehrmacht to restrain it, what would prevent the Red Army from swarming through Romania, then crossing the Danube into little Bulgaria? The outlawed Communist Party had tried to kill him years ago on the Araba-Konak road; they intended the bomb in Sveta Nedelia for him. With the Soviet army standing behind them…

His only hope was time: time to delay, to maneuver. As Metropolitan Stefan sang the Christmas liturgy, Boris prayed there would be time enough.

14

January 1943

D obri could hear the music as soon as he opened the back door of the car. The Hotel Bulgaria blazed in the winter night like a lighthouse with a thousand beacons; soldiers in full-dress uniform glided up the front steps with ladies on their arms. And soon he would be among them.

He stepped around to the sidewalk and opened the door for Daria. She took his arm and got out of the car, and for a moment Dobri had to just stand and look at her.

"What? Is something wrong?" she asked, nervously touching her hair and the front of her dress.

"Yes, I'm afraid so."

"What? Have I torn something?" She was searching frantically now.

"No, not at all. It's just that I'm afraid the orchestra won't be able to compete with the music in your eyes; we may spoil the dancing for everyone else."

"Oh, please. Enough of your Bailovo blather. Let's get inside before we both freeze."

Dobri waved the driver on. With a playful leer at Daria and a mock salute, Corporal Sedjiev pulled away from the curb.

"I still don't see why you insisted on the car," Daria said, taking his arm as they turned toward the hotel entrance. "The palace is just across the street."

"No, my dear. This is a special night, and you should arrive at the ball like all the other lovely ladies. Besides, it's cold, and you're too beautiful to risk frostbite—at least, not until we've had a turn or two on the dance floor."

Daria laughed. "It sounds as if your military candor has completely left you tonight, Sergeant Dimitrov."

"Oh, not at all. I only say what I see. Any man here would speak the same way."

They went inside and checked their coats. At the other end of the foyer, the red-carpeted stairs swept up in a luxurious curve to the mezzanine and the doorway of the grand ballroom of the Hotel Bulgaria. Dobri smiled and waved at the men he knew and even a few he didn't. Daria was so beautiful, and he was so full of joy, he felt as if he were the equal of any man here, officer or noncommissioned.

The dance floor was jammed with swirling couples, but Dobri pulled her almost into the center of the mob. The orchestra was playing "Tonight We Love," arranged as a lively bounce. Dobri was a little surprised to hear American music, but Daria reminded him it was really Tchaikovsky, only slightly modernized.

"Well, officially we're at war with both countries," he said, "but since the Russian legation is still open, I guess it's permitted."

The next song was "Come Back to Sorrento," and though Dobri's waltz was a little rusty, Daria's coaching soon had him gliding smoothly, one-two-three, one-two-three across the floor. Her touch was as light as a bird's wing, and his eyes never left hers. The plaintive Italian melody swirled them around and around the ballroom, and they might have been the only couple there, for all he knew.

When the orchestra started a tango, they made a strategic retreat to the refreshment table. With champagne flutes in hand, they found seats in a corner.

"Can I confess something to you?" Dobri asked.

"What is it?"

"It took me three days to figure out how to ask you to come to the Midwinter Ball with me."

She gave him a puzzled smile. "Why?"

"Well, I couldn't get it to sound exactly right. I rewrote it five or six times."

"You wrote it?"

"Sure. Five or six times."

She laughed and shook her head. "And all the time I was afraid you weren't going to ask me."

"Really?"

She nodded. "Two or three of the domestics at the palace have beaus in the military. I'd overhear them talking about what they were going to wear, where they were going after the ball, and I'd think, 'I wonder if Dobri has ever gone to the Midwinter Ball. I wonder if he's interested in things like that.'" She gave him an embarrassed look and took a quick sip of her champagne.

Dobri took her hand. "The thing is, I was afraid."

"Of what?"

He looked down. "Well, I'm just a sergeant, and I've only been out of Bulgaria two or three times in my whole life. I come from Bailovo, and…"

"Dobri."

He looked up at her.

"You are a good man. Especially in times like these, that's more important than all the savoir-faire in Paris and Rome put together."

"All the what?"

She laughed. "Never mind. Just know this: I would rather be here, with you, right now, than anywhere else in the world. And as far as that goes, you're not the only one who feels…"

"Who feels what?"

Now Daria looked away. "I know you must get tired of hearing me talk about it. But to be Jewish, right now—"

"And you think I care anything about that?"

"No, not you, maybe. But not everyone feels the same way you do."

"That's a good thing. Because…" *No, Dobri. Don't say that.*

The orchestra began to croon a slow and lilting "La Vie en Rose." Dobri stood and held out his arms. Daria moved into him, and they rocked slowly back and forth, barely moving their feet. Dobri held her and thought that if Christ chose that very moment for his second return to the earth, Dobri Dimitrov of Bailovo would wing his way to eternity having realized every dream worth owning in this life.

The next two hours fled quicker than any time in his life. Before he knew it, the orchestra was playing "Good Night, Sweetheart," and couples were drifting toward the stairs.

The line at the coat check was long. As they stood in the crowd, waiting their turn at the counter, Dobri gradually became aware of a loud voice not far in front of where he was. Through the shifting gaps in the queue, Dobri saw the fellow and realized it was Lyuben Bojilov, the man whom he had replaced as sergeant in the household guard. Bojilov was drunk as a piper. He was hanging all over the woman he was with, who looked as if she was more than ready to be rid of him. Those nearby were doing their best to ignore him, but it was hard, since Bojilov seemed to be getting louder by the moment. And then the crowd parted just long enough for Bojilov to spot Dobri.

"Well, look there! If it isn't Dobri Dimitrov! How are things in the palace, Dimitrov? How do you like the job? You know, the one you stole from me?"

Dobri felt his face growing stiff with embarrassment. He tried averting his eyes and pretending Bojilov wasn't there, hadn't said anything. But Bojilov wouldn't be denied.

"Yo, Dimitrov! I'm talking to you, boy! Or are you palace boot-wipes too good to speak to soldiers who work for a living?"

"Come on, Lyubcho, you're drunk," his woman said, tugging him toward the coat check. "Let's get our coats and—"

Bojilov shoved her away and stumbled through the crowd toward Dobri. Dobri could feel Daria's eyes on him. He turned his head slightly toward her, without taking his eyes off Bojilov. "Daria, dear, I think you'd better step away. This fellow's drunk."

"Dobri, what—"

"I'll be fine. Just move over there a bit, out of the way."

"Who's that with you, Dimitrov?" Bojilov said, staggering closer. "Cute little trick." He stared at Daria, looked her up and down, and Dobri felt his hands clenching into fists.

"I'll tell you something, sweetheart," Bojilov said. "Your boyfriend here? Dimitrov? He got my job. Six years I was in the King's Guard, and the next thing I know, I'm out on my duff, and for what? What? Does anybody know for what?" He wheeled himself around to peer drunkenly at the crowd, most of whom found something else to look at. "I'll tell you why: because I'm not afraid to speak my mind. It's a crime that our armies aren't doing their part in the war against the Bolsheviks and the Jews, and I don't care who hears me say so!"

There was an angry murmur starting in the crowd, but no one made a move toward Bojilov. He turned toward Dobri and took a step closer. "But Dimitrov, here, he's a good boy, see? He keeps his mouth shut, I'll bet. Why's that, Dimitrov? Huh? Why so quiet? Is it your little lady here?" He jerked a thumb toward Daria. "Oh, I know who she is, all right. The queen's personal servant. Daria Ree*chett*ee," he said, in a slurred, mock-Italian pronunciation. "She's one of Tsar Boris's pet Jews. Did you know that, Dimitrov?"

"You're drunk, Bojilov," Dobri said, doing his best to keep his voice level. "You don't know what you're talking about. Why don't you just get your coat, go home, and sleep it off?"

"Sleep it off? Yeah, I'll sleep it off…in a stinking staff room in a stinking barracks in Bankia. And tomorrow I'll be back on my stinking job: teaching green recruits how to take their rifles apart without shooting their fingers off. Thanks a lot, Dimitrov! I owe you—I owe you big."

Bojilov's punch was surprisingly quick and accurate, a sudden left jab that caught Dobri just below his right eye. But Dobri rolled with it and counterpunched with an overhand right hook that crashed into Bojilov's jaw and snapped his head to the side. Dobri felt the anger pulsing through him as his left fist arced upward, his knuckles connecting with Bojilov's chin. Bojilov lurched forward, trying to get a shoulder into Dobri's chest and force him backward, but Dobri sidestepped and sent another right into Bojilov's midsection, followed by an elbow against the side of his head. Bojilov doubled over, but Dobri couldn't stop; his fists had minds of their own, pounding Bojilov's face with uppercut after uppercut, until finally Bojilov staggered to one side and crumpled to the floor, his face a mask of smeared blood.

Dobri stood over him, panting and grinding his teeth. He felt hands on his shoulders, heard a man's voice in his ear.

"That's enough, Dimitrov. He had it coming, but he's finished."

Daria!

He wheeled around and found her, cowering against the wall, trembling like a poplar in the wind.

"Come on, Daria. Let's go. He was just drunk."

She wouldn't look at him; her eyes were like those of a trapped animal.

He wiped his hands on his uniform trousers and put an arm around her shoulders. He guided her past the place where two or three men were helping Bojilov to his feet. The crowd parted for Dobri and Daria as they made their way to the coat-check counter. A few of the women put a hand on Daria's arm as they passed. "Don't worry about it, dear…" "Don't let that drunk upset you…" "Forget about him. Nobody listens to him…"

Dobri realized his commanding officer, Captain Kalayev, was standing beside the counter, watching him.

"Captain Kalayev, sir, I'm so sorry—"

"Nice dance tonight, wasn't it, Sergeant?"

"Sir? I…I just want to say—"

"Yes, a very nice dance. So good to see you, Sergeant. And you, Miss Richetti. Well, you'd better run along now. Back on duty in the morning, right, Sergeant?"

Dobri stared at the captain for several seconds. He nodded. "Yes, sir. I'll be there right on time, but—"

"Fine. Here, Miss Richetti; I believe this is your wrap?"

The captain held Daria's coat as she slipped her arms into the sleeves, then he reached over the counter and took Dobri's from the coat clerk.

Dobri tried one more time as he put on his coat and hat. "Captain Kalayev, about what happened back there—"

"What? I heard a little noise, but I couldn't really see what it was about. How about you, Stefcho?" Kalayev said, turning to an officer standing nearby.

The officer shook his head. "Didn't see a thing, Alexei."

They came down the front steps of the Hotel Bulgaria, and Dobri was relieved to see the Renault idling by the curb, right on time. He pronounced a silent blessing on Corporal Sedjiev and all his descendants. He put Daria into the backseat and hurried around to the other side.

"Well, how was it, Sergeant?" Sedjiev asked, grinning at them over his shoulder.

"Never mind, Corporal. Just get us to the palace on the double."

Sedjiev's eyes widened. "Yes, Sergeant." He pulled into the traffic on Alexander Battenberg. "Everything all right, Sergeant?"

"Yes. Just a little trouble as we were leaving, that's all."

Daria wouldn't look at him. She leaned against him, but her posture was that of a frightened child. He leaned close and spoke to her quietly.

"You heard what the others said; nobody listens to him. You mustn't let him frighten you."

She wouldn't answer.

Sedjiev pulled into the park behind the palace and stopped at the doors to the winter garden. Dobri thanked him as he helped Daria out of the car. Then he shepherded her inside the palace.

The winter garden was dark; a little light from the side foyer at the bottom of the stairs came through the half-open doorway. Dobri took both her shoulders and brought her around to face him.

"Daria, look at me. Look at me. There, that's it. Now, you must speak to me. You can't let that stupid man have so much control over you."

Her lips were trembling. She gave him a lost, pleading look. "He called me a Jew in front of all those people. He told them I was a Jew. That awful man said it in front of everyone."

"Yes, well, you're a Jew. I don't see anything bad about that."

And then the dam burst. She crumpled against his chest, weeping in great, shuddering sobs. "They can see," she said. "They know."

He held her for a long time, until by degrees the fear and embarrassment and shock was bled from her. He whispered to her over and over, "Daria, my dear. Shh, Daria…"

She leaned away from him, tilted her face back, then took his chin and turned his face toward the light from the doorway.

"Oh, Dobri. Your eye is swollen."

"Well, a lucky punch."

She took his hands and looked at them. "Your knuckles are bloody."

"It's not all my blood."

"You fought for me."

"And I'd do it again, a hundred times over."

She was looking at him as if seeing him for the first time.

"Daria, listen. I'm not a very smart man, and I'm not too good with words. But I think that in this world there is no safe place, not really. There's no place where you can hide, because sometimes the thing you fear most is only inside your head anyway, and even if you can hide from everybody else, you can't hide from yourself. You can get so busy trying to feel safe that you miss life. I…I don't want to miss you."

She was holding his hands, and her face was turned up to him, and there was nothing else, never anything else in the whole world he could do. He bent to her, lowered his lips to hers, and drank in a moment so sweet, so pure and full and perfect that for a few moments nothing else existed except the warmth of her touch.

Lily was transcribing the notes of Alexander's last meeting with the department heads when the two men came in. One looked older than the other, and the younger one wore the black uniform and insignia of the SS. Both had hard, serious faces. The older man began speaking to her in German. Lily shook her head and said the only German words she knew: *"Nicht verstehe."*

The older man gave her an exasperated look. He said, "Belev."

Alexander had people in his office and didn't want to be disturbed. Lily looked at the men, trying to figure out how to make herself understood, when one of the clerks from the Agency Activities section walked through. Lily knew he spoke German.

"Christo! Come here a moment."

The young man walked over to her desk.

"These two gentlemen don't speak Bulgarian. Can you please tell them that the commissar has people in his office at the moment and ask them if they'd care to wait?"

Christo turned to the men and began relaying Lily's message, but the SS officer cut him off. He spoke a few sentences, punctuated by a lot of pointing and sudden waves of his hands.

"These men are from the German embassy. This is the Gestapo attaché, Adolf Hoffmann," Christo said, indicating the older man, "and this is Hauptsturmfuehrer Dannecker. They say they have some urgent business with the commissar."

Lily studied the Germans and bit her lip. She went to Alexander's door and rapped lightly, then went inside. Alexander looked up from behind his desk, and the two men sitting in front of the desk turned to look at her.

"Pardon me, commissar, but there are two—"

"Ah! Herr Hoffmann, *guten Tag!*" Alexander said, rising from behind his desk and smiling at the two Germans who, Lily realized, had followed her to the door and were already pushing past her into Alexander's office.

"Gentlemen, please excuse us for a moment, won't you?" Alexander said to the men he had been meeting with. "I need a few minutes with Herr Hoffmann and—I'm sorry, sir, I didn't catch your name. Ah… *Bitte, entschuldigen Sie mich, mein Herr; ich kenne nicht Ihren Namen.*"

"*Ich bin Hauptsturmfuehrer Theodore Dannecker. Wir müssen mit Ihnen privatem sprechen, bitte.*"

"Yes, yes, of course. These gentlemen were just leaving, yes?"

Alexander hustled the two men out the door, motioned Lily back to her desk, and closed himself in with the Germans.

Twenty minutes later Dannecker and Hoffmann walked out of Alexander's office, and he hurried to her desk.

"Miss Panitza, please come in here at once."

As soon as she closed the door behind her, Lily could see Alexander's excitement. "I want you to get all the department heads and section chiefs in here as soon as possible. If they've got appointments, tell them to cancel. I want everyone here this afternoon at three o'clock sharp."

"What's going on?"

"Don't worry; you'll find out about it soon enough. Just make sure everyone gets called. I want them here—no excuses."

That afternoon Lily, notepad in hand, crowded into Alexander's office with the rest of the personnel he had summoned. There wasn't room for another chair; Lily had to stand in the corner farthest from Alexander's desk. One of the managers suggested moving to the conference room on the ground floor.

"No," Alexander said, "I want everyone in here for a reason. Anybody in the hallway downstairs can hear everything that goes on in the conference room, and what I'm about to tell you must be kept absolutely confidential. Don't tell your wives, your girlfriends, your mothers—anybody. All of this stays here—understand?"

The men nodded. Some of them shrugged.

"All right. This morning, I met with Adolf Hoffmann, the Gestapo attaché to the German embassy, and Hauptsturmfuehrer Theodore Dannecker from Berlin. Herr Dannecker is our special SS advisor for Jewish matters. We're about to kick into high gear our campaign to cleanse Greater Bulgaria."

A few of the men looked at each other; the room became very still.

"Dannecker and Hoffmann have already met with Interior Minister Gabrovski. We're ready to begin deportations of Jews to Poland, where the Reich will receive them for permanent processing. By the time we're finished, there won't be a Jew left anywhere in this country. But the interior minister and our German allies have agreed that the logical place to begin is with the Jews in Macedonia and Thrace, the territories now under our administration. These people are anarchists and troublemakers, and besides, we need to keep the Jews still within the old borders for a while, until they've finished some roadwork and other projects. But don't worry. We'll get rid of them, too.

"Now, I don't need to tell you that if any of this leaks out beforehand, the Jews and all the misguided Jew lovers in Bulgaria will scream bloody murder. So to keep our job as simple and manageable as possible, everything has to be done very quietly, behind the scenes. If anybody talks about this in the wrong place, it could cost him more than his job. Do I make myself clear?"

Alexander stared around the room, and Lily felt her face stiffening with fear. Of course, Alexander didn't look at her. He would never imagine he had any reason to.

"We estimate there are between ten and twelve thousand Jews in Macedonia and Thrace. We will have to organize departure points, train schedules, freight cars, and a certain amount of food and water. The security forces in each town will need advance notification, complete with lists of addresses. We will need transit compounds within the old borders with shelters, latrines, and, of course, sturdy fencing. And all of this has to come together at once; we don't want the Jews from Skopje taken one day and those from Bitolya the next, because by the next day there won't be any Jews left in Bitolya, or else they'll make trouble for the security forces. So every one of you has to execute his responsibilities to the letter and at the exact moment ordered. Failure will not be tolerated.

"In the next few days, each of you will be receiving from this office a list of specific tasks and responsibilities. We will launch this operation at the beginning of March—about four weeks from now. It isn't much time, given how much there is to do. So be ready. That's all."

The men went out of Alexander's office, most of them with grave faces.

A few had hints of the same exhilaration Lily had seen in Alexander. No one was speaking, just the sound of shuffling feet.

When they had all left, Alexander motioned her toward his desk. "Tonight I need to meet with the executive committee to finalize the plans. After that, I'll have a document for you to type and send to Minister Gabrovski. I want you to type it as soon as tonight's meeting is concluded."

Lily felt the urge to wince—a cold and late supper again tonight—but she suppressed it. Instead, she nodded.

"Good." He smiled at her, and despite herself, Lily felt her heart quicken. "Lily, this is a historic moment in Bulgaria. And I'm the one they picked to make it happen."

"Yes, Alexander. How wonderful for you."

15

Once the Jews have crossed the border, it is understood that they are automatically deprived of their Bulgarian citizenship, if they were Bulgarian citizens prior to being transported. They will be permitted to take only clothing and some food for the journey; no valuables or currency will be permitted. Those transported from the recently liberated regions of Macedonia and Thrace will be collected in transit camps inside the old borders of Bulgaria prior to being transferred to German territory.

Liliana Panitza couldn't believe what she was typing. The Jews might as well have been some inferior grade of cattle, instead of human beings. How could Alexander be doing this?

In the interest of minimizing panic or insurrection among the Macedonian and Thracian Jews, it is imperative that this operation begin simultaneously in each town and village referenced in the plan. Otherwise, we can expect the Jews to escape (or attempt escape) and join partisan or Communist underground units.

Furthermore, the Interior Ministry is strongly urged to press for the continuation of this plan to Jews from within the old borders as well. Once the operation begins in Macedonia and Thrace, the Jews in Bulgaria proper can hardly be expected to remain calm. Unrest could result. At the very least, all Jewish men from the old boundaries should be recalled to labor camps and put under the strictest control.

Alexander's note went on to describe the exact steps needed to round up the Macedonian and Thracian Jews, the locations of the transit holding points, the buildings to be constructed, and a method for utilizing the property confiscated from the Jews to pay for the entire undertaking. He outlined a cover story for the deportation to keep the Jews from becoming unduly desperate. They would be told they were being sent to resettlement camps within Bulgaria for the remainder of the war. In no case should they be told their destination was Poland or Germany, Alexander stressed; that would only lead to trouble.

> Even if the deportation of the Jews from the old boundaries is not decided at this time, the Commissariat for Jewish Questions urges most strongly that we should still seize this opportunity to extend the operation beyond Macedonia and Thrace. To this end, we recommend increasing the total number of transportees above the estimated Jewish population of Macedonia and Thrace—for instance, to 20,000 persons, instead of only 12,000. I believe our German advisor will agree readily to this.

Lily had no doubt Alexander's assessment was correct. She hoped Hoffmann and Dannecker didn't find it necessary to come to the commissariat too often. They made her nervous, and not just because they didn't—or wouldn't—speak Bulgarian.

As she finished typing Alexander's report, she was trying to think of a way to let the palace know about this latest effort. Her last message to Daria Richetti hadn't been answered. She'd heard about some unpleasantness at a military ball involving Daria and assumed that had something to do with it.

Maybe it was time for another tactic. So far, Lily had seen little visible evidence of Tsar Boris's intentions to oppose the Jewish measures. Maybe it was time to go directly to the people most affected. She decided to contact her attorney friend, Nissim Levi.

Pavel Grouev took up his cognac and leaned back in his chair. He smiled expansively at the young man seated across the table.

"Your problem, Stanislav, is that you are too trusting. Let's suppose, as you say, that we were able to realize the Marxist ideal. Let's say we could miraculously redistribute all the property in Bulgaria so that every single person was included in the means of production. Then, go forward in time, say, ten years. What do you think will have happened? Do you think that selfish, ambitious people will have stopped being selfish and ambitious? No, they won't. Instead, they will have placed themselves and their cronies at the top of the apparatus of state. They'll have villas and private beaches—which they hold in the name of the people, of course—and private accounts in Zurich. And remember, 'religion is the opiate of the people,' so they won't even have the constraint of the church and its ethics. And the peasants in the villages will be worse off than ever, because they don't even have the incentive of ownership. The sheep they graze, the plots they tend, the rose oil they process— all of it belongs to the collective. It belongs to everybody, so it belongs to nobody. And the only ones getting fat are the comrades at the top of the pyramid. That's the inevitable outcome of your worker's society."

Stanislav Balan took a drag on his cigarette and exhaled a stream of smoke above Pavel's head. "Now, Mr. Grouev, remember, I'm not a Communist. I'm just playing devil's advocate here. But can't you at least admit that Marx and Engels were right about the plight of the modern worker? Surely you can't ignore the sweatshops and the children forced into virtual slavery? You've read Dickens."

"I can admit the disease, but I don't admit that decapitation is the cure. The trouble with Bulgarians, Stanislav, is that most of us suffer from an exaggerated impulse to save the world, and to do it right now. Five hundred years of Ottoman rule made us confirmed haters of injustice—and that's good. Injustice should be thoroughly despised and opposed. But it also made us quixotic. We're an impulsive, emotional people, Stanislav, very susceptible to the simple curatives Marx and Engels seem to offer—and to the manipulations of Stalin and his agents provocateurs. Please don't mistake my meaning: I completely understand the appeal of socialism. A man under twenty who isn't a socialist probably has no heart. But a man over twenty who's still a socialist has no head."

The Tsar Osvoboditel Café was crowded with its usual mix of politicians, bureaucrats, intellectuals, and military officers—active and retired. General Loukov had somehow again managed to squeeze his bulk into his usual corner booth. He sat there now, holding forth to the young Legionnaires and other hard-line right-wingers who usually surrounded him. A few times, over the noise of the café, Pavel had heard the general's forceful statements about the "weak-willed policies of this government" or some other such choice expression. Pavel, of course, studiously avoided seeming to notice. Let Loukov bluster, Pavel reasoned; Tsar Boris had put him in his place with a few well-chosen words to the Fuehrer last spring. The king's intelligence sources had noted Loukov was getting a much cooler reception these days in the offices of the German air attaché. No doubt the corpulent retired general sought to make up for the loss of his German contacts by increasing the volume of his bullyragging in Sofia.

But Tsar Boris still worried about the influence of Loukov and his Ratnik and Legionnaire cronies. Every so often the king's Berlin contacts would report rumors of Gestapo dossiers casting doubt on the policies of the Sofia government and lauding the pro-Nazi efforts of Loukov and his kind. Tsar Boris tended by nature to be a little suspicious—and who could blame him? But such rumblings as one sometimes heard from Berlin made him justifiably fearful of a right-wing coup. Last summer the king had denied a German travel visa to a Legionnaire sympathizer based on just such concerns. No coup materialized, of course, but Tsar Boris still kept an eye over his right shoulder.

"I don't know, Mr. Grouev," Stanislav Balan said. He swirled the remains of his brandy and stared pensively into his glass. "I still say Communism has some claims that will have to be heard and dealt with."

"Oh, I don't doubt it, Stanislav. Especially if the Red Army keeps pushing the Wehrmacht back on its heels after the spring thaws."

"Is the Russian front collapsing so quickly?"

Pavel shrugged. "Since the Sixth Army surrendered at Stalingrad, the Russians have taken back Kursk. It's still touch and go, but it's safe to say Hitler isn't going to be riding through the streets of Moscow anytime soon."

"Surely His Majesty would seek an understanding with the United States and Britain if Germany were to falter?"

Pavel tugged on his watch chain and thumbed open the case. "My goodness! Look at the hour. I'd better start home, or Mrs. Groueva will toss out my supper." He smiled at the secretary and pushed his chair back. "I always enjoy talking with you, Stanislav. You remind me of myself—many, many years and more than a few kilos ago."

They shook hands. There was a roar of laughter in the corner. The Loukov party was breaking up also; Pavel saw the general struggling out of his booth.

"Well, I think I'll take my leave before our portly colleague gets to his feet. I'd just as soon not exchange pleasantries with him," Pavel said. With a final nod at Balan, he left the café.

Boris hurried into the small meeting room and quickly motioned the others to sit down. "What's the situation? How much do we know?" he asked a very worried-looking Pavel Grouev.

"He was shot by a man and a woman right at the front door of his home," Pavel said. "The watch chief says he received a call from Loukov's wife about nine thirty. She was barely coherent, poor woman, after having witnessed the whole thing—and their daughter, too. He had gone with one of his friends to a movie after leaving the Tsar Osvoboditel Café around six thirty." Pavel glanced at the king. "I was there at the same time. I saw him—at his usual table."

"Go on," Boris said.

"He apparently stopped for a quick drink after the movie, and he and his companion parted. The general walked home alone, and of course the assassins took this as their opportunity."

"Do we have any idea who the attackers were?"

"We have some idea, Your Majesty," said Chavdarov, the chief of police, seated across the table. "From the few details we were able to glean from Mrs. Loukova and her daughter, we think the female accomplice may be Violetta Yakova—"

"Yakova! A Jew!" said Interior Minister Gabrovski. He sat beside Pavel Grouev, but Pavel appeared to be doing his best not to notice Gabrovski's presence.

Boris motioned for quiet. "What steps have we taken to apprehend them?"

Chavdarov opened his hands in a gesture of uncertainty. "Naturally, my men have thrown up blockades on the main roads out of the city. They've gone to the houses of known dissidents and questioned them. But so far—nothing."

"I tell you, Your Majesty," Filov said, "we must take this opportunity to step up the struggle against the Communists and their Jewish abettors! General Loukov had many friends in the German embassy—"

"Yes, Mr. Prime Minister, I'm quite aware of the general's popularity. But I hardly think that an indiscriminate propaganda campaign based on guesswork is likely to shed much light on this matter or help us solve the murder."

Filov's round face reddened. He clamped his jaws and stared at the tabletop in front of him.

"Your Majesty, I beg your pardon," the chief of police said, "but within minutes of receiving the call from Mrs. Loukova, twenty or thirty of the Legionnaires were brandishing fists in the face of my watch chief, demanding that we come here, to the palace, and arrest the 'royal agents' who had silenced the one man who dared to speak up for what he believed in." The police commander carefully studied the backs of his hands as he finished speaking.

"You see!" Gabrovski said, thumping the table with his chubby fist. "The government is getting blamed for this act of terror. We must take stern measures, Your Majesty. We cannot afford for Berlin to think we're soft on the enemies of the Reich."

Boris got up from the table and paced to the wall. He looked at Pavel, then away. Filov was coming as close as he dared to speaking openly of a Berlin-sponsored coup; that much was plain to Boris. How much public opinion would line up behind the prime minister? In the bad days, just after he had taken the throne following his father's abdication, such tactics were far too common. Boris still remembered with a shudder the pictures of the mutilated hands of Prime Minister Stambolisky. But he had worked so hard to change all that! Would most Bulgarians sincerely believe his government was capable of the cold-blooded murder of its critics? Boris didn't think so. But what would Berlin think? That was another matter.

He felt the room closing in on him, hemming him in. He shut his eyes, trying to remember the feel of the wind above Tsarska-Bistritza, blowing in his face as he hiked the trail up to Moussala Peak. He would give away almost anything he owned to be there now.

But he wasn't. The men at the table were watching him, waiting for his next words. Just as always. He was the king. He had to decide, to act. It was his responsibility, his curse.

"The security forces will immediately begin rounding up all known Communist cells," Boris said. "Conduct house-to-house searches if you must; I will even order a complete blockade of the city, if you need it."

Chavdarov nodded.

"The prime minister is right; we must spare no effort to root out the Communist threat." Boris leaned ever so slightly on the word *Communist*. The emphasis wasn't lost on Filov and Gabrovski; the prime minister clenched his jaw and continued staring at the tabletop while Gabrovski shook his head ever so slightly.

"Gather every scrap of information you can. And let me know how many Special Security details you need."

"Thank you, Your Majesty. I'll see to it," the chief said.

"Mr. Grouev, please extend our condolences to Mrs. Loukova and her daughter. Her husband was a great man, a patriot. He will be missed.

"That will be all for now, gentlemen. Keep me apprised of any further developments."

Boris opened the door of the room and turned to face the men at the table. The police chief went out first, giving the king a little bow as he shook his hand. Gabrovski went out without speaking. Filov leaned close as he passed.

"Your Majesty, I must speak to you further on this topic, and soon."

Boris gave him a tight nod, then turned to face Pavel Grouev. He laid a hand on Pavel's arm and watched as the other two men receded down the hallway.

"Pavel, I need to know what the prime minister does in the next few days: whom he contacts, where he goes, even how long he stays there. All of it. Everything is important. Can you see to it?"

Grouev nodded.

"Thank you, Bacho Pavlé." Boris pinched the bridge of his nose. There was a tiny pain in the center of his forehead, like a minuscule gremlin trying to dig a hole from the inside of his skull. He knew the pain would soon be getting worse.

The blood dripped onto the carpet. Should a man dead so long still have blood in him? His father was shouting, accusing him. He had to leave, but he had no idea where he could go, how he could release this burden. Something told him he couldn't; even if he tried to put it down, it would cling to him of its own accord.

With shame burning his face and his father's taunts ringing in his ears, he turned and walked away. He wanted to talk to the soldier, to ask him what it was like to die. He wanted to beg his forgiveness. But to talk to him, Boris would have to look at him, and that he couldn't do. The soldier's face would tell him more than he wanted to know. More, maybe, than he could endure. So he kept walking, walking... Why couldn't he find the door?

On the day of General Loukov's funeral, Boris was at his retreat in Tcham-Koria. He had tried but failed to convince himself to attend. Each time his imagination brought him to what would no doubt be a packed service, his memory returned to the ruined dome of Sveta Nedelia nearly twenty years before—the disaster that was intended for him. In a way it was his loyalty to the dead that had saved him from their number that day. That, and Pavel Grouev's habitual lateness...

Boris still didn't know why the initial fusillade from the slopes above the highway had missed him, nor could he rationally explain surviving the cross-fire as he dashed for the motorbus following the royal car along the mountain road. By the time he could return with a detachment of soldiers from the barracks back in Orhanié, Professor Ilchev and Kolyanov, the royal game warden, were dead in the ditch. Colonel Stamatov was still returning fire from the roadside ditch, his two companions' dead bodies beside him. The soldiers gave chase, but the attackers quickly lost themselves among the crags.

Not three hours later, many miles away in Sofia, General Gheorgiev was gunned down. The incidents were very much related, as Boris would learn to his sorrow.

Professor Ilchev was an entomologist, one of Boris's favorite camping companions. With the game warden and Colonel Stamatov, they had been enjoying the spring air in the West Balkan range. And now, because he had been riding in a car with his sovereign, Ilchev was dead.

On the morning of General Gheorgiev's funeral, Boris went to Bali-Iskar, the village of his game warden, to attend the funeral. Upon his return to Sofia, he went first to visit Ilchev's widow. "I always admired Delcho's knowledge," he told her. "He was one of the very few men in Bulgaria who cared enough about butterflies to spend more than five minutes talking with me about them. My grief is as nothing compared to yours, of course, but I will miss him very much." Mrs. Ilcheva seemed touched, even in her sorrow, by his visit, Boris remembered. Her face for some reason made him think of his mother.

He was supposed to pick up Pavel Grouev at his office, and they would go together to General Gheorgiev's state funeral, to be held in Sveta Nedelia Cathedral, less than a block from the palace. But Pavel wasn't there at the appointed time. Boris waited and fumed. Pavel finally arrived, huffing and puffing as he apologized for underestimating the time he would need to get into his formal clothing. They were walking out the door to the garage, Boris chiding Pavel for being late yet again, when they heard the explosion.

It was the worst act of political sabotage in Bulgarian history, one of the worst in Europe. Later the intelligence service pieced together the plot: the Communists had killed Gheorgiev, knowing that the death of a person of his prominence would command a lavish state funeral, attended by every high-ranking official, including the king. They had either bribed or coerced the sexton of the cathedral, himself a Communist, into hiding the explosives and giving them access to the crawlspace above the central dome of the church.

It would be a long time before Boris would again tease Pavel about being late.

Boris knew that his absence from General Loukov's funeral would be noted. He told himself that it was not a lack of courage that held him at Tcham-Koria—after all, what was his life worth to him these days anyway? No, the real reason was much less obvious, more difficult to explain, even to himself. Bulgaria herself was at risk. Who else had the patience and tact to steer the middle course, the course that would avoid as long as possible grounding the nation on either the reef of a German defeat or the unthinkable mayhem of a Russian-sponsored Communist coup? No, the similarities between Loukov's death now and Gheorgiev's eighteen years before were too striking to be ignored. Boris decided Bulgaria couldn't afford the risk.

He returned to Sofia the day after the funeral, and the day after that, Sergeant Dimitrov admitted Bogdan Filov to his office at the palace.

"Good morning, Mr. Filov," Boris said, seated behind his desk.

"Good morning, Your Majesty. Thank you for receiving me." Filov hung his hat on the rack and removed his coat.

"Of course. How was the funeral?" *Might as well have it out in the open.*

"Very moving, Your Majesty. Very peaceful actually."

He stared at Filov for maybe five seconds. "Very well. You had matters to discuss?"

"Yes, Your Majesty. This may sound crass, but I want to speak to you about the use to be made of General Loukov's untimely death."

Boris stared at the prime minister. Filov shifted uncomfortably in his chair.

"Hear me out, Your Majesty. I'm only trying to say that we shouldn't keep from the people of Bulgaria the real perpetrators. In our communications, we shouldn't speak of 'enemies of the state' or 'unknown foreign agents.' We should use the public concern as leverage for the cleansing of the nation. Clearly we cannot tolerate the presence of murderers and anarchists in Bulgaria. We must act decisively to purge them and the elements of society that spawn them."

In the lap drawer of his desk, Boris had a report from his intelligence service. He had read it for the third time just before Filov's arrival. In the past week the prime minister had been to the German embassy no less than fourteen times. He was known to have spoken privately with Ribbentrop's special envoy on at least four of those occasions. The SS advisor for Jewish questions had been present at two of Filov's interviews. It wasn't difficult for Boris to imagine some of what his prime minister had discussed—albeit indirectly—with the upper echelons of the Reich. It was not unlikely that Filov had received demands—their contours softened to resemble diplomatic requests—for some proofs of Bulgaria's intentions and plans for getting rid of the "undesirables" in her midst. The death of one of the Reich's most enthusiastic Bulgarian supporters would only have added to the urgency of the German efforts.

Boris passed a palm over his scalp. "What do you suggest, Mr. Filov?"

"The Interior Ministry has a plan. As early as next month, we can begin rounding up dissidents and sending them out of the country en masse."

"Dissidents?"

Filov wouldn't look at him. "Mr. Gabrovski tells me that the Reich's special advisor suggests starting in Macedonia and Thrace."

Naturally. Take the Jews out of the territories where Bulgaria has the least leverage. We can't very well refuse, can we? Eight hundred thousand German troops in and around our country...

"One of Mr. Gabrovski's aides has prepared a complete outline of train schedules, provisioning, gathering points, and—"

"Spare me the details, Mr. Filov. You have a plan. What else do you need from me?"

"So you agree this is necessary, Your Majesty?"

"I agree that it is unavoidable."

There was a lengthy silence. "Very well, Your Majesty. I'll notify Mr. Gabrovski."

The prime minister stood and began gathering his wraps.

"Tell me something, Mr. Filov."

"Yes, Your Majesty?"

"Is it a good trade, do you think?"

Filov's forehead furrowed. "I don't understand, Your Majesty. What trade do you mean?"

A few trainloads of Jews for one general. "Never mind, Mr. Filov. Forgive me."

Agreement for the deportation at first of 20,000 Jews from the
new Bulgarian lands Thrace and Macedonia to the German eastern
regions...

Liliana Panitza stared at the handwritten document. Alexander had everything mapped out. The Jews from Radomir, Dupnitza, Gorna Djumaya... The Jews from Skopje... All the lists she had typed, the lists of names she had requested from the district offices—all of it had come down to this, a contract between A. Belev and T. Dannecker, to be typed in Bulgarian and translated into German. The Bulgarian Commissariat for Jewish Questions guaranteed that "only Jews" would be included in the transports, excluding Jews from mixed marriages and those with contagious diseases. There would be lists in triplicate of all those consigned to each trainload of one thousand Jews. Two copies would go to the German escorts, and a single copy would go to the Reich's plenipotentiary in Sofia. Efficient touch, that. It was probably Alexander's idea.

Twenty thousand human beings.

Alexander had been working with manic energy these last weeks. One night, when he had kept Lily late to prepare packages of documents for mailing to the district offices, she had made herself tell him that what they were doing was wrong.

"You don't get it, do you, Lily? The Germans will take them anyway. You think Macedonia and Thrace really belong to Bulgaria? We're just getting credit for it, that's all."

And that was what finally mattered to him, she guessed.

He stuck his head around his office door. "I need that finished immediately, Miss Panitza. The Hauptsturmfuehrer is coming by this afternoon to sign it. Stop staring and start typing."

Lily twined into her typewriter two pieces of paper separated by a carbon. She typed the date at the top: February 22, 1943.

16

The last tones of the bell before the final benediction always reminded Stefan of the trilling of a bird heard from far away on a crisp morning in the mountains. He could never understand why, exactly. The two sounds had little in common except their purity. Still, each Sunday at this point in the Mass, he allowed the final reverberations to fade into silence before raising his hand and giving the dismissal.

"May the blessing of the Lord and His mercy come upon you through His divine grace and love always, now and forever and to the ages of ages."

"Amen," the congregation responded.

He nodded to the deacon, who took up the salver holding the antidoron. The worshipers began queuing up in front of the iconostas to receive fragments of the blessed loaf.

Stefan ducked through the curtains behind the altar. He went to the robing chamber, and an acolyte helped him remove his miter and vestments.

Stefan felt ready for a cup of hot tea and a bowl of good soup. He stepped down the hallway toward his private chamber. He was reaching for the door handle when a sudden movement startled him.

A man was standing in the shadows beyond the door of the chamber. The man in the dark suit.

"Well, it's the famous Stefan, metropolitan of Sofia."

"Who are you? What are you doing here?"

"Forgive me, Your Eminence. I've taken you aback."

The man took off his black broad-brimmed hat. He put his hand into his coat. Stefan's nostrils flared in alarm. Was he about to be shot?

"Here," the man said, holding out a calling card.

Rabbi Daniel Tsion
Comparative Theologian, Scholar, Teacher, Counselor
Chiprovzi 45, Sofia

Stefan looked at the card, then at the man. Tsion was short and stocky, with a grizzled beard straggling down his cheeks and across his chest. His hair was thinning on top. He stood watching Stefan, his lips a straight line that denoted maybe a habitual sense of purpose. He wore spectacles with thick lenses.

"I still don't know why you're here, Rabbi Tsion."

"To talk to you, of course. Why else would I be waiting outside your room?"

"I've seen you before."

"Yes, I've been listening to your speeches for some time now. And wondering."

"Wondering what?"

Rabbi Tsion lifted his chin and gave Stefan a flat, demanding look. "That is best explained out of the hallway."

Stefan opened the door to his chamber and gestured for the rabbi to enter. The room's primary furnishing was the bookshelves lining the walls, along with a simple oak desk and two chairs. Gray winter morning light came through a window behind the desk. As Stefan closed the door and moved to the chair behind his desk, Tsion stood with his hands behind his back and peered at the spines of the books on the shelves just inside the doorway.

"Stefan Zwieg…Thomas Mann…Albert Wasserman…Kafka…Freud… For a chief prelate in the state church, you have wide-ranging literary interests," Tsion said.

"I choose my reading to suit the interests of the well-informed mind, not political expediency."

Tsion nodded, his back still turned. "So I see. I'm not surprised."

Stefan had felt first apprehension, then curiosity, but he was now approaching the frontier of annoyance with his unusual guest. "You have something to tell me?"

Tsion wheeled and gave Stefan another enigmatic, appraising look. "Not I, Your Eminence." He raised a gnarled finger and pointed upward. "The Holy One."

"Indeed?"

"You may mock, if you wish. That's nothing new to God's prophets. Even the other rabbis look sideways when I try to tell them."

"Rabbi Tsion, I assure you, I intended no mockery. It's just that it's not every day one meets a…prophet."

Tsion stepped toward the desk and leaned over it, so that his face was on the same level as Stefan's. Behind the thick lenses, his eyes were fixed and unwavering.

"A great persecution is coming toward Israel," he said, "a terrible evil that cannot be imagined. The Lord says that he is sending this evil as a test for the nations. Those who are caught up in it, who turn their hands against the children of Abraham, Isaac, and Jacob, will be judged severely in the court of heaven."

Stefan stared at the rabbi for several seconds. "Rabbi Tsion, I assure you—"

"The leaders of this land must heed! God will winnow the earth, and he will spare no nation that causes harm to his people. He has sent me to you, Your Eminence. He has persuaded me that you are a man who desires righteousness. That is why this word has come to you now."

Stefan realized he was tracing the sign of the cross with his forefinger, over and over again on the arm of his chair. He was an educated man, a well-traveled man. He doubted that anyone who knew him would be inclined to describe him as either gullible or superstitious. But there was something about Rabbi Daniel Tsion's bearing, or perhaps the force of his simple words, that would not permit easy dismissal.

"It may be that the Lord has given you a word for this nation," Stefan said finally. "What shall I do? How may I assist?"

Tsion stood away from the desk. He reached again into his flowing black coat and brought out a piece of foolscap, folded in three parts. He laid it on the desk in front of Stefan. The paper had writing in a small, precise hand on both sides.

"I've written everything down," Tsion said. "I've brought you the first copy, and I will take a copy to the king's chancellor, the minister of the interior, the prime minister, and the majority and minority deputies of the Sobranje."

Stefan took up the foolscap and glanced at it. It appeared to contain much the same message Tsion had just delivered, except in greater detail and with more repetition. Stefan doubted that it would make much of an impression on Gabrovski, but he still idly wished he could be a fly on the wall when the rabbi marched into the Ministry of the Interior with his oracle from the Most High.

"Rabbi Tsion, I will of course continue to do everything I can for the relief of our citizens of Jewish faith, but you must know I have been speaking against the Law for the Defense of the Nation since the day it was first debated, and—"

"Maybe it's time for you to stop speaking and start listening."

Stefan was again stumped.

"You travel the country, do you not?"

Stefan nodded.

"Talk to the Jews. They have eyes and ears. They have voices that must be heard."

Tsion turned around and walked out of the chamber, closing the door behind him.

Stefan stared at the foolscap for several seconds. He got up, slid the rabbi's message into the inside pocket of his jacket, and reached for his overcoat and hat.

Buko Lazarov tilted the glass and let the *slivovitza* drain down his throat. He gave a contented sigh as the volatile liquor burned a path toward his belly.

"That's good stuff, Michael. I'll husk corn all night, as long as the *slivovitza* holds up."

Michael Abadjiev gave him a quick grin, then looked away. "Glad you like it, Buko. Here—take these ears. My stack seems to be going down slower than anybody's."

"Maybe because your glass is emptying faster," said one of the other men.

"You should talk, Leon." Abadjiev said. "You're going through the tobacco faster than we are the corn."

The men chuckled. For a moment, the only sound was the dry rustle of the husks as the men tore them from the corn.

"Is this Yambol leaf?" Buko said, looking at his cigarette.

Michael nodded.

"You know your stuff, Buko," one of the men said.

"Yes. Well, I used to, anyway. It's been a while…"

There was another long silence; more husks drifted to the ground.

"Well, I've got to visit the toilet," Buko announced. He stood and took a long pull on his cigarette; he watched the ember creep closer and closer to his fingers, then at the last moment dropped the butt to the flagstone and ground it with the ball of his foot. He crossed the courtyard toward the house. Through the half-closed curtains, he could see the women in Abadjiev's parlor, sipping their glasses of wine or beer and chatting in twos and threes. Anka was sitting with Michael's wife, Georgina, and another woman whose face was obscured by the curtain. Anka looked like someone doing her best imitation of a person having a good time. Again Buko wondered why he and Anka were the only Jews at the party. He fingered the small yellow star on the front of his jacket.

When he came out of the house, Michael was waiting by the door.

"Buko, I have to tell you something."

"What, you've run out of tobacco?" Buko, chuckled, then realized his host was looking at him with the expression of someone who had drawn the short straw in a bad-news contest.

"What is it, Michael?"

"Buko, a few days ago Zakhari Velkov came to see me at my office. He works for the commissariat."

Buko didn't have to ask which commissariat.

"I'm in charge of the local government requisition program, and Velkov wanted to know about commandeering the tobacco warehouse."

"Fernandes?"

Abadjiev nodded. "He wouldn't tell me why at first, but I pressed him. He made me swear silence; he said it was a high-level government secret."

Buko felt his throat going dry.

"He said that an agreement had been signed in Sofia, an agreement for deportation. He said that all the Jews in Kyustendil are to be arrested and impounded in the Fernandes warehouse or somewhere like it, then put on trains for deportation camps elsewhere in the country. From there…" Abadjiev swallowed and looked away.

"Michael?"

"Buko, you're my friend. We learned to read together. We played on the same football team, for heaven's sake. I tried to keep this to myself, but I haven't slept in a week. I had to tell you."

Buko stared at the ground beside Abadjiev's feet. *If they're taking us, what about the Macedonian Jews? What about my sister? Dimo?* Buko's heart was loping against his rib cage. He reached out and touched the wall to steady himself.

"Look, it's after your curfew," Michael said. "I'll walk to your house with you and your wife. That's why I invited you here tonight, anyway—to warn you without alerting anyone. You must let your people know, Buko. Maybe somebody knows someone who can get this craziness stopped. You've got to get out the word."

As if drawing a heavy bucket out of a well, Buko dragged his eyes up to meet Abadjiev's. "Michael, when is all this supposed to happen?"

Abadjiev looked as if he was about to be sick. "March 10. Less than a week."

When they arrived home that night, Buko sent Anka upstairs. She didn't ask him where he was going—she didn't even look at him. Buko watched her slowly climb, hoping she had the strength to reach their apartment.

He slipped through the alleys and along the fences to the home of Pinhas Comforty, the president of the Kyustendil synagogue. Within moments Comforty had sent word to the other local Jewish leaders, and within the hour a handful of men were sitting in Comforty's darkened parlor, listening with slack faces as Buko told them what he had heard at the attorney Abadjiev's house. Buko finished, and Haim Behar spoke up.

"I've heard about this too—and from a different source."

"Where did you hear it?" Comforty asked.

"I was in Sofia a few days back, visiting my cousin. Iosif Vatev, who does some work for the commissariat, told me in exchange for a bribe."

Someone spat. "Vatev. You can buy a baptismal certificate from him— even a birth certificate that makes you a gentile. He's as crooked as the Iskar."

"Still, we have to accept it as corroboration," Behar said.

"There's something else," said another man. "My cousin lives in Radomir, and he says that, for days now, empty boxcars have been stacking up on the sidings there."

"There is one more piece of information," Comforty said. "Yesterday evening I received an order from Tasev, who heads the commissariat police in this district. He told me I had to collect several hundred pails and ladles, coal shovels, kitchen knives, pans, axes, beds, tables, basins... I'm supposed to gather these from the Jews here and take them to the commissariat head-quarters tomorrow."

"Equipment," someone muttered.

"For a camp," Buko said. "We have to get word to Skopje. My sister and her children are there. That's where they're planning to start the deporta-tions—in Macedonia and Thrace."

"I have a friend who'll let me use his telephone," Comforty said. "I'm going to call the Sofia Central Consistory and find out what they know."

The men emptied their pockets; among them, they had thirty leva. Buko said he thought it was enough to bribe the cable operator to get out of his bed and send an urgent telegram to Skopje and maybe Dupnitza. The men agreed to meet again the following day to pool information and make further plans. None of them would sleep that night, Buko knew.

He went straight from Comforty's house to the home of the telegraph agent he knew best. He knocked on the door, staring about him in the dark—fearing at any moment to be accosted by a constable or, worse, a gang of Brannik youth roaming the streets in search of someone to bully. Finally the door opened a handbreadth.

"Listov! It's me, Buko Lazarov. I need to send an emergency cable."

"What? Don't you know what time it is, Buko?"

Buko put his shoulder against the door and half fell into Listov's house. "I don't have time to argue, Dimitri! They're going to round up the Jews, and I have to send a cable to Skopje. My sister and her children are there."

Buko was prepared to fight Listov if he had to. But he wasn't prepared for what he saw. In the faint swatch of moonlight coming through the half-open door, Buko saw a look of shame and pity on the telegraph agent's face.

"Buko, I… There are bad things ahead for you, I'm afraid."

"What do you know?"

Listov wouldn't look at him. "Come on. I'll take you down to the office."

The telegraph office was a small first-floor room near the railroad station. Across the river, the Fernandes warehouse hulked in the darkness. In months past, Buko had stared at the building, wishing himself back there. Now he couldn't bear to look at it.

Listov let Buko inside, then locked the door behind them. Buko could hear the shuffling of his feet as he groped his way toward the narrow counter that divided the tiny waiting area from the operator's station.

"Leave the lights off," Listov said. "I don't want anybody wondering why I'm sending a cable at this hour." There was a rattle as his hand struck something on the countertop. Buko heard him cursing under his breath. The hinges on the countertop squeaked as Listov let himself behind it.

Buko heard the striking of a match, then saw the pinkish glow of the flame, sheltered between Dimitri's hands, as he lit a stub of candle. Dimitri hunkered over the candle, his body a dark, flickering shadow. There was a click, then the hum of the equipment warming up. Buko watched as Listov raised the candle and squinted at the scrap of paper on which he'd written his sister's address in Skopje and the message.

Dear Anna,

I think you need to get out of Skopje for a few days. Why don't you meet us in Melnik? Be sure to bring Dimo and Elena. It will be good for us all.

Buko

Buko had fretted over the wording. Anna would know it was urgent, since Buko had never sent her a telegram before. He prayed she would understand the signal.

Listov was working the telegraph key.

Too late Buko thought of a problem. "Dimitri, can we trust the operator in Skopje?"

The clicking paused. "What choice do you have?" The clicking resumed.

In a few seconds, Listov had keyed the message. He switched off the equipment and snuffed the candle. The countertop gate squeaked again, and Buko heard him coming back. Listov was about to put his key into the lock when Buko grabbed his wrist.

Footsteps were coming down the street just outside the door: a single person, moving unhurriedly. Then tuneless whistling. The steps paused outside the door. The door handle turned back and forth, then the door rattled. The footsteps moved on down the pavement.

Buko would have sworn his breathing was audible all the way to the train station, but the steps didn't come back. After maybe two minutes, Listov put his key back into the lock. He leaned toward Buko.

"If the way is clear, I'll knock once."

He went outside and closed the door. A second or two later Buko heard the tapping of his knuckle on the doorframe. He stepped outside and waited as Listov locked the door. As soon as they could, they got off the main street, walking away from the receding footsteps.

On a side street just across the river, Listov turned to Buko. "The cable will be in the Skopje office in the morning. It should be delivered before noon. You can come by the office tomorrow afternoon, and I'll tell you if I've had a reply."

"Thank you, Dimitri. I won't forget this." Buko reached into his pocket for the thirty leva.

Listov put his hand on Buko's arm. "Keep the money, Buko. Give it to your people. God knows you'll need it." He turned and walked toward his house.

"I saw it, Daria. I typed the agreement, and I saw the signed copies. The commissar drew a line through the words 'from the newly liberated lands.' They're going to try to take the Jews from the old borders as well." Lily Panitza's eyes flickered here and there; her face was haunted.

They kept their voices low as they moved at a leisurely pace through the crowds in the market, but even in the midst of the throng, Daria felt as if every eye was turned in their direction. She was forcing herself to take deep, slow breaths. She realized her fingernails were digging painfully into her palms.

"Whom else have you told?" Daria said.

"Some Jewish leaders who are friends of mine. This has to be stopped, Daria. You have to go to the king."

"Do you honestly imagine Tsar Boris doesn't know what's happening?"

"I don't know. But you have to try. You have to try everything."

All afternoon, since that conversation, Daria had been numb. She sat in the winter garden, watching the crown prince and Princess Maria-Louisa working on their lessons, but she hardly noticed anything they did. Prince Simeon had to ask her three times to divert her eyes to the arithmetic paper he wanted her to check. The numbers scrawled in his childish hand were like random marks; they made as much sense to her as the patterns in the bark of a birch.

And then, from some faraway place within her, a place she wouldn't have suspected or been able to name, an idea came. It arrived at the threshold of her consciousness, tapped patiently at the barrier of her dread, and waited. She carried it with her for the rest of the day. That night, as she lay on her bed trying to sleep, the idea sat down with her and began to speak.

"Yes," she thought after a little while, "tomorrow I will get a message to Lily. One she won't likely be expecting."

Pavel Grouev was reading his favorite French novel when the knock came on the door. He gave his wife a questioning look, and she gave a slight shake of her head. The children were at the kitchen table, finishing their lessons. Radka looked at him.

"Well, Papi? Aren't you going to see who it is?"

A little cross at the interruption, Pavel carefully placed his bookmark in the novel. He went to the door and laid a hand on the latch.

"Yes, who's there?"

"Pavel, it's me—Mikhail Simoniev. You must let me in."

Pavel unlocked the door, and the entire Simoniev family filled the parlor: Mikhail and his wife, Betty, with their two children, Benjamin and Zizi.

"Zizi!" Radka pushed away from the table and started toward her friend, grinning as she held out her hands. Then she faltered.

"Zizi, why are you crying?"

Mikhail grabbed Pavel's hands. "Pavel, please, you must hide us. There's a rumor going around that tonight the police are going to round up the Jews in Sofia."

"What? There must be some—"

"Please, Mr. Grouev," Betty Simonieva said, her voice breaking. "We're so scared."

Pavel stared open mouthed, first at the Simonievs, then at his family, now gathered in a silent huddle behind the couch where his wife had been sitting. Radka was the first one to move.

"Come on, Zizi. You can sleep in my bed, and I'll make a pallet on the floor beside you."

Mrs. Groueva got up from the couch and went to Betty Simonieva. She drew the other woman aside, her arm about Betty's shoulders.

"Of course," Pavel said. "Mikhail, you and Betty can have our bed. And I'm sure Benjamin can tuck in with our boys without any problem. We'll sort this out in the morning."

At the stroke of noon, Buko was standing in front of the telegraph office, waiting for a chance to speak privately with Listov. Finally the single remaining customer walked out, and Buko hurried to the counter.

"Dimitri? Any answer to my cable?"

Listov looked at him, then reached toward a shelf under the counter. He placed in front of Buko a copy of the cable he had sent, with a single word stamped across it: "Undeliverable."

"What does that mean?" Buko said. "I wrote my sister's address very clearly—"

Listov put a hand on Buko's arm. "I know, I know. I cabled back immediately, requesting the reason. Buko, the address is right. But there's no one there."

That night Buko awoke from an uneasy sleep. He lay in the darkness, listening to Anka's breathing, then realized something was amiss. It was a sound: the sound of rail cars being shunted back and forth along sidings at the station, just across the downtown area. In all the years he had lived in Kyustendil, Buko had never heard such a sound from the station at this hour of the night. Something was going on. With dread pooling in his stomach, he decided to investigate.

He hadn't gone far in the brisk spring air when he realized there was another sound: a moaning, sighing sound, like wind through the pines on the high slopes, but higher pitched, less rhythmic. Then he heard children weeping. His feet broke into a trot.

By the time he neared the railroad station, the sound was almost unbearable: not loud, but heartbreaking—a wordless anthem of suffering. Only with the greatest concentration was he able to discern individual cries among the ebb and flow of the mourning; it was like a tightly woven cable or like a river of sound pouring unheeded over the sleeping town.

There were no lights on at the station—everything was being done in darkness. Guards, some in plain clothes, some in the uniforms of the commissariat police, roved along the cars, now and then striking with their sticks at an outstretched hand or even a face pressed to the slats of the rail cars. Buko heard the guards cursing at their captives, albeit quietly; they didn't want to wake anybody.

Most of the guards seemed to be on the side of the train nearest the station. Buko slipped from one shadow to the next until he was on the far side. He moved among some empty boxcars, watching what was happening, trying to find a way to take in a scene too horrible to contemplate.

Where were these people from?

He crept up beside the nearest freight car. A voice came from inside: "Please, whoever you are, get us some water."

"I...I don't have anything to—"

"What place is this?" another voice asked.

"Kyustendil," Buko said.

He heard a scrambling, shuffling sound, saw dim movement in the darkness through the slats of the boxcar. Someone was trying to reach the side. Buko felt his gorge rising; they were crammed into the cars like cattle. The smell of urine and excrement assaulted his nostrils.

"Kyustendil, you said? Listen, you have to go find my father!"

"Shh! Quiet, Marta! Do you want to bring the guards?"

"My father," she went on in a hoarse whisper. "He lives on Tsarska Street, just down from—"

"I need a drink. I'm thirsty." It was the voice of a child. "My mama won't move. Can somebody get me a drink?"

Buko felt himself teetering on the edge of panic. He backed away from the car, saw the arms reaching toward him. He moved down a little farther and thrust his face toward the slats, asking, "Where were you taken from?"

"I am from Giumurdjina..." "Dede Agach..." "Ksanti..." "Seres..." "Kavala..." "Skopje..."

"Who is from Skopje?" Buko said. "I want to talk to someone from Skopje."

They shifted themselves to and fro, like dreary, human-size playing cards, trying to make room for someone moving from the center of the car. A grayish face appeared at the slats. "I am from Skopje," the man said.

"My sister lives in Skopje—Anna Gamilha? She has a son, Dimo, and a daughter, Elena. They live on Pirotska Street. Has anyone seen her?"

"I don't know," the man said. "There are some more people from Skopje on the next car, I think. You might ask. But...can you bring some water?"

Buko hurried to the next car, his breath rasping in his throat. "Is anyone here from Skopje?" he whispered at the slats. "I'm Buko Lazarov. I'm looking for Anna Gamilha."

His request passed among the car's inmates, a verbal note handed back and forth from one side to the other. He pressed himself toward the side of the car, his ears tuned at a fever pitch for the crunch of gravel beneath a guard's boot.

"Uncle Buko?"

The words came as a ragged half whimper from a place a few meters down from where he stood. Buko's heart was pounding. He hurried to the place.

"Dimo?"

"Uncle Buko, oh, Uncle…" Buko heard the young boy sobbing. He worked his fingers through the slats and stroked his nephew's grimy face.

"Dimo…in God's name, what—"

"They came for us at three in the morning," Dimo said. "There was a rainstorm outside, but they didn't care. 'You have fifteen minutes to pack,' they said. 'One suitcase per adult.' They herded us into the street, down to the tobacco warehouse. There were guns everywhere, all of them pointed at us. They kicked us, slapped us. I saw an old man, walking with a cane, stumble in the mud, and two of the police beat him and cursed at him until some of us picked him up and carried him.

"When we got to the warehouse, they took our suitcases and bags from us. They looked at everything. They smashed the cheeses—I guess they thought we'd hidden our diamonds in there." Dimo gave a mirthless laugh. "They…they even searched our mouths and inside our bodies. The women, too."

Buko realized tears were streaming down his face, but his grief and shock were too big for sound.

"I don't know how, but I still have this—" Dimo pressed something through the slats, and it fell onto Buko's palm.

It was the bracelet from Buko's mother, the one he had just sent to his sister by Dimo.

"But I gave this to you—"

"They'll just find it on me the next time they search us, Uncle. Keep it. As a remembrance."

The cars clattered together; somewhere ahead the engine was preparing to pull away from the station.

"Dimo, I have to talk to your mother, to Elena—"

He shook his head. "The men who searched them were very rough. They haven't spoken or moved since. We had to carry them onto the train."

The car was starting to move. Buko walked beside it, desperation clawing in his chest like a trapped beast. "Dimo, where are they taking you? Maybe I can send something? Some help?"

"They just said we're going to camps inside Bulgaria," Dimo said. "But

I don't know how long we'll stay there. Or how many of us will be dead before we get there. The nights are cold, and there aren't many coats among us. No food."

Buko was trotting now, not caring if he was seen. "Dimo, don't give up!"

"Uncle Buko…keep the bracelet. Don't forget…"

Buko ran beside the car, holding his hands against the slats beside his nephew's face. He ran until he tripped against a large stone in the roadbed and fell headlong in the gravel. The train rolled past above him, gathering speed. He was sobbing now. He opened his fist, and the bracelet was there. He held it against his face, and grief poured from him—a grief as black as the enclosing night.

17

I think you are mistaken to try to include the Sofia Jews in this order," the German ambassador said. "The populace of this country, with very few exceptions, has no concept of the struggle against worldwide Jewry. They lack the cultural and scientific sophistication to comprehend the pernicious nature of the Jewish infection. If you act prematurely, the public outcry of the ignorant could jeopardize everything you've done so far."

Lily Panitza watched as Interior Minister Gabrovski smiled to himself and straightened his tie. That wasn't a good sign; it usually meant Gabrovski was fighting to control his emotions.

"My dear Herr Beckerle, I think you're blowing this out of proportion. After all, we have a signed contract." He glanced at Alexander, who sat beside Gabrovski, staring fixedly at the top of the table. Lily knew Alexander's fingers were twined together in his lap, furiously kneading as he struggled with the anxiety and frustration the ambassador's objections must be causing him.

"Consider, Herr Beckerle," Gabrovski said, "that alone, among all the nations of Europe, Bulgaria has made specific covenants with the Reich for the transfer of her Jews. We alone have agreed to pay for their transport across our borders. We alone have guaranteed that the Reich is in no way responsible for returning them once they have passed the Bulgarian frontier. And Commissar Belev here"—Gabrovski put a hand on Alexander's shoulder—"has done such a marvelous job of creating special train schedules, providing for transit camps, taking care of all the details. How can you be so pessimistic?"

Beckerle shook his head. "I don't know, Mr. Gabrovski. Some of the Jews, especially in Sofia, have friends in high places."

"And we're prepared to deal with that," Alexander said in a voice edged with impatience.

Careful, Alexander, Lily thought. *Remember who sits across from you...*

"We've identified those most likely to cause trouble," he said. "They'll be on the first train out of here."

Beckerle stared at Belev for several seconds. He pursed his lips, then gave a tight nod. "Very well, Mr. Gabrovski. We'll see. But I tell you again: the last thing the Reich wants is a messy public debate over the Jewish question—in Bulgaria or anywhere else. Secrecy is our watchword."

"I understand, Your Excellency."

Beckerle rose from the table and left.

As soon as the door closed behind him, Gabrovski turned to Alexander. "Mr. Belev, I hope you understand the seriousness of the situation."

"I believe I do, sir."

"If this mission is compromised, we will be very embarrassed in front of our German allies."

Alexander nodded.

"Good. Double-check your networks. Our information must not fall into the wrong hands; that would be a disaster."

"I understand, Mr. Gabrovski."

"Miss Panitza, did you get everything Herr Beckerle said?"

"I believe so, Mr. Gabrovski."

"Very well. I suppose that's all, then, Mr. Belev. You may go. And keep me informed."

Alexander was taciturn on the ride back to the Dondukov Boulevard office. Lily could tell he was fretting over the interview with Beckerle. She rested her palm on the back of his hand. He stared out the window and wouldn't look at her.

When she got back to her desk, she noticed a phone message from A. Taenova, the code name Daria Richetti used to contact her. There was a phone number; Lily recognized it as the number of one of the small cafés ringing Alexander Nevsky Square. She looked at her watch; Daria would be there soon if she followed their usual plan.

Lily shuffled some paperwork and made a few notes on some files. When she thought the time was right, she left her desk and went downstairs, then crossed the street to the small bakery.

"Good morning, Miss Panitza," the baker's wife called. She was sweeping the layer of flour and crumbs that seemed to resettle on the floor as soon as the broom passed; Lily had never come in when this woman was not sweeping.

"Good morning, Mrs. Tenukova. If it's not too much trouble, may I borrow your phone?"

"Ah, the government forgot to pay its bill again?"

"No, I just… This is a call I don't want everybody in the office listening to." Lily gave her a shy grin.

"Oh, the boyfriend again? Well, of course, of course. You know where it is; just help yourself."

Lily dialed the number on the note and heard Daria's voice after the second ring.

"Yes, what is it?" Lily said.

Daria told her.

"Are you sure?"

She was. Then the line went dead.

After giving Mrs. Tenukova another embarrassed little smile and shrug, Lily walked back to her office. She was very confused. She hoped Daria Richetti knew what she was doing.

Stefan cupped the water in his hand and slurped noisily. He straightened, wiping his beard with a satisfied sigh.

"My son, you're one of the few people whose drinking makes more noise than the fountain," Father Ilarion said.

"The water of the Rila Monastery is the best in Bulgaria," Stefan said. "For me, drinking it is like taking communion with the land."

Ilarion smiled and put a hand on the metropolitan's shoulder as they walked the uneven cobblestones of the courtyard. I'm glad you came to see me, Stefan. I've been wanting to talk to you for some time. It was good to catch up."

"You're one of the wisest men I know," Stefan said. "And these days a hardheaded man like me needs all the wisdom he can get."

"Ah, you're too rough on yourself. Hardheaded, maybe, but good hearted."

Stefan made a dismissing gesture.

"Where will you go from here?"

"To Dupnitza. Some men have asked to see me."

Father Ilarion pursed his lips. "I think you won't hear good news there."

"I've gotten used to that."

They were at the wide archway. Stefan clasped Ilarion gently to him and kissed the old priest's hand. "Grace and peace to you, Father."

"And to you, my son."

Driving down the winding mountain road from the monastery to Rila village, Stefan thought about Father Ilarion. The old monk was one of the foremost experts in the Balkans—maybe in Europe—on textual variants among the ancient codices. He had a brilliant, encyclopedic grasp of the historical and social forces behind the formation of the New Testament canon. He could have taught at any Orthodox seminary in the world. Yet he had spent his entire life at the monastery, working in the library, puttering in the flower gardens, even taking his turn in the scullery. Once, after a particularly challenging discussion over some point of Scripture, Stefan had chided Ilarion about hiding his light under a bushel.

"A scholar of your caliber has no business stuck up here like a rock badger in a hole. You should be teaching young priests what you've learned."

Ilarion had smiled and looked away over the red-tiled rooftops of the monastery. "Someone must tend the wells," he said, then turned to look at Stefan, "so that others may come and drink."

As he approached the railroad crossing at the outskirts of Dupnitza, the barrier started down. Stefan braked, grousing under his breath that the stupid train would make him late for his appointment. The engine chugged past, then the coal car…and Stefan felt his heart freezing in his chest.

The train consisted of open-slatted livestock cars—crammed with human beings.

The metropolitan got out of his car and stood helplessly as the train rolled past the crossing, car after car of pathetic human freight. He saw women with babies in their arms, other women far advanced in pregnancy. There were old men, boys and girls, their clothing sodden and ripped, their faces grimed by the cinders blowing back from the engine stack. They were packed into the cars so tightly that there was no room to sit. And still, Stefan saw bodies lying tangled among the legs of those still upright: those who had died and slid to the floor, like deadfall in the underbrush of a forest.

A loud cry went up from them, a wailing like the souls of the damned. Without realizing it, Stefan had stretched out a hand toward them: a pathetic, useless gesture—too little and far, far too late.

The train passed, and the sound of the wheels faded into the distance. Stefan realized that he had fallen to his knees in the roadway, that he was weeping.

They have eyes and ears… They have voices that must be heard…

But how was he to know that their eyes were windows onto despair? How could he have guessed that the voices were the cries of those who had lost all hope?

The train was routed north, one can only guess toward the Danube— and then, presumably, to Poland, a place that promises a fate so horrid that even the babes in arms know to fear it.

These are human beings, not cattle, and it is a shame to highest heaven that they be forced to travel in such a way. Their conditions are unbearable, and we must beseech Your Majesty in the strongest terms possible, in the name of Christ himself, to relieve the undeserved suffering of these wretched people who are passing your borders on their way to a nightmare end.

Pavel Grouev took a final look at the telegram and let it fall to the desk. "It bears the seal of His Eminence Stefan, metropolitan of Sofia."

Tsar Boris leaned back in the chair behind the desk, massaging his cheekbones and the bridge of his nose. His eyes were closed.

Pavel waited for maybe three full minutes, and still Tsar Boris remained silent. As soon as this telegram had arrived at the palace, Pavel knew he needed to bring it here, to the royal residence at Vrana, though it was the weekend and the king was supposed to be spending time with his family. Pavel knew he had to bring it, and he had dreaded this moment since first reading it.

Pavel cleared his throat quietly. "Your Majesty will, of course, want to respond?"

Tsar Boris's hands fell to his lap. He stared at the ceiling. His mouth opened and closed. Pavel felt a stirring of anxiety.

"Draft a letter to His Eminence," the king said finally, "stating that all possible legal measures will be taken. Say that we regret the taking of persons from the areas under German authority, but that our ability to act in their behalf is limited by the terms of our administration of the territories concerned."

"Yes, Your Majesty. I'll see to it as soon as—"

Boris sat bolt upright in the chair, as if he had received an electric shock. "What do they expect of me, Pavel? What would Stefan have me do? Defy the German military? Make Bulgaria a new Yugoslavia?"

Pavel shook his head and shrugged.

"I saw a German map, Pavel. Do you know how they had Macedonia and Thrace labeled?"

Pavel shook his head.

"'*Unter bulgarische Verwaltung*—Under Bulgarian Administration.' They weren't even the same color as the rest of Bulgaria." Tsar Boris began chuckling, but the sound didn't remind Pavel of anything to do with mirth. "They call me 'King Unifier.' I'm nothing of the kind, Pavel. I'm pathetic. I'm the king of technicalities. I don't even have the power to prevent the abduction of my own subjects—no, wait! Not subjects, administrative clients. That's what they are. And now, thanks to the Reich and Gabrovski, they've been reassigned to another administration."

He looked at Pavel, a wild, unhealthy light in his eyes. "Reassigned! That's what we'll call it from now on, Bacho Pavlé! I'm sorry, Mrs. Simonova, you and your children have been reassigned…"

"Your Majesty, shall I go now and prepare the response to Metropolitan Stefan?"

Tsar Boris put his hands to his face, then rubbed his palms slowly across his scalp. He took a deep breath. "Yes, Pavel. Please draft the response and bring it to me for my signature as soon as it's ready."

There was a tap on the door. Pavel opened it slightly. He turned to Tsar Boris. "It is Miss Richetti, Your Majesty."

Daria came in. "Your Majesty, the queen wished me to tell you that she and the children are waiting for you in the dining room. Luncheon is ready."

But Tsar Boris gave no appearance of having heard anything Miss Richetti had said. Instead, he was staring at the collar of her gray suit, staring at the yellow star pinned there.

"What... Miss Richetti, what is... Why are you wearing that?"

Pavel saw the color leaving her face, but he also saw the set of her jaw and the way her eyes were locked on those of the king.

"It is the law, Your Majesty. I am a Jew. Therefore I must wear the star."

"Daria, you... I never intended..."

From the look of her, Pavel guessed there were many things she might have said at that moment, but she chose to voice none of them. Instead she simply said, "What shall I tell Her Majesty?"

Tsar Boris stood slowly; he looked like a man who had just been bludgeoned in the stomach. He wouldn't look at Miss Richetti.

"Call the garage," he said in Pavel's general direction. "Tell them to get the Packard ready. I...I have to drive...somewhere." Then he strode from the room.

Apparently the epidemic was spreading. When Pavel walked into his house that night, his daughter Radka sat at the kitchen table with a yellow star, fashioned of construction paper, fastened to her black school dress.

"Radka! What is this foolishness? Everyone knows you aren't Jewish."

"If Zizi has to wear the star, then I'm wearing it too."

Pavel looked at his wife, but she only shrugged and went on stirring a pan on the stove.

"Radka, my dear, I know you love your friend. And you must believe me; everything possible is being done."

"But Papi, Zizi says there's an order for deportation. She says the Jews will be loaded on trains and taken to Poland and killed."

"That is not—"

"They're so afraid, Papi. The Nazis hate them. They're Bulgarians, not Poles. Why should they have to go away? Why can't His Majesty put a stop to all this?"

"Radka, you don't—"

His daughter looked at him; her eyes trembled with tears. "What if it was me, Papi? What if my name was on a list somewhere? What if I had to get on a train, and I would never see you again? What would you do?"

Pavel looked at the face of his beautiful child, and he knew he had no answer for the questions burning in her heart. He sat down and held his head in his hands, as if by doing so, he could still his own mind. *Oh God in heaven, whatever shall we do?*

Buko looked around at the other men gathered in the side room of the synagogue. "We have no choice," he told them. "Once we're on those trains, our last hope is gone." For a moment, the sight of his nephew's face, forced between the slats of the cattle car, swam before his eyes. "The orders for this deportation originated in Sofia. That's where we must go to get it stopped."

"We can't travel to Sofia!" someone said. "We can't even walk down the street. We're under house arrest."

"We can obey the house arrest and die like cattle, or we can make a start toward Sofia and die like men," Buko said. "I'm going. I've known Dimitar Peshev since we were in grade school. He's a good man, and he's the deputy speaker of the Sobranje. If I can talk to him, he can get the right people to listen."

"I'll go with you, Buko."

Everyone turned around. It was Assen Suichmezov. Assen was a Christian, but everyone in the synagogue knew him; he'd grown up in a Jewish neighborhood in Kyustendil. He'd called Buko's father "Uncle Sabo" until the day he died.

"I've gone around to some of my business associates," Assen said. "We've collected three hundred thousand leva. Maybe if we spread some of the money around the commissariat, we can buy some time."

Pinhas Comforty walked over to Suichmezov and embraced him. Several of the other men did the same.

"I'll go too," Georgi Yeremiev said. He was the president of the local union of reserve sergeants.

"And Levkov from the chamber of commerce has pledged to go," Assen Suichmezov said, "as well as ten or twelve of the downtown merchants and businessmen. They've started hiring taxis. We'll go in a convoy."

"But how will we get there in time?" someone asked. "The district governor has control of all the gasoline supplies. He'll never release enough fuel to do this."

"Then we'll go on the five o'clock train," Buko said. "We've got more than enough money for tickets."

"There are police surrounding the railroad station right now," Pinhas Comforty said. "Can you even get on the train?"

"I plan to find out," Buko said. "What is there left to lose?"

The others who had volunteered for the delegation arrived at the synagogue one or two at a time. About a quarter past four, after a long succession of prayers and blessings, the handful of men left the synagogue. Assen Suichmezov asked if he might drop by his shop to pick up a valise some of his associates said they were bringing, containing some additional funds hastily collected for the delegation.

But the Brannik youth had gotten there first. The windows of Suichmezov's business were all smashed, and the words *Kike* and *Traitor* were splashed in ugly red paint along the front walls. Word traveled fast in Kyustendil.

"Buko, turn your collar under so your star doesn't show," Assen Suichmezov said. "Stay close behind me, and keep your cap pulled down. Maybe we can bluff our way past the guards, and they won't check too closely."

With each step closer to the train station, Buko felt his heart hammering harder against his breastbone.

They crossed the plaza in front of the station, and a policeman stepped in front of them. "Where are you going?"

"We've got tickets for the five o'clock train to Sofia," Suichmezov said.

"What's your business in Sofia?"

"Since when does a Bulgarian citizen have to give an excuse for traveling on the train?"

"I'm afraid I'm going to have to see some identification," the officer said.

Buko felt a cold sweat starting on his forehead.

"This is an outrage!" said Levkov, stepping in front of Assen Suichmezov. "I'm a member of the chamber of commerce here, not some back-country yokel you can push around." He made as if to step past the officer, but the policeman whipped out his nightstick and jabbed Levkov in the solar plexus, doubling him over as he gasped for breath.

"Now, as I said, I need to see identification for anyone who's planning to get on a train leaving Kyustendil. We have our orders."

Other guards were approaching their position, some of them already brandishing their sticks.

"We'll just do this one at a time, all right? You first." The officer held out his hand and stared at Assen Suichmezov. Slowly Assen reached inside his coat and withdrew his wallet. He opened it and withdrew his papers, which the officer peered at for several moments.

A whistle blew—the first warning for those planning to depart for Sofia. The sky was reddening toward evening. They were running out of time.

"All right, you next," the officer said, turning toward Levkov. The businessman was still trying to regain his breath, but he managed to hand his wallet to the policeman.

"Thank you for your kind cooperation, Mr. Levkov," the guard said. "Next, please."

This was Ivan Momchilov, a local attorney. He flipped open his identification under the guard's nose. The guard took it between a finger and thumb, as if it were a dirty handkerchief, and took a long, leisurely perusal.

The second whistle blew.

Buko was next in line, and there was no way he would get past this checkpoint. He was desperately trying to think of some ruse when he heard rapid footsteps approaching behind him.

"Officer, let these men through at once, by order of the People's Sobranje of Bulgaria!"

It was the tall, thin, gray-haired Peter Mikhalev, the other local Sobranje deputy from Kyustendil—Dimitar Peshev's legislative colleague. He strode up to the checkpoint, gesturing imperiously.

"I'm an officer of the government, and these men are traveling with me. If you prevent us from getting on that train, I'll see to it that you and anyone who cooperates with you not only loses his job but also faces a special tribunal for obstruction of governmental business."

The officer stared at Mikhalev, and for the first time his sneer wavered. "I wasn't informed about any official travel purpose for this train."

"And there are probably a world of other things you don't know as well," Mikhalev said. "Now are you going to get out of my way or not?"

Buko hardly dared to breathe. He kept his face turned down, tried to remain part of the background.

The officer jerked his head toward the station, and his underlings stepped aside.

"Come on, gentlemen," Mikhalev said. He put a hand on Buko's shoulder and urged him forward. "Our Sofia contacts will meet us at the central station. We must hurry."

Buko's legs felt as though they might give way at any moment. He forced himself to keep walking, to stay up with the older Mikhalev's long-shanked stride, to put as much distance as possible between himself and the guards behind them.

When the five men had boarded the train and enclosed themselves in a car all to themselves, Peter Mikhalev said, "I'm sorry, gentlemen. I was meeting with constituents in Boboshevo. I got back to Kyustendil late this afternoon." He turned to Suichmezov. "If your son Gregor hadn't caught me as I was entering my house and told me about the meeting, I wouldn't have gotten here in time."

"God bless you, Peter," Suichmezov said. "Then you know what we're about."

Mikhalev looked at them all and finally at Buko. He put a hand on Buko's shoulder. "I went to the district governor's office. Tasev from the commissariat was there. I...I cannot believe..." He turned his face away.

The train gave a jerk and began to move. They could see the Kyustendil train station move past. And then, on the sidings beyond, they could see line after line of empty boxcars waiting in the gathering dark.

18

March 1943

Apart of Daria's mind found it amusing—watching the palace staff trying desperately not to look at her yellow star. In the past day there had been many eyes flickering to it, then away, many smiles of greeting that hesitated for an instant. At first she tried to keep count of those who showed surprise, as opposed to those who showed nothing at all— or thought they did. But she had soon lost track.

She had dreaded most of all seeing Dobri for the first time. His protective instincts would be aroused; he would say everything he could think of to convince her to remove the star. He might even become angry—or, perhaps worse, distant.

How could she explain to him what she was doing? She couldn't even explain it to herself. All she knew was that in the depths of her hopelessness, the seeds of something like courage had taken root. Maybe not courage—call it doomed resignation or the anger that comes with desperation. When Panitza revealed to her the plan to deport the Macedonian and Thracian Jews, then the further intent by the commissariat to include the Jews from the old boundaries, Daria knew there was no more room to hide, no more time for the doubtful protection of anonymity. Whatever it cost her, she had to assert to herself: "This is who I am, and that at least I will keep."

And on that first morning, when Dobri came to relieve the night watch commander, his eyes gladdened at her face, then went stark when he saw the yellow star. Almost…almost she repented of her foolhardiness for the sake of this simple, good man whose affection for her made him a hostage to circumstance.

He walked up to her, his eyes fixed on the star. He reached out a finger to touch it. Then, his eyes filling with understanding as warm and helpless as tears, he looked at her and touched her face. He walked away from her, toward his duty station, and he never said anything, but she knew what his silence cost him; it meant everything.

The queen, of course, realized what she was doing, even as she choked back with a palpably physical effort the anxiety that leaped to her face each time she saw Daria wearing the star. But Her Majesty was far too gracious to mention the matter one way or the other. That was one of the things Daria had loved most about Queen Giovanna ever since she had known her: a chief mark of her nobility was her ability to ennoble others.

The children were a different matter. Crown Prince Simeon, always brimming with curiosity, wanted to know if Daria had won a medal.

"No, Your Royal Highness, it's not a medal."

"Be quiet, Simeon," Princess Maria-Louisa said. "It's a Jewish star."

"But why is Mademoiselle Daria wearing it?"

The princess gave Daria a guilty look, then scowled at her younger brother.

"It's all right, Your Royal Highness. I wear the star because I'm Jewish. The law says Jews must wear the star."

"Am I Jewish?"

"No, silly," Princess Maria-Louisa said. "Don't you know? You were baptized in our chapel by Metropolitan Stefan and the rest of the Holy Synod. You're Orthodox."

"Why isn't Mademoiselle Daria Orthodox then? She's just like us."

"Your Royal Highness, I'm… Maybe you should begin working on your lessons; your tutors will be here before long."

"No! I want to know about the star!"

Behind the crossed arms, behind the scowl pressing down on his little forehead, she could see the worry, the childish, stubborn sense that something here demanded explanation, demanded redress. She was up against this little boy's immutable, heartbreaking need for things to be fair—for the world to behave according to the proper rules.

Oh, dear God, where to begin?

"Let's sit down over here, shall we? Now then. Of course, you understand about the war."

"Yes. We're on the side of the Germans, but some people don't think they can win."

Daria stared at him for a heartbeat. "Yes, well… The Russians are fighting against the Germans, and the Russian government is Communist."

Crown Prince Simeon nodded. "The Bolsheviks killed my father's godfather, Tsar Nicholas."

"Quit interrupting, Simeon," Princess Maria-Louisa said.

"Some people think the Communists and the Jews are secretly working together," Daria said.

"Are you a Communist, then, Mademoiselle Daria?" the princess asked.

"Absolutely not! But some people don't understand that you can be a Jew and also be a loyal Bulgarian citizen."

"Why don't you just tell them?" Crown Prince Simeon said. "Why doesn't my father just make a new law?"

"Oh, Your Royal Highness, it's not that simple. Your father can't always do just as he wishes. He must listen to the Sobranje and his cabinet and…"

Daria felt the princess's hand slipping into hers. "Nothing bad can happen to you, Mademoiselle Daria."

The crown prince's eyes were big; they glistened like melted glass. "Mademoiselle Daria, can't you just take off the star? Then nobody will know. I won't tell on you, and Maria-Louisa won't, and Mother won't, and—"

Daria shook her head. She reached out to touch the crown prince's cheek. "No, Your Royal Highness. That is something I can't do." She stroked his hair and gently squeezed the princess's hand. "Sometimes—how can I say this?— sometimes it's wrong to hide. It isn't always like this, but sometimes hiding can be like telling a lie. For me, this is a time like that."

The crown prince laid his head in her lap, and Princess Maria-Louisa scooted in beneath her arm. A stillness descended, a hush like the silent shivering of the air after the last stroke of a bell has died away.

Daria heard a tiny sound, the brush of a leather heel on the marble tile near the doorway of the children's room. She looked and saw the silhouette of Tsar Boris just beyond the nearly closed door in the darkened hallway. For a few seconds he stood there, very still, then turned and walked away without making a sound.

"Pinhas! Can you hear me? It's Buko Lazarov, in Sofia. Pinhas!"

The connection was terrible. Buko was about to go out of his mind already, and now he had to strain every nerve to hear the words coming through the curtain of static on Dimitar Peshev's telephone.

"Did Gregor answer the phone?" Suichmezov was asking over Buko's shoulder. "Did you tell him to get Comforty on the line?"

Buko nodded impatiently. "Pinhas! Are you there?"

"Buko?"

"Pinhas, we are here, in Peshev's apartment, in Sofia. Can you tell me what's going on there?"

Through the squealing and popping on the line, Buko could hear voices in the background, the sound of a crowd. Why were there so many people in Assen Suichmezov's house this early in the morning?

"Police…this morning…curfew…all day. But everyone…tonight…Fernandes warehouse. And then to the trains."

"What? Pinhas, it's hard to understand you."

The other men were sitting and standing around him, staring as if they might extract the message from his face, his eyes.

"Everyone is saying they'll come tonight," Pinhas said, shouting over the distortion. "The police have imposed a citywide curfew. I had…sneak… this call."

"Pinhas, how…" Buko faltered, knew it was wrong, but couldn't help himself. "How is Anka? And her mother? Is anyone there with them?"

"Everything is in an uproar," Pinhas said. Buko didn't know if he'd even heard the question. "Christians are offering to hide valuables for their friends, or else they're buying their things to raise money. Everything…hopeless. Time…out."

"Pinhas, listen to me. Can you hear me? Listen. Tell everyone—we are here with Dimitar Peshev, and he will speak to the leadership. Pinhas, tell them to hang on. Do you understand? Tell them—"

Buko stared at the dead phone. He put it back in its cradle, then looked around at the others.

"It sounds as if there's a daylong curfew in Kyustendil. For everybody. Tonight they'll arrest the Jews and take them to the Fernandes warehouse."

A few seconds of stunned silence passed.

"This is impossible!" Dimitar Peshev said. "I am deputy speaker of the Sobranje! How can something like this be happening in my own hometown without my having heard a word from anyone?" He strode back and forth across the apartment, his hands shoved into his pockets. He turned to look at Buko, who sat in the chair beside the phone, feeling as if the life was draining from his body.

"Buko, you know me! You know Mikhalev. How could we ever believe the Law for the Defense of the Nation would come to this?"

Buko tried to frame an answer, but all he could do was shake his head.

"The interior minister himself has assured the Sobranje over and over that the Jewish question will be settled peacefully and humanely. Those were his very words."

"If everything is done in secret, at night, then it might well happen peacefully," Assen Suichmezov said. "They want to make their problem disappear. Then they'll have peace."

There was a knock on the door. The men looked at each other, and Peshev went to the door. "Yes, who's there?"

"Dimitar, it's Yako Baruch. You've got to let me in."

Peshev opened the door, and Baruch hurried in. "Thank God, you're all here," he said to the somber group, still gathered near the phone. "We've received terrible news from—"

"We know. We've come from Kyustendil to warn—"

"No, not just Kyustendil," Baruch said. "Plovdiv, Sliven, Pazardjik, Dupnitza…all the Jews are under house arrest. And trains are gathering at the stations."

Buko stared at him. "They mean to take us all. Every Jew in Bulgaria."

"The trains from Thrace and Macedonia have already started moving toward the Danube," Baruch said. "My cousin in Dupnitza saw it all. They unloaded them in a camp outside Dupnitza. One doctor and two nurses were supposed to tend to the sick—almost a thousand people. What could they do? The people were crying for water, for bread. They were trying to get messages to their families. They were drenched and shivering from traveling through rainstorms in the open cars; almost none of them had coats. Children were looking for their parents; babies were squalling in their own filth. It was sickening. Then the commissariat police loaded them back on the cars, whipping them and cursing at them like cattle. And the trains pulled out—headed north."

Peshev was staring out the window of his apartment, onto Neofit Rilski Street. Outside, the traffic was moving as usual, Buko guessed. Children in their black uniforms were walking to school. The buses and trams jangled their way through the early morning. But inside this apartment, disaster hung like a fog.

"I must go to the Sobranje," Peshev finally said. "I'll find out what's happening with my colleagues. And I will make Filov and Gabrovski listen to reason."

"I'll be with you," Peter Mikhalev said.

"Suichmezov, will you come to the Central Consistory and speak to the assembly?" Yako Baruch said. "I'm afraid there will be a riot unless someone who knows something can come and tell us what's being done and what we should do."

"I'll come," Assen said. "If I can say anything that will help…"

"What about me?" Buko said. "What can I do?"

Peshev laid a hand on Buko's shoulder. "Stay here, Buko. Keep the door locked; you'll be safe. And keep trying to call Kyustendil if you feel like it. But first try to get some rest. You're the one who's brought us this far. You should be still. Let someone else carry the load for a while."

Pavel Grouev slumped at his desk, barely able to hold himself upright. He had not slept a minute the night before, as far as he could tell. The Simonievs were back at his apartment, wild with fear. Like apparently every Jew in Sofia, they had heard about the deportation orders. Zizi was inconsolable; all night long Pavel had heard the sound of her sobbing through the closed door to Radka's room. Betty Simonieva had carried with her a leather valise and an electric lamp. Mikhail told Pavel that the lamp was the first thing he had ever bought for Betty after their wedding, and she would not leave it in the apartment, no matter how much he tried to persuade her. This morning, before he had dragged himself to the palace chancery, Pavel's wife had told him that she had glimpsed the open valise. It contained no clothing or valuables—only pictures of the Simonievs. "It was like she was trying to pack all her memories," Dafina said, "and forgot about everything else." Pavel told Radka she could stay home from school that day. It was the first time in family history such a thing had taken place, but what else could he do? Sending her away under such circumstances seemed useless at best, cruel at worst. When he left, his daughter was sitting beside her friend on the couch, holding her and rocking her, like a mother comforting a child.

Tsar Boris sat in the corner of the office, in his favorite overstuffed leather armchair. If anything, he looked worse than Pavel felt. He had some papers in his hand that he sifted through, but Pavel didn't think he was actually reading them. He had been here when Pavel arrived. Naturally, the king had shaved and was wearing fresh clothes, but his face, his eyes, told the tale.

It wasn't unusual for Tsar Boris to come into Pavel's office several times each day from the adjoining room where he often worked; he liked to chat about the reports he read, the current situations in the government, or the progress of the war. Actually, the "chats" usually consisted of Tsar Boris speaking to Pavel, who responded *"Oui"* or *"Non"* at what seemed the appropriate moments.

But today the king sat motionless in the corner, pretending to read, making no attempt at conversation. At this moment, Pavel guessed, Tsar Boris was the loneliest human in Bulgaria.

Pavel's phone jangled in its cradle, jarring the silence of the office. He picked it up. "Grouev."

"Mr. Grouev, it's the prime minister. He says it's a matter of greatest urgency and asks to speak with the king."

Pavel thought for a few seconds. "Very well. Put him through."

"Mr. Grouev, I must speak to His Majesty at the soonest possible moment," Filov said as soon as the palace operator connected him. "Is His Majesty in residence today? And if he isn't, I must know his location. We have a crisis on our hands."

Pavel's eyes widened. Filov sounded as if the barbarians were pummeling at his office door.

"I…believe His Majesty is in residence, Mr. Filov. I may be able to find him for you. When did you need to see him?" As Pavel spoke, he watched Tsar Boris's face. The king winced but didn't shake his head no.

"Right now, if possible," Filov said. "I cannot stress enough the seriousness of the situation. We need a decision immediately."

"Well, Mr. Prime Minister, I can't promise you anything like that, but if it's as urgent as you say, I'll see if I can rearrange His Majesty's schedule to—"

Pavel stared in surprise at the phone. Filov had hung up.

"*Qu'est-ce que c'est?*"

Pavel shrugged. "*Je ne sais pas. C'est le premier ministre.*"

"What does Filov want now, a license to hunt Jews on the streets of Sofia?"

"Well, he sounds rather upset, Your Majesty. Something or other seems to be quite the matter. I gather he's on his way here right now."

Tsar Boris covered his eyes with his hand and leaned his head on the back of the chair. "Bacho Pavlé, I'm so tired. I don't know if I can deal with another crisis."

"*Oui,* Your Majesty. I understand."

"I should just abdicate. I should just go get in one of my cars, put my wife and children in with me, tell everyone we're going for a holiday in the Swiss Alps, and never come back."

"I'm sorry, Your Majesty. I know it must seem intolerable at times."

Boris spread his hands in front of him and gave Pavel a look of pure desperation. "No matter what I do, I'm wrong."

"I don't believe that, Your Majesty."

Boris sagged deeper into the chair. He shook his head. Pavel hoped he could find the strength to endure whatever situation he was about to face.

"Why don't you move over here, behind the desk, Your Majesty? Most likely, the prime minister will come directly here."

Boris nodded. He levered himself up out of the chair and moved across the room, shuffling his feet almost like an invalid. Pavel felt his chest constricting in fear and compassion for this man who was both his king and his friend.

"Remember this, Your Majesty: 'The king's heart is in the hand of the LORD; he directs it like a watercourse wherever he pleases.' From the Proverbs."

Tsar Boris looked at him and tried to smile. "Thank you, Bacho Pavlé. I know you mean to console. But at the moment, my heart feels more like a dammed-up sewer than a watercourse."

A moment later Sergeant Dimitrov knocked on the door. "The prime minister is here—"

He had barely gotten the words out when Bogdan Filov barged past him into the room, closely followed by Peter Gabrovski. Filov started talking before he was seated in the chair in front of the desk.

"Your Majesty, there has been a most serious breach of security that threatens the operations of the Interior Ministry—"

"The Jews all know about the deportation plans," Gabrovski said, grabbing the chair Pavel had hurriedly offered him. "They told—"

"Dimitar Peshev was in my office first thing this morning," Filov said, giving Gabrovski a cold stare, "demanding to know why he wasn't informed about the latest plans to resettle the Jewish population in…other areas. He had names, he had places—everything."

"I told him nothing," Gabrovski said. "I told him of no plans, gave him no information, but it didn't matter. He knew. He even said the district governor in Kyustendil had confirmed everything."

"And you denied knowledge of these plans?" Tsar Boris said.

Filov's face was crimson. "We were caught off guard, Your Majesty. This has been one of the government's most closely held secrets, most of the details of which were known only to the cabinet and the Commissar for Jewish Questions. What should we have done, simply turned tail and handed Peshev a full admission at his first question?"

"Dimitar Peshev has been no friend of Your Majesty's government," Gabrovski said.

"He is a duly elected deputy of the Sobranje, and he votes with the majority," the king said.

"Yes, but he opposed our favored candidate for deputy speaker, as Your Majesty remembers. The opposition used him as a lever against our efforts."

"I think that has more to do with you than with me, Mr. Prime Minister," Boris said. "But to return to the question at hand: how did you leave Mr. Peshev?"

"He was scurrying up and down the halls of the Sobranje, trying to find anyone who would listen to his talk about the Jewish plan. His Kyustendil colleague Mikhalev was in his office, making phone calls. And there are meetings going on right now, I'm told, with the Jewish leadership and others. There could be a lot of trouble over this, Your Majesty. A big uproar—something Berlin won't be pleased with at all."

"They have always insisted on the utmost secrecy," Gabrovski said.

Boris looked at the two men across his desk and fought the absurd urge to smile. *Yes, the devil does his best work in the dark, doesn't he?* And then he thought of Daria Richetti and the yellow star blooming on her collar at precisely the most disadvantageous moment in history.

Where was he? Somewhere in the unfocused, ill-defined middle. King of a country, yet less free to follow his conscience than his wife's personal aide. Sickened by the foul array of his available choices, yet shackled to them by compassion for his people.

He knew what Gabrovski and Filov wanted right now; he would give it to them.

"It seems to me, Mr. Prime Minister, that discretion has become the better part of valor." His teeth stung with the irony of the characterization. "You are correct in asserting that we cannot afford a public outcry over the Jewish question. I think you had better suspend your plans toward that end. Otherwise, we risk the appearance of anarchy, and the Wehrmacht is not known to take kindly to such unsettled conditions along its rear guard."

Filov sat back in the chair and gave Gabrovski an embarrassed, confirming look. Gabrovski appeared almost relieved. Boris wondered how the interior minister would explain this little fiasco to his German handlers. No doubt, that worry would insert itself into his mind soon enough. Right now, he had angry Sobranje deputies to deal with.

"Was there anything else, gentlemen?"

"No, Your Majesty. We just needed your…thoughts on this matter."

Boris stood and extended his hand. "Very well. Do what you can to re-assure Mr. Peshev and his colleagues that no measures are being carried out."

The two ministers bowed and started toward the door.

"Oh, and, Mr. Prime Minister?"

Filov turned to face him.

"Someone had better remember to inform the Jews."

Hauptsturmfuehrer Dannecker stood across from Alexander Belev's desk. From her place just outside Alexander's office, Lily could hear every word; Dannecker hadn't bothered to close the door behind him. He pointedly ignored Alexander's request that he take a seat.

"You have failed to live up to your end of our agreement," the SS commander said.

So, Lily thought, *he can speak Bulgarian when it suits him.*

"Herr Dannecker, that's not quite true. We've transported nearly twelve thousand Jews from the newly liberated—"

"We could have taken the Macedonian and Thracian Jews anytime we wanted them, and you know that," Dannecker said. "Our agreement called for twenty thousand Jews. You delivered twelve thousand."

A long silence crept past. Lily felt her heart pounding. Poor Alexander—what would happen to him?

"I must report this to Berlin," Dannecker said. "I'll let you know what your further instructions are."

The SS officer marched out of Alexander's office and through the outer office without looking at anyone. As soon as the doors to the stairwell had closed behind him, Alexander slammed his office door so hard that the glass pane cracked.

19

Yaroslav Kalitzin walked into the commissariat office on Dondukov Boulevard, whistling and smiling to himself. He nodded in a friendly way at Lily Panitza.

"Good morning, Miss Panitza. I'm here to give my report to the commissar."

"He isn't seeing anybody."

Kalitzin gave her a confused look. "What do you mean? He told me as soon as my operations in Thrace were concluded to come and give him a complete report. Everything went like clockwork; I'm here to give him the good news."

"You don't know what's happened," Lily said. "Things went terribly wrong, starting in Kyustendil. None of the deportations scheduled for the rest of the country took place. The whole operation was canceled."

"You're kidding."

"Do you think I'd make jokes about something like that? I'm not as flippant as you. The commissar is not seeing anyone until the general meeting at ten o'clock. The interior minister will be here then; you can tell him your wisecracks if you want."

Kalitzin stared open mouthed at Panitza, then looked around the office. No one returned his look. The atmosphere was as tense and guarded as a courtroom waiting for a verdict.

At ten o'clock sharp the large conference room on the first floor was filled. Alexander sat on one end, and the department heads and their assistants were scattered along both sides of the long, polished table. The chair at the head of the table was vacant, and everyone avoided looking at it. It would soon be occupied by Interior Minister Gabrovski, and no one was looking forward to hearing what he had to say.

Lily was seated halfway along the table, her notepad and pencils at the ready. She knew Alexander was holding a letter of resignation; she had typed it this morning.

At three minutes after ten, Gabrovski came in. In absolute silence he removed his topcoat and hat. He sat down in his chair and spent some seconds straightening his tie. Then he looked down the length of the table.

"Never in all my years of government service have I been so humiliated," he said. "We have been made to look stupid in front of our German allies. We have been discredited with the people of this country. And right now, over in the Sobranje, the deputy speaker is gathering names on a petition to force the prime minister to reverse the policies of the government toward the enemies of the New Bulgaria. They even knew about our agreement with Herr Dannecker, for heaven's sake!"

In the silence that followed, Lily wondered how many people seated around the table actually knew about the agreement Alexander had signed with the Hauptsturmfuehrer.

Alexander stood, holding his letter in his hand. "Mr. Gabrovski, as Commissar for Jewish Questions, I assume full responsibility for the failure of this operation. I hereby offer my resignation." He handed the letter to the person sitting next to him, and it passed from hand to hand, like a live coal, down the table to land in front of Gabrovski. Alexander sat down, looking like a man who had just had a lung removed. Lily forced her eyes back to her pad, readied herself to continue taking notes.

Gabrovski picked up Alexander's letter and glanced at it. "I appreciate the gesture, Mr. Belev. But I didn't come here looking for scapegoats. I came here looking for answers."

Alexander cleared his throat. "With all due respect, Mr. Gabrovski, if the order for cancellation had come only a few hours later, it wouldn't have mattered anymore. The Jews would have already been on the trains."

"Do you think I'm unaware of our schedules, Mr. Belev? Do you think I didn't use every delaying tactic I could think of, trying to buy us some more time? Next time, I'll send the Sobranje deputies directly to you, and let you convince them nothing is amiss!" He fingered Alexander's resignation letter. "And so I eventually had to concede the cause as lost and cancel the operation. But the point is, the plans made here in the utmost secrecy were somehow leaked to the leadership of the Sobranje and, worse, the entire Jewish population of the country."

The interior minister's eyes traveled the table and halted at Borislav Tasev. "Mr. Tasev, you were sent to Kyustendil to prepare for the deportations there, were you not?"

Tasev nodded, carefully keeping his eyes on the center of the table in front of him.

"Can you offer any explanation as to how, within hours of your request for supplies from the Jewish community, meetings were being held in secret, planning a propaganda campaign against the action?"

"The Kyustendil Jews raised millions of leva," said Popov, the inspector general of the commissariat. "They probably bribed someone—maybe someone in Tasev's organization."

"You have no proof of that, Popov," Tasev said. "Besides, I was the one who found out about the delegation to Peshev. And I was the last to be informed about the cancellations. When I went to the synagogue in Kyustendil to collect the last consignment of supplies, the president of the synagogue made me look like a fool in front of my men. He knew about the change in the orders before I did. After about five phone calls, I got the order to come back here. You can't expect us to operate with such a lapse in communication."

"It could have been worse," said the district chief for Plovdiv. "We were proceeding according to our orders when Metropolitan Kyril showed up at the school where we were holding the Jews. He demanded to come in, and my men, naturally, refused. Then this crazy priest climbed the fence and went inside anyway, daring my men to stop him. 'I will lie across the tracks in front of any train that tries to leave Plovdiv with these people,' he said. What were we supposed to do? Shoot a priest?"

Gabrovski held his head in his hands. "So it's come to this. The heads of our own church are openly defying the laws of the land."

There was a long silence.

"If I may, Mr. Gabrovski," Alexander said. "The deportations of the Macedonian and Thracian Jews are still in process. Many of these people are being held in transit camps in Bulgaria, and as far as they know, these are their final destinations; they shouldn't be told anything different. I suggest that we go forward with this part of the plan. We can tighten the security around the camps and restrict highway access to these areas, if we must. The transport craft are already waiting at the port in Lom, ready to sail to Vienna as soon as the trains are unloaded. We estimate confiscated property from Macedonia and Thrace to be in the neighborhood of fifty million leva."

Gabrovski's eyebrows rose.

"The expected cost of transportation is considerably less, so funding is not a problem," Alexander said. "Perhaps in the meantime things could change in our favor."

Gabrovski looked at Belev. "This is the first reasonable thing anyone has said since I got here. Thank you, Mr. Belev. Maybe your resignation is a bit premature after all."

Lily saw Alexander's jaws clench and his cheeks redden.

"Here is what we will do," Gabrovski said. "We will execute the deportations already under way, as Mr. Belev suggests. As far as anything else, we will all—each and every one of us—keep our mouths firmly shut. We will not speak about this to anyone, and we will let this little storm in the Sobranje blow over. Then later…we'll see."

Gabrovski stood and reached for his coat. "Mr. Belev, I'll keep you informed as the situations develop."

He turned around and walked out.

The icy fist clenching Dobri's heart loosened its grip the moment he heard that the deportations had been cancelled. The first thing he did was say a silent prayer of thanks. The second thing he did was pace the palace hallways until he found Daria, speaking with one of the chambermaids just outside Tsaritza Giovanna's private suite.

Without thinking, he dashed up to her and took her in an embrace that lifted her off the floor. The chambermaid giggled, but Dobri didn't care. The fear he had felt for Daria had nearly crushed him, and having it lifted felt like being reborn. He wanted to dance with her; he wanted to hold her until he couldn't stand up any longer. He wanted to look into her dark eyes and know he would never again risk losing the sight of them.

"Dobri, please put me down," she said, her voice muffled in his shoulder. "I'm not a stuffed animal."

"No, you are my treasure, my Daria, and I was so afraid I might lose you, and I haven't, and I don't ever want to take such a chance again. Is there somewhere we can go—to talk?"

Daria looked at the gawking chambermaid. "That's all, Anika. You can go tell the others what I said."

Anika scurried away, covering her grin.

Daria led Dobri into a side chamber. He looked at her, and he could see the weary tracks of fear on her face. He wanted to cup her cheeks in his hands and gently smooth away all traces of the recent dangers; he wanted to take her to a place where no harm could ever touch her.

"Daria, I've been doing a lot of thinking these past few weeks, especially with everything that's happened the last couple of days. When I saw you yesterday, with all that's in the air, I was so afraid I might lose you. I don't know if I could live after losing you, Daria. I want to be with you. Daria, I—"

She placed her finger on his lips. She gave her head a small shake. "Dobri…don't. You can't. Not now."

"What do you mean? I love you, Daria. I don't ever want to be without you. I know that more clearly now than I've ever known anything in my life."

"Oh, but, Dobri, don't you see? This isn't over."

He stared at her as her hand strayed to the yellow star on her collar.

"This is a risk I can't ask you to bear, Dobri. This belongs to me. And it would be unfair—"

"But there are exemptions! Don't you know? Jews married to non-Jews aren't subject to the Law for the Defense of the Nation. And…I don't know, there must be something…"

Dobri felt the desperation leaking into his voice, but he didn't know what to do about it. Surely she could see, couldn't she? She loved him; he knew it. She had to see.

"I'll speak to the queen. I'll speak to anybody you say, Daria, just please say that you'll think about it."

"Dobri, I have thought about it. I've thought and brooded on it longer than you can imagine. And I can't turn my back any longer on the plight of the Jewish people. Because that would be like denying who I am. I'm sorry, my dear. But I couldn't marry you now, not like this, not under this threat. It would be a lie. And I would never be able to forgive myself—or you."

Dobri felt something collapsing inside him. He couldn't possibly be hearing these words from her.

What should he do? The jilted lover was supposed to walk away in a fury, vowing never to return. Wasn't that the way it usually played out? Should he tell her she was a fool to refuse his love? Or should he simply turn and walk away and never look back?

He knew it was useless. He was snared by her as surely as a bird in a net, and he couldn't think of anything to be gained by pretending otherwise. And she hadn't said no…not exactly. More like "not yet." *Fools put their hope in such maybes,* he thought. *Well, Dobri Dimitrov, it's not the first time you've thought yourself a fool.*

"I understand, Daria. I think I do. Some of it, at least." Dobri's throat felt as though he'd swallowed a toothpick sideways. "And I… My offer is still good. If I can do anything to protect you, I'll do it at a moment's notice. I'll wait. And I'll hope. And who knows? Maybe someday…"

She touched his cheek, and her fingertips drifted to the hollow of his neck. He could feel their gentle pressure riding the crests of his pulse. A tear leaked from the corner of her eye and spread along the curve of her cheek.

"I believe you, Sergeant Dimitrov," she said in a hoarse whisper. "As you say, who knows?"

"Our request is that when undertaking any measures, only the real needs of the state and the people would be taken into account," Pavel read. "We cannot oppose measures imposed by security needs—"

"Generous of him," Boris said.

"We cannot believe that the deportation of these people out of Bulgaria has been envisaged; this intention has been ascribed by a malicious rumor to the Bulgarian government."

"Imagine that, Pavel. Our government doing such a thing."

"The honor of Bulgaria and her people is, above all, an element of her policy. It is a political asset of the greatest value, therefore nobody has the right to waste it without the approval of the entire nation."

"Brave bit, that last," Boris said. "Filov will be furious."

Pavel nodded. "Our sources in the Sobranje indicate Mr. Peshev has collected signatures from more than forty of the pro-government majority deputies. Some of the opposition deputies have tried to sign, but Peshev is clever. He knows Filov could easily play that off as the usual complaints from the malcontents in the legislature. Peshev wants to make it clear to Filov that his own majority opposes the Jewish measures. It's looking like a full-scale parliamentary revolt."

"What will the prime minister do? Call for a vote of no confidence?"

"It's possible, I suppose. He may think new elections on the Jewish question would give him a more docile Sobranje. But I don't think so," Pavel said, scratching his beard. "I think, instead, he'll bring pressure to bear on the signers, try to get as many as he can to recant."

"He wants to meet with me in the next few days," Boris said. "I suspect Mr. Peshev's letter will be our main topic of conversation." Boris shook his head and heaved a sigh. "Of course, my intervention on behalf of Peshev is impossible. He won deputy speaker only with the support of the Communist-leaning and other opposition members, and Filov has never forgiven that. Matters with Germany are too delicate right now; I simply can't risk alienating Filov."

"Of course not, Your Majesty."

"But I can't help admiring Peshev's courage."

"Certainly."

Boris stood from his chair and walked to the bookcase on the wall adjacent to the door to Pavel's office. He ran his index finger along the spines, then pulled a volume. He looked at the title and opened the book. He aimed a surprised look at his chief of cabinet.

"Rabelais? Really, Bacho Pavlé, I would never have suspected it of you."

Grouev blushed, which was the whole reason Boris had made the comment in the first place. He loved the predictability of Pavel's prudish sensibilities.

"He was a great writer," Pavel said, looking anywhere but at Boris. "I read him for the educational value, as would any well-cultured person."

Boris smiled as he thumbed through the volume. "*Gargantua and Pantagruel*. Who wouldn't love such a life as he wrote for his merry giants? They did just as they pleased. That was the chief lesson of their lives."

Pavel busied himself with some papers on his desk.

"Does anyone ever live such a life, truly, Pavel? Did Rabelais, for example? Or did he merely write what he wished he could experience in fact?"

"We are all obliged at some time or other, Your Majesty."

Boris nodded with a sad little smile, leafing through the book a final time before sliding it back into Pavel's shelf. "I think you're right, Pavel. I think all of us are obliged—even the rakes and the rebels. At some time, soon or late, life catches us out, forces us to own the cost of whatever we've been. Or whatever lot has been chosen for us. Don't you think?"

"It seems to me the key is to choose well, Your Majesty."

"And what is our reward for doing so, do you think?"

Pavel gave him an odd look. "The consolation of a life well lived, I suppose."

"Ah, yes. But who decides whether the life was well lived?"

"Only God sees the heart, Your Majesty." Pavel was fidgeting. This metaphysical interlude was disturbing his habitual, methodical manner of getting through the day. Boris smiled at him, though Pavel didn't see; he was back to shuffling his papers.

"If the prime minister calls, tell him I will be available to him any morning the rest of this week."

"Yes, Your Majesty."

Boris gave the spine of *Gargantua and Pantagruel* a final, wistful caress with his thumb. He went back to his suite, just on the other side of Pavel's office.

As Boris suspected, Prime Minister Filov was still fighting mad at what he viewed as Dimitar Peshev's betrayal of his position as a majority deputy.

"I mean to call for new elections, Your Majesty," he said, emphasizing his words by jabbing his index finger on the desk in front of him. "This question strikes at the heart of our stewardship of this government, and I intend for Mr. Peshev to feel the full weight of his actions."

Boris leaned back in his chair and made a tent of his fingertips. "Perhaps you're right, Mr. Filov, but have you duly considered the potential use Peshev and his allies could make of the recent difficulties? Surely you don't imagine the majority of Bulgarians will suddenly come around to agreement with what they perceive as the more odious aspects of government policy? Do you really want to parade the boxcars at Kyustendil in front of voters?"

Filov looked uncomfortable. "Yes, that was handled badly," he said. "If Gabrovski's people had done their jobs, the Thracian and Macedonian Jews would have left the country quietly and efficiently, and very few people would have been the wiser."

"And yet, as you pointed out not long ago, the proverbial cat is out of the bag. I think you should consider carefully before declaring new elections—the Bulgarian people are notorious for having minds of their own."

Filov chewed on this for a moment. "But I must do something, Your Majesty! Dimitar Peshev has made a mockery of the majority's solidarity. He himself voted for the Law for the Defense of the Nation! And now that we seek to implement it, he becomes maidenly and skittish. And he undermines our authority."

"Are you sure there isn't a less public arena where you can accomplish your goals?"

Filov began nodding slowly. "Yes, it's possible. It won't be easy, but it's possible."

Pavel Grouev seated himself in the balcony just as the prime minister ascended the podium at the front of the Sobranje. Looking around the chamber, he could see the many scowls and whispered conversations that indicated this would be a stormy session. He waited for Bogdan Filov to look up, to notice him sitting in his usual place for important speeches in the Sobranje, but the prime minister never raised his eyes above the level of the deputies' floor. Pavel guessed Filov either assumed the king's chief of cabinet was here on his behalf or was so intent upon avenging himself on Dimitar Peshev that he didn't care.

It was too bad. Dimitar Peshev was a good man. He came from a well-to-do family in Kyustendil and had trained for the law before being called to military service in the Great War. Afterward, he served successful terms as a judge in Plovdiv and Sofia. When Kiosseivanov formed his government in the midthirties, he recognized Peshev's talent and fairness and appointed him minister of justice. Dimitar Peshev was one of the very few majority deputies in the Sobranje who had the trust, not only of his own side of the house, but the opposition side as well. Grouev knew Filov well enough to know that the prime minister, with the backing of the pro-German elements firmly behind him, would not be satisfied until Peshev was thoroughly discredited. He wished for the hundredth time His Majesty hadn't asked him to come and observe what was certain not to be one of the Sobranje's finest hours.

After calling the plenary session to order, the Speaker of the Sobranje called upon the prime minister, who began by reading the full text of the letter Peshev had written and circulated among the deputies. Pavel watched as the deputies of the People's Sobranje grew more and more uncomfortable. Pavel wondered how many of them were uncomfortable because of the evident danger to the solidarity of the pro-government majority and how many were reacting to the unpleasant truths Peshev's document was forcing them to confront.

But the prime minister had no intention of debating the merits of the Jewish question on this day. As soon as he finished reading, he cast the sheets of paper aside in a theatrical motion of contempt.

"Gentlemen of the People's Sobranje, what you have just heard is an affront to the duly enacted policies of this government, a nose-thumbing of the cabinet, and a severe threat to the discipline by which we maintain order in this legislative body. I hardly know how to adequately express my disgust at such a caviling, self-serving display by one who voted for the very law authorizing the actions it purports to disclaim. Furthermore, this sort of demagoguery is a threat to the authority of our government. Therefore, I call for an immediate vote of confidence in the government and its policies."

Filov sat down, and the Speaker returned to the podium. "Will the secretary please poll the members?"

Pavel watched in fascination as all of the 114 deputies present—Peshev and the signatories to the letter included—raised their hands to express their support of the government and its overall policies.

"Thank you," Filov said when the tally was complete. "I think we can now dispense with any foolish notions of this government's incapacity to act on behalf of the nation."

Peshev stared uncomprehendingly at the prime minister. Pavel could easily imagine what he was thinking: *Just because we decided not to dismantle the house doesn't mean there aren't rats living in the cellar.*

The Speaker glanced nervously at Filov. He cleared his throat. "Now I call for a vote for the censure of Dimitar Peshev."

"What?" "This is unconstitutional!" "Shame!" The cries from the floor erupted spontaneously, and the Speaker pounded his gavel furiously. Pavel briefly wondered if he was going to need the security guards to restore order.

A scene ensued that made Pavel squirm, even as detached as he was from the actual proceedings. The secretary called each majority deputy's name and required him to stand and give his vote on the question. And, as if that weren't embarrassing enough, Filov interrogated each member, jotting notes as they responded to their reasons for supporting or opposing Dimitar Peshev. It took more than an hour, and at the end, sixty-six deputies had voted for Peshev's censure, thirty-three against, and eleven—amazingly, given the almost-unbearable pressure being brought to bear by the prime minister—abstained. Four deputies got up and left the session as the voting began. Pavel couldn't blame them.

Then, in an astounding breach of procedure, Filov called on one of the majority members to read a motion to remove Dimitar Peshev from his position as Deputy Speaker of the People's Sobranje.

Peshev jumped to his feet. "I request the floor, Mr. Prime Minister! I demand the right to submit my own resignation!"

Filov ignored him, and he also disregarded the flurry of requests from members of the opposition to address the assembly.

"This is illegal!" shouted Nikola Moushanov, an opposition deputy, but well respected and one of the senior members of the Sobranje. More cries of "Shame!" erupted from the floor; members were banging their hands on their desks.

But in the end, Filov's powers of intimidation brought about his desired result: by the barest of margins, the motion to relieve Peshev of his office was adopted. The smirk on Filov's face as the outcome was announced made Pavel turn his face in disgust.

A few of the opposition members weren't finished though. They demanded the right to speak and loudly insisted that the Jewish question be discussed. Moushanov defended Peshev's actions on humanitarian and constitutional grounds. A few of them described in gruesome detail the suffering of the Jews deported from Thrace and Macedonia, speaking to the almost constant accompaniment of the Speaker's gavel. But the louder he pounded and the more Filov tried to shout them down, the angrier and more insistent they became.

"The only moral capital of a small nation is to be a righteous nation," one of them said. "Only a righteous Bulgaria can demand that her rights be respected by stronger nations."

"This question is not before the house!" Filov said, nearly screaming. Pavel was embarrassed for him; it was pathetic that the Sobranje was so violently divided that its presiding officers could not even govern themselves.

"The next person who attempts to introduce matters for debate which have not been agreed upon will be forcibly ejected," the Speaker said. A few of the security guards moved a pace or two forward from their positions along the walls.

By threat and intimidation, Filov and the Speaker managed to recess the assembly. A few deputies gathered around Dimitar Peshev, who sat at his desk, staring ahead like a man who has just seen his fondest dreams wadded up and thrown in the refuse pile.

Pavel had heard a few of the rumors Filov's operatives had spread: Peshev had received millions of leva in bribes to create a furor over the deportations; Peshev had only instituted his parliamentary actions because he wanted to discredit Filov and become prime minister himself; Peshev was secretly half-Jewish and was only trying to save his own skin.

Pavel couldn't believe any of it. Peshev was simply a good, honest man caught between the human tragedy of the Jews and the need of an almost defenseless country to survive a brutal war. Pavel rose from his balcony seat and sidled toward the aisle and the stairway, wishing there was a drink somewhere strong enough to wash the rank taste from his mouth.

20

The German diplomatic courier snapped his heels together and gave Dobri the stiff-armed salute of the Reich. He took a key from his pocket, opened the locked pouch, and handed Dobri a letter bearing the seal of the German embassy. He popped off another rigid salute, executed an about-face, and marched away down the corridor. Dobri guessed the rate of the clicking of his heels was probably according to some regulation or other.

Dobri had never exchanged words with this fellow, only the sealed correspondence between Ambassador Beckerle's office and Tsar Boris. Being a career military man himself, Dobri could appreciate spit and polish. But something about this particular soldier gave Dobri an itch he couldn't scratch. Fortunately, their work didn't require them to be chatty, only efficient.

Dobri knocked on the door of Pavel Grouev's office. The older man looked up from his desk. "A message from the German embassy, Mr. Chancellor. For His Majesty."

Pavel nodded and waved a finger at the door leading to the small office where Tsar Boris usually preferred to work. Dobri tapped on the door.

"Your Majesty, a packet has just arrived from the German embassy."

"Thank you, Sergeant Dimitrov. Come in."

Dobri saluted the king, then laid the packet on the small desk where the king sat, reading his correspondence for the day. Dobri turned to leave.

"Wait a moment, Sergeant Dimitrov."

Dobri faced the king. "Yes, Your Majesty?"

"Sit down, Dobri." Tsar Boris gestured toward the chair in front of his desk.

Dobri sat, wondering why the moment had suddenly moved into the personal sphere. Tsar Boris rarely called him by his Christian name. Dobri was at once flattered and a little uncomfortable.

"How are things with Daria?" His Majesty asked.

Dobri realized his mouth had dropped open. "I…well, Your Majesty, we… With all that's been happening lately, there hasn't been—"

"Dobri, I wonder if you might humor me for a moment by letting me tell you a story?"

"A story? Well, yes, Your Majesty. I would be honored."

"Don't be honored, Dobri," Tsar Boris said, smiling. "Just listen. I know a man—we'll call him 'Mr. K.'"

Dobri nodded.

"We were great friends, K and I. I've known him all my life. He was always bigger and stronger than I was, though younger, but I was the one who kept him out of trouble. He called me 'Bo.'" Tsar Boris chuckled, shaking his head at some memory or other.

"Often we were together at my family's estate at Euxinograd on the Black Sea coast. Have you ever been there, Dobri?"

"Once to the coast, Your Majesty, but never to Euxinograd."

"Ah, the park at Euxinograd, Dobri! You should have seen it in those days when my father terrorized the groundskeepers, and every blade of grass was perfect! For us children, it was a mysterious jungle, an enchanted forest. We had secret meeting places in some of the hedges.

"But the coast, Dobri…the beaches. As you can perhaps imagine, the older K and I got, the more interested we were in strolling the beaches and observing the native species.

"Mind you, bathing suits in those days were very tame, compared with what you see nowadays," Tsar Boris said. "Skirts to the knee, and dark hose all the way to the ground. But still, Dobri, for that day it was something no boy wanted to miss.

"K developed a deep infatuation for a certain girl we saw rather frequently. Everyone knew who I was—how could they not? A boy walking along the beach trailed by a dour chaperon and at least two officers in military uniform? And naturally, as long as he was in my company, K was subject to the same notoriety. But the thought of this girl fascinated him. He used to talk about her in the evenings when we were sure none of the adults could hear. 'I want to speak to her, Bo,' he would say. 'Do you think I dare?' It was the greatest, darkest secret two friends could share."

Dobri blushed, thinking unaccountably of the first girl he had ever kissed—a gangly twelve-year-old with straw-colored hair and a small mole on her chin. He thought her name was Katya, but he wasn't sure.

"K has acquired a rather different reputation now," Tsar Boris said, "For those who know this, his shyness in those days must be rather hard to comprehend."

Dobri studied his fingernails. It was obvious Tsar Boris was speaking of his brother, Prince Kyril, whose amorous exploits were an open secret in Sofia. It was said that a certain street in a certain neighborhood was the first in the area to be paved with macadam, since it enabled a more silent approach for Prince Kyril's motorcar on its late-night arrivals at a certain house.

"He is a good man, Dobri, despite his, ah, moral weaknesses. He loves me, and he loves his country. But—and this is the point of my story—do you know that he never worked up the courage to speak to that young girl on the beach? He never allowed his enthusiasm full rein. For some reason I still don't understand, he lacked the will to follow his heart. Who knows? Maybe the thought of making such a visible overture to the girl was too much for him. But the point is, he never did. Never got any message to her.

"Later he learned to satisfy himself in other ways. But Dobri, as far as I know, K has never truly fallen in love—at least not for longer than a few nights at a time.

"And I can't help wondering how different his life might have been had he simply walked up to that young girl on the beach at Euxinograd and spoken to her."

Tsar Boris was looking at him with a strange expression. Dobri tried to think of some words that might make sense, that might allow the king to see that he had tried, in the only way he knew how, to say to Daria the truth of what he felt for her. He had not kept silent or secret. But how, then, to explain the shame of the refusal? How to talk around the hurt that still kept him awake some nights, looping around and around his mind like an annoying song he wished he'd never heard in the first place?

"You don't have to explain it to me, Dobri," Tsar Boris said, as if somehow divining his confusion. "I just want to tell you this: Risk is always at the heart of anything worth having. Risk, and the patience to endure it, I think."

Slowly Dobri allowed his eyes to engage with the gentle gray green eyes of his sovereign, seated across the desk, a gentle half smile teasing the corners of his lips.

"Thank you, Your Majesty. Your words bring me comfort."

Tsar Boris nodded. "Good. That was my object, Sergeant." He smiled at Dobri a moment longer, then reached into the lap drawer of his desk for a letter opener. He slid the tip of the blade beneath the flap of the packet from the German embassy. The talk was at an end.

Dobri stood, and though Tsar Boris's eyes were on the letter he was opening, he gave the king a salute that contained all the fervor and love he could muster. Then he slipped out, closing the door softly behind him.

Boris hadn't read many lines of the letter before his anxiety was back. It was a summons—worded, as always, as a polite invitation—to come to Berchtesgaden for a meeting with Adolf Hitler. The request that started the gnawing in Boris's stomach was the line specifying that "His Majesty will wish to bring also the esteemed General Konstantin Loukash, Chief of the General Staff of the Bulgarian Army, for consultation with us on matters deeply touching the conduct of our great struggle for freedom."

Matters were deteriorating on the Russian front; everyone knew that. Even though the Wehrmacht had managed a last-ditch counterattack in the Ukraine that regained them Kharkov, the general feeling was it was only a matter of time before the beleaguered Germans had to begin yielding ground toward central Europe. Hitler's general staff had to be growing frustrated as they watched their losses mount, then contemplated the untouched divisions of their Bulgarian allies with duty no more taxing than controlling traffic in Thrace and keeping an eye on the Turkish frontier.

There was no question of refusing the meeting. Boris summoned to his mind the litany of usual excuses for keeping the Bulgarian army out of the fight with the Soviets: the increased responsibilities in the newly liberated territories, the ever-present potential for an Anglo-Turkish offensive from the east, the still-outdated condition of Bulgarian armaments, the importance of safeguarding the German rear along the Black Sea and Aegean coasts…

These arguments were beginning to seem tired even to Boris. How much longer would they continue to be effective?

The first thing to do was to consult with Filov. By now, Boris was fairly certain that much of what the prime minister heard or suspected about the Royal Palace's policies and attitudes ended up on the desk of either Ambassador Beckerle or the Gestapo attaché Hoffmann. The prime minister might as well be brought into the conversation early. The more Boris could make his discussions in Berchtesgaden seem to Filov like his own ideas, the better. Boris checked the date on the communiqué: March 31—four days away. He picked up his phone and called Pavel Grouev.

The prime minister came to his office the next morning. Boris told Filov of the request from Hitler. "He wants me to bring Loukash with me."

Filov's eyes narrowed. "A request for troops?"

"That's what I'm afraid of. You know how I feel about that, given the possibility of our expanded duties in postwar Greece and the complications that are bound to develop when the Reich finally gets around to negotiating with us on the permanent status of Macedonia—which they must, given any sort of positive military outcome."

Filov nodded, a thoughtful look on his face. "Yes, our troops are stretched thin already and with too little and outdated matériel."

"Precisely my thinking. And don't forget the persistent rumors about the Anglo-Turkish talks. The last thing we want is to have all our forces off in the Ukraine with an English-reinforced Turkish army moving up the Maritza valley."

"I think we should do our best to maintain the same position we've been holding," Filov said. "But, Your Majesty, we can't forget that in any postwar negotiations, the advantage is always on the side of those allies who have contributed the most to the victory. Has Your Majesty's thinking on that ultimate matter shifted to any great degree? Perhaps this would be a time to at least hedge ourselves slightly in that direction."

Boris pursed his lips. How could he give Filov just enough to satisfy him without providing still more grist for the rabid pro-German propaganda mill?

Lately the intercepts from the Reich's communications had been worrisome. They included assessments casting doubt on the commitment of Bulgaria's "highest leadership" to anything but furthering its own territorial demands in Macedonia and Thrace while doing little in any concrete way to support those who might make such gains possible. Filov would need something, some sop to toss to those pressuring him on the right. But how to do it without making a commitment Boris had no intention of carrying through?

"I see dangers in both positions, Mr. Filov, as you well know. I am very concerned about Germany's strategic position right now."

"But Your Majesty, the Reich's cause is far from lost! And consider: if the Wehrmacht is in a difficult position in Russia, so too is the Red Army. The outcome still hangs very much in the balance. And if Bulgaria can be the pebble that tips the scale in the favorable direction…"

Boris actually smiled at Filov. "Mr. Prime Minister, your optimism is indefatigable, isn't it? To paraphrase Agrippa's answer to Saint Paul, 'Almost thou persuadest me to enter the fray.' I will certainly listen carefully to any reasonable proposal the Fuehrer makes. That is all I can promise."

Filov looked disappointed, but he hid it quickly. "Of course, Your Majesty must do what wisdom and conscience dictate."

"I very much appreciate your confidence, Mr. Filov."

The Fuehrer's private plane arrived at Vrazhdebna Airport early on the morning of March 31, and Boris and his traveling companions were soon aboard. They landed a few hours later at Salzburg and within a half hour were motoring up the switchbacked road to Berchtesgaden and the Eagle's Nest.

As the cars pulled up in the large circular driveway, Boris was chagrined to notice that Joachim von Ribbentrop stood immediately to Hitler's right. Boris didn't like Ribbentrop and thought he was a bad influence on the policies of the Reich. But it was likely he would be spending at least some time in conference with the Reichsminister. He hoped Balan had remembered to pack his headache and ulcer medication.

After a perfunctory champagne-and-caviar reception, Boris, General Loukash, Hitler, and Ribbentrop were seated around a large round table with a map of Europe spread before them. General Loukash was much more interested than Boris in the various red, black, and blue solid and dotted lines drawn on the map. He continually peered at the chart, nodding and rubbing his chin, even when he was responding to a question posed to him by either Hitler or his foreign minister.

Boris waited apprehensively for the request to come: "When can you send some Bulgarian divisions across the Danube to…" He didn't know what would follow that opening. It could be "…reinforce our supply lines in Romania and Hungary" or "…relieve our divisions along the Dnieper River." Whatever it was, it would throw Bulgarian troops into direct conflict with the Soviet Union, and Boris dreaded the ultimate consequences of such an action, however innocuous the Reich leadership made it seem.

But the meeting wore on, and the request never came. Ribbentrop opened by warning of the heightened concerns over Turkish communications with Britain. Secret talks had been held between the British and Turks at Adana, Ribbentrop said, and while the Reich still believed Turkey would remain neutral, it would be well for Bulgaria to heighten her vigilance on her eastern borders.

As Loukash was nodding his head in response to this, Boris said, "This is grave news indeed, Herr Reichsminister. This only points up what I have stressed from the beginning: Bulgaria can best serve the Reich by remaining ever watchful along our eastern borders and the Black Sea and Aegean coasts. We are your best line of first defense against some unexpected adventure from either quarter."

"If the Allies try anything in the Balkans," Hitler said, "we're ready for them. My general staff has drawn up a three-part line of defense: along the Aegean Islands, on the Greek coastline, and with your excellent assistance, in Bulgaria."

Boris smiled and congratulated the Fuehrer on the balance and strategic wisdom of the defensive plan. Ribbentrop looked bored.

Hitler went on to talk about his plans for a summer offensive in the Ukraine. "We will push down from Orel through Kursk, then neutralize their divisions in and around Kharkov. From there the Dnieper Valley will lie open before us, and we expect to quickly consolidate a position that will enable us to strengthen our hold on Kiev and the surrounding region."

Loukash put a finger on the map and traced the plan described by Hitler. He made interested noises. Boris prayed he kept his mouth closed and made no statements that resembled an invitation to consider Bulgarian troops as assets in the described campaign.

"An interesting plan, Your Excellency," Boris said. "And wise, no doubt, to wait until the summer, when the blitzkrieg style favored by your Panzer divisions will be more practicable."

Hitler smiled. "Thank you, Your Majesty. Well, I propose that we take a short walk around the grounds, get a bit of fresh mountain air."

The four men scooted their chairs back from the table and trooped toward the flagstone steps leading up to the heavy wooden door. Ribbentrop got there first and held the door for the other three men, smiling and gesturing them through.

When they were outside, Ribbentrop fell quickly into step beside Boris. Hitler was entertaining Loukash, and the general looked as pleased as a boy getting an impromptu lesson from his favorite football star. Boris would not be so lucky, it appeared.

"It's too bad about the problems with your recent deportation attempts," the Reichsminister said, without preamble. "We had hoped for a much larger consignment."

"Yes, Herr Reichsminister. Well, as you know, the Jews from the Bulgarian-administered territories were included. As far as the Jews from the old boundaries, I intend to send only a few of the more radical elements—Bolsheviks and their sympathizers, known troublemakers. The rest are still urgently needed for public works. Of course, plans are already under way to intern the remainder of the Jewish population in work camps within our boundaries, for security purposes and to increase their availability and efficiency as a labor force."

Ribbentrop made no answer for several moments. *Why don't you say something, you cold fish?* Boris thought. The two men's feet crunched along the graveled path; up ahead, General Loukash was laughing at some joke the Fuehrer was telling.

"You know, of course, Your Majesty, that the Reich regards a radical solution as the only proper solution to the Jewish question."

Boris gritted his teeth against the words that wanted to come out. "Certainly, Herr Reichsminister. And yet I wonder if you have a full appreciation of the great differences in attitude between the average Bulgarian and populations elsewhere in Europe. Our Jews are, by and large, Sephardic, more Spanish and Italian than anything else. They don't occupy positions of influence, generally speaking, in our country. They are assimilated, you might say. The average Bulgarian peasant probably couldn't tell you if his neighbors were Jewish, Orthodox, or Roman Catholic, unless his wife dragged him to church on Sunday and he stayed awake long enough during the service to notice who was or wasn't sitting around him."

Ribbentrop favored him with a thin smile. "Yes, Your Majesty. I know things are different in Bulgaria. But in our view, Jews are Jews, plain and simple. And as to influence...one wonders. One hears rumors."

Boris took several paces before he could permit himself to reply. "Yes, well, Herr Reichsminister, it's a wonder rumors travel so fast when they so often don't have a leg to stand on."

Ribbentrop shrugged. "Speaking of such things, Your Majesty, I wonder if you could clarify something for me? Our sources tell us of a certain citizen of Bulgaria, a Mr. Poulev. Apparently, this man Poulev traveled to Istanbul recently, using a diplomatic passport, and was seen meeting privately with Earle, the American ambassador there."

"Poulev...Poulev. Hmm. I seem to recall meeting someone by that name, some time or other, a minor functionary in the Ministry of Foreign Affairs. But I haven't heard his name for quite a while now. I would guess he hasn't been a government employee in these last few months. I imagine he just retained his diplomatic passport because it made travel more convenient. I have no idea why he would have been in Istanbul, unless he was there on some business errand or other."

"More convenient... Yes, I see. Well, I know the Fuehrer would appreciate anything you could do to make sure Mr. Poulev can be trusted. These are dangerous times, you know. We can't be too careful."

"I quite agree, Herr Reichsminister."

All morning the crowds had waited in the misty April drizzle as, one by one, the large black cars circled to a stop in front of the huge main entrance to Alexander Nevsky Cathedral. Each car disgorged a man dressed in long, flowing black robes and a tall "chimney pot" hat with a black veil draped down the back. From Plovdiv, from Vidin, and from Vratza they came, the princes of the Bulgarian Orthodox Church, the Holy Synod—the ten men who, collectively, spoke for all the faithful in the country. Stefan watched them coming in, making their way to the central siege of the cathedral, where they would deliberate. It was like a gathering of large, dour crows just before the breaking of a storm. As far as Stefan was concerned, there was only one matter worth discussing.

When the ten metropolitans were seated in the thrones circled in front of the Great Altar, Neofit of Vidin, the president of the synod for that year, signaled that they should rise for the invocation. He intoned the blessing, and the other nine chorused "Amen." Before they seated themselves, Neofit added, "Let us not fail to offer prayers and petitions for our brother Filaret, who is prevented by illness from attending."

Each of the metropolitans bowed toward the empty throne, intended for their absent colleague. More "amens" were muttered. Neofit remained standing as the rest of the clerics settled themselves and arranged their robes.

"Brothers, I don't need to tell you that evil has grown strong in our land these last days. Three years ago this body met and petitioned the government to repeal the unjust law shackling our Jewish citizens. Two years ago we registered our strong protest over the new provisions of that law forbidding marriages between Orthodox citizens and baptized, catechized persons of Jewish origin. Last year once again we asked the rulers of our nation to show mercy, to modify or abate the unfair restrictions of the Law for the Defense of the Nation and its unconscionable persecution of innocent Jews.

"Now, though, my brothers, the wickedness of unreasoning hatred has gone so far as to pen like cattle innocent men, women, and children. To load them onto cars hardly fit for the transport of beasts, and to send them out of our country to a fate we cannot imagine."

Neofit looked around the circle. "I myself sat in the office of the prime minister of this nation, begging him, as a Christian and the leader of a Christian nation, to show mercy and humanity toward the suffering people. Do you know what he told me? Do you know what he said? 'Millions of people are suffering on battlefields all over Europe, Father. The suffering of the world is the fault of the Jews and their Bolshevik sponsors.'

"Can you believe it?" Neofit's fists were clenched so tightly they were almost shaking. "This man has no more regard for the common decency one human owes another than a rabid dog."

Neofit sat down, and Kyril of Plovdiv fairly leaped out of his seat. It was commonly known Stefan and Kyril were not generally on speaking terms. Kyril had let it be known more than once that he considered the metropolitan of Sofia a little too friendly with the world to be a true ambassador of Christ. For his part, Stefan had been heard to be openly impatient at what he regarded as Kyril's pigheadedness on certain matters of tradition. It would be interesting to see on which side of today's question the two found themselves.

"On the night of March 10, I went to the place they were holding the Jews of Plovdiv, waiting to load them onto the trains," Kyril said. "When the commissariat guards and police tried to stop me, I climbed the fence to get inside. I told the poor people, frightened out of their wits, that wherever they were sent, I was sent. I told the guards that I would lie down on the tracks before I would permit a train to take Bulgarian citizens who have committed no crime whatsoever out of their own city."

Kyril shook a finger at the rest of them. "I sent a cable to the prime minister, the minister of the interior, and to the Royal Palace. I told them that, though I have all my life been a loyal citizen of this country, when its laws violate the commandments of God, I will no longer consider myself bound by the laws of the land. I told them that I would reserve for myself full freedom of action, bound by the dictates of my conscience and my duty to God—not by an unjust and inhuman law of their concoction."

Kyril sat down with his arms crossed, and most of the other metropolitans nodded their agreement.

Joseph, metropolitan of Varna, rose slowly from his seat. "Brothers, you all know that in times past, I gave my support to the Law for the Defense of the Nation. I love this country, and the thought of Bulgaria falling under the sway of a foreign power—any foreign power—was and is hateful to me.

"But now I see things differently. This law, which has its origins not in the Bulgarian constitution but someplace else, is intended exclusively to punish Jews and take away what is rightfully theirs—including the common right of human beings to live without fear. It is a cruel law, and it is being applied inhumanely. It is no more truly a Bulgarian law than the Packard driven by His Majesty is a Bulgarian car. And unlike the king's car, it serves no useful purpose whatever. This law does not defend our nation—it brings shame upon it."

Paissi of Vratza was next, and like the others, he made a plea for the synod to oppose plans to deport Bulgarian Jews from their homeland. It was interesting to Stefan that no one bothered to raise any doubts about whether such plans were actually in place.

Sofroni, metropolitan of Turnovo, slowly got to his feet. "My brothers, I must start by making a confession and asking your forgiveness, because I fear I have misused my office as a priest."

The stooped old man paused, and the other metropolitans looked around at each other. Nobody had any idea what might be coming next.

"A young man in my church—I won't say his name, of course—came to me for confession. 'Father,' he said, 'I must ask your forgiveness for a sin I haven't committed yet.'

"Well, I've been a priest longer than many of you have been alive, and this was a new one on me. 'What is this sin, my son, and if you know it is coming, why can't you avoid it?'

" 'Because I'm a member of the special Commissariat Guard, and they're going to make us round up the Jews, and if I refuse to follow orders, I'm afraid of what they'll do to me or my wife or my baby.'

" 'My son,' I said. 'When are they going to make you do this terrible thing?'

" 'Two nights from now. We're supposed to gather all the Jews into one of the warehouses downtown and put them on trains to camps somewhere.'

" 'Don't worry,' I told him. 'I will take care of this for you so that you don't have to have this terrible sin on your conscience. Go your way, your sins are forgiven in the name of the Father, the Son, and the Holy Spirit.' "

Sofroni looked around the circle, and his expression was like that of a cat with canary feathers sticking out of its mouth. "I'm afraid I didn't keep the privacy of the confessional, my brothers. I went and talked to every Jew I could find in Turnovo and told them to come to the church on the night after next. There must have been at least a hundred people in the church, and their faces were full of fear.

"My brothers, I still have my old infantry rifle. It's old, as I am, but it will shoot. And I stood at the doors of my church, and when the guards from the commissariat came, as I knew they would, I had my gun leveled at the squad leader.

" 'Sirko Djevrev, I baptized you when you were born,' I said to him, 'as I did your father before you. Your grandparents were the first couple I married when I came to this church. And before God and all the holy apostles, I give you my most solemn oath that I will shoot you dead where you stand if you or any of your men make one move toward these innocent people.'

"Well, we stared at each other, the soldiers and I, for a little while, until Sirko told his men to stand down. They went out of the church, and I stayed there for the rest of the night with the Jewish families until word came to Turnovo that the deportations from the old boundaries were cancelled."

Sofroni looked around at them. Like Stefan, most of the other metropolitans were hiding smiles behind their hands.

"And so you see, brothers, not only did I break the secrecy of the confessional, but I also threatened violence to a child of God. And so, I humbly ask for your forgiveness and submit to whatever penalty you assess." He sat down, his snow-white head bowed—the very picture of humility.

Stefan moved first. He got up from his chair, crossed to where Sofroni sat, kneeled before him, and kissed his ring. One by one, the others followed suit.

Each of the leaders of the Bulgarian church rose and excoriated the Law for the Defense of the Nation, the brutality of the commissariat police, and the immorality of the current forces in government who seemed intent on carrying out such plans.

Then it was Stefan's turn. For a long moment he stood, looking around the circle, eying each of his colleagues in turn. When he came to Kyril of Plovdiv, something like approval passed silently between the two habitual rivals.

"Fathers, fellow shepherds of God's flock, there is no need for me to add words of warning or to express yet once again the horror that has already been so eloquently stated. What we must do is clear. The Jews know that no one with any authority will speak for them, unless we in the Bulgarian Church do it. Especially for those of Jewish birth who have accepted the Pravoslav faith and received the holy sacrament of baptism, we cannot fail in our vigilance.

"The Law for the Defense of the Nation is being implemented and masterminded by a man who lacks sound judgment on these and possibly other matters. If we do not intervene forcefully and decisively, we can only expect worse cruelties and outrages to follow.

"The state cannot give an answer to the question of what the Jews of Bulgaria have done to deserve such treatment. Everything has been taken from these people, and now that the commissariat is attempting to take away their lives, they have asked for the defense of the church. We cannot refuse this summons.

They have voices that must be heard...

"Five years from now, or ten, or twenty, will we look back on this moment in our history and feel shame because we failed to heed the call of human compassion, because we failed to imitate the mercy of Christ? Or will we—those of us left alive after the struggle—feel at least the satisfaction of having done all our hands found to do in our country's time of need?"

Neofit, as acting president, proposed a letter demanding a meeting with the leaders of the church, the king, and the prime minister. A second letter of censure was to be dispatched, on behalf of the synod, to the prime minister, with a copy sent to Tsar Boris. Stefan drafted the censure letter and, with the approval of the others, added these words to the end:

"The church reminds you of the words of Christ from St. Matthew's gospel: 'With the measure you use, it will be measured to you.'"

21

Lily finished typing the last line of data from the last card in her stack. She wound the sheet out of the typewriter and put it in the overflowing tray. She leaned over and looked at the carton on the floor beside her desk. She sighed and rubbed the back of her neck. The carton was still maybe one-third full of the postcard-size "Family Cards" that were flooding into the commissariat offices from all over Bulgaria.

The cards listed data on each Jewish family in the country: parents on both sides, children, names, ages, occupations… And all the data had to be transferred into the notebooks Lily was compiling. When Alexander had ordered the effort, he had told her the transcription of this information took priority over all other work for every secretary in the office, including her. Lily's only slight moment of enjoyment since this whole thing began was the time she got to tell that Damonova woman she would have to put aside whatever she was doing and begin immediately with the transcription work.

"But Director Kalitzin told me he had to have this report ready to turn in by tomorrow."

"Well, I guess you'll just have to stay late tonight," Lily had told her. "The commissar says the data on these cards is our first priority now, and they're stacking up all over the office. So you'll just have to tell Director Kalitzin to wait awhile."

Damonova's stack of cards was taller than Lily's. She looked out of sorts, and that suited Lily just fine. Why should she sit at her desk filing her nails when there was work to be done?

Why was Alexander suddenly compiling all this information? Lily wondered. When the deportation attempt from the old borders was thwarted, she was afraid for him. He had put so much effort into it that she thought he might be capable of harming himself. He wouldn't come to bed at night. He lay on the couch in the living room and smoked. Some mornings she found him sprawled there, his hair mussed and his mouth gaping open, a butt still smoldering in the dented aluminum ashtray on the floor beside the couch. At first, during the days, he cloistered himself in his office and wouldn't see anyone. His temper flared at the slightest pretext. Once, after he hung up his phone, Lily heard a shattering sound in his office. She rushed in and realized that he had slammed a paperweight onto his desktop with such force that he had shattered the heavy glass top. She tried to help him clean up the mess, but he shouted at her to just get out.

But then, gradually, officials began meeting with him, advising him to withdraw his resignation. Even Dannecker, the haughty SS officer, came back from Berlin and urged Alexander to remain in charge of the Commissariat for Jewish Questions. Everyone knew Alexander's determination, his dedication to the task. There was no one who could be counted on to replace him.

And now, it seemed, he was devising another plan, something even bigger than the actions in early March. The last time she was in his office to deliver the completed data sheets for the large black notebooks he was compiling, she saw a requisition form on his desk. The description read, "For the acquisition of twenty-five wooden huts, capable of housing a hundred people each…" And on his calendar she had seen the words, scribbled in Alexander's hurried hand, "Sofia—census." The date was about two weeks away.

Lily gathered the completed data sheets from her tray and walked toward Alexander's office. She tapped gently, then went inside. He was poring over the sheets, putting them into his notebooks. He barely glanced at her. "Yes, just put the next stack on the corner of my desk. Have we gotten the cartons from Sliven yet?"

"I think they came in this morning, Mr. Belev. But they're still in the mailroom downstairs; there's no place outside to put them yet."

"Well, just get to them as soon as you can. These sheets will be very helpful. Very helpful, indeed."

Lily set the completed pages on the corner of his desk and turned to go back to her desk. But just as she did, she noticed a stack of sheets near the center of the desk, and something drew her eye to the one on top. At the bottom of the neat, typed rows of information, Alexander had penciled in and circled something. A name: Daria Richetti.

The first thing Boris saw when he entered his office in the Palace Chancery was the stack of correspondence Balan had laid out for him, and on top was a large, thick envelope bearing the seal of the Holy Synod. Boris knew what it would say, but he was not quite prepared for the scalding tone the fathers had adopted. "Scandalous…inhumane…criminal…persecution…" He forced himself to read it in its entirety, though with each paragraph his mood darkened a little more.

Boris wondered briefly what Metropolitan Stefan would have said to Ribbentrop's veiled inquiries about the status of the Jewish question in Bulgaria. What if he forwarded a copy of the Holy Synod's letter of censure to Herr Beckerle?

And yet…he could not bring himself to be angry with the church fathers—not really. They were good men, all of them, if sometimes a bit near-sighted.

He would have to meet with them, of course, as they had requested—no, demanded. He would have to listen again to their quotations from Scripture, their appeals to the justice that became a godly king. What was it Pavel had quoted to him recently? *The king's heart is in the hand of the LORD…* Maybe his heart was there, but Boris's head felt like a tennis ball hammered back and forth between the pro-German majority in the government and the pro-Jewish agitators like Stefan and the others. And now the Communists were tying themselves to the Jewish problem as well. Boris's sources told him it was one issue where the insurgents found themselves on the side of the angels as far as the general population was concerned. If the Red Army followed the collapsing Wehrmacht into Bulgaria, there would no doubt be a long chapter in the history books reserved for the heroic Communist efforts to save the Jews of Bulgaria from the evil, Fascist government that would have sent them away.

"Jews are Jews, plain and simple…"

"With the measure you use, it will be measured to you…"

Boris picked up the phone, and Stanislav Balan's voice answered.

"Stanislav, I need to schedule a meeting with the prime minister and the interior minister. As soon as possible."

"I have come to the conclusion that we need a new, stricter policy toward the Jews of Bulgaria," Boris began. He saw the looks of pleasure and satisfaction on his ministers' faces. Good. Let them hold that attitude.

"It is necessary that we immediately mobilize absolutely all the Jewish men to labor camps, dispersed throughout the country. We must assure ourselves that there are no exceptions, and that the organization is efficient. The small efforts made earlier at road- and bridge-building were insufficient. We must demonstrate to our German allies that our need for the Jewish labor force is real and bears a strategic benefit for the Reich and for us as its ally.

"I expect a detailed plan on my desk in one week, Mr. Gabrovski," Boris said, fixing the interior minister with his sternest gaze. "The slipshod attempts that characterized your last action are unacceptable."

Gabrovski's face dipped toward the tabletop. He gave an embarrassed nod.

"Mr. Filov, I expect you to do everything possible to support this new initiative. At this critical juncture in the war effort, when every available man is needed for the defense of our country's eastern and southern borders, we cannot afford to have a free labor force taken from us and sent to Poland or anywhere else. I intend to get every ounce of use from our Jews. I expect to see results before the end of May. Do I make myself clear?"

"Yes, Your Majesty."

Boris stood. "That will be all, gentlemen."

The two ministers left, and Boris could see the surprised glances they slid each other. They gave him a quick bow, which he returned.

As the door closed behind them, Boris slumped back into this chair.

Oh, dear God. If this doesn't work…

Dobri Dimitrov picked up the phone. "Yes?"

"Sergeant, the prime minister's car just passed the guard station."

"Thank you. I'll inform His Majesty. Anything suspicious?"

"No, sir. Everything is quiet out here."

"Good. If you see or hear anything at all, contact me immediately."

Sofia had awakened that morning to news of the assassination of Sotir Ianev, a member of the majority in the Sobranje. The Bolshevik partisans were still active, and that made Dobri more tightly vigilant than usual. He intended for his men to feel the same urgency, even here in the relative remove of the royal residence at Vrana.

Dobri walked down the hall to the large meeting room, where Tsar Boris sat at the head of a long, highly polished table of burled walnut.

"Your Majesty, the prime minister is here."

"Good. Bring him here immediately, then be sure to tell me when the priests arrive. Please ask them to wait in the salon until ten o'clock."

"Yes, Your Majesty."

Dobri fretted as he went toward the front door to welcome the prime minister to Vrana. Something big was happening, and he couldn't help thinking it had to do with the Jews. And when Dobri thought of the Jews, Daria filled his mind.

He had taken Tsar Boris's words to heart: he had decided to risk everything for her. And right now, that meant doing almost nothing. It was maddening in a way. Dobri was trained as a soldier. You encountered a situation, you analyzed the obstacles and your resources, you decided on a plan of action, and you executed the plan. You solved the problem. But this situation with Daria was shrouded in a fog. It was bound up in the whole political atmosphere of the country. There was no enemy to advance against, except perhaps Daria's own attitude toward her ancestry—but that was part of her, wasn't it, and how could he do anything against that without doing something to harm her, to destroy the trust in him that he longed, more than anything in the world, for her to have?

It was a puzzle with no solution. Sometimes, in his darkest moods, Dobri thought he had no business involving himself in such matters. *You're just a peasant from Bailovo, Dobri Dimitrov; she's above you, anyway. Let it go—let it all go, and when the war is over, go back home and find that girl with the mole on her chin and marry her and have a houseful of kids and tend your sheep and drink rakia every night and fall asleep and forget that you were ever involved in great questions of the world. Leave that stuff to men like His Majesty, who were bred for it.*

And then he would see her, caring for the children or speaking with Tsaritza Giovanna about some household matter or simply sitting in a sunlit corner, reading a book, and he knew. *Risk lies at the heart of anything worth having.* She would look at him, and her eyes would tell him, "Yes, Dobri, but not yet." And the *when* of that *not yet* both tortured him and filled him with the most dire, indispensable hope.

The entry bell sounded. Dobri opened the large, ornately carved front door and crisply saluted the prime minister, who stood waiting on the doorstep.

"Welcome to Vrana, Mr. Prime Minister. His Majesty is waiting for you in the conference room. May I escort you there, sir?"

"Thank you, Sergeant."

Dobri led Filov through the foyer, past the salon, and down the hall to the tall double doors of the conference room. He tapped twice on the doors, then opened them and bowed the prime minister into the room. He heard the king greet Filov, then closed the doors behind the prime minister.

"Thank you for coming early, Mr. Filov," Boris said, gesturing the prime minister to a seat near the head of the table. "I expect this interview with the Holy Synod to be somewhat, ah, complicated, and I thought it best that you be present."

"I'm honored by your trust, as always, Your Majesty."

"Yes. Now, when the priests arrive, I want you to sit at the opposite end of the table." Boris pointed to the end of the conference table nearest the door through which Filov had just entered.

"As you wish, Your Majesty."

"They will have some remarks, and then I have prepared a statement, which I hope you will do me the favor of reading." Boris picked up a sheaf of papers and offered them to Filov.

The prime minister took his spectacles from his coat pocket and sat down to read. Boris watched him. Filov nodded here and there, even gave a few grunts of satisfaction. When he had finished, he looked up at the king.

"An admirable statement of our position, Your Majesty. It strikes just the right tone, I believe: firm, yet tolerant and humane wherever possible. I don't see how the Holy Synod can object." He handed the papers back to the king.

"Oh, they can, and they will, never doubt that. But the important thing is, Mr. Filov, that we must communicate to them that this government is firmly taking charge of the Jewish question. Not Berlin, not the German embassy—ourselves. We have our Jewish situation in hand, and we intend to carry it out in our own way."

Filov nodded. "A wise message to present to them, Your Majesty."

"I'm glad to have your approval." Boris looked at his watch. "Well, it's almost time for them to be here. You'd better take your position." He smiled at Filov. "The curtain is about to go up."

Filov gave him a smile in return and moved to the opposite end of the table.

There was a tap at the door, and the black-robed priests filed into the room. Boris and Filov offered customary deferential bows as the clerics found their seats around the table. When Neofit of Vidin took the seat closest to the king, the rest of the metropolitans sat down, followed by the king and the prime minister.

"I'm sure, Holy Fathers, that you all grieve, as do we," Boris said, "at the untimely and brutal death of Sotir Ianev, a faithful servant of this nation, who died at the hands of anarchists who believe they can win their aims by terror."

There was a short silence. "I believe I can speak for all the Holy Synod, Your Majesty, when I say that we pray for the soul of Mr. Ianev and also for the souls of those misguided persons who committed such an act," said Metropolitan Neofit.

"Amen," Boris said. "And yet, Holy Fathers, we live in times that demand not only prayer and faith but also vigilance. We must remain on our highest guard against those enemies, both within our country and without, who would wreck the peace and prosperity of Bulgaria in the name of some misguided ideology. These people, and those who harbor them, must not be tolerated. As monarch of this nation, I am duty bound to take whatever actions are necessary to protect the greater good of Bulgaria."

Boris picked up the letter he had received on behalf of the synod. He looked at Neofit. "If I didn't know you better, Father Neofit, I would have been shocked and perhaps a bit insulted by the tone of this letter."

Neofit's eyes flickered across the table toward Metropolitan Stefan. "Your

Majesty, the church cannot do other than speak for God's people—all of them. We regret causing Your Majesty any pain in addition to the heavy load you carry on behalf of the nation, but…"

Boris allowed the silence to lengthen. He was a bit surprised that Stefan didn't fill the breach; he was usually not shy about expressing himself. But in the presence of the sitting president of the synod, he seemed to feel the need to allow Neofit to lead. Boris looked down the table at Filov, then picked up his prepared statement.

"With your permission, Fathers, I will make a few comments on the Jewish situation." He cleared his throat slightly, then read, "In recent days our government has come under harsh criticism for its decisions regarding a certain segment of our population. I speak, of course, of the Bulgarian Jews. But I fear that those who are the harshest in their criticism fail to see the larger context in which these decisions have been taken. I hope, in these few words, to clarify that context, as well as the policies this government intends to follow with regard to this ongoing and potentially divisive question."

The king then referred to the gentle treatment historically afforded to Jews in Bulgaria but noted the extensive sociological and scientific evidence presented by some of the most eminent German social scientists for the conclusion that worldwide Jewry constituted an unproductive drain on the vitality of the people among whom they lived. "While we in Bulgaria have chosen to ignore the evidence of social science presented elsewhere—perhaps because of our historically tolerant attitudes toward those of different races—we can no longer afford, in this time of world conflict, to coddle or tolerate any potential source of danger to the nation, however benign we may have formerly considered it."

Boris referred to the "innately profiteering spirit" of the Jewish race and the damage it had inflicted on the human race for centuries. He traced the beginnings of the current world conflict to the influence of this racial trait and noted that all across Europe, other nations were rising to the challenge by removing Jews from their positions of influence in government, finance, the military, and industry.

"The Law for the Defense of the Nation, enacted for similar reasons by due process of the People's Sobranje, is intended as a protection of the vital interests of Bulgaria, and the Pravoslav Church of Bulgaria cannot afford to present a conflicting message."

As the diatribe wound down, the king promised, in the name of human fairness, to examine all complaints about the treatment of Jews and to do whatever was possible and lawful to minimize their suffering. "It should be noted, however," he said, "that this nation can no longer afford the luxury of an unproductive segment of society. We intend to see to it that all our nation's resources, human, material, or otherwise, are brought to bear, either willingly or by force, in the furtherance of our war efforts and the improvement of our country. The times are too critical for anyone, Jew or otherwise, to be permitted to avoid doing his share."

Boris finished reading and looked again at Filov. The prime minister looked like a teacher's pet who had just been moved to the head of the class. The priests, on the other hand, were mostly staring at the center of the table, unable or unwilling to meet either each other's eyes or the king's.

When Boris judged the silence had become sufficiently long and uncomfortable, he stood, bowed to the seated prelates, and exited the room, followed closely by Filov.

When they were in the hallway, Filov grasped the king's hand and pumped it vigorously. "Excellent, Your Majesty! Excellent! This is precisely what they needed to hear. The church cannot, in time of war, place its interests above those of the nation."

With a deep effort, Boris forced his attention to his prime minister. "Thank you, Mr. Filov, for being here. And now I am very tired, and I must rest."

"Of course, Your Majesty. That must have been very draining."

Boris showed Filov to the front door. Sergeant Dimitrov opened the door for the prime minister, saluted, and closed it behind him.

"Dobri, I am very tired. Please see that the Holy Synod find their way out to their cars. I'll be in my apartment."

"Yes, Your Majesty."

But he didn't go to his apartment. Instead, he went to a small reading room just across the hall from the conference room and closed the door all but a small crack. He listened to the angry voices of the priests as they left.

He closed his eyes and leaned his head on the back of the chair and listened as he was characterized as Fascist, anti-Semitic, high handed, and a puppet of the Nazi pseudoscientific ideologues. He waited until the angry rumble of voices and shuffle of black robes had moved down the hallway and the doors of his house had closed behind them.

He got up and walked slowly across the hall into the conference room, to the end of the table where he had sat. He picked up his speech and tucked it into the breast pocket of his coat. For a few moments, he stared at the chair where Filov had sat. He thought about the enthusiastic report the prime minister would deliver to his contacts in the German embassy.

He went outside. It was a bright spring day in mid-April, and a fresh breeze tossed the tender, greening leaves on the branches of the tall elms and larches. He took the speech out of his pocket and separated the first sheet. With the precision of someone performing a religious ritual, he tore the sheet in half, then in quarters, then in eighths. He continued until the pieces in his fist were the size of postage stamps. Then he opened his hand to the wind and let the cleansing April breeze carry the fragments of paper away, scattering them into anonymous hiding places among the grass and shrubbery of the large yard. He did the same thing with the second sheet, then the third, until the entire speech had been offered up to the careless embrace of the hurrying wind.

22

Buko received his notice on the same day as most of the other men from his synagogue. It came in a plain white envelope, marked only with an address on Dondukov Boulevard, in Sofia. Inside was a printed form on cheap paper: "By order of His Majesty, Tsar Boris III, all Jewish men of _Kyustendil_ will report to the local train station or other place designated by the local office of the Commissariat for Jewish Questions for immediate transfer to work camps, where further information will be given and duties assigned. You are to report on the date shown below."

Kyustendil and the date to report—_May 4, 1943_—were the only hand-written words on the document. A final, ominous note added: "Failure to report as directed will be grounds for imprisonment, in accordance with the provisions of the Law for the Defense of the Nation. There are no exceptions."

Just in case someone might be missed, the police were tacking up the notices in public places throughout Kyustendil, starting with the front doors of the synagogue.

At night, behind closed curtains and huddled around the meager light of candles, worried men talked about this sudden order and what it might mean.

"They told the Jews from Thrace they were being sent to camps in Bulgaria too. They sent them there, all right—then reloaded them onto the trains that took them to Lom, where they put them on the barges that took them to Austria."

"This one specifically mentions the king. That's different. Usually everything just has 'by order of the commissariat.' What does His Majesty have to do with this, I wonder?"

"What about our women and children? Once we're out of the way, what happens to them?"

Buko tried to talk to Anka, but she wouldn't answer. She wouldn't even look at him. He wondered if, to her, he was already dead. He came home every night, sat at the table, and ate bread and cheese. He gave her the little bits of money he made doing the work he was able to find, and she took the money to buy food, to pay the meager, diminished rent Baba Marika's landlord allowed himself to collect. But she wouldn't talk to him. The closest she came was remembering something out loud, something from past days, better days. She would say, "I remember the time when my brother Nissim won some money on a horse race in Blagoevgrad. He was so proud, thought he was so smart. But when he got home and told Papa, Papa was so angry at him he made him go out right then, that night, and give the money to the rabbi." Something like a laugh might come from her; she might shake her head at the memory. "What was Nissim thinking? He was always such a foolish boy."

Buko would try to enjoy the moment with her, would chuckle or say something clever, maybe. But it made no more difference to Anka than the sound of the wind in the door or a dog barking in the street outside. He might as well have been somewhere else. For her, he was no longer there.

He had tried to be angry with her, but he couldn't sustain it with any success. Maybe the constant dread and uncertainty had already taken her mind away. Maybe the only part of his wife that was left was the fragment that knew how to prepare food, to care for her old mother, to sweep, to remember the times when danger wasn't a constant companion. Maybe it was better that way. Maybe he shouldn't try to awaken her again, to resurrect the woman who used to laugh at his jokes, scold him for being late, argue with him about money, and allow him into the tender places of her body and her heart.

"Anka, I have to go tomorrow," he told her on the evening before his departure. "I have to get on the train. They say they're taking us to Yambol to work on the roads and bridges. I'll send back some money if I can, Anka. When they let us, if they do, I'll come back and see you and Baba Marika."

But they were only words in the dark, whispered to a motionless form that looked like his wife.

Buko lay down and stared at the ceiling and tried to sleep. Tomorrow he would get on the train. No one knew what else to do; they had spent everything they had on halting the deportations in March. And besides, this order came from the highest place, from Tsar Boris himself. Who was left to whom they could appeal? Dimitar Peshev was powerless now, stripped of his position of authority in the Sobranje. "It's just the men this time," some people said. "Maybe it really is a work camp."

Maybe. Buko wondered if, somewhere in Anka's mind, her spirit said *Kaddish* for the husband who was no longer there. He wondered if he should be saying *Kaddish* for her.

MEMORANDUM

SECURE COURIER ONLY; READ AND CLASSIFY
TO: Minister of the Interior, Peter Gabrovski
FROM: Commissar for Jewish Questions, A. Belev
DATE: 4 May 1943
SUBJECT: Deportation of all Jews out of Kingdom of Bulgaria

This plan comprises a method for complete execution of objective by September 30, 1943. By this date, all Jews presently residing in the Kingdom of Bulgaria will have been transported to the eastern regions of the Reich. Approximately 48,000 persons will be involved: 25,000 Jews from Sofia and 23,000 Jews from elsewhere in the provinces. All transfers of Bulgarian Jews will occur in the Danube ports of Lom and Somovit.

The capacity of the national railroad system allows for the transport of 16,000 persons per month, with the first transports to begin May 30. Prior to this date, all Jews in the Kingdom will have been concentrated in transport camps outside the major metropolitan areas, facilitating their quick and nondisruptive departure for the transfer points in the north of the country. Once the transportees are loaded onto the vessels at Lom and Somovit, responsibility for them is transferred to the officials of the Reich.

The key element in this plan is secrecy. Under the current plan recently enacted by the Royal Palace, it should not be difficult to devise a propaganda campaign designed to convince Jewish women and children that they are being taken to temporary camps in the provinces, to further facilitate the work projects already authorized by

His Majesty. The Jews from Sofia should be the first transportees, with preference given to those persons known to be malcontents, leaders, or influential in the Jewish community and other segments of society. Once they reach these areas, the Jews will be lodged in schools, Jewish homes, or other locations where maximum normalcy of life can be maintained, to minimize the possibility of negative propaganda.

Twenty-four hours before the arrival of the transport trains, local authorities will be alerted, via certified couriers only, that warehouses and large buildings will be needed to concentrate the deportees. The transfer to the holding points will be carried out at night, using commissariat security forces and special forces coopted from local police. It is imperative that the local Jews and the transferees leave on the same trains; no persons of Jewish origin should be left behind. Once the trains have departed, they should have express clearance all the way to Lom or Somovit, whichever is their destination.

Temporary camps will be needed in Lom, Somovit, and perhaps Tziber, in order to hold the Jews until they can be loaded onto the boats. If the final deportation is not decided upon, a permanent camp will possibly need to be constructed at Tziber to maintain the transportees in a single location until final disposition is made.

At the same time the trains are dispatched to pick up the transportees, special shipments of staple food goods should be made to the principal rail stops along the way. Adequate water supplies should also be secured. One medical professional should be on hand at each stop to certify the condition of the transportees. Circulars concerning the issuance of food and the requirements of the medical inspections will be made through the commissariat offices in each region. With the authority of the Ministry of the Interior, the necessary clearances for the transportation authorities will be issued in the same way.

It is estimated that 10,000 Jews per week can be accommodated by the methods outlined above. By the end of the fall of this year, our goal can be accomplished and the future of Bulgaria assured.

I await your response to this memorandum.

Lily's eyes were bleary by the time she had finished transcribing Alexander's handwritten draft. She looked at her watch; it was almost eight thirty in the evening. She had taken him the final batch of transcriptions for his notebooks when he had handed her the sheaf of paper and asked her to have two copies ready for him in the morning.

"I won't be home tonight," he had said. "I've got to go see a man about a special job. Just leave me something on the stove, if you get a chance."

Everyone else was long gone. Lily took the sheets from her typewriter. The top copy, the original, would go to the interior minister. The carbon beneath would go into Alexander's file.

The third copy was a bit blurry but still legible. She folded it and put it in her purse.

Alexander didn't have to wait long for his answer. The day after Lily posted the memo by secure courier to the Interior Ministry, a smiling Gabrovski strode into the offices on Dondukov Boulevard. He went into Alexander's office. "My boy, you've done it this time," Gabrovski said as he closed the door, and even through the closed door, Lily could hear the sound of congratulatory backslapping.

The interior minister was in Alexander's office for maybe an hour. When he came out, smiling and waving to everyone in the office, Alexander motioned her inside. As usual, there were reams of notes he wanted her to type. "The interior minister has approved the plan, Miss Panitza," he said, a boyish grin spreading across his face. "All of it. He's even suggested some additions, and that's mostly what this is." He passed her the handwritten sheets.

"How wonderful for you, Mr. Belev," she said. "I'll get right to work on these."

"Yes, please. Some of them require immediate planning and action, so every second counts."

Of course, Gabrovski had signed off on every component of Alexander's plan. There was also to be an anti-Jewish exhibition to be installed in the Bulgaria Hall section of the National Theatre. It was to be a cooperative effort between the Interior Ministry and the propaganda ministry of the Reich. Lily's eyes widened at the amount of money budgeted for the exhibit. She knew something about the ministry budgets; the Reich had to be paying the lion's share for this latest round of anti-Semitic misinformation. There must have been twenty or thirty separate exhibits described, and they were all to be in place by May 15—less than a week and a half.

There were also press releases to be typed, linking the assassination of Sotir Ianev and the attempted assassination of a radio-station operator named Yanakiev to Communist agents who were also Jewish, and reminding anyone who might have forgotten about the killing of General Loukov by "the known Jewess and Bolshevik killer, Violetta Yakova." These propaganda fliers, thinly disguised as news, were to be sent to newspapers all over the country for immediate release. And the Interior Ministry would see to it they all ran on the front page.

Lily thought about the hazy carbon of Alexander's memo, still folded in a secret place in the bottom of her purse. She had to let somebody know—and soon.

When Lily came home that night, Alexander and a stranger were in their apartment. He was a soldier; his uniform was unbuttoned, exposing a stained undershirt. Alexander saw her and motioned her in. She felt like running away, but she moved with tiny steps into the parlor.

"Lily, you're home! Good! I want you to meet an associate of mine. This is Lyuben Bojilov, a sergeant in His Majesty's army. Lyuben, meet my friend, Miss Liliana Panitza."

Bojilov looked at Lily in a way that made her skin crawl. He slid onto his feet, set down his half-empty glass, and did a drunken imitation of a gentleman greeting a lady by planting a sloppy kiss on the back of her hand. Though Lily had her hand stretched so far from her she looked like someone disposing of a dead mouse, she could still smell the *slivovitza* on Bojilov's breath.

"Sergeant Bojilov was just leaving, weren't you, Lyuben?" Alexander said. "I think we've pretty much covered the business we needed to discuss."

Lyuben drained his glass and gave a wistful glance at the bottle of liquor on the table beside Alexander's chair, still more than half-full. "Oh well, leave it to a government man to kick an honest soldier out onto the street just when the party's getting interesting."

Alexander gave a polite laugh and stood, pulling Bojilov out of his chair on the pretext of giving him a pat on the back. "Come on, Lyuben, you don't want to wear out your welcome."

"No, I guess not, Mr. Belev, I guess not. Well, I'll take care of that little matter—"

"Fine, fine," Alexander said, laughing a little too much, Lily thought. He put an arm around Bojilov's shoulders and herded him firmly toward the door. He gave him a final wave and closed the door behind him.

Lily heard the soldier's boots clunking unevenly down the stairs. "Alexander, what need do you have of someone like that?"

He looked at her for several seconds. "Never mind. I have a job that he's just right for. Did you get the documents completed from the meeting with Gabrovski?"

"Yes, Alexander. Everything went out today, just as you asked."

"Ah, Lily." He smiled and opened his arms to her. "What would I ever do without you? You are a model of efficiency, do you know that?"

She let him hold her, trying to ignore the part of her mind that hated herself for being here, for working at the commissariat and for loving the feel of this man's arms around her at this very instant.

"Tell you what, Lily," he said, holding her shoulders and tilting back his face to look at her. "Let's go out tonight and eat somewhere nice. What do you say? Where would you like to go?"

"Oh, Alexander, I'm so tired. Really, I could just go down to the corner baker and—"

"No, no, none of that. Not tonight. Lily, we're on the verge of our greatest triumph. Even Dannecker says so. We deserve a little celebration, you and I. Come on. I'll put my tie back on while you freshen up. I won't take no for an answer."

Buko stood in line with the rest of the men, holding his dented metal bowl. His palms were raw and bleeding. Some of the others told him it took about two weeks on the rock pile for the calluses to form. Some of the newcomers had tried to fashion crude gloves by tearing away pieces of their shirttails and wrapping their hands, but Beshkov, the commandant, just happened to visit the rock pile that day, and he had the guards beat the gloved men for "wearing unauthorized equipment."

The blood on Buko's hands made it hard to hold his bowl; it kept threatening to slip from his grasp. One evening an inmate had dropped his bowl, just as he was getting to the front of the line, and the guards beat and kicked him out of the line. "The soup's not good enough for you, kike? You can do without then." Some of the other men saved bits of whatever meager vegetables they could find in their bowls that evening, slipping them into their pockets and taking them to their comrade back in the barracks.

Dragomir Beshkov was perfect for the position of camp commandant: not only was he a virulent anti-Semite, he was also a sadist. Buko had seen him challenge a man on one of the crews who was bent over, trying to lever the wooden wheel of a rock-laden barrow out of a mudhole. "Where's your star, Jew? You're supposed to display your yellow star at all times, don't you know that?"

"Here, Commandant, here!" the man shouted, jumping to his feet and pulling back the lapel of his ragged jacket to show the yellow star he was wearing.

"Don't raise your voice at me, Jewish pig!" Beshkov screamed. He struck the man with his fist, and the worker dropped like a stone. Beshkov kicked him a few times and then walked away, whistling tunelessly. It was more frightening than if the commandant had kept ranting and raving.

Buko worked at the rock pile, hammering at the stone to break it into marble-sized gravel that could be mixed with asphalt. Sometimes, from the top of the stone piles, he could look across the flood plains of the Tounzha and see the tobacco fields, sprouting green in the May sunlight. They used to get some good leaf from the farms around Yambol. Buko remembered one of the managers—Dragoniev. Always a pleasant fellow. His name didn't sound Jewish, though. Buko wouldn't have ever thought of that before.

The barracks where they slept looked as if they'd been thrown together with about as much care as chicken coops. There were two shelves running around the walls, and men slept on the shelves with a thin camp-issue blanket for cover. One man's feet would be jammed up against the next man's face. Sometimes the barracks were so crowded that men had to sleep on the bare dirt floor. Some of the men traded their blankets for an extra coat if somebody showed up in the camp still in possession of a decent garment. Sometimes men arrived at the camp barefooted, since they'd made the mistake of wearing good shoes to the train. If a guard anywhere along the route wanted a man's coat or shoes, they were taken. Sometimes there were extra shoes at the camps from the workers who were too old or sick to tolerate Beshkov's regimen. But sometimes the newcomers just had to wrap their feet with whatever rags they could find.

At night, when quiet had fallen over the camp, the men exchanged information in cautious whispers—at least, the ones with enough energy to do anything but fall immediately into a deathlike sleep. Aaronov, a bricklayer from Pazardjik, told Buko one night that the order canceling the March deportation reached their town late. They were already herded into the local tobacco warehouse when the release order came. The Jews of Pazardjik went home to find their houses ransacked, everything of value taken. "They knew what they were doing, and they were organized," Aaronov said. "It took them less than four hours to clean out the whole neighborhood." Buko asked the bricklayer what he thought happened to his things.

"Sold," said Aaronov, "or just stolen. I saw a woman wearing my wife's new coat, the one I had just bought for her birthday. She was the wife of the local commissariat director."

But then Buko told Aaronov about what happened to him the day he went to the station in Kyustendil to get on the freight car with the rest of the men. As he left his house, Sotir Podorov was standing in the street at the bottom of the stairs. Tears were streaming down his face. "Buko, I just came… I wanted to tell you good-bye."

The handyman grabbed Buko and kissed him on both cheeks. He held him the way a father holds a son. He stuffed a hand in Buko's coat pocket and said, "For your trip. Hide it. I will pray for you, Buko, every day. I will light a candle for you at the shrine of the Blessed Virgin." And then he was gone.

Buko put his hand in his pocket and withdrew a hundred-leva note. For some reason, the guards at the Kyustendil station didn't ask him to take off the scarred, down-at-heel work shoes he was wearing on the day he boarded the train.

"I still have that note," Buko whispered to Aaronov. "I could have used it to bribe a guard for cigarettes or some sausages from the village or…I don't know. But, somehow, I'd rather have that note. When I feel it, I can remember the way it felt when he jammed it into my pocket. I can remember his tears and the feel of his arms around me. And that seems better somehow."

Some of the men told stories of camps where conditions were better. One fellow from Karlovo, a farmer named Leviev, said his brother was called up to someplace near Stara Zagora where they worked on the railroad bridges. "He was one of the first ones they took," Leviev said, "and he said the guards were easy to get along with. They'd let them save up their meat rations and trade for cigarettes, whatever. He even came home one weekend to visit his family. He said the commandant didn't care, as long as he didn't catch anyone sneaking back—and as long as they didn't get behind on their work quotas."

Such stories were hard to believe at the Yambol camp. Each morning started with the guards pounding on the doors and walls of the barracks, then kicking and cursing anybody who was slow getting up. One old man, a stoop-shouldered graybeard who always slept on the ground near the door, nearly got his ribs caved in by the guards one morning. Buko and some of the others gathered around and got him on his feet. They carried him to the breakfast lineup, the old man's toes dragging in the dirt. By the time they'd handed out breakfast, he was able to walk a little.

Breakfast was usually a piece of bread no bigger than a man's palm. On lucky days, there was a thumb-sized rind of hard cheese. On some days, according to no system Buko could decipher, some of the men got mail. The envelopes and packages had always been rifled, of course, but the letters made it through. Some of the men at least got news from their families and friends.

Buko knew Anka wouldn't be able to bring herself to send him anything, but he thought maybe one of his friends from Kyustendil would drop a line and let him know if things were any worse there.

One thing all the men at the camp agreed on: so far the trains all were coming in; none were going out. They were alive and not being sent any-where worse. That was something.

Daria had nearly finished the pile of socks Giovanna had asked her to work on when she heard the sound of the queen and Princess Maria-Louisa return-ing. She was sitting in one of the small parlors on the second floor of the family wing, her favorite place in the afternoon; the shade from the large maple and elm trees outside gave a pleasant, leafy cast to the light from the large windows. This was where she and the queen most often worked on the knit-ting projects with which the queen kept herself occupied during the after-noons and evening hours.

She heard the sound of the elevator ascending from the ground floor, then the sliding of the doors. There was a scuffing of feet on the parquet just outside the door, and Daria looked up to see a very cross Maria-Louisa. Gio-vanna stuck her head in the door just long enough to say that she'd be in to help Daria finish the knitting as soon as she hung up their jackets.

"Princess, would you like to come help me work on these scarves for our brave soldiers?" Daria asked. Maria-Louisa loved to help with the knitting, though her help most often took the form of questions about why one had to hold the needles just this way or why the soldiers wouldn't enjoy more gaily colored scarves.

But Maria-Louisa sank onto a stool near one corner and made no answer other than a shake of her head.

Daria put down her needles; she looked carefully at the princess. "Is something wrong, Your Royal Highness?

Maria-Louisa wouldn't look at Daria. She sat slumped over and twined her fingers in her lap, two habits that Giovanna especially disapproved of. Clearly, she was troubled about something and didn't have the words to express it—or didn't want to say the words.

Daria decided to try a different tack. "How was your outing with your mother, Mrs. Filova, and Frau Beckerle? It must have been exciting to be with three such great ladies and listen to what they—"

Maria-Louisa covered her face with her hands. She tried to keep the sob quiet, but Daria crossed the room and knelt beside her in an instant. She put her arms around the princess. "Oh, my, Princess. Please tell me what is troubling you."

Daria heard a quiet footfall outside the door. It was Giovanna, but she quickly signaled Daria that she didn't want her daughter to know she was listening. All of Daria's inner alarms were activated by this time. She held the princess and kissed her hair, smoothing a few stray tendrils back from her forehead. After a few seconds, Maria-Louisa was able to speak.

23

May 1943

It was very nice at first. Frau Beckerle and Mrs. Filova came to pick up Mother and me in a long black car that had the red flags with the black spiders on it. Everyone on the street turned to look at us, and I liked that. Mrs. Filova and Frau Beckerle were very polite, and they even talked to me a little. I told them French was my favorite subject, and they asked me some easy questions *en français,* and I did rather well. I noticed Mother's look and stopped talking before I talked too much."

"It sounds to me as though you handled yourself very well on such an important outing."

"It was later. We went to a special performance at the National Theatre, and it was in Bulgarian, and Mother or Mrs. Filova had to keep leaning over and translating for Frau Beckerle, and it was about some old kings and battles with tin swords. It was hard enough to be interested in the story without having to hear it being whispered in German."

"That doesn't sound like much fun, but you were very patient to—"

"After that," Princess Maria-Louisa said, "when we were leaving the theatre, Frau Beckerle said why didn't we just pop around to the Bulgaria Hall and view the new exhibit there? Mother said she hadn't heard about it, and I could tell something was wrong because Mrs. Filova got a funny look on her face. And when we walked around to the other side, there was a huge sign draped across the front of the Bulgaria Hall, and it said…it said…" The princess put her face in her hands. The next words came out in a mumble, between her fingers. "It said, 'The History of the Crimes of the Jews.'" Princess Maria-Louisa doubled over completely, covering her head with her arms.

Daria held her for a while, slowly rubbing her back. A part of her was feeling deep sorrow for the deception of an innocent child, and another part of her was angry and afraid. What new evils were being heralded by this latest round of anti-Semitic lies?

"Can you tell me what happened after that?" Daria said.

"Mother stared at the sign for a few seconds, then turned away. She said something in German, and I know I'm not supposed to be studying it yet, but I know what she said. She said, *'Das interessiert mich nicht,'* and she turned right around and started walking toward the car." Princess Maria-Louisa turned one eye toward Daria. "Mother told them she wasn't interested in seeing that exhibit, isn't that right?"

"Yes, that's exactly what she said."

"But Mrs. Filova, and especially Frau Beckerle, were angry at Mother after that. They sat differently, and they talked differently, and they didn't ask me any more French questions."

Daria kept her hand moving up and down the princess's back, trying to gentle her, trying to think of something to say that might smooth away the hurt or the mistrust or the fear or...

Queen Giovanna stepped quietly into the room. Daria felt her hand brush across her shoulder. She knelt in front of her daughter and put her hands on the girl's arms.

"Maria-Louisa. Look at me."

Like a tightly wadded piece of paper released from a strong grip, the princess unfolded until at last her eyes found her mother's face. She was still curled around herself, her elbows pulled in as if ready to fend off an unexpected blow. But she looked at her mother and waited. Queen Giovanna put a hand on her daughter's cheek. A long, silent moment settled as the two women who knew so much more than they wished to know surrounded this girl who felt so much more than she had words to say.

"My dear, I don't know how to explain to you what you saw," Queen Giovanna said. "You know, of course, you feel within yourself the wrong of it."

"Mother, Mademoiselle Richetti is a Jew, and she has committed no crime. She could never—"

Queen Giovanna softly placed her fingertips against the princess's lips. "No, my dear. You're right. And you're right about so many more people than Mademoiselle Daria, whom you know and have loved since your eyes opened on the world. There are hundreds, thousands of people just like Mademoiselle Daria who do not deserve the name associated with that hateful sign you saw on the front of Bulgaria Hall."

"But how, Mother? How can Mrs. Filova believe it? How can Father allow it? Frau Beckerle I can partly understand, because she's German and can't help it, but—"

"No, Maria-Louisa. That is wrong. Being German doesn't make a person evil any more than being Jewish does. Frau Beckerle and Mrs. Filova and…and even your father are in the grip of forces so big and so powerful that they are doing what they think they must—what they think they have to do. They think they have no choice. But—and this is what I want you never to forget, my child—there is always a choice. Even if the only place the choice exists is down in the deepest corner of your heart, there is a choice. And no one—not the Fuehrer, not me, not Father, not even God himself— can take that choice away from you. It is the most precious gift we have as human beings. And you must use it wisely."

Princess Maria-Louisa stared at her mother for a long time. "Has Father made a choice?" she said finally.

Queen Giovanna nodded. "Your father makes many choices every day, and most of them he tells to no one."

"Why?"

"To protect us, my dear."

Princess Maria-Louisa reached over and touched the yellow star on Daria's collar. "And you have made your choice, Mademoiselle Richetti?"

Daria felt the tears burning at the corners of her eyes. She forced as much of a smile as she could and nodded.

The princess looked at her mother, and her face hardened. "I will never choose hate. I will never choose a lie."

Queen Giovanna took her daughter's hands in her own. "I believe you, dear."

Bojilov sauntered down Alexander Battenberg Square. He took a pull on his cigarette, then flicked the ash with his thumb. He kept watching over his shoulder, in the direction of the Royal Palace. He'd heard the Richetti woman sometimes took walks. He was hoping he might see her today, find out if she went out alone or accompanied. He heard a man's voice, shouting, somewhere to his left. It was a street preacher or something, from the sound of it, over by the Vazov Monument. Bojilov leaned against the lee of a building and watched the crowd start to gather.

Lily walked up and down the sidewalk in front of the Russian Church, looking at each face that passed her for as long as she dared without seeming to challenge.

It was madness to meet Daria this close to the palace, but there was no time. Did the courier put the note in the right place? Did Daria find it, or someone else? The orders were going out soon; if she couldn't get word to the palace today, she'd have to run the risk of contacting some of her acquaintances in the Jewish community.

"Just keep walking, and don't look at me," said a voice by her elbow. It was Daria. Lily resisted the urge to look behind them. She would trust Daria's senses.

They continued along in front of the church and turned left along Rakovski.

"Let's get among the crowds around the Vazov Monument," Lily said.

There was an orator standing at the base of the monument, spouting off about the war, about Russia, about the Western powers. He was a wild-looking character, dressed in traditional folk attire, and the main purpose of his diatribe seemed to center on the rusted coffee can at his feet into which people occasionally tossed a few stotinki.

Lily and Daria strolled the margins of the crowd, keeping their eyes on the speaker. "The commissariat is planning another round of deportations, and this time there won't be anybody left behind."

"Starting when?"

"Soon. The notices will start going out in the next few weeks."

"Who knows?"

"No one but the commissar, the interior minister, and the directors in the towns most directly concerned. A few of the railroad officials. Not many."

"You said the towns most directly concerned—"

"The places where the transports terminate."

"Where?"

"Lom. Somovit. Tziber. And I think Pleven and Shumen are on the list also."

There was a long silence. "All Danube ports, or directly connected by rail," Daria said in a voice barely above a whisper.

The speaker was doing an impression of Stalin that had the crowd roaring with laughter. Absently, Lily wondered how much longer such entertainment would be available in Sofia.

"Can you get word to the leadership of the Central Consistory?" Daria asked after a few seconds.

"I don't see how. Alexander—the commissar keeps us all so busy. Every minute we are typing forms for the railroads, requisitions for this and that, lists, memos. I was there until nine o'clock last night, and one of the drivers was under orders to bring me directly home as soon as I finished the last project I was assigned."

"Then I have to find a way to tell them."

Standing in the middle of the crowd, their eyes staring blindly at the street entertainer, Lily's hand gripped Daria's.

"I'm going to walk away now, " Lily said, "toward the Levski Monument. Don't watch me. If you manage to get word to the Central Consistory, send me a message by the usual method. If you can't do that, at least get in touch with Dr. Benaroya. He's a gynecologist; you could make an appointment with him without arousing suspicion. He knows everyone important. He can help get the word out. But there isn't much time."

Lily started to move away, then she felt Daria's hand on her arm.

"Lily. I don't know how to thank—"

"Never mind that. Just get the word out. That's all that matters now." And she vanished into the crowd.

For a few moments, all Daria could do was stand and absorb the terrifying reality that Panitza's words had begun to create within her. It was a time for action; the responsibility lay with her, and there was no avoiding it, no passing it off—to the queen or anyone else. No one else could sponsor her this time. This burden had selected her with a deeply personal precision.

Since she had begun wearing the yellow star, a small part of her thought perhaps that was sacrifice enough. Maybe, just maybe the bravery of flinging aside the camouflage afforded by her position was enough. Maybe that was her contribution to the great cause. Maybe no other risk would be needed.

But now came the burden of this choice. What was the old Roman phrase she had learned as a girl—"The condemnation of a vow"? She was condemned by the consequences of her own decisions. She could refuse it and become something she hated, or she could accept it and enter more deeply into the fear of the one who risked all for the sake of a hope that was anything but certain.

She waited, pretending to listen to the street performer, so that Lily's departure would seem unconnected to her own. Then she turned down Moskovska Street with her arms tucked around her despite the balmy warmth of the May morning.

Bojilov watched the Richetti woman walking away, toward the Royal Palace, and he made note of the time. Maybe she felt the need for a little stroll every day about now. There was no chance of taking her from the palace. It would need to be done quietly, with no fuss and preferably no witnesses. That was what Belev said he wanted—no fuss. It looked easy enough, from what Bojilov had seen: the Richetti woman had ambled along toward the crowd, drawn by the fool on the monument base. She had spoken to no one, as far as Bojilov could tell. No one was expecting her. No complications. Daria Richetti would become just another Jew among hundreds of Jews headed for Lom or someplace like it. And her privilege wouldn't do her any good where she was going. And that was what Belev most desired.

Bojilov didn't care about any of that so much. But this particular Jew had cost him a humiliation not so long ago, at the Midwinter Ball, and that was something he did care about. Dimitrov had made him look like a fool in front of everyone there. The memory of it still stung. This Richetti woman had some good looks about her. Who knew? Maybe there would be a little extra time before he handed her over to the boys at the commissariat. A little time to even a personal score.

And besides, the money Belev had promised him if he executed the plan as agreed upon was too good to pass up. A hundred thousand leva for the snatching of one little Jewish girl. With that kind of money, Bojilov could leave Sofia—even Bulgaria. He could drop his army uniform in the trash and go someplace safe until the war blew itself out and the pickings were easy again.

Bojilov followed her at a safe distance all the way to the palace grounds. He noted which gate she used, how many guards were there, everything he could think of that might be useful later. That was how you stayed alive, Bojilov thought. You noticed things—things that might give you a slight advantage when the time came. And if what Belev had told him was true, the time was coming soon.

Bojilov ran down his mental list of those from his time in the Royal Guard who were still on palace duty. Was there someone on the inside who owed him a favor? Someone who might be willing to pick up a few thousand leva for keeping his eyes open and making a phone call at the right time? Maybe even one of the women, the domestics. Bojilov smiled, remembering a certain laundry girl—Karina? Kalena?—who hadn't minded being backed into an out-of-the-way corner once or twice. She might serve Bojilov's purposes if she was still managing to keep the queen or one of the senior domestics from smelling the booze on her breath.

Yes. There were several ways of keeping tabs on Miss Ree*chett*ee. And when the time was right, Bojilov would be ready.

Daria didn't sleep at all that night. But by morning she had a plan. Despite what Lily had said, Daria had decided the slightly indirect route was the safer. Anyone who went anywhere near the Central Consistory or the Central Synagogue was surely being watched, probably photographed, and had his name on a list in the commissariat offices. And it wasn't just the risk to herself that she had to consider; any direct action she took would reflect on His Majesty. There were plots within plots within plots, and Daria knew she couldn't afford to run afoul of some stratagem she didn't even suspect.

In the morning, her eyes raw and her hands trembling from lack of sleep, she dressed herself and, as early as was permissible, went to the queen's suite.

"My dear! You look awful," Queen Giovanna said as soon as Daria rose from her curtsy.

"Yes, Your Majesty, I'm afraid I'm feeling a bit under the weather. It seems to be a rather…feminine matter, and—"

"Well, you must see Dr. Kajilov at once. He's been attending me since before the birth of Princess Maria-Louisa, and there is no more discreet—"

"Actually, Your Majesty, please forgive me, but I have had a referral to a certain Dr. Benaroya. Jacques Benaroya, I believe? And if I might, I was hoping I could have the use of a car to go to his offices this morning."

Queen Giovanna looked at her, and Daria didn't dare meet her eyes; the queen was likely to see far too much. *Please, Your Majesty, just give your permission. You know what you know, but you must surely also know that I must do what I must do.*

An uncomfortable silence crawled by, then Queen Giovanna gave Daria a smile that didn't quite reach her eyes. "Well, of course, Daria. You must do as you think best. I would never insist on your using my doctor if there was another whose services would be more…appropriate. Dr. Benaroya is, of course, quite well known in several circles. And I'm sure you'll be able to tell him exactly what he needs to know in order to take precisely the proper action."

Daria felt her shoulders drooping even more. In all the years of her service, this was as close as she had come to telling Queen Giovanna a lie, and they both knew it. The queen was angry with Daria for taking this risk but far too respectful to command her to refuse it. That was why Daria would love this woman with the last breath of her body.

Dr. Benaroya stared at Daria, and she could see fear competing with calculation behind his eyes. "If they really mean to do this, they'll start with the most influential Jews—the Sofia elite," he said.

Daria nodded. "That would be my guess, Doctor. My source says the eviction notices will begin going out very soon."

"How soon?"

"My source wasn't sure. But it seems to be a matter of days rather than weeks."

The tall, slim, olive-skinned man shook his head and ran a hand through his thinning, salt-and-pepper hair. "This is impossible. I have to get word to Levi and Farhi and the rest, and naturally they're being watched round the clock. I never know when I leave here in the evenings if the men in the dark coats behind me will allow me to arrive at my house or…" He stopped and looked at her. "Please forgive me for running on, my dear. You've shown great courage in coming here, in helping us sound the alarm. You've done enough."

"Thank you, Dr. Benaroya. I'm glad I was able to do something."

"When you go out of the examination room, tell my receptionist that I want to see you again in two weeks." He gave her a sad little smile and a shrug. "The way things are, you may be the only patient on my calendar in two weeks. But still, it's best to keep up appearances. You never know who's watching, or where."

Daria swallowed and nodded.

He put his hand on her arm. "Miss Richetti, we know—all of us—that His Majesty is not behind any of this. We know how his hands are tied by the Fascist majority and our friends in Berlin. But, please, if there is anything you can say…"

"Of course, Doctor."

Daria left the office and walked down the flight of stairs to the car waiting in the street. Corporal Sedjiev hurried around to open her door. "Everything all right, miss?"

"Yes, thank you, Corporal." For an instant, Daria's mind flitted back to that night at the Hotel Bulgaria—which had begun as a wonderful evening and ended in ugliness and hatred—and then the unforgettable, redeeming touch of Dobri's lips on hers. Sedjiev had been their driver that night. When they got in the car after the fight, his first question to Dobri had been almost the same as his words just now.

They pulled away from the curb, and Daria looked up at Dr. Benaroya's window, thinking about the last thing he'd said. What could she ever say to Tsar Boris to affect the fate of Bulgaria's Jews? Even the queen didn't discuss matters of state with her husband; she had made that clear to Daria on more than one occasion. It simply wasn't done. The women had their sphere, and the men theirs, and to try to pass from one to the other was a breach of everything that held together life as Daria had always known it.

No, Tsar Boris was no Xerxes, and she was certainly no Esther. Purim was months past; the time for deliverance was gone, maybe. What did Daria know of deliverance? What did the Jews of Macedonia and Thrace know of it? What sense did it make to believe in it in a world that seemed driven to tear itself apart?

But still she had come here, and she had delivered her message. Maybe that was worth something. Maybe the deliverance was in the effort, the will to believe that an action, taken or not taken, could make a difference. Maybe somewhere such things were remembered and gave meaning both to those who survived—and to those who didn't.

Interior Minister Gabrovski stepped into the office of Pavel Grouev and gave the chief of cabinet a pleasant smile. "Please have Mr. Balan inform His Majesty that I am here."

"Good morning, Mr. Gabrovski. I've already called Balan. He'll be here shortly to take you to Tsar Boris." Grouev said all this without looking up from the papers he was working on. Gabrovski decided to ignore the slight. After all, if this meeting went well, his supreme moment of triumph would become a certainty. He could afford to be generous.

In a few minutes Stanislav Balan came into the room and shook Gabrovski's hand. "This way, please, Mr. Gabrovski. His Majesty will meet with you in the upper salon."

Gabrovski was surprised; the king's custom was to do business in the small office behind Grouev's. The salons were normally reserved for decorous affairs of state. He began to feel even more confident about the outcome of this meeting.

They climbed the marble stairs to the second floor and passed along a wide hallway until they came to a set of double doors covered with elaborate moldings and secured by two Royal Guards. One of the soldiers stepped aside and opened the door, and Balan bowed Gabrovski through.

Tsar Boris was seated at the opposite end of the room at a Louis XIV table of gilded wood that was topped by black marble veined in gray. He wore his white summer dress uniform, and he watched the interior minister approach him, crossing the parquet floor, much as a judge might watch a defendant enter a courtroom. Suddenly Gabrovski realized he had never felt more like a supplicant than he did at this moment.

And yet he had to carry this through. Belev had already ordered the printing of the expulsion orders. Support for the Jews in the Sobranje was effectively crushed with Peshev's downfall, and Dannecker and his superiors were becoming more and more insistent on visible results—any kind of results.

"Give him two options," the Hauptsturmfuehrer had said at their last meeting. "Plan A: Deport the Jews immediately to the Danube ports for transfer to our eastern regions. Plan B: Banish the Jews to the provinces— starting with the most influential—from Sofia and the other major cities. Then you can claim at least a partial victory, and it will be easier to take them from there to the Danube, if and when the time comes."

Gabrovski had believed that even Plan B, if endorsed by the palace, could lead to eventual victory over the Jews. Who knew? Boris might even look the other way, as he'd seemed to do on other occasions, while the trains from the provinces shuttled the remaining Jews from the kingdom.

Gabrovski reached the chair at the opposite end of the table from His Majesty. Tsar Boris looked at him for a few seconds with absolutely no change of expression. Then a tiny smile appeared. "Good morning, Mr. Interior Minister. I believe you requested this meeting?"

24

P avel Grouev opened the door of his house onto a scene of pandemonium.

The Simoniev family stood bunched together in the middle of his living room. His wife, the boys, and Radka were holding them and hugging them and trying to speak to them, but to little avail as far as Pavel could see. Radka's face was red from crying, and Pavel wondered how much longer the neighbors would tolerate the wailing before calling the police.

Mikhail Simoniev saw him and came toward him, waving a sheet of paper. "Three days, Pavel! We have to be out of our house in three days!"

"What? Let me see this." Pavel took the notice from Mikhail. It was printed on the letterhead of the Commissariat for Jewish Questions.

TO: Simoniev, Mikhail V. and family, as listed below:
         Elisabeta ("Betty")—age 38
         Suzanna—age 18
         Benjamin—age 12

EXPULSION ORDER #1,456

You are hereby ordered to vacate your current residence, _Tsar Shishman Ave. 1278, # 38-B_, by _24 May 1943_. You may bring with you two bags for each person, containing only the most essential belongings. When the officials of the Commissariat for Jewish Questions arrive at your residence on the above date, you will immediately remit a detailed listing of all furniture, personal effects, and other belongings to be left in your residence. You will remit this list, together with all keys to your residence, to the official. You will report to the central station, _track 4_, and you will board the train for _Vidin_, departing at _2:12 p.m_. You will not be required to purchase a ticket. All expenses for this transport will be assumed by the Commissariat for Jewish Questions. You must bring this notice with you to your assigned departure point.

Pavel looked up at his friend. "Mikhail, I…I don't know what to say—"

"Vidin, Pavel! They're sending us to Vidin! On the Danube! They're sending us to Poland, to the death camps!"

"Yutch Bonar is a madhouse," Betty Simonieva said. "People are wandering through the streets, saying farewell to everyone they meet, Jewish or not. People don't know whether to buy suitcases and backpacks or to try to sell everything they own and hide the money with non-Jewish friends. No one knows what to do."

"At least we're all going to the same place," Mikhail said. "I saw one man whose notice was sending him to Russe, and his eighty-year-old mother's notice said she had to go to Lom. She's sick, he said, and won't live a week without someone to take care of her."

"They don't want us to live," Zizi said, sobbing into Radka's chest. "They want us all to die—they're going to kill us."

Benjamin was looking at one family member after another, and the panic on his face made Pavel want to weep. What comfort could he offer these people, his friends? Tsar Boris had met with Gabrovski; Pavel had to assume the king knew what the interior minister could and could not authorize.

"Stay here, Mikhail," Pavel said. "At least for tonight. Don't go back to your house. I'll return to the palace and see what I can find out. Maybe… I don't know. But stay here, and I'll see what may be done."

Mikhail grabbed Pavel's hands. "Bless you, Pavel. You're a saint, a savior. Talk to His Majesty. Please tell him we aren't bad people. We're loyal subjects, we're—"

"Now, now. I'll see what's going on," Pavel said, unsettled by it all. "Just stay here. No one will harm you."

When Pavel reached his office, the first call he made was to the Jewish Central Consistory. "Give me Nissim Levi," he said. "This is Pavel Grouev, chief of His Majesty's cabinet."

"Grouev! Thank heaven you've called," the attorney said when he reached the phone. In the background, Pavel could hear the sound of many voices; he guessed at least thirty of the leaders of the Jewish community were gathered, trying to make some sense of this desperate situation.

"Nissim, tell me as much as you can about what's going on."

"Well, it's all very confusing, Mr. Grouev. At six o'clock this morning, someone pounded on the door of my home and shoved into my face a notice from the commissariat. Pardo, Colonel Tadjer…they say much the same happened to them. It's as if they wanted to make sure they got the leadership of the consistory before they did anything else."

"Are all the notices for destinations on the Danube?"

"Most. Some are to places like Kyustendil, close to the southwestern border. A few to Pleven and other rail centers."

"Can you tell how many notices have been served so far?"

"The highest number I've seen so far is 2,550. But every time someone new comes along, the numbers get higher. They're taking everybody, Mr. Grouev: military invalids, families of men who are already at work camps. Just a little while ago I heard of some people who are trying to organize a mass protest on the twenty-fourth, the day of the evictions. And we also heard of a young man who hanged himself when he got his notice."

Pavel rested his forehead on his hand. *How is it possible that my country has descended to this?*

"You must speak to His Majesty, Mr. Grouev. We know he isn't a Jew hater, like Gabrovski and some of the others. Some of us are going to get in touch with the Holy Synod. Some of our women will go in the morning to Madame Karavelova. The papal nuncio is here from Istanbul, and Benjamin Arditi has agreed to speak to him and ask him to intervene with Tsaritza Giovanna."

"It sounds like you've thought of everything," Pavel said.

"Everything—and nothing, Mr. Grouev. There is panic in the Jewish community. People are piling their furniture on the sidewalks. Women are selling their household silver for a few stotinki. Peasants from the outlying villages are loading housefuls of goods in their donkey carts. We are doing our best at the consistory to maintain calm, but it's beginning to seem more and more like the end of the world.

"Please, Mr. Grouev, tell His Majesty: we can't let this happen. Not to us—and not to Bulgaria."

Pavel hung up the phone and suddenly realized: May 24 was the Feast Day of Kyril and Methodie.

Lily went to Alexander's door and announced the two men. "Rabbi Yeremiev and Dr. Geron are here to see you, Mr. Belev."

The two men, both with ashen faces, shuffled toward the office door of the Commissar for Jewish Questions. Alexander didn't rise when they entered, barely glanced at them as they took the two seats in front of his desk. He didn't bother to ask Lily to close the door.

"What do you want?"

The two men looked at each other. "Mr. Belev, I would like to read you a letter, drafted by Colonel Damian Velchev, a person I think you know—"

"A radical who ought to have been executed in 1936, just as he was sentenced. If it hadn't been for the meddling of bleeding hearts like Peshev, he'd be dead right now. Why should I care about anything he has to say?"

"There was a time," Rabbi Yeremiev said, leaning forward in his chair, "when visitors to this office were received respectfully, Mr. Belev."

"Well, things have changed, haven't they? You Jews and your Bolshevik allies are the enemy of my country, and the time has come for us to quit coddling you."

"To Your August Majesty, Tsar Boris III, king of the Bulgarians," Geron read. "Only the most dire circumstances could cause the undersigned to address this letter to you during these difficult days. Please, Your Majesty, hear with your heart and act in the way that becomes the King Unifier of a just and peace-loving land..."

Belev snorted and leaned back in his chair. He stared at the ceiling, but he let Geron keep reading.

"The expulsion of the Jewish population of Sofia, which will undoubtedly lead to their deportation from the country of their birth, is a grave and inhuman measure that cannot be condoned by any right-thinking people. Bulgarians cannot countenance this action; by their very nature they are a tolerant and peace-loving nation. This dreadful miscarriage of justice must be cancelled by Your Majesty, because only Your Majesty gathers together, in your own person, the power of the government and the love of all people of this nation. Your Majesty is Bulgaria. The responsibility for protecting the integrity and reputation of our land falls now on you."

He looked up. "This is signed by Colonel Velchev, former Prime Minister Kiosseivanov, former Prime Minister Tzankov, Metropolitan Stefan, and nineteen various other influential—"

"Stefan! The biggest traitor to this nation since the Great War! Don't you know that every time he climbs into his pulpit and attacks the government, the Bolsheviks reprint his words and use them as propaganda?"

"Mr. Belev, I don't believe you can prove any connection—"

"I don't have to prove anything to you Jews! If you came crawling in here to frighten me by threatening me with His Majesty's disapproval, you might as well know that Interior Minister Gabrovski has Tsar Boris's approval for everything we're doing."

Alexander let this information have its effect on the two men. Lily realized why he hadn't shut the door: he was enjoying this and wanted her to watch.

"There will be no exceptions to the expulsion orders," Alexander said. "By this time next week, not a single Jew will remain in Sofia." He pointed a finger at Geron's face. "And you, *Doctor* Geron, are on the list," he said with a sneer.

Dr. Geron drew himself up in his chair. "I will share the fate of my people, Mr. Belev, but I will be the last to leave, and until the moment I am gone, I will do everything in my power to see that this malicious anti-Jewish policy is abolished."

"Power! You no longer have any power! Get out of my office."

Alexander swiveled his chair away from them, pretending to read some papers with his back turned to the two men.

For several seconds they just sat there. Lily didn't know what to do. She went to them and placed her hands on their shoulders.

"I'm sorry, gentlemen. The commissar…has another appointment waiting. I have to ask you to leave now."

The two men pushed themselves out of the chairs as if using the last of their strength. Lily walked them to the door, then closed it behind them. She went with them to the stairs that led to the street. As she passed the window by her desk, she could see the ring of guards stationed on the sidewalk all around the commissariat offices, guards made up of special forces from the Sofia Police Criminal Investigation Forces and put directly under Alexander's command for the duration of this operation.

"This way, gentlemen," Lily said, indicating the stairway doors. "I'm…I'm very sorry."

Dr. Geron looked at her. "Young woman, it's obvious that you still have a human heart beating in your breast. How is it that you are able to work in this place of evil?"

Lily opened her mouth to answer, but no words would form in her mind. She looked away, and by the time she had looked back, the two men had gone through the doors. She heard their footsteps descending the stairs, moving down, down…then gone.

The phone rang in the guardroom. A corporal answered it, then stiffened involuntarily. He held the receiver toward Dobri. "Sergeant, it's His Majesty. He's asking for you."

Dobri took the phone. He was puzzled; he wasn't on duty until tomorrow. With all the uproar going on about the latest round of deportations, he had planned to spend this day as close as possible to Daria—though he wasn't sure exactly what he could do or what she would even permit him to do. He could hardly force himself to think of anything but Daria, but she seemed composed, almost calm. In a way, her attitude made him even more fearful for her.

"Yes, Your Majesty?"

"Sergeant Dimitrov, I need you to bring my car to the rear entrance. Bring clothing for several days. I must leave Sofia at once."

"I… Yes, Your Majesty, but—"

"Sergeant, I realize this is a rather unusual order, especially at this time, but I must insist that you do it immediately."

"Of course, Your Majesty. I will be there in fifteen minutes or less."

"Thank you, Dobri. And I must also insist that you say nothing to anyone about this."

"Of course, Your Majesty."

Dobri hung up the phone, completely nonplussed. Leaving Sofia? With so much turmoil taking place?

The corporal was looking at him, the obvious questions hanging on his face.

"Djevrev, call the motor pool. Tell them to have the Renault ready to go in five minutes. I'll be there personally to pick it up."

Djevrev stared at him.

"Corporal, did you hear me?"

"Yes, Sergeant. Of course. I'll call them right now."

Dobri went to his quarters and began packing a duffel bag. The actions of his hands were automatic, ingrained. But his mind was pacing back and forth across the terrain of his confusion. There was near panic in the streets among Sofia's Jews; the Yutch Bonar district was a powder keg. Commissariat and special police forces were everywhere. Delegations of Jewish leaders and government officials were arriving almost hourly at the palace. Metropolitan Stefan himself had been here maybe twelve times in the last two days, demanding to see His Majesty, Pavel Grouev, the prime minister—almost anybody connected with the upper echelons of government. And Chancellor Grouev—the man looked as if he might fall over dead at any moment. As chief of the king's cabinet, it was his duty to meet with those demanding to see the king, and apparently the king was refusing all such meetings. Poor Grouev was receiving the brunt of all the protests, and all he could offer in return was his solemn promise that His Majesty would be told everything, that all possible measures would be taken, that above all everyone should remain calm. Dobri pitied him. A soldier, at least, had clear-cut orders to follow. But a diplomat, it seemed, operated in a different world, where lines were always shifting and nothing was ever clear.

And His Majesty was leaving? For an instant, Dobri heard a whisper of doubt in his mind. But he couldn't permit himself to start that path. Unswerving obedience to his sovereign was the bedrock on which everything else in his world was built. Dobri needed, more than anything, to believe that Tsar Boris knew what he was doing.

Daria… But no—she would be safe in the palace. Tsaritza Giovanna would never permit anything to happen to her. Would she? Ever since Daria had donned the yellow star, something had changed within her. She had become firmer, somehow, less predictable—and infinitely more precious to Dobri. Suppose her name really was on some list at the commissariat. Dobri tried to imagine one of the commissariat police knocking on the palace door, trying to serve an expulsion order on the queen's personal attendant. No, it was impossible. It couldn't happen. Daria would be safe.

He would go with His Majesty on whatever urgent mission was required, and he would perform his duty, and that would be his salvation, as it had always been.

He glanced at his watch. Three minutes until the time he had promised to be at the door with the car. He grabbed his duffel bag and hurried toward the garage.

Dobri downshifted for the hairpin turn around the shoulder of the mountain. Tcham-Koria was about four kilometers ahead. He glanced in the rearview mirror. Tsar Boris was staring out the window, much as he had been doing since they had left Sofia just over an hour ago. As they rounded the tight curve, he spoke for the first time since they had left the palace.

"Sergeant Dimitrov, I wonder. Did you ever know anyone who was truly mad?"

"Well, there was old Bochko, who used to sit on the wall of the church-yard every Friday morning and crow like a rooster as the sun was coming up."

"This was in Bailovo? You were a boy?"

"Yes, Your Majesty."

"And you saw him do this?"

"I heard about it. It was common knowledge, you might say. Sort of a village joke. Now and then, when my father was rousting me from my bed, I heard him. After a while, people stopped talking about it. Unless there were visitors."

"Crowing in the sunrise… Did this Bochko do anything else unusual?"

"No, not that I remember, Your Majesty. He did odd jobs around town. Sold a little firewood, hired out as a goat boy, worked during the haying season. He used to sleep behind the wall of Yosef Khojukharov's shed during the summer, where there was a thick pile of leaves from the elm trees back there. And when it got cold, I think he slipped in among Yosef's livestock."

Tsar Boris chuckled. Dobri was glad to hear the sound.

"Is this Bochko still living in Bailovo, do you imagine, Sergeant Dimitrov?"

"Oh no, Your Majesty. Khojukharov found him dead one winter morning when he went to milk his goats. Bochko was lying there, and Yosef nudged him with a toe, as he usually did, but old Bochko didn't move. Then Khojukharov noticed his eyes were open, but with the glaze of the dead. He said Bochko's face was turned toward the door of the shed, where it faced to the east. It was still dark, because it was the middle of winter."

Tsar Boris was quiet for a while. "What do you think, Dobri?" he said in a voice almost too quiet for Dobri to hear. "Was he watching for the sunrise?"

"I…I don't know, Your Majesty. I was only a boy. To me, it was just the death of a funny old man."

"Was he Orthodox? Do you know?"

"Yes, Your Majesty. They buried him in the churchyard. On his tombstone, they carved a rooster outlined by a rising sun. I remember seeing it the last time I went to visit my parents' graves."

"Who paid for his burial?"

"He had a few leva in his pocket when Khojukharov found him, and some people chipped in here and there. The village loved him, I guess, after its fashion. At least enough to give him a decent Christian burial."

"A man could be remembered for worse reasons," Tsar Boris said. "He gave a few smiles, he led a simple life, and he died in a warm place. His people loved him enough to do the final duties by him. There have been many worse deaths."

He was still using that quiet voice that seemed to Dobri as if the words he said wanted to mean something else, but Dobri had no idea what.

"So what do you think, Sergeant Dimitrov? Madness—is it a good thing or a bad thing?"

They were driving through the main street of Samokov. The car's head-lights washed over the buildings at the center of the village, mostly small, two-storied brick structures covered with stucco. The ground floor of many of them were shops of some sort with living quarters upstairs. Most had the overhanging second story typical of traditional village architecture. If they had gotten here an hour or two earlier, before the evening light faded, old men would have looked up from the chess games set up on casks in front of the stores. Women with freshly bought bread or sacks of beans under their arms would have had to step aside in the narrow street to let the car pass. They might even have had to wait for someone to guide a herd of goats or sheep or cows across the road.

Bailovo was much like Samokov, though not so high in the mountains. Dobri had lived there until he left for the army. How could he possibly answer Tsar Boris's question? And yet he had the feeling that whatever he said next would be important—would matter in some way that he couldn't begin to guess. Tsar Boris was a man in torment. He carried a load of which Dobri had no notion. But now, in the darkness of this automobile, Dobri was suddenly thrust among the councils of the great. And he realized he would rather be alone, facing a squad of enemy soldiers, than have the burden of this moment.

God help me.

"All things being equal, Your Majesty, I would rather not be crazy. But if I had no choice, then I suppose the madness of Bochko was a good thing. At least he never harmed anyone, so far as I knew."

Dobri heard the squeaking of the leather seats, then he felt Tsar Boris's hand on his shoulder. "Thank you, Dobri. Thank you."

"You're welcome, Your Majesty, but…for what?"

Dobri could have bitten off his own tongue for his impudence, but in that moment his confusion and sudden anxiety were too much for his habitual discipline.

"For comforting me as best you could," Tsar Boris answered. "There's only one thing that worries me."

"With Your Majesty's permission, what is that?"

"There is more than one kind of madness, Dobri."

"Yes, Your Majesty."

And may God and all his saints protect my Daria from such madness…

They took the steep, winding path from Tcham-Koria up to Tsarska-Bistritza. Dobri was surprised to see another vehicle parked in the circular drive in front of the royal residence.

"Stop in front, Sergeant, and leave the engine running. Tap on the front door. Svilen, my valet, will answer. Ask him to give you the field telephone, then bring it back here and we will go on up to the chalet at Yastrebetz."

"Yes, Your Majesty."

Dobri went to the door and found everything just as the king had said. The old man handed him the field telephone, then touched Dobri's sleeve as he was turning away.

"You didn't bring any guns with you, did you?" he said.

"Only my service revolver," Dobri said. "But what business is that of yours?"

Svilen nodded. "His Majesty doesn't want any noise—not even the sound of hunting rifles. Very strange. First time he's ever come up here without wanting to have his hunting gear all laid out when he arrives."

Dobri carried the field telephone back to the car and put it in the trunk. Then he drove slowly around the gravel driveway and onto the rough, switch-backed trail up to the chalet. Dobri had never been to the chalet before; from the vegetation, he guessed they must be above two thousand meters.

Tsar Boris asked Dobri to pull the car all the way into the small garage and close the door. Dobri opened the trunk. There was precious little in the way of luggage: his duffel bag, a large leather valise for Tsar Boris, and the field telephone.

"I'll get the valise," Tsar Boris said.

When they closed the door of the chalet behind them, Tsar Boris turned to Dobri. "Sergeant Dimitrov, no one is to know we are here. If the prime minister himself calls on the field telephone, you will tell him you do not know my whereabouts. Do you understand?"

"Yes, Your Majesty."

Tsar Boris looked up the winding staircase that led to the second story of the chalet. "You know, Dobri, this is the first time in my life that I won't be in Sofia on Kyril and Methodie Day."

"I…I'm sure the rest of the royal family will enjoy the day."

"Yes, I expect they will. I've asked Captain Kalayev to be especially vigilant."

Oh, Daria!

"I'm sorry we—that is, you—can't be there, Your Majesty."

"Yes, so am I. But sometimes, Dobri, the right choice appears strange to those who don't understand. This, I think, is one of those times."

"I'm not sure, Your Majesty. But I trust Your Majesty's judgment."

He gave Dobri a sad little smile. "Thank you, Dobri. I pray your trust is not misplaced."

Tsar Boris picked up his valise and began climbing the stairs.

Hauptsturmfuehrer Dannecker pounded his fist on Pavel Grouev's desk. "This is ridiculous! Do you mean to say that you are the chief of the royal chancellery, and you have no idea of the king's location?"

The German was red faced, and his teeth were grinding. Pavel gave him an even, calm look and said, "Herr Dannecker, that is precisely what I mean to say. If you will give me the message you wish him to have, I will see that it is passed through the channels—"

"Oh, this is absurd," the SS officer snapped. "Come on, Hoffmann. We'll have to finish the job properly once we get them all out of Sofia. In this *arschenrückwärts* country, there's no point in trying to do anything organized or sensible."

Dannecker spouted angry German all the way to Pavel's door and much of the way down the short hallway to the main foyer of the palace.

Stanislav Balan came into the office and handed Pavel a stack of papers. "These are transcripts of radio broadcasts from Allied as well as Communist stations, warning against the consequences of allowing the deportations. The Communist cells are calling on the people to oppose the action by all means possible."

Pavel shook his head. "Stanislav, His Majesty has already decided what he will allow. Thank you for keeping me informed, but—"

"I understand, Mr. Grouev. Ah, I believe Metropolitan Stefan is next in line, sir. One of the switchboard operators has him holding for you."

Pavel took a deep breath and puffed out his cheeks. He tried to smile. "Somehow that seems fitting, don't you think, Stanislav? Please tell the switchboard to connect His Eminence at once."

Gingerly he picked up his telephone. He heard several clicks, then the voice of the metropolitan.

"Mr. Grouev, I have a delegation of the leaders of the Jewish community in my home at this moment, and I cannot possibly describe to you the scene at this place. My house, my courtyard, and the street in front of my house are full of Jews begging for the protection of the church from this despicable relocation scheme. It is time for His Majesty to say one word: 'Enough!' He can end this stupidity with a simple order to the so-called authorities. The mercy of Christ demands it, and the people of Bulgaria demand it too."

When Stefan paused for a breath, Pavel quickly said, "Your Eminence, you may be assured—and you may assure those with you now—that I will convey your message to His Majesty, just as you have conveyed it to me."

"Well, confound it all, man, where is His Majesty? Is he the king of Bulgaria or not?"

"I was not told His Majesty's location, but—"

"The king must show the statesmanlike wisdom for which he is justly famous, Mr. Grouev. He must come back to Sofia and put a stop to this horrendous injustice. And you can tell him I said those exact words."

"Yes, Your Eminence, I will. And may I further suggest that at tomorrow's holiday celebration, you take the opportunity to speak to Prime Minister Filov. He is deeply involved in these matters and would certainly be a competent authority to—"

"Involved? Oh yes, I'd say he was involved, all right. Up to his anti-Semitic eyeballs, he's involved. Thank you for that brilliant bit of advice, Mr. Grouev."

The line went dead.

Pavel stared at the phone for a moment, then returned it to its cradle like someone putting a raw egg back into its carton. He held his face in his hands for a few seconds. He looked at his clock. It was almost time to place the call to the number Tsar Boris had left with him. What would he tell the king? That the city was trying to tear itself apart? That Sofia was the frayed rope in a deadly tug of war?

Pavel thought about the last words Tsar Boris had said to him before getting in the car and disappearing to...wherever he was. "If I'm not here, they can't force my hand," he said.

But who did the king mean? Metropolitan Stefan and the anti-German faction, or Gabrovski and his commissariat? Or someone from Berlin perhaps? Pavel didn't know what kind of cat-and-mouse game Tsar Boris was playing. He only hoped that when he returned to his palace, there was still a country left to govern.

25

K yril and Methodie Day dawned bright and sunny. Any other year Stefan would have regarded the weather as a blessing on the national holiday. He would have most likely been smiling and whistling as he made his way from his house to Alexander Nevsky Square, where the festivities would begin. He would be in a good mood, despite the weight and heat of the gold-embroidered vestments and the tall miter rising like a chimney from the top of his head.

But today the metropolitan was not in the mood for celebration. He was going to Nevsky Square, of course, because it was his duty, but his mind was chewing endlessly on the Jewish problem. Confound Boris! Why the king should choose this day, of all days, to disappear into the countryside...

Stefan suddenly realized he was in the middle of a crowd of people. Then a short man dressed in black stepped forward and gave him a frank, apprais-ing stare.

"Rabbi Tsion. How can I help you?"

"I think you know, Metropolitan Stefan." The square-built rabbi ges-tured around him. "The Jews of Sofia have nowhere else to turn. Everywhere we are met with deaf ears. Some of us have had commissariat police raid our houses this morning, on a day of national celebration. Some of us have been subjected to unlawful interrogation and beating. A few have been arrested. If nothing is done, God will punish this nation, Your Eminence, as I warned you in my message of prophecy. You claim to speak on behalf of God. What will you say?"

A few of the other people around Tsion looked away, uncomfortable that such harsh words were directed at the chief cleric of the church in the capital city. But Tsion gave Stefan his customary unyielding, matter-of-fact look, as if he had just asked a question of a student in midrash.

Another rabbi moved up beside Tsion. It was Asher Hananel, the chief rabbi of the Central Synagogue. Hananel was almost in tears.

"This morning, Your Eminence, Rabbi Tsion and I led a great crowd of our people in prayer—a crowd that was locked out of the Central Synagogue, its own house of worship. We are the descendants of the Maccabees, Your Eminence. We know how to die on our own soil."

Stefan looked at the two men, then at the crowd, all wearing yellow stars. He closed his eyes for a moment.

"The ceremonies can wait. Rabbi Tsion, Rabbi Hananel, come with me to my rooms. We can talk there."

Crown Prince Simeon was tugging at his mother's hand. "Come on, Mother! We'll be so far back we won't be able to see anything!"

Daria, walking behind and holding on to Princess Maria-Louisa, headed toward the steps of Alexander Nevsky, dragging behind her a deep sense of dread. She had overheard enough of the worried conversations among the palace diplomatic staff to know that something unexpected might happen today. There was talk that the Communists were trying to organize some kind of protest against the Jewish expulsions. Daria had even heard that some of the young men in the Maccabee and Betar Zionist groups were getting together some kind of plan—she wasn't sure whether it had to do with aiding the protest or preventing it. Daria had always loved Kyril and Methodie Day. But today all she could think of was observing the festivities and getting back behind the palace gates as soon as possible.

Bojilov trailed along behind the tsaritza, the two children, and the Richetti woman. With the crowd gathering for the ceremony at Nevsky, it was easy to keep them in view and still stay concealed. And with all the extra security around the palace, no one gave much thought to one more uniform in the crowd moving along the gold-painted paving stones of Alexander Battenberg Square.

There was no chance of taking her now. Even if he couldn't see the plain-clothes Royal Guards encircling the queen and her party, the crowd around would turn on him like mad dogs if they thought he was threatening the crown prince or his sister.

Where was Dimitrov? Bojilov would never have imagined that the bumpkin from Bailovo would be anywhere except beside his sweetheart today, unless he'd been called away by the king.

And that was another thing. People were saying Tsar Boris was nowhere to be found. Bojilov had never heard of such a thing.

Oh, well… Maybe he had Dimitrov with him, shooting mountain goats somewhere at one of his lodges. So much the better. It would make grabbing the Richetti wench and claiming his hundred thousand from Belev just that much easier. All he had to do was wait for the proper moment. And the way the rumors were running, the moment was likely to create itself.

Boris paced along the ridge line, then paused, bending to examine a small pattern of lichen on a rock. *An excellent example of Acarospora aeruginosa. I don't think I've ever seen it at this low an elevation, though.*

He straightened. As far as he could see, ridge after ridge of the Rila Mountains surrounded him. The silence was crystalline. Since he had left Sergeant Dimitrov at the chalet, he was the only human—indeed, the only moving thing—he had seen.

He lifted his eyes to the heartbreaking blue dome of the sky, and the beauty was almost more than he could bear. Had his Uncle Albert felt the rending pain of such beauty before his fall from the rock? Wouldn't that be a moment in which to die! The self-crushing weight of the glorious creation around you, a single slip of the foot, and you would awaken…where?

Where did kings go who abandoned their country in its hour of greatest need?

No. It wasn't like that. Had he stayed, Filov and the Germans would likely have brought all their pressure to bear. Internment camps could be bad, but at least the people would be alive.

Lord God, please protect my poor country today. And if you have some time left over, please guard my wife and children.

Just down the spine of the ridge, Boris found a rock to rest his back against. There was a little shade—not unwelcome in the late May sun, even at this altitude. He leaned his head back and thought about Sergeant Dimitrov, probably fretting below in the chalet because the sovereign he was sworn to protect was out of his line of vision.

Gabrovski had laid the two documents side by side in front of him. He had explained it all quite carefully and requested Boris's signature on either the order that would authorize the Jews' eviction to the provinces or the writ that would authorize their shipment to the death camps across the Danube.

Boris had signed the eviction order without comment. He slid it across the marble tabletop to the interior minister, who quickly countersigned it and tucked it under his arm. He gave the king a slight bow, then strode quickly from the salon. Boris watched him go: a stocky man in a gray woolen suit, a man who had obtained a signature that meant he had arrangements to make and people to see.

The deportation order still lay on the table. Boris was completely alone in the salon. He picked up the document and tore it down the middle, then tore it again the other way. He slid the pieces into the pocket of his uniform and later slipped them into a burning grate in one of the hallways.

Boris opened his eyes and looked around. He took a deep breath of the mountain air. About five meters away a boulder sat just outside a small ring of pines. As Boris watched, a young rock badger crawled out of a hole beside the boulder and tested the air with its wriggling nose. The small animal sat on its hind legs, facing Boris. He decided to address the animal.

"And by this bold, decisive action, Tsar Boris III, king of the Bulgarians, sentenced his fifty thousand Jewish subjects to humiliation, to exile within the borders of their own country. And then the bold Boris got in his car and drove out of the city, hoping that by the time anyone found him, the awful music would be over and the few dancers left at the party would have already gone home."

The badger's nose was still working at the air.

"And what do you think of such a king, Monsieur Badger?"

The badger raised its head in Boris's direction, jerking it from side to side.

"Can't decide what sort of predator I am, can you?"

The badger sat very still.

"Let me give you some advice, my dear *Meles meles:* if you've got a good hole, you should stay in it if at all possible. If they manage to drag you out, bad things can happen."

Boris stood and tipped his hat to the badger. The animal flinched toward its cover, then halted, watching him.

"Thank you. You've been a most attentive audience," Boris said.

Surely lecturing a badger on politics isn't madder than crowing from the top of a church wall. Especially if the badger seems willing to listen...

Dobri made Svilen read the message once more to make sure he'd gotten it exactly right. Just as he hung up the field telephone, His Majesty walked in the front door. Tsar Boris hung his hat on the hook by the door and propped his walking stick in the rack. He looked at the note in Dobri's hand.

"Well, Sergeant Dimitrov, it appears you've had some messages. Would you care to give them to me?"

"Yes, Your Majesty. Whose do you want first, Interior Minister Gabrovski or Metropolitan Stefan?"

Tsar Boris winced. "The devil's own choice. Still, I think I'd prefer to hear what Stefan has to say. It ought to be entertaining at least."

Dobri read the words he had transcribed from Svilen, who had, in turn, taken them down directly from Chancellor Grouev, he said. Boris listened patiently until Dobri finished.

"Sergeant Dimitrov, I would like you to make a return call to Svilen and have him relay it immediately to Mr. Grouev, who will contact the metropolitan. You are to tell him that we have ordered that all transportees are to be well treated, even those who were taken from the area of Hitler's military command. Now we will again take His Eminence's appeal into account, to offer the maximum possible relief in the course of the implementation of the laws of Bulgaria concerning the Jews' rights and fate within our borders. The Law for the Defense of the Nation was duly passed by our government in consideration of our obligations to our military ally, Germany, and we are not completely free to repeal or cancel its provisions on our own initiative."

Dobri nodded as he wrote down the king's words. When Boris had made a few corrections to the document, he handed it back to Dobri. He went toward the door and reached again for his hat.

"Why don't you make your phone call, Sergeant, while I take a little more mountain air? And then, if someone should happen to ask the whereabouts of the king, you can say with all truthfulness that you don't know." He smiled at Dobri and was gone.

Dobri looked at the paper in his hand, then at the field telephone. He took a deep breath and began turning the generator crank.

Metropolitan Stefan walked out onto Alexander Nevsky Square. He ascended the speaker's stand and took a firm grip on the lectern. Behind him sat Filov, Gabrovski, and many of the other ranking ministers. He made the sign of the cross over the multitude gathered in the square.

"Shall we pray. Oh, Lord, look down upon thy people this day, and sanctify and consecrate to us the memory of the blessed brothers, Saints Kyril and Methodie, thy servants who brought unto thy people in this place the blessings of learning. And may our actions as a nation be as those of the righteous and full of knowledge, and not as those of the wicked who do not follow the path of true wisdom. In the name of the Father and the Son and the Holy Spirit, amen.

"In past years," he said, looking out over the crowd, "we have always enjoyed, on this, our most special national holiday, the participation of all Bulgarians, regardless of race or creed. And rightly so, since the blessings of learning brought to us by the brothers, Saints Kyril and Methodie, extend equally to all men and know no boundary, either geographical, political, or personal.

"But this year our celebration is flawed. It is cheapened and—it is not too strong a word—disgraced by the treatment being accorded our Jewish countrymen. This year we make a mockery of the traditions of Bulgaria, because the Jewish students are not here."

Stefan knew Filov's eyes were boring into his back. He could hear someone behind him nervously clearing his throat.

"Look around you, students. Where are they? Where are the children who stood beside you in previous years? Was there a Leviev in your class? A little girl named Abramova, perhaps? Don't you remember them, children? Don't you remember your classmates who, one day, came to school wearing a yellow star, an emblem forced upon them by an uncaring bureaucracy whose only interest was in marking them out as somehow different from the rest of you? Have you forgotten, children of Bulgaria? Have the men who make the rules also made you—even you—turn your backs on those who yesterday were your playmates?"

A few of the students, standing at rigid attention, shifted their eyes this way and that. Some of them even turned their heads. Some let their eyes fall, as if weighed down by the realization of what they were hearing.

"I stand before you, citizens of Bulgaria, as your spiritual shepherd and appeal to the state authorities not to shackle the freedom-loving, democratic, and instinctively tolerant spirit of our people to any foreign indoctrination, influence, or ultimatum.

"The persecution of Bulgaria's Jews, which is being carried out at this moment, on this day that should be a day of national happiness, is an outrage and a stain on the history of our small but proud land. This criminal discrimination is directly contrary to the spirit of Bulgaria herself. On this day devoted to our great teachers, I beg those who steer the ship of state: you must immediately remove, nullify, and cancel any policy of this government that promotes division, estrangement, and persecution."

Stefan sat down at the end of the dais. The crowd of students and onlookers was clearly stunned by the harshest Saints Kyril and Methodie Day speech they had ever heard. Instead of the traditional praise of the students and the paean to the benefits and blessings of learning, they had received a chastisement.

The leader of the nearest column looked nervously at Stefan and the other dignitaries on the dais, then, rather doubtfully, gave the signal for his class to begin the procession of students. In place of the usual smiles as the students passed the reviewing stand, there were averted eyes.

At the edge of his vision, Stefan could see Filov staring fixedly ahead like a bronze statue of himself. No doubt he was barely able to contain his anger. *Well, let him stew. And I have a few more words for him as soon as the students' parade is finished.*

Daniel Tsion walked with heavy steps toward the synagogue in Yutch Bonar. Metropolitan Stefan was a good man who wanted with all his heart to do justice, Tsion believed. But he wasn't sure even the powerful and fearless metropolitan would be able to sway the determination of the pro-Nazi government majority. Stefan, Madame Karavelova, Nikola Moushanov—all the leading figures of the country who had listened to the delegation in Stefan's house had pledged their unflagging efforts and influence, and Tsion had no doubt they would deliver them. They were all good, moral people. But what good was moral persuasion against an evil that respected only brute force? And Tsar Boris was not in the palace, if reports were to be believed. The old man didn't know what to make of it. The word from the Lord had been as clear in his mind and heart as if he were speaking to a friend sitting in his living room: *There will be a terrible punishment against this nation if my people are harmed.* And yet so far the message had been without effect. As far as he knew, the commissariat police were still hauling people out of their homes and marching them to the central train station.

He heard the sound of a crowd. Tsion looked up and realized that the throng he and Rabbi Hananel had left in front of the synagogue after this morning's prayer service was still there and had even grown. He took a deep breath and squared his shoulders. So. It was time again for the famous mystic Tsion to say some words to his people—some of whom thought he was crazy, especially after his prophetic word. Were they afraid enough by now to listen to one even as crazy as Rabbi Daniel Tsion? Despite himself, he smiled and shook his head. No wonder God had to call prophets. No sane man would apply for the job.

Some of those in the front of the gathering saw Tsion's approach, and they soon quieted the rest. Somebody had dragged a bench from a nearby sidewalk, and the rabbi grunted as he climbed onto it. He looked out across a sea of faces that stared back at him like the mirror of his own fears.

"My people, we have spoken with Metropolitan Stefan. We have sent emissaries to Madame Karavelova, who has pledged her full support. Moushanov and other members of the Sobranje are doing what they can to persuade the prime minister to cancel the evictions."

He could see Nastia Isakova moving among the crowd, whispering in an ear here and there. Tsion knew that she and her fellow Communists had sneaked from house to house in Yutch Bonar last night after the curfew, rallying everyone they could to come out this morning to "a meeting at the synagogue." Tsion was afraid of the extent to which the Communists might be willing to exploit the atmosphere of dread and hopelessness. No doubt, Vulka Goranova and Betty Danon, though they dared not show their faces in public, were pulling as many strings as they could to ensure the party's influence over the day's events. It was a mark of his own sense of desperation that Rabbi Tsion himself wasn't sure whether that was a good or a bad thing.

"I don't know whether this day will bring deliverance or not," Tsion said. "The story of our people is the story of deliverance beyond all hope, of provision in the midst of poverty, of covenants kept and promises coming to pass when blessing seemed impossible. Maybe today will be a part of that story. But I don't know, my people. The only advice I can give you is to put your trust in the Eternal One."

Tsion closed his eyes and reached skyward; the crowd fell absolutely silent. Maybe he was hoping to grasp a hint, some divine basis for even the merest guess. Maybe he was trying to pull at the sash of heaven, to gain a purchase, to clamber over the sill and see beyond some view he could offer to the people besides the fear and helplessness that covered them now like a shroud.

But there was nothing. He sighed, lowered his arms, and shook his head.

"I'll tell you something else about our story," someone said, jumping onto the bench and bumping Rabbi Tsion roughly to the sidewalk. Tsion looked up. It was Gosho Leviev, one of the young, angry ones.

"Jewish brothers and sisters, we can't accept this situation! Are we going to go meekly to the slaughter? Rabbi Tsion is right: our history is full of liberation coming unlooked for, but sometimes the chosen people have had to strike the first blow, to show the Lord that their hearts were ready to give everything to remain faithful to the promise. Don't forget the Maccabees! Don't forget the patriots of Masada!"

Cheering started somewhere near the middle of the crowd and rippled outward. People were raising their fists in the air. Tsion watched, a great sadness coming over him. Of course they were listening to Gosho. What else could they do except lie down and die?

"I say we go out into the streets and show the commissariat and everybody else what Bulgarian patriots' blood looks like," Leviev shouted. Another man—Tsion thought his name was Assenov—had found a Bulgarian flag. He jumped up on the bench beside Leviev and began waving it. The crowd began chanting; Tsion wasn't even sure what the words were. Leviev and Assenov leaped from the bench and started off up Klementina Boulevard.

Rabbi Tsion watched them go, shaking his head. He understood all too well the urge to fight, to lash out against the oppressor. He felt in his own sinews the need to do harm to the one seeking to harm him.

But it was futile. He had seen it—in no way he could explain, even to himself. He knew that deliverance, if it came, would not be by opposition of arms.

Daniel Tsion had never felt more weary in his life. He turned toward his house. He supposed he should pack a bag and help his wife prepare for the long ride into whatever fate awaited them.

When he reached his small house with its roof of crooked red tiles, two men were standing in front of the door. Sarah stood just inside the open door, weeping and wringing her hands.

"Daniel Tsion, by order of the Commissariat for Jewish Questions, you are under arrest for inciting a riot," one of the men said. "You must come with us."

"Yes, yes, of course I must. May I at least say good-bye to my wife?"

The men looked at each other, and the one who had spoken gave him a tight nod. "Yes, but be quick about it."

Tsion stepped into the doorway and took Sarah in his arms. What words could he say to her? Words of comfort, which might well turn out to be lies?

"There, there, my dear," he said, patting the back of her neck. "There, there."

He touched the mezuzah on the doorpost as he stepped back outside, then turned and had a final look at the front of his house. The stones of the walls were crooked, like the tiles on the roof, yet for almost forty years it had sheltered him and Sarah and the three children they had raised. He raised a hand to Sarah, then turned and walked away with the two men.

"Mother, why was Metropolitan Stefan so angry today?" Crown Prince Simeon asked as they crossed Alexander Battenberg Square, headed back toward the palace gates. "That didn't sound like what he used to say on Kyril and Methodie Day."

"No, my dear. I'm afraid it's a rather unusual Kyril and Methodie Day," Queen Giovanna said, hurrying through the dispersing crowds and looking about her as she went.

"I didn't see anyone with a yellow star like Mademoiselle Richetti's," Simeon said. "Where were they? There are usually a lot of them on the street."

They were almost to the gates when they heard the sound: sirens to the northwest, coming from the direction of the Yutch Bonar. Queen Giovanna and Daria exchanged a worried look.

Daria pushed Princess Maria-Louisa toward her mother. "Quickly, children, get inside the palace with your mother," she said. She turned, slipped between the escorting guards, and ran down Alexander Battenberg in the direction of the noise. She heard Queen Giovanna shouting at her, ordering her back, ordering her to come inside the palace gates with her and the children.

And for the first time in her life, Daria disobeyed her sovereign and friend.

Bojilov's eyes widened as he watched the Richetti woman running away from the palace. He saw the tsaritza shouting after her, saw the children clinging to their mother in fright as their nanny made straight for the one place no Jew in Sofia should be on this particular day.

And he began to smile. This was going to be easier than he thought.

Squads of soldiers were mustering, surrounding the palace. He ran along with them to the place at the north end of the palace where Battenberg Square joined with the short out-turnings of Moskovska and Turnovo streets. Then, at an opportune moment, he slipped away. He turned aside long enough to dash into a shop. The proprietor looked at him with surprise.

"I need your phone," Bojilov said. "There's trouble. Quick!"

The man pointed, and Bojilov grabbed the phone and dialed a number. "Bring the car. There's an alley between Tsar Samuil and Boris I. Park at the east end, out of the street. Got it?"

Bojilov slammed the handset back into the cradle and ran outside, down Dondukov, in the direction he had last seen Daria Richetti running.

26

The last column of students had left Nevsky Square, and the dignitaries were leaving the dais. Stefan strode over to Bogdan Filov and planted himself in front of the prime minister.

"Mr. Prime Minister, you must surely see that nothing is to be gained by persecuting this minority population. Bulgaria is a small country. We have little but our reputation, and that is being compromised by—"

"I am not prepared to discuss this with you, Your Eminence," Filov said. "The veiled demands in your antipatriotic speech are unbecoming a person of your responsibilities and position. You are interfering in matters that do not concern you."

"Since when does human suffering not concern the church?"

"The Law for the Defense of the Nation is a law of necessity, duly enacted by the Sobranje—"

"Except for the parts written in the closed-door sessions of your Fascist cabinet—"

"And as such, this law will not be cancelled; it will be fully implemented. And I warn you," Filov said, jabbing a finger at the metropolitan, "to stop meddling in politics. Your badgering of His Majesty and this government will get you nowhere."

"And your senseless persecution of Jews will get you into the hottest bonfire in hell!" Stefan said as Filov wheeled around and walked away.

The metropolitan shook his head as he watched Filov's receding back.

Ah, Sovereign Lord. Why have you put me in the middle of such wretched days?

He heard the sirens, then saw the soldiers clattering across Battenberg Square and taking up positions around the Royal Palace.

"Lord save us, what's happening now?" Stefan muttered. He would go to his house and call the Central Consistory. Someone there could tell him what was going on.

Daniel Tsion looked up when he heard the shuffling of feet. A group of about ten men was being shoved down the stairs by a squad of police. The police were carrying clubs, and two or three of them had guns drawn. The police manhandled them against the wall, and the gun-wielding officers pointed their weapons at the men while another of them fiddled with a large key chain. The lock on the cell clicked, and the hinges squealed as the guard swung the door open.

"All right, get in there, you filthy kikes, unless you want to be shot where you stand!"

The men against the wall were battered and bloody. Some of them looked to Tsion as if they were no more than thirteen or fourteen. The oldest of them might have been in his thirties. When one of them didn't move fast enough to suit one of the police, he received a jab in the kidneys from a club, which buckled his knees and gave the police a good excuse to kick and club him some more, to set an example for the others.

The cell door clanged shut behind the ten prisoners, who sank to the floor panting and moaning.

"Don't get too comfortable," one of the guards said as the rest of them trooped back upstairs. "There'll be plenty more coming, and you'll have to make room for them."

The prisoner nearest Tsion, lying on his back and bleeding from his mouth, turned his head and saw the rabbi.

"Looks like they were ready for you," Tsion said. He reached out a hand and stroked the young man's sweat-and-blood-soaked hair. "What happened?"

"We turned into Klementina by the synagogue. Some of the Central Consistory Council tried to stop us, but we brushed them off. Then some of the Maccabees and Betar tried to link arms across the intersection of Klementina and Opelchenska to keep us from getting any closer to the palace. But we overran them also—"

The young man coughed, and gobbets of blood spattered the floor between his head and Tsion's leg.

"Be quiet now; save your breath," the rabbi said, stroking the boy's cheek.

"They knew we were coming," another man said, sitting nearby. The entire left side of his face was one angry bruise, and he had bloody spaces where teeth had been knocked out. "The police were there in buses. Then there were mounted police and commissariat guards on motorcycles. They beat us with their rifle butts and their clubs. I saw a woman fall, and three of them dragged her to a commissariat van, kicking her and hitting her with their fists as they went."

"They chased us down the side streets and the alleys," another fellow said. "They rode us down with the horses and threw us into the vans. My little brother was beside me, and they dragged him away from me, threw him in a different van. I was holding on to his arm; he was screaming my name." The man covered his face with his hands.

"They'll hunt us from house to house," someone said. "They'll load us all up and take us to the Germans."

"Has anybody seen Rabbi Hananel?" Tsion said. "Rabbi Hananel? Was he with the crowd when you ran into the police?"

A few shrugged or shook their heads. "There were too many of us, too much going on," one man said. "I didn't see him, but that doesn't mean he wasn't there."

Surely Asher Hananel had enough sense to take himself out of trouble's way, Tsion thought. *Somebody has to try to stay free, to guide the few that remain, to comfort the families with missing ones.*

Daria raced down Dondukov until it reached Maria-Louisa Boulevard. The commotion was off to her right and ahead of her, so she ran north on Maria-Louisa. Soon she started seeing buses lining the wide street, with perhaps hundreds of police getting out of them, all helmeted and carrying clubs and with rifles strapped to their backs.

Were they simply going to start shooting Jews in the streets? She stared at the ranks of forming guards and heard the hoof-clatter of the mounted patrols.

Pirotska Street was to her left and seemed mostly unobstructed. She dashed that way, her heart pounding against her ribs. After a few blocks, the shouting was louder to her right, so she turned down a side street that ran north and emptied onto Tsar Simeon Avenue. And there she stood, frozen by what she was seeing.

Police were battering at a line of marchers, one of whom held a Bulgarian flag and tried to wave it, even as two commissariat guards beat him in the ribs with their clubs. The mounted police rode into the crowd like cavalry, laying about with their clubs as if they were fighting the footmen of an invading army.

Daria realized she was screaming. "They're Bulgarians, you fools! They only want to be heard; they don't want to fight! They're Bulgarians!" She was weeping as she cried out, and soon the words became unintelligible even to her.

And then a hand was clamped over her mouth, and an arm thrown around her waist was squeezing the breath out of her.

"Hello, Miss Reechettee. Remember me? From the Midwinter Ball?" The voice was beside her ear; she felt the scratch of his unshaven face on her cheek. "Where's your boyfriend, Miss Reechettee? Where's Dobri Dimitrov, your knight in shining armor?"

She twisted her head about until she could see his face. It was the drunken soldier Dobri had fought with as they were leaving the ball—Bojilov. Her eyes were wide with fear.

He dragged her back down the side street, then pulled her into an alley. "We'd better move from here, Miss Reechettee, don't you think?" he said as he shoved her in front of him. "Little bit of trouble in this part of town right now, and we can't afford to get mixed up in it, can we? No, we'd better go somewhere else."

He shoved her down the alley. His callused hand was clamped tightly over her nose and mouth; she could barely breathe. She flung her head violently and managed to partially free her mouth.

"Why are you doing this, you beast?" she said. "Where are you taking me?"

"Beast? Is that what you think I am?" he said in a quiet, almost hurt voice.

The next thing Daria felt was his fist slamming into the side of her face. Everything dimmed, but she willed herself not to relinquish consciousness. She had to see, had to notice everything. Surely someone would come to find her. She had to keep her eyes open and her wits about her.

"I know I'm not as charming as your sweet Dobri," Bojilov crooned.

Daria cringed as his lips brushed her ear. "But I'm hardly a beast, Miss Reechettee. Or may I call you Daria? That's your name, isn't it? Daria. Such a lovely name. Such a lovely girl."

She felt the arm clamped around her waist moving upward toward her breasts. She twisted and fought, clawing at his eyes, biting at the hand he tried to clamp over her mouth. She managed to twist halfway around, until she was facing him, and she brought her knee up sharply, landing a solid jolt squarely in his groin.

Bojilov grunted, and his grip slackened. Daria twisted out of his grasp and dashed for the alley entrance. An old, battered car was there, but there was enough room for her to sidestep it and get out onto the next street.

But just as she reached the car, the driver's door flew open, and another man in uniform leaped out. To her horror, Daria realized it was Corporal Sedjiev. He grabbed her.

"I'm sorry, Miss Richetti," Sedjiev said. "I'm sorry. I'm so sorry you're mixed up in all this."

"Corporal Sedjiev, how can you assist this—this animal? Let me go, at once!"

"I'm sorry Miss Richetti." It was all he would say.

Bojilov was limping toward her. The look on his face made Daria want to cry, but she refused to give him the satisfaction.

"Well, you've got some fight, I'll say," Bojilov said when he reached her. He gave her an evil smile. "But that won't matter too much where you're going. They know how to take care of that."

Daria thought of shouting, but with the clamor in the streets nearby, she knew she wouldn't be heard. She forced herself to look Bojilov in the eye. Then she spat in his face.

Bojilov backhanded her, then punched her. He opened the back door of the car.

"Put her in, Sedjiev. You drive. I'd better ride back here with her. Make sure she doesn't do anything else stupid. You know the place."

They shoved Daria into the backseat, and Bojilov got in behind her. "Oh no, my dear, you don't sit in the seat. It wouldn't do for you to be seen by any chance observers, now would it?" He shoved her onto the floor and held her there. Sedjiev got in, and the car started and moved forward, out of the alley, into the street.

Dear God, please… Please…

"Mr. Grouev, I have reliable reports of Jewish homes being ransacked, of innocent Jewish citizens being arrested and held without charge in the city jails, of young Jewish men being beaten nearly to death in the streets of this city… I could go on and on. What will it take to cause His Majesty to act? In the eyes of the world, such criminal assaults against our Jewish citizens can mean only one thing: We are prisoners of Hitler's mad anti-Semitic delusions.

"The prime minister? With all due respect, Mr. Grouev, Bogdan Filov is part of the problem, not part of the solution. Only His Majesty can, once and for all, remove the world's suspicions. He must do something and do it quickly."

Metropolitan Stefan hung up the phone without waiting to hear Grouev's reply. He thought a moment, then picked up his phone again and dialed the number for the nearest telegraph office. He grabbed the note he had written a few moments before.

"This is Metropolitan Stefan. I wish to dictate a cable. It is to be addressed to His Majesty, Tsar Boris III, at the Royal Palace. Yes. The message is, 'Don't persecute, lest you be persecuted yourself.' Stop. 'With the same measure you measure others, you'll be measured.' Stop. 'Know, Boris, that God is watching your acts from heaven.' End of message. What? Yes, I'm certain that's what I want to say. Send it just like that, or so help me, I'll come down there and do it myself!"

Stefan rubbed his eyes. He hadn't slept all night. Each time he phoned the Jewish Central Consistory, the news was worse. Against the advice of the leaders of their community, some young Jews had decided to march to the Royal Palace, to demonstrate their protest against the relocations from Sofia and the other cities. The police and commissariat had been merciless in their repression of the mostly unarmed marchers. Rabbi Tsion had been arrested. Rabbi Hananel was a fugitive in the streets.

Someone was pounding his front door. Stefan pushed himself up from the table and went to the door.

It was Marta Hananel, the rabbi's wife. Stefan quickly opened the door and let her in. The poor woman was near hysteria.

"I told Asher not to come home, and he did it anyway," she said, her words tumbling out one after another. "I told him, 'Asher, they're looking for you; don't come home.' But he did, and now the commissariat has him, and God knows what they'll do with him. Oh, Metropolitan, you're the only hope we have left."

"No, Mrs. Hananel, our hope is in God, where it has always been. Here, sit down. Try to calm yourself. Can you drink some tea?"

When he handed her the glass, he also showed her the note from which he had dictated the telegram to the palace.

"I have tried to warn His Majesty, Mrs. Hananel; other eyes than those in Sofia and Berlin are watching what happens in our country. There is an Eternal Judge, and I only pray that he will be merciful. But if something doesn't change soon…"

The rabbi was brought into the office, half-carried between two commissariat guards. Lily Panitza looked at him and had to resist the urge to put her hand to her mouth. His face was bruised. He held his arms around his middle like someone protecting a wound. She went over and put her hand beneath the rabbi's elbow, gently supporting his shoulders with her other arm.

"This way, please. The commissar has asked to speak to you."

Hananel managed a weak nod, and Lily escorted him toward Alexander's office. She knocked, then opened the door. Alexander was facing the doorway, and he started shouting at Hananel as soon as he saw him.

"Why do you Jews keep trying to influence the king and the rest of the government? Don't you know that the government has entrusted this commissariat with your fate? This morning your wife was seen going to the house of that provoker of unrest, Metropolitan Stefan. I despise Stefan! You and your troublemaking people are the enemies of our country!"

The battered, exhausted man standing beside Lily drew himself as straight as he could. He looked at Alexander and said, "Mr. Commissar, you have no right to insult me or my people in this way. I was an officer in the Bulgarian army. I fought in the war; I was wounded and received the Cross of Valor from the tsar himself. This is my country as much as it is yours."

"Shut up! Shut up, do you hear me? Your words are fine for Metropolitan Stefan. They don't impress me. You and your people have been parasites on the body of this nation for years, hoarding your wealth and driving up prices. You're just waiting for the Bolsheviks to come in and give everything to you, and the only thing standing between Bulgaria and your greed is the German army. The Germans understand your kind, all right! They know what should be done with the likes of you. I only wish..."

Alexander looked out the window, and when he spoke, it was as if he had forgotten anyone else was in the room.

"I only wish you didn't have soft-hearted friends in high places. Then we could do with you as we like—as we should!" He swung around again to face Hananel. "Yes, you'd better be thankful for those who support you. And one day soon even that won't be enough. One day I'll have every one of you shipped out of this country to the place where you really belong!"

"Why did you bring me here, Mr. Commissar? Just to shout at an old man who can't possibly do you any harm?"

Alexander gritted his teeth. "Miss Panitza, this man is free to go. We can't hold him any longer. But I warn you," he said, pointing a finger at the rabbi, "you're under house arrest. If you stick one foot outside, I'll have you thrown back in jail. You are not to contact any authorities under any circumstances except through me or my organization. Is that clear?"

"Quite clear, Mr. Commissar."

"Get him out of my sight."

Dobri drove the Packard to the garage and turned the keys over to the chief mechanic. Then he hurried to the palace. He and Tsar Boris had been gone for three days, and judging from the calls he had received on the field telephone and the king's replies he had transmitted back, he guessed that yesterday's Kyril and Methodie Day was anything but typical.

After all he had heard and what he had managed to put together for himself, Dobri longed more than anything to see Daria and know for himself she was safe. He checked in with the officer of the watch and hurried toward the private wing of the palace.

Tsar Boris had gone no farther than the anteroom on the second floor. Tsaritza Giovanna was there, and the look on her face as she spoke to her husband made Dobri's heart pound with alarm. They both looked at him as he came in.

"I beg your pardon, Your Majesties, I was actually looking for Miss Richetti. I had no idea... I didn't mean to interrupt." He turned to go.

"No, stay, Sergeant Dimitrov," Tsar Boris said. "Dobri, I... A terrible mistake has been made."

Dobri stared at the king. He had called him "Dobri" in front of the queen. He felt the blood roaring in his ears, felt the sinews around his knees trembling, like cables with too much weight on them. Still, he kept his eyes locked on Tsar Boris's and waited to hear whatever doom was about to be pronounced.

But it was the queen who moved first. She came to him and put her hand on his arm. She told him what happened the day before, when the sound of the sirens in Yutch Bonar had drawn Daria, despite everything the queen could do.

Dobri's eyes flickered from the queen to Tsar Boris.

"Gone? And no word from her?"

A single tear trickled from Queen Giovanna's eye. She gave the slightest shake of her head.

"Dobri, I swear to you that no effort will be spared," Tsar Boris said. "We will find her and bring her back here, where she belongs."

Where she belongs... That was the trouble, Dobri realized. Daria thought she was going where she belonged when she ran to the aid of her people being truncheoned by police on horseback. She disobeyed the queen because she was obeying a higher calling.

And if he had been here yesterday, where would his place have been? With the oppressors or the oppressed?

He realized the king was speaking to him.

"Please forgive me, Your Majesty. I...I didn't hear what you said."

Tsar Boris's eyes peered into him, a soft gray green that seemed to pierce him like a searchlight. But there was no anger—only understanding and sympathy. "Dobri, I asked you to go to your commander and tell him I wish to see him immediately. And after you have sent him to me, tell Chancellor Grouev that I must see him at once."

An order to carry out.

Clinging to the thought like a lifeline, Dobri saluted, wheeled about, and was gone.

Boris looked at his wife. "We'll find her, Giovanna. I swear it."

She returned his look for several seconds. She tried to smile but couldn't manage it. She turned away and said over her shoulder, "When you can, you'd better come see the children. They've been worried about…things."

"I don't care what the decree says, Father Nikolai. This supposed relocation to the outlying areas of the country is only the first step. They started shipping them from the central station in Sofia this morning, and there hasn't been any letup. Of course the commissariat means to send the Jews to the Germans. Now, as I told you, I am contacting all the churches and authorizing the priests to baptize any Jew who comes professing such a desire. No, of course they won't have been catechized. These are desperate times, Father! We are trying to save these people's lives; we'll tend to their immortal souls later. Now will you do as I say or not? That's better. And when you've baptized them, be sure you contact the local registry office of the commissariat and notify them that the religion of the person has been changed from Jewish to Orthodox. We'll beat these scoundrels at their own game."

Stefan hung up the phone. Some of these small-town priests didn't understand the urgency of the situation.

He smiled to himself; he'd heard reports that lines were forming at some of the smaller churches in Sofia. The would-be converts were avoiding Nevsky, the Russian Church, and Sveta Nedelia, of course, because of their proximity to the center of the city and the government offices. But elsewhere Jews were asking to be baptized, and Stefan intended to make sure his priests accommodated the demand.

His telephone rang.

"Your Eminence, this is Sarafov, director general of the Ministry of Religion. We have reports that Jews are seeking baptism in order to avoid the consequences of the government regulations. I must inform you that we have decided not to recognize the validity of any baptismal certificate issued to any Jew since January 1 of this year. They cannot avoid relocation by some last-minute farce of conversion."

"Since when does the Ministry of Religion or any other government department decide who is and who isn't an Orthodox Christian?"

"Your Eminence, this charade you are carrying out is in direct defiance of the Law for the Defense—"

"Since, in my opinion as the chief prelate of the Pravoslav Church of Bulgaria, this latest decision of yours flies in the face of the mission of the holy church, I shall compose a letter that will go to each priest in every parish in Bulgaria and reaffirm that any person, regardless of former religious background, who wishes to be baptized should immediately be granted this request."

There was a long silence on the line. Sarafov cleared his throat. "Your Eminence, I hope you appreciate the significance of what you're doing. Interior Minister Gabrovski—"

"Oh, so that's who's really jerking your chain, is it? This isn't about the Ministry of Religion at all, is it, Sarafov? Well, you can tell Interior Minister Gabrovski exactly what I said. In fact, you can tell him that by this time three days from now, every parish priest in the whole country will be talking about the relocation of the Sofia Jews and also informing his congregation of the official position of the church."

Stefan slammed down the phone. He flung himself up from his desk and paced his study. "Won't recognize the validity of the baptisms! Who do these idiots think they are?"

He stuck his head into the hallway and shouted for his clerk. Anton Dunovski came hurrying toward the study. "Anton, I need you to take a letter. At the moment I'm so angry I don't think I can hold a pen."

The young man scooted into a chair in front of Stefan's desk and waited, pen in hand. Stefan dictated the letter to the parish priests, just as he had promised Sarafov. When he had finished, he said, "See that this is typed and enough copies are made to send to every parish in the country. And, Anton, I want it done by tomorrow morning."

Dunovski nodded and hurried from the room.

A few minutes later the phone rang again. It was Sarafov again.

"What does Gabrovski want now, Mr. Sarafov?" Stefan said.

"The, ah, Interior Ministry has determined that, in order to prevent excesses in connection with the baptism of the Jews, the Sofia churches will be closed for a while."

For approximately seven seconds, Stefan was too astounded to speak.

"Do I understand you correctly, that the interior minister thinks he can take under his authority the governance of the churches of this city?" Stefan said, in a voice so soft that it surprised even himself.

"Ah…yes, I believe that's the gist of it," Sarafov said.

"The church shall not obey this order! I protest against this miscarriage of law, I defy the interior minister to carry out his directive, and I shall order the Sofia churches to hold services according to the usual schedule!"

Stefan strode across his study and yanked open the door. "Dunovski!"

The clerk stepped into the hallway. "Yes, Your Eminence?"

"That letter I gave you—I want it typed and copied and ready for mailing by this afternoon! And be sure to send a copy to the attorney general!"

He went back into his office and grabbed his phone. He dialed the number for the sitting president of the Holy Synod, Metropolitan Neofit, in Vidin.

"Father Neofit? Stefan here. You won't believe what this government is trying to do now."

Daria hadn't been able to feel her arms or legs since sometime during the night. She was tied to a chair in a dark room. A rag was stuffed in her mouth, and her jaws were tied shut; the strips of dirty cloth around her head were so tight they were cutting into her skin.

From the sound of the traffic outside, she was on the bottom floor of a building somewhere not far from the central station. She could hear the trains coming and going, the clanging of the cars as they were changed. She wondered how many of her people had already been loaded onto trains and sent out of Sofia. She wondered which train she would be on and how soon.

On the way to this place, Bojilov had lain on top of her to keep her from raising herself enough to be seen. The smell of his breath on her face, his hands groping her, the things he whispered in her ear—it nearly turned her stomach inside out.

"Stop it!" she said once, her face muffled by the floorboard of the car.

"Come on, Sergeant," Sedjiev said from the front seat. "We're in deep enough already. Don't make it worse."

"You're just jealous, Corporal," Bojilov said. "Too bad you can't take a turn guarding Miss Ree*chett*ee."

Daria was actually relieved when they reached their destination. They had parked the car beside the building, then Bojilov had tied her wrists behind her back and blindfolded her. "If you try to call attention to us, Miss Ree*chett*ee, the knife I have pressed against your back will pierce your lungs and heart so quickly that you'll be dead before you hit the pavement. You'll be just another dead Jew for the street sweepers to find during the night. Do you understand?" He let her feel the point of his blade between her shoulder blades, and she nodded.

He shoved her into the building, then into the room where he tied her. "You should be thankful," he said as he bound her. "You don't have to stay in jail with the others. It wouldn't do to have Tsar Boris's favorite Jew somewhere she might be found by a nosy palace guard named Dimitrov, now would it? No, you'll stay right here until it's time for your train to leave."

"Sergeant, when do I get my money?" said Sedjiev, watching nervously as Bojilov finished securing his prisoner.

"Shut up, Sedjiev. You'll get paid when I do, all right?"

"They'll come looking for her, Sergeant," Sedjiev said. "Tsar Boris will never rest. If anybody finds out—"

Bojilov spun around and grabbed the corporal by the throat. "And if you don't stop your whining, boy, you won't be spending your money anyway. Got it? Now go get those civilian clothes out of the car. We've got to get rid of these uniforms."

Sedjiev left; he wouldn't look at Daria.

She'd been here all of one night and maybe half a morning. She was stiff from being tied to the chair, and her throat was burning with thirst.

Then someone had come in the other room—apparently someone Bojilov and Sedjiev were expecting. Through the closed door into the adjoining room, she could hear the voice of Bojilov and another man's voice that wasn't familiar to her. It sounded as though an argument was building between them.

27

I want to be very clear on this, gentlemen," Tsar Boris said, letting each man at the table feel, in turn, the full weight of his sternest look. "This young woman has been in Her Majesty's family since the queen was scarcely more than a girl herself. I will not tolerate any laxity in your efforts. Chief Chavdarov, if you must post an officer at every gate of every train station in this city, and if they must personally inspect each woman who embarks, that is no more than I expect. Do you understand?"

The chief of police nodded. Tsar Boris turned to the chief of royal security.

"Captain Kalayev, I expect to be kept informed of any rumor, any hearsay, anything at all unusual that might provide a clue to Miss Richetti's whereabouts. And when those responsible are found, they will be shown no mercy. Is that clear?"

"You can be sure of it, Your Majesty."

"Unfortunately, I must be away on urgent diplomatic business. I expect to be gone three days. When I return, I will want a full briefing. And, Captain Kalayev?"

"Yes, Your Majesty?"

"It is my special desire that you involve Sergeant Dimitrov in your efforts as much as possible. He will be staying here; I've made other security arrangements that I believe are more than adequate. I think you know Sergeant Dimitrov is…very close to Miss Richetti."

Dobri bowed his head, partly from embarrassment and partly from gratitude. He had assumed he would be on the plane to Austria in the morning. It was probably wise, actually: a man whose heart was breaking with worry didn't make the most attentive bodyguard, no matter how professional he claimed to be.

"I understand, Your Majesty," Kalayev said. "We'll keep Sergeant Dimitrov informed."

"Very well then. Mr. Grouev, have you spoken yet to the officials at the commissariat?"

"I am scheduled for an interview with Mr. Belev this afternoon, Your Majesty."

"Good. I know you'll convey the gravity with which we view this situation."

"I shall do my best, Your Majesty."

"I'm telling you, every informer and secret police agent in Sofia will be swarming this area. She's the queen's personal servant. Don't you understand that? I say we get her on the next train out of here and be finished with her." It was Bojilov's voice.

Then the other man said something in a calmer tone, which Daria couldn't quite make out, except for the words *special* and *timing*.

"That's all fine for you," Bojilov said, "but we're the ones with our necks on the line. Unless…" Then he said something in a quieter voice.

"I wouldn't try something like that if I were you," the other man said, his voice rising now. "I didn't get where I am by not knowing how to cover my tracks. They'll never trace her back to me. You'll be hanged as a deserter or worse, and the money you could've had will still be right where it is. So don't get any ideas."

Bojilov grumbled something inaudible. Then Daria heard Sedjiev's complaining tone. The other man said something short. There were quick footsteps, and Daria heard the street door open and close.

Bojilov made a noise like an animal roaring, and Daria heard a fist slamming into the door in front of her. Then the door opened, and he stalked toward her, a teeth-bared scowl on his face.

"Well, Miss Ree*chett*ee, it sounds as if you'll be our guest a little longer than I planned. I suppose we'll have to feed you something, give you something to drink. I don't think they're taking corpses on the trains—not yet, at least.

"Sedjiev!" he said over his shoulder. "Go buy some bread and cheese. And find something to fill with water. And if there's enough money left over, a little *rakia* might be nice." He turned back toward Daria. He leaned over her and leered into her face. "Don't you think so, Miss Ree*chett*ee?"

When the men from Sofia began to arrive at the camp, Buko really started to worry. There were lawyers, doctors—people of position and influence. A few women came off the trains too and were hustled off to the women's camp that Buko and some of his fellow conscripts had hastily constructed on the other side of the dusty road that led into Kermon, the nearest village.

In the huts at night, all the whispered talk was speculation about the possible meaning of this latest round of deportations.

"'Relocations,' they're calling them," said Sirko Danielov, who said he'd owned a tailor shop on Dondukov Boulevard, just down the street from the headquarters of the commissariat. "They kept telling us, 'You will be sent to camps in the interior of the country, where you will complete work projects.' But everyone's afraid of the next train—the one going north to the Danube."

"My wife and daughters are in that camp over there," another man said, pointing toward the camp across the road. "What are they going to have the women do?"

"Whatever they can think of," said Levov, a man who had been at the camp as long as Buko. "They don't care what happens to any of us here, man or woman."

"Rabbi Hananel and the others at the Central Consistory are doing everything they can," said another man. "And Metropolitan Stefan gives them fits every chance he gets."

"God bless him," someone said. "Amen," said another.

Boris liked best to sit in the cockpit, beside Hans Bauer, Hitler's personal pilot. Bauer humored Boris's fascination with all things mechanical, talking endlessly with him about aerodynamic theory, the latest gadgets on the Fuehrer's Junkers, whatever crossed Boris's mind. Since Boris's interest was surpassed only by his knowledge, Bauer actually found himself enjoying the time spent with his royal copilot and sometimes said so. He even allowed

Boris to take the control on a few occasions, and Boris was sure the pure delight on his face as he operated the aircraft reminded Bauer of his children on Christmas morning.

"We are about thirty kilometers from Salzburg Airport, Your Majesty," Bauer said to the king.

"Thank you, Captain Bauer. I suppose I should go in the back and make sure I'm ready to present Bulgaria's best face to the Fuehrer."

Bauer nodded and smiled. Boris and the real copilot sidled past each other in the doorway of the cockpit, and Boris walked back down the aisle to the seats where Bardarov, Balan, and Svilen were waiting.

"Well, we're beginning the final descent, Bauer says. Svilen, you brought the case with the medals?"

"As always, Your Majesty."

"Colonel, please bear in mind at all times that the Russian front is a dangerous topic for us. You should certainly not offer our hosts an easy lead in that direction, and if the subject does come up, you must be as noncommittal as possible."

Bardarov nodded.

Boris leaned back in his seat and closed his eyes, trying to clear his mind for the diplomatic slalom course ahead. *Mustn't let him think Bulgaria is wavering in her support, but mustn't commit troops to the eastern front. Stay away from the Jewish question. Play down any rumors about feelers to the West. Be as encouraging as possible, without giving away resources we can't afford.*

The wheels scraped against the tarmac, and as the Junkers taxied toward the gate, Balan had his binoculars out, inspecting the welcoming committee.

"Goering is there, surely," Boris said. He knew the Reichsmarshall was supposed to meet with him on this trip.

"Actually, I don't see him, Your Majesty," Balan said.

"Really? Hmm. Here, Svilen. Take back the Air Force Eagle, and give me the Austrian Military Merit Cross. The Fuehrer should appreciate an award from his homeland, and that can't hurt anything."

Svilen put the diamond-studded eagle back in the valise and handed Boris the red-and-white ribbon with the large cross in matching colors, awarded to Boris when he was the crown prince, patrolling the trenches alongside the kaiser's own troops during the Great War. Boris pinned the cross in a prominent place on his uniform, and then it was time to line up to exit the aircraft.

Hitler greeted Boris with his usual warmth. "Your Majesty, how good of you to come on such short notice," he said, saluting and then giving Boris's hand a hearty shake.

"I was a bit surprised that Reichsmarshall Goering isn't here. I was under the impression he had specifically requested some time with me."

Hitler's smile chilled slightly. "The Reichsmarshall was indisposed today. He can join us later, if you like."

"Yes, if it's convenient."

So it's true, Boris thought. *Goering and Hitler are at odds these days. Interesting.*

As they walked toward the waiting cars, Boris, as was his habit, fell back a bit to greet Hitler's attendants.

"So good to see you again, Your Majesty," one of them said. He leaned close and half whispered. "The Fuehrer is always in a good mood when he knows you are coming. It makes things more pleasant for all of us, if you take my meaning."

"So happy to be of service, Herr Linder," Boris said, clapping the fellow on the shoulder. "It's good to be back in your beautiful country."

I only wish I really felt that way.

"Mr. Belev, this woman is practically a member of the queen's family," Pavel Grouev said. "I hope you understand that His Majesty holds your office responsible for finding and returning her."

"My office had nothing to do with this," Alexander said, his eyes flickering toward Lily to make sure she was recording everything that was said. "You can search the files yourself, Chancellor; Daria Richetti's name is not on any list of Jews scheduled for relocation."

Of course not, Alexander. You penciled it in, as you thought of it. Then you erased it, very carefully. Maybe even typed a whole new sheet, just so no one would ever see the erasure.

"Be that as it may, this is the Commissariat for Jewish Questions, Mr. Belev. His Majesty and the government have entrusted you with the orderly execution of your…duties. And Miss Richetti was expressly beyond the scope of those duties. His Majesty would view with great favor any assistance you could provide."

"With all due respect, Chancellor Grouev, how do you know this woman has been transported? How do you know she hasn't simply tired of her work in the palace and gone off with some traveling salesman to start a life somewhere else, more to her liking?"

Pavel Grouev slapped his hands on the desk and thrust himself to his feet. Lily's eyes widened. Chancellor Grouev was widely known for his even temper, his absolute control and calm, even in the most stressful situations. Alexander had clearly crossed a line.

"Mr. Belev, regardless of what you so flippantly suggest, I am here by direct order of His Majesty, and I am telling you that you had better, at the very least, give the appearance of doing your best to find Miss Richetti. Do I make myself clear?"

Alexander stared at the older man for a long moment. Then he nodded.

"Very well. I'll be back in two days to receive your progress report." Grouev nodded toward Lily, settled his hat firmly on his head, and strode out of the office.

Lily stared at Alexander. "Aren't you afraid at all?"

"Of whom? Grouev? The palace? They can't blame anything on me."

"Is there anything for them to blame on you?"

He gave her a hard stare. "Just transcribe those notes. And quit asking so many questions."

Boris had requested that his visit to Berchtesgaden be kept secret, so his host had installed him in the Bechsteinhaus, the smaller chalet next door to the Berghof, where important diplomatic guests usually stayed. The talk over a light lunch this day was all of Hitler's worries about Italy and the North African campaign. "If the Americans land in Sicily, we'll have some serious rethinking to do," Hitler said.

"If, on the other hand, they open a front on the Peloponnesus or western Greece, Bulgaria's support could become crucial," said Ribbentrop, seated on the other side of Hitler.

They're thinking south and west, rather than north and east, Boris thought. *That's something.*

"We believe Bulgaria should extend its occupation of Serbia and Thrace," Ribbentrop said. "Perhaps as far as Salonika."

"I beg to differ, Herr Reichsminister," said Boris. "Your Italian allies will see that as undermining their interests in the region. I believe Salonika should remain under German administration, for the benefit of the pact."

Hitler pursed his lips and nodded. "That could be true, Your Majesty. Perhaps we ought to send a military mission to your country to take a closer look, make a more informed assessment."

"That seems wise, Your Excellency," Boris said.

"I suppose it couldn't hurt," Ribbentrop conceded.

"And if I may be so bold, Your Excellency, if Bulgaria is to extend its duties in the Balkans, there is still a matter of some outstanding armaments that were agreed to but never delivered."

"Yes, yes, we'll see to all that." Hitler rang for the maître d' and ordered the dessert course. "I've got a new schnapps I want you to try after dessert, Your Majesty," Hitler said with a mischievous smile. "I think you'll find it rivals your *slivovitza* for potency."

"What are you trying to do, Your Excellency," Boris said with a laugh, "get me drunk in the middle of the day and then have me sign something I'll regret tomorrow?"

Hitler chuckled. "Your Majesty, I wouldn't use schnapps for that."

Now Ribbentrop was grinning. Boris gave Hitler a slightly confused look, then smiled politely.

During the briefings that afternoon by a succession of German generals, Boris listened intently for any hint of how things were going on the Russian front, but the topic was conspicuous by its absence. Now and then, there was mention of "holding positions in the north" or "strategic fallbacks in preparation for a major breakout," but no details were forthcoming. Instead, most of the talk seemed to focus on the Germans' concern with the Balkans and the possibility of a southern European front being opened by the Western allies. Once again, it began to appear that his fears of a German demand for Bulgarian troops to move north toward Russian were unfounded—at least for the time being. And the Jewish question never came up at all.

Dobri came into his duty station and stared in surprise at the corporal sitting at the dispatch desk.

"Zabounov? What are you doing here? Today's Sedjiev's day, isn't it?"

Zabounov shrugged. "He called in sick."

"Oh. Anything going on I need to know about?"

Zabounov shuffled through the papers on top of the desk, then wheeled around to look in the folders in the wall racks behind him. "Doesn't look like it. The tsaritza's going to visit one of the hospitals this afternoon, but that detail's already covered. The captain thought it might be smart, considering everything—"

Zabounov gave Dobri a guilty look. "Oh, Sergeant. I'm sorry. I didn't mean—"

"No matter, Corporal. Just make sure you mark me off on the duty roster."

"Yes, Sergeant."

Dobri started out the door, then half turned back toward Zabounov. "When did Sedjiev call, exactly?"

Zabounov looked at a clipboard. "Around four o'clock yesterday, looks like."

"Poor fellow. He must have something bad to know that far in advance. Well, all right then. Carry on."

"Yes, Sergeant."

Dobri walked out of the duty station and down the hallway of the palace. Something was nagging at him, but he couldn't put his finger on it. Something about Sedjiev.

Anatoly Sedjiev was a small-town boy, like many of the noncommissioned recruits in the Bulgarian army. His story was probably a lot like Dobri's: not much opportunity where he was, a chance to draw regular pay and eat fairly predictable meals. Sedjiev wasn't exactly one of the best and brightest, but he had managed to get himself assigned to the Royal Guard, so he must have something going for him somewhere. Dobri had always liked

Sedjiev well enough. That was why, when he needed a driver for his night with Daria at the Midwinter Ball…

The Midwinter Ball…Bojilov… *She's one of Tsar Boris's pet Jews. Did you know that, Dimitrov?*

Dobri spun and sprinted back to the duty station. "Zabounov! Get me the commander of the Bankia barracks!"

Wide-eyed, Zabounov grabbed the phone, quickly consulted a list of the military installations around Sofia, and dialed a number. Dobri could barely hold still, waiting for the phone to be answered.

"Colonel Bouresh, please. It's the Royal Guard calling."

Dobri grabbed the phone from the corporal and waited for what seemed an eternity for the colonel's voice on the phone.

"Yes, what is it, Kalayev? Haven't you boys at the palace got anything better to do than bother working soldiers?"

"Colonel, I beg your pardon, sir, but this is Sergeant Dobri Dimitrov of the Royal Guard. I apologize for the breach in protocol, but I need to ask you a simple question on a matter of great urgency, sir."

There was a long silence, and Dobri prayed silently that Bouresh didn't give him a round cursing for presuming to call a superior officer and then hang up.

"Well, what is it?" Bouresh said finally.

"Sir, I simply need to know if Sergeant Lyuben Bojilov is on duty today, sir."

"Bojilov… Bojilov… Oh, yes, the shooting-range instructor. What do you want with him?"

"Sir, I beg of you, all I want to know is if he's on duty."

"Well, by all the saints, Dimitrov, hold on a minute, and I'll see if I can find out." There was a rustle on the phone, and Bouresh's next words were muffled. "Hey! Lieutenant Blagoev! Check out at the firing range and see if Feldwebel Bojilov is on duty today."

"Bojilov?"

"Yeah, some boot polisher up at the palace wants to know."

Dobri waited, and waited, and waited some more. After nearly seven minutes, he heard an indistinct voice some distance from the phone at the

Bankia barracks commander's office. He couldn't tell what the messenger was saying. Then he heard a clunk as Bouresh picked up the phone.

"Hmm? That's odd. Hello, Dimitrov? My man says Bojilov's been gone for four days on family leave, according to his commanding officer. Says his mother is sick somewhere in the southern part of Sofia, and he's the only one she's got who can—"

"Colonel, thank you very much. That's all I need to know. Thank you."

Dobri tossed the phone toward Corporal Zabounov and dashed out the door toward Captain Kalayev's office.

Captain Kalayev, with Dobri at his heels, pounded up the stairs of the small building where Sedjiev's apartment was located. "What's the number again?" the captain asked.

"Two seventeen," Dobri said as they reached the second-floor landing. "This way," he urged, hurrying along the dark hallway to the right.

They reached the door. Kalayev knocked loudly. "Corporal Sedjiev, this is Captain Kalayev. Open the door immediately."

Up and down the hallway, doors were opening; curious faces poked into the passage.

Kalayev knocked again. "Sedjiev, if you can hear me, open this door." He waited a few seconds, then turned to one of the other men. "Break it down."

The burly soldier kicked the door three times, and on the third kick the latch splintered from the frame. Dobri, Kalayev, and the four other guards spilled into Sedjiev's apartment, weapons drawn. They went through both rooms of the tiny flat, throwing furniture about, looking behind every door, even tossing clothing out of closets and shoving aside the scant provisions in the tiny pantry.

"He isn't here, Captain," one of the men said. "Hasn't been for a while, from the look of it."

Kalayev looked at Dobri. "Well, your hunch was correct, Sergeant. But why would Sedjiev get mixed up with a no-good like Bojilov? And why would either of them do something so crazy as grabbing the queen's personal assistant?"

"I can't explain it, sir. But that night at the Midwinter Ball, I had the feeling that he really hated Daria—Miss Richetti—simply because she was Jewish. And the fact that I have the job he was fired from didn't help anything."

"Sir, this may be something," one of the other men said, holding up a piece of paper. "There's an address here. Does anybody know what Sedjiev's handwriting looks like?"

Kalayev took the paper. "Lom Street, one forty-seven. Over by the central station."

Dobri was already running for the stairs.

Stefan opened his door.

"Ah! Dimitar! Thank you so much for coming."

The writer gave the metropolitan a little bow. "Your Eminence, how could I do anything else? You sounded most urgent."

"Please, come sit down. I've got some freshly brewed tea…unless you'd care to join me in something stronger?"

"Tea will be fine." Stoyanov seated himself in one of the large, overstuffed armchairs in Stefan's parlor. The room was awash in the vigorous sunlight of spring. Stefan handed his guest a steaming cup, then poured himself another glass of *slivovitza*. He took a large swallow, then seated himself across from Dimitar Stoyanov. The writer took a sip of his tea, then set the cup carefully back in the saucer. He smoothed his flowing white mustache and waited for the metropolitan to speak.

"Dimitar, I need an emissary to the palace."

He cocked his bushy white eyebrows in a surprised expression. "My dear Metropolitan! I've never known you to be one who lets anyone speak on his behalf."

Stefan shook his head. "No, listen. Things have gotten completely out of hand. I've berated Filov from the pulpit. I've cajoled and urged His Majesty in every forum and on every occasion I could use. And still the Jews are being shipped to God knows where. I need someone who can speak to Tsar Boris with a fresh voice—someone whom he respects. Someone like the eminent author Ellin Pellin."

Stoyanov took another sip of tea. "And what shall I say to the king, I wonder, that hasn't already been said?"

"I don't know. Remind him of your long personal friendship. Appeal to his humanitarian instincts. Talk about protecting Bulgaria's reputation. Anything, Dimitar! Our citizens are in desperate danger of being sent out of this country, and once that happens, their fate is sealed. You know this. Please, Dimitar, as a patriot and as a caring human being, you must speak to His Majesty. I've said everything and said it every way I can think of, with little effect. Dimitar, help me."

Stoyanov took a deep breath. He stared at a corner of the ceiling beyond Stefan. "These are dreadful times, aren't they, Your Eminence? What has our country come to, that it has become so difficult for the voices of sensible men to be heard?" He looked at the metropolitan. "Yet I will do what I can. I will go to Tsar Boris. I'll say…something. What else can I do?"

"Thank you, Dimitar. God bless you." Stefan took another draft of liquor. More to himself than to his guest, he said, "I only hope it's not too late."

28

T he carful of Royal Guards drove slowly past the address, then parked
around the corner.

"There's an alley between 147 and the building on this side of the block," Kalayev said. "Dochev, you cover it in case they try to come out the back way. Kurtev, you work your way around the buildings to the opposite side, maybe in the opening of that alley, in case they come around that way. Ghergiev, you stay here with the car and watch this side. Dimitrov and I will go around the front. Keep your eyes and ears open. This may be nothing, or they may be here. Either way, we can't afford mistakes."

The men nodded.

"All right, Dobri. Let's go see if we can find Miss Richetti."

As Dobri and Captain Kalayev left the vehicle, the other men deployed silently behind them. They edged along the building, ducking beneath the few windows on the street, until they rounded the front on the short street named after the city on the Danube far to the north. Around the corner was Sveta Nedelia Church. *If they are here, they are hiding right out in the open,* Dobri thought. Sometimes crowds gave the greatest concealment. Besides, Lom Street was on the side away from Maria-Louisa Boulevard, so it was more of a side street than a main thoroughfare, the kind of place people pass every day on the way to work but never really notice.

They had reached the front door. Pressed against the wall, Kalayev reached over and silently tried the latch. It was locked. He motioned for Dobri to take a covering position on the other side of the door. Dobri quickly crossed in front of the captain and flattened himself against the wall. Both drew their side arms.

Two black-clad old women, most likely on their way to the church, stopped and stared for a moment, then hurried away.

As Dobri watched, his heart pounding, Kalayev held out one finger, then two, then three. Then he whirled about to face the door and slammed his boot into it, breaking the latch.

As they rushed into the room, Dobri had a fleeting glance of a wide-eyed Sedjiev, sitting at a small table with a piece of bread in his hand. He flung his arms up and tried to say something, but his mouth was full of bread, and Dobri was already spinning toward the other corner of the room, where Bojilov was leaping for his service revolver on a shelf by the wall. Two shots rang out, and holes appeared in Bojilov's shirt, just below his armpit. He clattered to the floor, his hand brushing the revolver on its way down, knocking the weapon off the shelf.

Dobri wheeled to cover Sedjiev, but the corporal hadn't moved; he was still sitting at the table with his hands in the air, a piece of bread in one of them.

"It was Bojilov, I swear it. I told him it was wrong, it was stupid, but he said the money was good and—"

"Shut up, Sedjiev," Captain Kalayev said, ejecting the two spent shells from his weapon. Training it again on the inert Bojilov, the captain reached out a foot and nudged the body on the floor.

"Well, I guess they'll be hiring a new shooting-range instructor at Bankia," Kalayev said. "Sergeant Dimitrov, I think I can manage in here. Why don't you check that other room?" He nodded toward the closed door in the wall facing Dobri.

Dobri opened the door, and, thank God and all the saints, she was there, wide eyed with fear but alive. The reality of seeing her was more than he had dared even to dream about for the last several days.

He realized his gun was still drawn. He shoved it into his holster and fell upon her. He kissed her cheek and tore at the strips of cloth binding her face and stroked her hair and cried and pulled at the cords holding her arms to the chair.

"Oh, Daria. I thought I'd never see you again." His voice was soggy with emotion, but he didn't care. "I was so afraid that I wanted to die rather than face the rest of my life without seeing your face again."

He loosed the cords binding her jaws, and she spat out the wad of cloth and leaned toward him. He drank in the sight of her mouth, her eyes, her cheeks, her forehead. He covered her face with kisses and rested his head on her shoulder and wept as if he had been the one who was lost and she had found him.

"When you get the chance, Sergeant, you might untie her legs," Kalayev suggested, grinning as he leaned in the doorway. "Hello, Miss Richetti. It's very good to see you again."

"Captain Kalayev." She nodded gravely. "Thank you."

He gave her a small bow, then turned away.

She couldn't stand; her legs were completely numb. Dobri lifted her in his arms, and she seemed weightless. He thought he might carry her like this all the way back to the palace.

"They were going to put me on one of the trains," she whispered, her mouth near his neck. He could feel her breath on his skin. "They were going to send me away with the others."

As he held her in his arms and breathed her into him, he knew he was receiving the answer to the most desperate prayers he had ever uttered. He couldn't speak. The only thing that came to his mind was a simple phrase that repeated itself over and over with no sign of stopping.

Thank you, God. Thank you, thank you, thank you...

As soon as Boris landed upon his return from Austria, he phoned Kalayev and heard the news of Daria Richetti's rescue. The second call he made was to Pavel Grouev to ask him about the general situation.

"Someone has requested a meeting with you, and I think you will want to see him," Grouev said.

"Who is that?"

"Dimitar Stoyanov."

"Yes, of course. Tell Ellin Pellin I'll see him at the first opportunity."

Two days later Boris was seated in his favorite chair in his personal study in the royal residence at Vrana. Stoyanov sat on a tapestry-covered divan. Between them was a small Italian rococo console holding a silver tea service. Both men sipped from porcelain cups bearing the Bulgarian national crest.

With his craggy face, his flowing, silvery hair, and his drooping mustache, Stoyanov had always reminded Boris of a Bulgarian Mark Twain.

"How was your time with Varban?" the writer asked, using one of the many code names he and Boris had made up over the years for various public figures.

"The Fuehrer was gracious, as always. Since I wanted to keep my visit inconspicuous, he even took his meals in the Bechsteinhaus where I was staying, rather than making me come to the dining room at the Berghof."

The writer nodded. "Thoughtful of him."

"With all that's been going on here lately, I suspect His Parrotlike Eminence has been rather busy, giving speeches and trying to stamp out fires of public discontent?"

Stoyanov smiled. "Well, Filov has had his hands full, yes. As he should have known." The smile faded. Stoyanov carefully placed his cup on the console's varnished surface and leaned forward, his elbows on his knees. He gave Boris an earnest look. "Which brings me to why I have asked to see you, Your Majesty. We have been friends for many years."

"And that has been one of the greatest honors of my life."

"You must know that I have always refrained from speaking to you on behalf of any political cause."

Boris nodded.

"But the time has come when I can no longer be silent, Your Majesty. In the week and a half since the relocations started, over fifteen thousand Jewish persons have been evicted from their homes, loaded onto trains with one or two bags of personal belongings, and shipped to camps out in the provinces, where many of them are living in conditions worse than those of the poorest peasant. Some are being housed in schools or warehouses. Some of them— the lucky ones—are being housed with local Jewish families. Better than a warehouse, but still a terrible strain on everyone involved. Their properties here in Sofia are being liquidated at fire-sale prices, and the funds are being channeled directly into the coffers of the commissariat—no doubt to pay for the whole pathetic enterprise.

"Your Majesty will remember that I was a signatory of the original Writers Union letter opposing the passage of the Law for the Defense of the Nation. I am here today to plead, as a friend, as a member of the Union, and as a Bulgarian patriot, for Your Majesty's firm intervention.

"What is happening to the Jews of Bulgaria is undignified to say the least, inhuman to say the worst. And this tragedy has affected your own household, Your Majesty, so you know what I'm talking about."

Boris swallowed and looked away. "We were very fortunate to find Miss Richetti—before it was too late."

"Yes, Your Majesty. But think of the thousands of families who have not been so fortunate. These people must be kept in Bulgaria at all costs, Your Majesty. They must not be delivered to the Germans, which would mean almost certain death. We must put an end to the persecution of our Jewish citizens. If we don't, history—indeed, heaven—will judge Bulgaria most harshly."

Boris thought of the copy of the letter he had received from the strange rabbi, Daniel Tsion: his "message from God" warning of dire consequences for Bulgaria if the persecution of the Jews was allowed to continue. He wondered if Ellin Pellin, like many other prominent public and government figures, had received a copy of Tsion's oracle.

"You know, I have one of your fellow villagers in my service," Boris said.

"Really? From Bailovo?"

Boris nodded. "A sergeant of the guard. Dobri Dimitrov."

"Dimitrov…Dimitrov… Of course, I've been gone from Bailovo such a long time…"

"In fact, Sergeant Dimitrov is rather deeply in love with Miss Richetti."

"The woman who was rescued?"

Boris nodded.

"Well. As a man who has loved, and as a fellow Bailovski, I'm glad for him. Please tell him I said so."

"I know he'll be happy to hear it."

Do it, Boris! You know he's right. Stefan and the church are right, Tsion is right—all of them! Be strong, for once.

But…the Germans…my country…

You have done everything possible to save your country's life. Now, at last, do something to save its soul.

And then an image came to him, an image so clear and sharp edged it might have been a picture painted by the hand of God: Daria Richetti, the yellow star pinned to her collar, looking at him through the doorway into the darkened hall where he stood listening to her talk to his children. What had she said?

Sometimes it's wrong to hide.... For me, this is a time like that.

He sent a wavering smile toward Ellin Pellin. "I wonder, could you excuse me for a moment, Dimitar? Please stay. I'll be right back."

"Of course."

Boris went into an adjoining room and picked up a telephone. He dialed the number of the Commissariat for Jewish Questions.

Lily Panitza's phone rang. It was the switchboard downstairs, and the operator was breathless. "Miss Panitza, it's a call for the commissar—and it's Tsar Boris himself on the line!"

Lily's mouth went dry. "Put him through," she said and heard the click of the call being routed to her phone. "Your Majesty, please hold while I connect you with Mr. Belev."

She laid the receiver on her desk and went into Alexander's office. Damonova was in there, waiting for Alexander to sign some papers, and Lily told her to leave.

Both of them stared at Lily as if she had spoken nonsense.

"Mr. Belev, I have a call holding for you. It's the king, and he wants to speak with you immediately!"

Damonova scurried out of the office, and Alexander's face went pale. "Well, ah, yes, Miss Panitza, connect His Majesty at once."

Lily pulled the door closed behind her, went to her desk, and put the call through to Alexander's phone.

He had been found out; she just knew it. The secret police had discovered the plot Alexander had hatched with that dreadful Bojilov to kidnap Daria Richetti, and Alexander was about to be imprisoned—maybe even executed.

She fought the urge to tiptoe to Alexander's door. She could hear his voice; he was speaking very little, and then only one or two words at a time. Mostly he was listening. After a while, she heard his phone dropping into its cradle.

There was a crash from inside the office. Lily leaped from her chair and ran to the door. Alexander was grabbing the black notebooks—the ones containing the lists of Jews scheduled for relocation—and he was flinging them against the wall. Papers fluttered through the air as he yanked the notebooks from his shelves, one after the other, and hurled them as hard as he could. Her heart pounding, she went inside.

He whirled to face her, and his expression made her want to call for help.

"Forbidden! Our kike-loving king has forbidden me to transport any more Jews!"

"Alexander! You're speaking treason!"

He gave no sign of hearing her. "He has ordered me to cancel all further operations until the government has conducted a full review. It's over, Lily! Over! We're finished!"

He made an inarticulate sound, like something that might come from a wounded beast. He picked up a wooden tray from his desk and hurled it blindly. It crashed into the wall not two feet from her head, splintering into pieces. Lily screamed and ducked back through the door and slammed it behind her.

Everyone in the office was staring at her. Looking at the floor and trying to regain her breath, she walked to her desk. She tried to find something to use to pretend she was working, to pretend she didn't notice the chaos breaking loose in the office of the commissar. She was the only one who was; everybody else was staring openly.

Just after noon, Interior Minister Gabrovski walked in, unannounced, and went straight into Belev's office. There was a lot of shouting and pounding on the desk, and after about fifteen minutes, Gabrovski left without speaking to anyone else.

The rest of the day hardly anyone in the office spoke above a whisper. They kept up only the appearance of work. Lily could hear the murmurs: "What's happened?" "Will he be arrested?" "What about the rest of us?" And periodically, the sounds of stamping feet or fists striking the wall or loud, inarticulate cries could be heard from inside the commissar's office. By midafternoon people were discreetly leaving for home.

Lily saw them looking at her as if for some cue, some idea of what they should do. How should she know? She kept her eyes on her desk, sorting through papers but seeing nothing except the terrain of uncertainty inside her own mind. At one point someone laid a hand on her arm. Lily looked up. It was Damonova, on her face something like pity. Then she left like the others.

When everyone was gone, Lily crept to the door of Alexander's office. He had not shown his face since the phone call from Tsar Boris. It had been quiet inside for an hour or two, and Lily feared the worst. She fully expected to go inside and see him lying on his desk in a pool of his own blood. She opened the door.

He was sitting in one of the chairs that usually faced his desk. He had dragged it to the window that looked onto Dondukov and was sitting with his back to the door, staring out over the busy street. He was perfectly still. Her heart pounding, Lily went toward him and looked into his face.

He was breathing. His face was still, even contemplative. He didn't move when she touched his shoulder, his neck. She couldn't see any obvious signs of harm on him. She stared at him for perhaps a minute, afraid to speak, even if she could have thought of something to say. Not knowing what else to do, she turned and began picking up the papers and notebooks strewn all over the floor of the office.

After maybe five minutes, without moving, he said, "One person. That's all it takes."

"What, Alexander?"

"One person. Think of it, Lily. I, Alexander Belev, signed a treaty with one of the world's most powerful nations. I planned its execution, down to the minutest detail. I set it in motion, and when difficulties arose, I figured out a way around them. We would have taken every single Jew out of Sofia and every other city in Bulgaria. It would have happened. And we would have eventually sent them to the Germans. The Final Solution would have been achieved. The future of the New Europe would have been secured, and Bulgaria would have done her part. All because of me, Alexander Belev. I could have done it, every bit of it…except for one person."

Lily scooped up an armload of lists and put them between the covers of one of the black notebooks. More than half afraid to hear his answer, she said, "And who is that one person, Alexander?"

Maybe he knows. Maybe he has known all along. Maybe now he will strangle me, and I will be dead and finished with this world where nothing turns out as it should.

She suddenly couldn't decide if she was fearful or exhilarated. To finish with it all—to bear no more responsibility, to be forced into no more decisions that set her heart at war with itself…

"Daria Richetti."

"What do you mean, Alexander?"

"If she, a member of the royal household, hadn't been drawn directly into the situation… Yes, I see it now. None of the rest of them could stop us—not even Stefan and the Holy Synod. But when Daria Richetti was taken, that was a mistake."

Lily picked up another armload of papers and sandwiched them into notebooks. Alexander's meticulous system was wrecked; she was just trying to clear the floor, to get the papers and the notebooks back on the shelves. For a long time she stole glances at the back of his head as he sat, motionless as a statue, gazing out over Dondukov.

"And whose mistake was it, Alexander?"

She held her breath, waiting to see if he would tell her the truth she already knew.

"That doesn't matter," he finally said. "The point is, when Tsar Boris felt such a personal stake in the issue, there was only one possible outcome. We can still fight for deportation; there are still a few more things we can try, but…"

She couldn't decide whether to hate him for continuing his deception or to be grateful she didn't have to decide how to handle a full acknowledgment.

She scooped up the final bundle of lists from the floor and laid them on his desk. She walked over to where he sat and put a hand on his shoulder.

"Come on, Alexander. There's no more to be done here tonight. Let's go home."

He sat unmoving for another moment, then rose from the chair like an obedient schoolboy. He walked past her, took his hat from the rack by the door, and walked out of the office toward the stairs.

Lily pulled his door closed. She reached the stairway, looked around the deserted office for a moment, then switched off the lights and followed Alexander down to the street.

Boris sat in the small office behind Pavel Grouev's and sifted through the reports in front of him. He looked at his chief of cabinet.

"You say they are unanimous?"

Grouev nodded. "Switzerland, Spain, France, Portugal—our embassies in all four places state that their consensus is against Germany winning the war. They urge the government to accelerate talks with the Western allies. The only alternative…"

"Is the Red Army overrunning the Balkan Peninsula? Of course. But will Washington and London intervene to the degree necessary to keep the Bolsheviks at bay in eastern Europe?"

"That is unknown, Your Majesty. But Romania continues to press for meetings with us, independent of the Germans, and they say they've been pressing Hungary for similar agreements also."

"That's saying something, considering their history with Hungary. But, Pavel, an alliance of foxes, no matter how clever, can't run the bear out of his cave. What hope do we have, unless we can make a separate peace with the United States and Britain?"

"We've pressed our Swiss contacts to wring anything they can from Dulles, but he continues to insist that we 'signal our willingness' in ways that can only be interpreted by Berlin as an outright abrogation."

"Such as?"

"Immediate repeal of the anti-Semitic laws, for one."

"We might as well issue Berlin formal notice of our intention to withdraw from the pact."

"And the Americans' response to our territorial questions was most disappointing, according to Kiosseivanov."

"Does German intelligence know we're using Kiosseivanov again?" Boris asked.

"Probably."

Boris blew out his cheeks in exasperation. "It's hard to tiptoe in a minefield, isn't it? Well, if the United States won't let us keep Macedonia and Thrace, any move toward them would be very unpopular—and not just with Berlin."

"I'm afraid so, Your Majesty."

"Do you think the Americans know about some of our pilots being involved in the air defense of Ploesti?"

"We've tried to keep that as quiet as possible, Your Majesty, but anything is possible."

Boris looked at his watch. "I have to go, Bacho Pavlé. It's the crown prince's birthday, and I promised him a trip to Turnovo to tour the military academy. We'd better get going if we want to have much daylight left when we get there."

"Travel safely, Your Majesty."

Simeon loved the drive on the mountain roads through the heart of the Balkans. As the car rounded the rising curves, he peered as far out and down as he could, even though the ravines, that deepened more and more as they climbed toward the spine of the mountains, scared him just a little—and thrilled him at the same time. Besides, his father was a good driver. He had heard some of the soldiers at the palace say that Tsar Boris knew every road in the country as well as he knew the streets around the Royal Palace.

Simeon had worn his favorite uniform today, bearing the insignia of his favorite regiment, the Forty-first Heavy Artillery, since Father promised him they'd visit the military academy. He had gotten up early—before daylight—and polished his boots and belts himself, without any help at all. When Mother saw him, she said she thought he could pass the strictest inspection any drill sergeant might care to give. She told the cooks to give him an extra piece of bread with jam. It was his sixth birthday, after all.

"Father, when I'm the king, what will you be?"

He could tell Father was thinking hard about his answer. His eyes changed, and he was quiet for a long time. He was quiet for so long Simeon wished he hadn't asked the question.

"When you are king, Simeon, I'll be…at peace."

Simeon wasn't sure he understood exactly what Father meant, but he was very sure he didn't want to know any more about it.

The visit to the military academy was everything Simeon had hoped. The cadets cheered his birthday, and there was a special cake, and then a pass-in-review and a twenty-one-gun salute. At the end, when the academy band played "Shoomi Maritza" and all the cadets sang, Simeon felt almost as tall as Father.

No trip to Turnovo was complete without a visit to the old castle. Father parked the car in a small gravel lot next to the high, arched, stone bridge that spanned the Yantra River from Trapezitsa Hill to Tsarevets Hill, "The King's Hill," where the ancient castle of the Second Bulgarian Kingdom stood.

A few sightseers were still going back and forth on the bridge, and naturally they all recognized Simeon and his father, especially since they were in uniform. Simeon had to be patient, because Father wanted to chat with everyone who came by. Simeon just wanted to get across the bridge and stand on the ancient stones of the castle.

They finally came to the portcullis, and just beyond it, along both walls, were all the organ grinders with their monkeys, gypsies selling trinkets and souvenirs, men with cameras offering to take pictures for two leva, and old women with hardly any teeth selling baskets or lace or whatever else. All of them bowed to the passing pair, and Father spoke some word of greeting to every one of them, and Simeon had to bite his tongue to keep from saying, "Hurry up!" But finally they were through the last gate and onto the castle grounds.

As they walked along the eastern edge of Tsarevets Hill, Simeon picked up a palm-sized stone. He pulled his arm back as far as he could and flung the stone into space, trying to make it splash into the Yantra River far below. But his throw was short of the river by many yards, falling among the trees that sidled at an angle along both sides of the stream.

Father smiled. He reached down and picked up a rock. His throw arced out over the empty air and splashed into the water, making a neat circle that was quickly swept away by the current.

Simeon pointed north along the ridge to an old stone structure that had begun to topple. "What's that there, Father, that place off by itself out at the end of the ridge?"

"Ah, now that's an interesting story, Simeon. Let's walk over there, and I'll tell you."

29

They walked the uneven pebbled path down the shoulder of the ridge until they came to the tumbled-down stones. Father put his hand against them and turned to Simeon.

"Do you know what this building is called?"

Simeon shook his head.

"This is Baldwin's Tower. Do you know why it's called that?"

Another head shake.

"Baldwin of Flanders was a Crusader. Tsar Kaloyan captured him in a battle near Adrianople. Do you know the modern city that is there now?"

"I learned this! Edirne, in Turkey."

"Correct! Tsar Kaloyan tried to make peace with Baldwin, but Baldwin would have none of it. And so, when they fought, Kaloyan was victorious, and Baldwin was brought here, to Turnovo, and imprisoned in this tower until his country ransomed him."

"Baldwin's Tower!"

"Yes. And there is a legend that over the years of his imprisonment, Tsar Kaloyan's wife came to like, then finally to love, the handsome Western king who was locked in this tower. It is even said that she offered to have him freed, to help him get away from the tower and the castle. But, the legend goes, Baldwin refused to leave—at first, because he demanded to be pardoned by Kaloyan himself, to keep his honor. But later, they say, he came to love Kaloyan's queen and refused to leave unless she would come with him."

Simeon wrinkled his nose again. "He stayed in this tower because of a girl?"

Father laughed. He snatched off Simeon's visored cap and rumpled his hair.

"No, I don't suppose that makes much sense to a young man six years old, does it?" Father turned to look at the tower, and for a long time he rubbed his palm on the stone, up and down. Simeon could tell he was thinking. When he spoke, his face was toward the stone wall, and it was in the quiet voice that Simeon knew wasn't really meant for him.

"Honor and love can be stronger than stone walls, Simeon. They can put you in places you don't want to be, places you can't get away from. But men have died for worse things. Many worse things."

Simeon didn't understand any of what Father said. But the words, and the sound of his voice, and the sight of the old stones, and the thought of Baldwin of Flanders staying here night after night and day after day—staying when he could have chosen to leave—all of it made Simeon sad in a way that he couldn't explain, even to himself.

"I'm ready to go home now, Father."

Father knelt in front of him and pulled him close. He held him that way for a long time.

"I am too, Son. Let's go back to the car."

"Stefan, you must listen to me," Neofit said. "And will you please stop that pacing and light in one place while I'm talking to you? It's like watching a tennis match, trying to hold a conversation with you when you're this way."

Stefan muttered something, but he sat down in a chair. He wouldn't look at the president of the Holy Synod, though, and that worried Metropolitan Neofit.

"We have reliable information that a meeting of judges and state attorneys has been gathered, their sole purpose to discuss the ramifications of issuing an indictment against you based on the provisions of the Law for the Defense of the Nation. They could be drawing up the arrest documents right now."

"But don't you understand, Father?" Stefan stood from his chair but forced himself back into it at Neofit's reproving look. "All Gabrovski and his Ratnik cronies want is for the furor to die down, for the people to look elsewhere, so they can do as they like with the Jews without any public outcry. If I stop speaking, if I allow the people of my churches the comfort of their Orthodoxy without reminding them of the suffering of their Jewish fellows, the Fascists have won!"

"Stefan, you are becoming too severe an irritant. They could take action."

"Let them! Let them put me in jail. I believe Saint Paul did some of his best work while in prison. I defy them, Neofit! I defy them to arrest me, when they know that the people are convinced I'm telling the truth."

Neofit sighed. "I thought you might respond so. And of course the Holy Synod is bound to uphold you as long as you are teaching Orthodox doctrine."

"Have you seen the latest fliers? They've even taken aim at Kyril in Plovdiv."

"Yes. At our next meeting, I plan to talk about these ridiculous attempts at defamation."

"Why should we just talk about it, Neofit? Why don't we do something?"

Neofit eyed Stefan warily. He was leaning forward, a gleam in his eye. The president of the synod was pretty sure that whatever the metropolitan of Sofia was about to suggest would not be aimed at placating anyone. "What do you suggest?" he asked, wincing.

"We should issue a full press release, stating the position of the Holy Synod with regard to the Jewish situation. And if the government tries to censor it, we should have it printed at our own expense and circulated to every parish in the country."

Neofit shook his head. "Well, you're a member of the synod, Stefan. You can make a motion for whatever action you wish. But if I were you—"

"Good!" Stefan slapped his knee and sprang up from his chair. "I'll have something drafted and sent around so the synod can read it beforehand and make suggestions."

Neofit sighed and cupped his cheek in his hand.

Alexander read the memo from Interior Minister Gabrovski, then dropped it on his desk. He swiveled his chair and stared out the window.

"What reply should I send to the interior minister?" Lily asked.

Alexander shook his head. "This tack they're taking with the church and Stefan is doomed. I despise the metropolitan as much as anybody, but there is no chance that we can credibly incriminate him."

"Then shall I tell the minister that you advise against—"

"No, absolutely not. He and Filov will figure it out for themselves soon enough. Here. I've made some recommendations for Hoffmann to pass along to Beckerle and Berlin. Type these up and get them off to the German embassy. They may buy us a little more time." He slid the papers across the desk with all the enthusiasm of a child at his mother's bridge party.

If he was beaten, why didn't he quit? Alexander was more than this program against the Jews… Wasn't he?

"Yes, Mr. Belev. I'll get these typed and sent immediately."

Kristiu Pastoukhov stood in the doorway of Pavel Grouev's office and smiled. "It's been a long time since I was welcomed anywhere near the Royal Palace," the old man said, "and now here I am, face to face with Tsar Boris's chief of cabinet."

"Come in, come in," Pavel said, hurrying from behind his desk and pulling Pastoukhov inside, quickly closing the door. Pavel hoped not too many people had seen the old Socialist and longtime opposition party member come to this office. Tongues were already wagging at the German embassy over the increasing communication between the palace and the pro-Western Kiosseivanov in Switzerland. It wouldn't do to give Berlin too many more reasons to question Tsar Boris's taste in diplomatic contacts.

"Please, Mr. Pastoukhov, sit down. May I offer you some tea?"

The gaunt, gray-haired man held up a hand and shook his head. "No, thank you, Mr. Chancellor. I am anxious to know why I have been invited—your messenger was very discreet, I might add—to the palace. Tsar Boris can hardly think I have changed my mind about the directions the government should be taking." He leaned forward in his chair, hands atop his cane, and stared at Pavel.

"No, actually, he doesn't. As a matter of fact, Mr. Pastoukhov, there is a possibility that the king, under certain circumstances, might be interested in your opinions on who might head up a government with a slightly, ah, more Western tilt."

"He doesn't think Germany can win."

Pavel smiled. "Well, I can't speak for His Majesty on such matters. But in these uncertain times it only seems prudent to think of all possibilities."

"The Americans and British are in Sicily. Mussolini is about as popular as the pox in Italy these days. The German offensive in Russia has stalled, and I'd wager you next week's grocery money the Red Army will be back in Kiev before the end of the year. I've said many critical things about Tsar Boris and his policies, Mr. Grouev, but I have never accused him of being stupid."

"Well, that's good to hear—"

"And I'll tell you another thing. No matter what happens in the war, Bulgaria can hold her head high because she refused to cave in to German demands to declare war on Russia. And I know how much credit Tsar Boris deserves for that. So what does he want from me?"

"As I said, certain changes in the makeup of the government may become advantageous, given certain eventualities. Tsar Boris would like your thoughts on these matters."

"Tell him I'll draw up the most anti-German cabinet this country has seen in ten years."

Pavel's eyes widened, but he managed a smile. "I'm sure you'll do what is in the best interests of the country, Mr. Pastoukhov."

The dapper old man levered himself to his feet. "I'll be in touch, Mr. Grouev. Shall I expect the same courier?"

"Probably, Mr. Pastoukhov. His Majesty will be most anxious to hear your thoughts."

The door closed, and Pavel looked at his clock. Almost time to go home. He was leaving a little earlier than usual this evening, because Radka's graduation ceremony from the Gymnasium was tonight, and he couldn't be late. He tidied up his desk, put a few things in his valise, locked the sensitive papers in a drawer, and left.

Walking home in the late afternoon sun was a special pleasure for Pavel. So often, duties and meetings kept him at the palace until twilight or later, even in the summertime. The air today was what he considered perfect: not yet laden with the heat of full summer, but just warm enough to be comfortable.

He looked up at the facade of the palace as he rounded its northwest corner. Pavel thought about what Pastoukhov had said. No doubt there were many who would very much like to see a less pro-German bias in the cabinet. But the Western allies were not trampling each other to welcome Bulgaria into the fold. The Wehrmacht might be encountering various difficulties, and Italy might be vulnerable, but the Reich was far from beaten.

Pavel thought about the soul searching, the seemingly endless political maneuvering Tsar Boris had carried on at the beginning of the war. Now that it was possibly entering its final phase, especially if you listened to people like Pastoukhov, it was the same dance, the same careful probing, the same politics of innuendo and discreet hints—all deniable, of course. Pavel didn't see how Tsar Boris held up under it all. He was looking very tired lately.

"It's good of you to receive me on such short notice, Your Majesty. I know these days your schedule must be very full indeed."

"Herr Beckerle, few things on my schedule are as important as maintaining good understanding with our valued German allies," Boris said, motioning the German ambassador toward a seat. They were in Boris's private office, just off Pavel Grouev's suite. He had never received the German ambassador here, and the more intimate setting, he thought, might be better for the sort of information he hoped to gain from today's conversation. Boris had never liked Beckerle, but he had found the Nazi ambassador to be somewhat easily influenced. He maintained cordial relations with him, hoping to use him to counteract whatever negative impressions were doubtless being conveyed by Filov and his right-wing constituents. So far, the balancing act seemed to be working. Boris's contacts within the German embassy assured him that the ambassador's communications with his superiors in Berlin were never overly critical of the Bulgarian government's willingness to cooperate with the Reich.

"I am here first of all to assure Your Majesty that the strategic fallback of the German armed forces to the Italian mainland is in no way seen by the Wehrmacht's general staff as a serious setback to our overall military plan."

And the retaking of Orel by the Red Army is probably just the result of a temporary feint by the Wehrmacht, to make Russia overconfident. "Of course, Herr Ambassador. The current, ah, instability in the Italian government is understandable, but no doubt your military commanders there have matters well in hand."

"Correct. The Reich has no intention of surrendering Italy, regardless of the propaganda being issued by Badoglio and the other pretenders. I want to assure you of that."

Boris nodded. *Of course, you foolish man, Marshall Badoglio was appointed by the king of Italy, who, you might remember, is my father-in-law.* "I have every confidence in the ultimate outcome of the war, Herr Beckerle, and I want to assure you that the kingdom of Bulgaria will continue to do its part."

Beckerle fidgeted for a moment. "Yes, Your Majesty, and that brings me to a rather uncomfortable question I'm afraid I must ask. I am receiving some urgent requests for assurances that the recent, ah, difficulties with the Jewish deportations do not signal some sort of retreat in Bulgaria's cooperation with the aims of the Reich." He wouldn't look at the king when he said it. Boris almost felt sorry for the bureaucrat, caught between Filov's staunch and continued assurances, no doubt, that the Fuehrer's Final Solution would be firmly assisted by his Bulgarian allies, and the evidence of Beckerle's own eyes that every attempt to move the Bulgarian Jews toward Poland was met with a public outcry that even guns couldn't counter.

"Well, Herr Ambassador, as I have explained—to the Fuehrer and Reichsminister von Ribbentrop themselves, by the way—the Bulgarian mentality is different from that of other European peoples. We have a different sort of relationship with our Jews—"

"Yes, yes, I have tried to explain that to my superiors."

"Good. Then you must know that we are doing everything we can to maintain the Jewish population in a situation where they can be kept under close watch and also aid the overall aims of our country as we continue to prepare for possible active involvement in the support of the Wehrmacht's rear. Surely the general staff have taken into account the eventuality of an Anglo-Turkish front or even a landing in Greece."

Beckerle nodded. "I have continually assured my superiors that Bulgaria is doing her best to support the ultimate aims of the Reich within the context of what is possible for her, given the particular circumstances here."

Boris smiled at the ambassador. "Herr Beckerle, I couldn't have said it better myself. I'm so glad we understand each other."

"Yes. Well, in these times, the Reich must be certain of its friends." Again Beckerle shifted uncomfortably in his chair. Boris readied himself for the forthcoming question that was apparently sticking in the German ambassador's craw. "Your Majesty, some of our contacts are…concerned about certain communications that appear to be taking place between highly placed Bulgarians and elements of the Western Alliance."

Ah. The obligatory scolding. They should have sent someone who knows how to do it. "Herr Beckerle, I must confess that you have me somewhat at a disadvantage. I have never authorized any person, in an official or any other capacity, to initiate contact with enemies of the Reich. As you must surely know after having been in our country so long, Bulgaria is a complicated land. Here we have endeavored to allow people their opinions, no matter how divergent, so long as their actions do not directly endanger the security of the country. No doubt some of my countrymen, acting on their strongly held and well-intentioned beliefs, have had conversations with certain people whose influence, they thought, would be beneficial for Bulgaria. I don't see how this government can possibly be held accountable for every stray chat some traveling industrialist or former diplomat has while he's in Geneva or Istanbul. I hardly think such matters can compare to the real evidence of Bulgaria's active support of our German allies. I ask you, Herr Beckerle: is there any country in Europe where your troops are treated so well?"

Beckerle pursed his lips and shook his head.

"Have we failed in any way to live up to our obligations to the agreement to administer the occupied territories in Macedonia and Thrace?"

Again Beckerle shook his head.

"And so, my dear Ambassador Beckerle, when viewed in such a context, surely you can see that Bulgaria continues in her firm support of the Reich."

"Yes, well, I personally see things much the same way as Your Majesty. But some of my superiors… At any rate, Your Majesty, before time completely gets away from us, I must give you this." He reached into the pocket of his coat and withdrew an envelope bearing the crest of the German embassy.

Boris opened it. It contained a communication from Hitler's northern military headquarters in eastern Prussia. Boris was "invited" to an urgent meeting with Hitler on matters of utmost importance concerning recent developments in the war.

He felt a warning in his gut. Hitler was feeling the pressure of the breakdown of his northern, eastern, and southern fronts. He was facing the real prospect of an Allied landing in Italy. He was calling in his allies to make absolutely certain that there would be no more surprises.

Boris folded the memorandum and put it in his pocket. He smiled at Beckerle. "Of course, Herr Ambassador, you may tell the Fuehrer that it will be my pleasure, as always, to meet with him."

They exchanged a few more pleasantries, then Boris stood to shake Beckerle's hand as the ambassador prepared to leave. When the door closed behind him, Boris sat heavily in his chair, retrieved the paper from his pocket, and stared at it, rubbing the bridge of his nose. After a few minutes he picked up the phone.

"Pavel? I've been summoned to Germany again. I leave in three days. Tomorrow I want a meeting with Filov. I have a bad feeling about this."

30

T he rabbi winced as the guard grabbed his ear and yanked.

"The sergeant is conducting roll call!" the guard, scarcely more than a boy, screamed into Tsion's face. Tsion could feel the flecks of spittle hitting his cheeks, his forehead. "You were clearly instructed to shout your name, you filthy Jew! Do you call that pathetic moan a shout? Now answer the sergeant correctly!"

"Daniel Tsion!"

"What?"

"Daniel Tsion!"

"One more time, for good measure!"

"I am Daniel Tsion!"

"That's better." The guard, a second lieutenant, strutted down the line of pathetic, worn-out men. "You Jews think you're the chosen people, don't you? You think you're something special, just because you're Jewish. Well, do you see how special you are?" he said, pointing at Tsion. "Do you see how much I care for one of your leaders? I care nothing for him! Nothing! I'll be glad when we get the orders to put the lot of you on the boats over in Somovit, to get you out of this country."

He stared at them for several seconds, then nodded toward the sergeant, who stood waiting, clipboard in hand, to continue the roll call. "Go ahead, Sergeant. And the rest of you, remember what I said."

The guard called the next name, and someone named Lev Chavdarov screamed out a response.

Daniel Tsion's ear was throbbing; he thought the lieutenant might actually separate it from his head. Ever since the freight cars had disgorged them at this camp near the Danube, the guards had singled him out for special treatment. "We know about you," one of them told him on that first night as they were being assigned to the ramshackle lean-tos called barracks. "You're one of the troublemakers. You got a message from God, did you? Well, how do you like God's answer?"

Tsion had looked at him, a tall, Slavic-looking blond fellow with a two- or three-day growth of stubble on his face. He was laughing with some of his cronies. And Tsion knew it was foolish and pointless, but for too many years he had become too used to speaking his mind.

"You're not God."

The guard stopped laughing and looked at him, the grin fading from his face. "What did you say to me, kike?"

Tsion clamped his jaw and stared straight ahead. The guard stuck his face inches from Tsion's and yelled, "I asked you a question, you filthy Jew! What did you say?"

Tsion could feel the eyes of the other prisoners trying not to watch and so draw attention to themselves, but they were unable to completely look away. The guard pulled out his truncheon and jammed it crosswise beneath the rabbi's chin, shoving it with both hands into Tsion's throat. The guard's voice, when it came, was not a scream, but a near whisper—more frightening than if he had continued to rant. "I'll put a dent in your skull if you don't tell me what you said." He was hissing the words in Tsion's ear.

"What I said was, 'You're not God.'"

The truncheon crashed down on his shoulder, numbing his left side, then into the backs of his knees, knocking him to the ground. The guard straddled him and leaned down into his face. "So, I'm not God? Well, let me tell you something, Daniel Tsion: while you're at this camp, you'd better think of me as God. Because I can snap my fingers, and you'll be gone. Do you understand me?"

More men arrived almost daily, and not all of them were from Sofia. There were Jews from Plovdiv, Dupnitza, Pazardjik, and other places. Many of them, Tsion learned, were leaders in their local synagogues or consistories.

The guards threatened them constantly with deportation. They were brutalized, grossly underfed, driven like pack animals during the day, and subjected to living conditions considerably worse than horrid. But weeks went by, and they stayed where they were. As far as Tsion knew, no prisoners were even transferred from one camp to another.

Each night, as he laid his aching, hungry body down on the hard ground in his barracks, Daniel Tsion recited some of the psalms. At first he just did it silently, as he thought of his wife and wondered what had become of her, what would become of any of them. Then one night, without quite realizing it, he allowed some lines of the ancient text to escape in a whisper from his lips.

> O LORD, how many are my foes!
>> How many rise up against me!
> Many are saying of me,
>> "God will not deliver him."
> But you are a shield around me, O LORD;
>> you bestow glory on me and lift up my head.

Before he knew it, the man lying next to him had joined in:

> To the LORD I cry aloud,
>> and he answers me from his holy hill.
> I lie down and sleep;
>> I wake again, because the LORD sustains me.

Then Daniel Tsion heard voices in the dark all around him, chanting the words that had sustained his people through the many dark days in the millenniums of their existence.

> I will not fear the tens of thousands
>> drawn up against me on every side.

> Arise, O LORD!
>> Deliver me, O my God!
> Strike all my enemies on the jaw;
>> break the teeth of the wicked.

From the LORD comes deliverance.

May your blessing be on your people.

After that night, Daniel Tsion was never afraid again. Careful, perhaps. But never afraid. And each night for the rest of the time in the camp at Somovit, the men of his barracks softly chanted a psalm: a quiet protest—a benediction of the afflicted, floating above them for a few precious moments, then out into the night.

For a full week after Daria was found, Dobri didn't leave her side for more than fifteen minutes at a time—except when she went to bed, of course. And even then, he left only after he had personally inspected the men stationed in the royal residence. They were his fellow soldiers, and they understood. But still, Dobri had to look each of them in the eye and receive each man's most solemn oath that he would be as watchful as if his own mother were sleeping inside.

After a time he had to return to his regular duty schedule; Captain Kalayev couldn't afford to lose his services indefinitely. But he still managed to arrange his routes so that he was often in the family wing of the palace, often pacing past the suite where Daria quietly spent her days. The tsaritza gave her no duties other than to rest. For a few minutes two or three times a day, she let the children in to visit with her, but that was all—and that was more for the children's benefit than for Daria's, Dobri guessed.

He burned to talk to her, to ask her again. But he was afraid. Who could say how this dreadful experience had changed her? For two or three days, she barely spoke at all.

When he could without her knowledge, he looked at her. He studied her as a commander studies the terrain of a battle or as a climber studies a rock-face. Could he still find some purchase on her heart?

And then his mind played out the possibilities. He rehearsed the words he might say and tried to imagine what she might say in return, and so far his fear of hearing no was mastering his hopes of hearing yes.

So he stayed by her side every minute he could, and he watched, and he waited, and he said very little. Sometimes she would look at him, and something in her eyes caused hope to leap suddenly within him. Then again, if she didn't turn to look at him as he walked past her door, he felt as beaten as any man can feel and still stand upright.

Dobri thought about Tsar Boris's words, that day in his office. *Risk, and the patience to endure it*... But for how long? And how much could a man afford to lose?

Daria watched him pacing the halls, watched him peering at her when he thought she wasn't looking. It had been days now, and still she didn't know what to tell Dobri. And the poor man was clearly suffering torments over it, though doing his best to hide it from everyone.

There was so much to be said, and she had no idea where to begin. Did she love him? Yes, she thought so. Did she trust him? How could she not? It was he who had found her, he who had lifted her and carried her when her legs were hopelessly numb from being tied to the chair for endless hours. For the rest of her life she would remember his face, his eyes streaming tears, as he picked her up. She would never forget the words that came from his lips over and over again, words he probably thought he was saying only inside his head: "Thank you, God. Thank you, God..."

But had anything changed, really? Her people were in camps scattered across the countryside, the threat of deportation constantly hanging over their heads. How could she accept the love of this good man, the safety it would bring, when the Jews of Bulgaria were still in such danger?

On the other hand, what was left for her to do? She had identified herself; she had come out from behind the camouflage of the royal household and let herself be seen for who and what she knew herself to be. She had not shrunk from the pain of her people. She had faced the beast of fear, and it had done its worst to her. And what did any of that have to do with holding poor Dobri at arm's length?

The day came when she could no longer lie on the daybed in her rooms. She rose and went looking for Queen Giovanna. She found her in her sitting room, occupied as she so often was with her knitting for the soldiers. Today she was working on woolen socks. She looked up, saw Daria, and smiled, patting the divan next to her.

Daria sat beside the queen and picked up a ball of yarn. Queen Giovanna handed her an extra set of needles, and she began looping the dull gray thread back and forth, back and forth.

For a long time they worked in silence. It was midafternoon, and the heat of early August was filtering past the shade of the huge beeches and elms outside the window.

"Shall I open the window a little more, Your Majesty—perhaps switch on the fan?"

Queen Giovanna's fingers never paused, but she nodded. When Daria sat back down beside her, the queen said, "I was wondering when you'd come out of seclusion. I'm glad you're here."

"Thank you, Your Majesty. I was wondering the same thing. And then, today… I don't know, I just knew it was time."

"Sometimes one knows when it's time, and that's good."

Daria bit her lip. Keeping her eyes on her work, she asked, "And what if one is unsure?"

The queen gave a tiny smile. "Absolute certainty is rare, I think. In science perhaps, matters can be nailed down with facts. In knitting, the pattern never changes; it can be completely known. But in art, for example, mystery is inseparable from the experience, it seems to me. And even Tsar Boris's generals don't go into their battles with all outcomes foreknown. Even soldiers must deal in risk. And of course, with the emotions, who can ever be certain?"

"But is that fair?"

Queen Giovanna looked at her. "To whom? Yourself? Or someone else?"

Daria felt her cheeks stinging. She took another turn of the yarn. For a long time, there was only the clicking of the needles.

"I don't know so much about fairness," Queen Giovanna finally said. "I know about seeing to my children, watching them grow, worrying about my husband, wondering how our country will manage when this war sorts itself out. But fairness? No, I'm not too sure about that. One lives the life one is given, makes the best decisions possible, considering one's choices, and prays for the best outcome."

Another long silence.

"And one recognizes when it is time to fight the battle," Queen Giovanna said, "and when it is time to tend to other things."

"Your Majesty, as you know, Vice Premier Antonescu continues to press for talks between Romania and Bulgaria—talks that would specifically exclude Germany—on the situation facing our two countries. They insist that such talks need not change our relationships with Berlin." Filov picked up a memorandum and slid it across the desk to Boris. "And yesterday I received this, by secure diplomatic courier, from the Romanian embassy."

Boris read the memorandum. After the usual diplomatic boilerplate about the critical nature of the days and the necessity for clear and thoughtful action by all parties, the Romanian ambassador posed two specific questions that, he alleged, came directly from the highest levels of his country's government:

1. Did the kingdom of Bulgaria truly believe that an Anglo-American occupation of the Balkans could hold back the danger of Bolshevism?

2. Was there concern in the kingdom of Bulgaria that some sort of agreement between Germany and Russia might be made—an agreement that might not necessarily take into account the best interests of Bulgaria and Romania?

"Our friends across the Danube are looking for the nearest exit," Boris said, sliding the memo back toward Filov. "Not that the Americans or the British are exactly inviting us with open arms."

The prime minister nodded. "Many attitudes would change, of course, with some really good news from the Russian front."

"Which may or may not be forthcoming. Well, Mr. Filov, it will be interesting to hear what the Fuehrer has to say this time. Thank you for bringing me up to date on this information. I'll keep it firmly in mind when I meet with the Germans."

"When do you leave, Your Majesty?"

"The day after tomorrow—Saturday."

Dobri woke up on Friday morning and knew that today he would again declare himself to Daria. He would take the consequences, whatever they were. As he polished his boots and belts, as he shaved, as he carefully settled his hat on his head for the short walk from his rooms to the palace, he felt a calm resolve. Either Daria would have him, or she wouldn't. If she would, then he would be the happiest man in Sofia. If not, then he would resign himself to a lifetime of thinking about what might have been. Maybe a woman would come along who could make him forget Daria, but he doubted it. Still, either way, today the tormenting question would be laid to rest. Dobri recognized the composed feeling settling on him; it was the same feeling that sometimes came to him before some difficult duty, one that would tax his abilities to the fullest. It was, he imagined, the calm he had heard some of the old-timers talk about feeling just before the onset of a battle. Everything became clear.

He went to his station at midmorning. He checked in with the corporal at the desk, then turned his face toward the private wing of the palace. He would go to her now, while his mind was focused. But then the corporal called out to him.

"Sergeant Dimitrov, I just remembered: Captain Kalayev wants to see you right away."

"What about, Corporal?"

"He didn't say. He just said to send you to him immediately when you checked in."

Dobri closed his eyes for an instant. Well. It would have to wait. He would find out whatever the captain wanted. Surely, sometime today he would see her, and the matter would be settled.

Kalayev looked up when Dobri entered. Returning Dobri's salute, he said, "Dimitrov, His Majesty is flying to Germany tomorrow for meetings with the big brass, and he specifically requested that you accompany him. Make sure your full-dress uniform is cleaned and pressed."

"Yes, sir. When do we leave?"

"Early tomorrow morning, from Vrazhdebna."

"Very good, sir. I'll be ready." He saluted and left.

When he arrived at the private wing of the palace, one of the chamber-maids told him she hadn't seen Mademoiselle Daria all morning. "I think she went with Her Majesty and the children to the park," the girl said.

"Who went with them?"

"Don't worry, Sergeant. There were at least three soldiers with them. Her Majesty isn't taking any chances these days."

After Dobri doubled back to the duty station and verified for himself that the men detailed with Daria and the royal children were all trustworthy, he breathed a little easier. But now he was becoming impatient. He couldn't hold himself in a state of readiness indefinitely. And he would require some time to prepare for tomorrow's trip. He didn't want to leave without know-ing which way things were going to fall.

Daria nodded her thanks to the soldier who held the door for the children and then for her as they entered the winter garden. "Thank you, Private, and your two companions, also."

The soldier bowed to her. "It was an honor, Miss Richetti."

The children scampered off to find their toys, and Daria walked slowly across the winter garden, hugging herself and thinking about what she wanted to say to Dobri. It was past time for saying, and though she thought her mind was settled, still she felt uneasy about the conversation. How would he react? She had rehearsed the words a hundred times these last few days, but even now she didn't know if she could get them out.

She saw a guard in the hallway, at the foot of the stairs, and asked him if he had seen Sergeant Dimitrov.

"Yes, Miss Richetti, he was here earlier this morning, asking for you. But I think someone told him you were out. I haven't seen him since."

"Thank you. I'm sure I'll find him."

So he was looking for her. What could that mean? Maybe he had come to a decision of his own. Maybe he was tired of waiting. Maybe the scene would be very different than the one she had scripted in her mind. But the only way to know was to find Dobri. She decided to go to her rooms. Surely, sometime today he would come there.

Dobri had never felt so frustrated in his life. Of all the days to be stuck on a side street in Sofia with a flat tire.

"I'm sorry, Sergeant. I'll get the spare, and we'll be back at the palace in no time."

A routine errand for Kalayev: just run down to the Central Police Station and pick up some intelligence reports the captain had ordered, then bring them straight back to the palace. A matter of fifteen minutes at most. Except for the jagged pothole in the shortcut that Corporal Kamchev had taken, and the thin tire on the right front.

"Sergeant, while I change the tire, do you think you should call the palace and let the captain know why we're running late?"

"Yes, Corporal, I think maybe I should. And don't worry, I'll tell him exactly why."

Kamchev turned toward the car's trunk with a guilty look, but Dobri didn't care. Of all days!

Daria was beginning to get angry. He was avoiding her! Trying to catch her out, put her at a disadvantage. For the past three weeks, he'd been coming around, regular as clockwork, and suddenly he made himself as scarce as an albino mountain goat.

She stomped over to her door and slammed it shut. If he came sneaking down the hall, let him knock, just like anybody else! She sat in her chair and fumed.

By the time Dobri and Kamchev had walked to the nearest garage, scrounged a tire to replace the spare that should have been in their car, put it on the car, and returned to the palace, the afternoon sun was settling behind the north-ernmost flanks of the Vitosha Mountains. Dobri sat in jaw-clenched silence beside the hapless Kamchev. When they stopped at the motor pool, he told the corporal to be sure to give the chief correct instructions on finding the garage from which they had commandeered the tire. "And stick to the main roads from now on."

He strode toward the palace and suddenly stopped. He looked down at himself. His hands and the front of his uniform were grimy from wrestling the tire onto the car. He was sweaty and probably smelled like a draft horse just in from the field. He couldn't go to Daria like this. In fact, he couldn't go to her at all. By the time he handed in the captain's reports, it would be time to go home and prepare for tomorrow's early departure.

Dobri walked into the captain's office. Kalayev was already gone, naturally, so he handed the dossier to the captain's aide. He pointedly ignored the stares the aide gave his filthy clothing and generally disheveled appearance.

As he walked down the stairs and out of the palace, he realized the date. No wonder—today was Friday the thirteenth. And tomorrow, on Saturday, he would be on an airplane to Germany. Dobri shook his head. He walked across the back of the palace grounds and turned a glance up, toward the windows of Daria's apartment in the private wing. When he got back from this trip, the first thing he would do…

31

August 1943

As soon as the airplane leveled off, Boris left the passenger lounge and knocked on the door of the pilot's cabin.

"Lieutenant Scherer, I wonder if you might allow me to serve as Captain Bauer's copilot for a few minutes?"

The young copilot, by now accustomed to Boris's fascination with flying, smiled and nodded, scooting out of the right-hand seat of the Junkers's cockpit and sidling past the king.

Bauer motioned to the headset Scherer had hung on the armrest of the copilot's seat. Boris settled the gear on his head as Bauer switched on the cabin intercom.

"Do you remember everything from our last lesson?" the pilot asked.

Boris nodded. "I think so, Captain. Would you permit me to take the control for a little while?"

Bauer released the control, and Boris felt a thrill go through him as the power of the Junkers's three engines vibrated in his palms.

"Take her up another two hundred meters," Bauer said. "You remember which dial is the altimeter?"

Boris nodded and carefully pulled back on the control. He felt the press of gravity as the airplane climbed. Exactly on the mark, he eased the nose forward and leveled the aircraft.

"Perfectly done, Your Majesty. You have a gift for flying."

"I love everything mechanical, Captain Bauer: automobiles, locomotives, boats... But flying is the greatest enjoyment I've found yet."

Bauer smiled and nodded. "When the air is smooth and clear, there's no place I'd rather be than up here."

They were still over a seemingly impenetrable forest in the Koenigsberg region when Bauer announced they were about to begin their descent. Boris edged past the copilot and returned to the passenger cabin, and everyone readied for arrival.

Seemingly out of nowhere, an airfield appeared below them, so well disguised that Boris didn't see how anyone could find it without precise coordinates and help from the ground. This was the *Wolfsschanze,* "The Wolf's Lair," Hitler's most closely guarded and northernmost command post. Boris understood that, since the defeat at Stalingrad, Hitler rarely left this place.

Ribbentrop greeted them, along with Field Marshal Wilhelm Keitel, Hitler's military chief of staff. They got into cars and drove through a bewildering maze of paths, completely overshadowed by the trees that served as a defense against detection by enemy bombers. They passed three heavily fortified gates before reaching the innermost zone of the complex, occupied only by Hitler and his high command.

"I wouldn't advise going for a stroll out here at night," Ribbentrop said, nodding toward the relatively open area surrounding the camouflaged concrete bunker that housed the inner zone. "This field is heavily mined."

"I appreciate the warning, Herr Reichsminister," Boris said, forcing a smile.

Hitler met them at the main entrance of the bunker, greeting Boris with something less than his customary warmth, it seemed. An SS captain showed the visitors toward their quarters and the officers' mess, while Boris went for a private lunch with Hitler, Ribbentrop, and several top military commanders.

Dobri had a cramped, uneasy feeling as he walked down the hall behind the SS officer. This bunker felt like something built by an ancient king—more like a tomb than a command center. At least that was what it was like for someone who'd grown up in the hills and forests around Bailovo. Probably the men who worked here all the time were used to it. He tried to think of other things. He would have struck up a conversation with the black-uniformed SS captain, but the man didn't seem to be the chatty type.

"I'd hate to be in any squad trying to capture this place," said Stanislav

Balan quietly, just behind Dobri's right shoulder. "I think the Fuehrer could hold off the whole Red Army from here."

"We like to think so," said the SS officer in almost unaccented Bulgarian. "The Fuehrer has a great appreciation for security."

Dobri looked at Balan out of the corner of his eye. He would keep his lips tight while they were here, he decided.

The food in the officers' mess was tasty, and Dobri tucked in with enthusiasm; it had been a long while since breakfast. After the meal he and Balan received a short tour of the command center, courtesy of the SS captain. He showed them the large conference room at the center of the complex, its only furnishings a large wooden table surrounded by chairs. The walls were covered with maps. To the left, the captain said, were the smaller meeting rooms where, most likely, "your king is now being interviewed by the Fuehrer and his top aides." Dobri suppressed a shudder. Judging from the way the SS officer had said the words, Tsar Boris was in for something less polite than an interview.

"On that side," the officer said, pointing to the opposite end of the conference room, "are the Fuehrer's private apartments. No one is permitted there." He stared at Dobri and Balan as if he thought they might try to sneak inside. Dobri and Balan nodded. Dobri tried to think of some clever way to break the silence, but nothing came to him.

"Well," the captain said, looking at his watch, "I believe the schedule calls for His Majesty to be in meetings for most of the afternoon. Perhaps you would like to go to your rooms and get some rest?"

To Dobri, it sounded less like an invitation than a command.

Except for a brief midafternoon visit, Dobri and Balan didn't see Tsar Boris until almost midnight, when he returned to the guest bunker. He looked tired and tense.

"How are the meetings progressing, Your Majesty?" Balan said.

Tsar Boris glanced at his secretary, then away. "Fine, Stanislav. Just fine."

The room where Dobri slept was small, and all he could think about as he lay down on his bed was what would happen if the forced-air ventilation system malfunctioned. Would they suffocate? He tossed and turned for much of the night, kept wakeful by the artificial silence. It was almost as if he could feel the weight of the concrete walls pressing on him. It was the worst night's sleep he'd had in a long time.

Boris lay on the narrow bed and stared up into the darkness. He had felt the pressure building during today's meetings. Though no one would come out and say the words, it was obvious that Hitler was desperate for reinforcements on the Russian front. Keitel, Zeitzler, and Jodl spoke in generalities and possible scenarios, but Boris could tell they were dancing around the unpleasant reality that the Wehrmacht was not only not advancing; it was breaking down under the steady pounding from the Russian army.

Hitler wanted Bulgarian troops to throw into the red maw of the northern front. And Boris could not let him have them. It came down to just such a simple proposition.

What would tomorrow bring? Would his arguments hold one more time as they had in the past?

It was dark, and he was stumbling along, unable to see anything. But he still carried the weight in his arms, and he still felt the soldier's lifeless limbs flapping against his legs as he walked. Where was he trying to go? When could he finally lay down this ghastly burden he carried? He had borne it for so long that it almost seemed a part of him. He wondered, if he really was able to release the corpse at last, would he still be the same? Did he know how to do anything but stumble in the dark carrying a weight that no one else could understand? He longed desperately to simply drop the body and run, but he was also afraid to do so.

Where was the light? Always before, there had been some light. And then he remembered, and became almost thankful for the darkness. Because when he saw…

Boris's eyes flew open, and at first he almost screamed, thinking he was still locked in the darkness of the dream—that the nightmare had become real.

But no, he was in the bunker, in the pitch black of Hitler's lair. Here there was neither day nor night. He could only wait in the windowless room until the next time came, until he was summoned once again to the table.

He felt a pressure ballooning in his chest and willed himself to slow his breathing, to pull the air in deeply, hold it, and release it slowly. It was impossible to gauge the passing of time in the darkness of the bunker; only the glow of his wristwatch marked the crawling of the minutes.

Finally, just before dawn, he drifted into a fitful sleep.

When Tsar Boris emerged from his room, Dobri was waiting, dressed and ready, in the hallway connecting the guest rooms.

"Good morning, Your Majesty. What are your orders for today?"

"Good morning, Sergeant Dimitrov. I believe I'm scheduled for meetings until midday. Be ready to leave early this afternoon, right after lunch."

He looked tired. Dobri wondered if the king had slept as little as he had.

Balan joined them in the hallway and received the same quick briefing from Tsar Boris.

"Did you sleep well, Your Majesty?" Balan said.

Tsar Boris shook his head. "It was like trying to sleep in a crypt. I hope I never have to spend another night in this place."

"I had much the same experience, Your Majesty," Balan said.

"I think perhaps Sergeant Dimitrov shares our opinion," Tsar Boris said, smiling tiredly as he looked at Dobri. "But he is too professional to say so."

"A soldier takes sleep when he can get it, Your Majesty. And when he can't, he does without."

"Well spoken, Sergeant."

As the three of them turned to walk down the hallway toward the main area of the command center, Boris clapped a hand on Dobri's shoulder. "That's why I especially wanted you on this trip, Sergeant Dimitrov. Every time I see you, I'm reminded of what fine lads make up the Bulgarian army. It makes me more mindful of my responsibilities."

Dobri detected something in the king's tone—was it worry? It was no secret that the war with Russia was not going well and that Tsar Boris was adamantly opposed to the deployment of Bulgarian troops against Russia. Dobri would not like to be in such a position. That was why God gave kingdoms to men like Tsar Boris and sergeant's stripes to men like himself.

"I'm proud and honored to serve, Your Majesty," Dobri said.

They reached the end of the hallway. The SS captain was waiting for Tsar Boris, motioning him toward the area beyond the conference room. Through the open doorway, Dobri could see a table glistening with china and crystal and a man in a white jacket standing at attention in one corner. Hitler stepped out of the room and beckoned Tsar Boris with a smile.

The SS captain turned toward Dobri and Balan. "The officers' mess, gentlemen—"

"Yes, thank you, we know the way," Balan said.

The breakfast was as delicious as the lunch and dinner yesterday. Given time, duty here could become tolerable, Dobri decided, if a man could eat like this at every meal. It might even be worth the constant feeling that the walls were closing in on you.

After breakfast, he and Balan went back to the guests' quarters to pack. Tsar Boris wanted to leave at once after lunch, and though there wasn't much to gather up, at least it gave them something to do to fill the time.

When Dobri had his quarters squared away, he went into Tsar Boris's room to help Balan. Dobri folded the king's clothing from yesterday into his valise, and Balan packed up the dozen or so bottles of various medicines that Tsar Boris habitually brought with him whenever he traveled.

"What do you think, Balan? Is there any advantage in being a king?"

"None that I can see," the king's private secretary said. "Not if he's the right kind of king anyway. He carries the weight of the nation on his back. He is less free than the poorest peasant, to my mind."

"The weight on him grows."

Balan nodded. "Every day I see it. He remembers what happened to Germany's allies after the first war. It haunts him, I know it does." He gave Dobri a guilty look. "I'm sorry, Sergeant. I shouldn't be so free with my opinions on such matters. Especially here." Balan looked around the small concrete room. "Though if they're listening to us, I don't know where they'd hide the device. These walls are as sterile as the moon."

All morning Boris listened to first one general, then another talk about the excellent prospects for the German cause, given the proper eventualities and a modicum of support from their allies. He nodded and listened but said as little as possible. Finally, around noon, the conference broke up. He had to restrain himself from bolting for the door. Instead, he smiled and shook hands with the German dignitaries, one after the other.

And then Hitler motioned him over.

"Your Majesty, I've asked my staff to prepare a lunch for us in my private suite. I'd like a few more words with you before you return home."

Boris felt the dull drag of dread on his mind as he smiled at the Fuehrer. "Your Excellency, I'd be most honored."

Hitler stepped closer. "Just the two of us, Your Majesty. Two men of Teutonic ancestry who understand the exigencies of command, yes?"

What was that supposed to mean? "Yes, of course, Your Excellency."

"Good. Right this way then."

They walked across the large central conference room to the forbidden side, Hitler's inner sanctum. A huge SS guard stood at the doorway to the suite, and he snapped to attention and gave a salute before opening the door for Hitler and his guest. Boris had to resist the urge to look over his shoulder when the door closed behind him.

They reached Hitler's private dining room. A smaller table sat in the center of the windowless area, and as at this morning's meal, it was laden with sparkling plates emblazoned with the insignia of the Reich, along with heavy crystal goblets. Hitler motioned Boris to one of the two chairs at the table, then struck a small silver bell.

A panel in the wall opened, and the inevitable white-jacketed men carried in trays of food. Boris wasn't sure he could stomach another bite in this fortress, this prison, but he knew there was no avoiding the formalities. He watched as the attendants loaded his plates with gravy-laden schnitzel, stewed potatoes, a cucumber salad, and the obligatory *Sacher torte* for dessert. Boris scooted the rich food around on his plate and tried to eat a bite every now and then.

"Your Majesty, my generals can't just come right out and say anything. They lecture and they theorize, but as usual, they leave it to me to do the dirty work of interpretation." He laughed and speared a bite of schnitzel. As the meat was halfway to his mouth, he looked at Boris and, smiling as if he were commenting about the weather, said, "We need to know when some of your divisions can move north, across the Danube, to support our troops facing the Russians."

Boris put down his fork. In what he hoped was a calm, even tone, he said, "Your Excellency, I thought we had long ago settled this matter. I believe my troops can be more useful to the Reich by staying where they are: guarding your rear along the Aegean Sea and keeping a watchful eye on Turkey. I believe we should remain neutral toward Russia."

"Well, I'm afraid it's a bit late in the day for that," Hitler said, jabbing the meat into his mouth and chewing vigorously. "For three years now I've allowed you to straddle the fence on Russia, Your Majesty, but matters are coming to a head, and I must know, plain and simple, where you stand."

Hitler wouldn't look at him; he busied himself with his food. But clearly, the burden of the next words was on Boris.

"Your Excellency, I repeat: I've made this clear—"

"You know what you remind me of?" Hitler said, now staring angrily and waving a finger in midair. "A little rich boy who's had things all his own way every day of his life. He sends everyone else to do his errands for him, but he can't be bothered. You've gotten back the Dobrudja because of our efforts. Your troops administer Macedonia and Thrace with our sponsorship. And still you want more of Macedonia, more of Thrace. Yet do you lift a finger to help those who've handed you these territories on a silver platter? You act as if you've gotten all this by your own efforts, when in reality, Your Majesty, with due respect, you're forever trapped between cupidity on one side and cowardice on the other!"

Boris sat in shock for several moments, considering how to respond to Hitler's tirade. He held the Fuehrer's eyes; to look away now wouldn't help matters. Across the table from him, the world's most powerful corporal stared angrily at the aristocratic king of a poor, backward country. Boris asked himself if it was beyond Hitler to leap across the table with a steak knife.

He had often wondered how it would feel, once he was backed into this final corner. He had wondered how he would react, how he would think. He looked within himself and realized that he felt nothing. His course was clear; it had been set ever since he came home for the final time from the horrors of the Great War's trenches, ever since an angry populace, bled white by his father's military adventures, had demanded the abdication of *Le Monarque* and the accession of his war-sickened son. Boris felt the insane urge to laugh; all this time he had been performing every maneuver he could imagine to avoid this choice, and when it came, as it turned out, there was no choice after all.

"Your Excellency, I can only say what I have already said. We have given the Reich our support, the use of our territory, the fruit of our fields and lakes. But when it comes to sending Bulgarian troops to fight against Russians, I must insist on our right to maintain neutrality. In that area, Your Excellency, Bulgaria must be allowed to follow her own course."

Hitler said nothing, but Boris could see the red rising in his cheeks. After what seemed a long time, he sat back in his chair and nodded. "So. That is how it will be. I see." He reached in front of him and rang the silver bell.

The wall panel swung open and a serving man appeared. *"Ja, mein Fuehrer?"*

"It appears we are at an impasse, Your Majesty," Hitler said in a flat voice, not looking at Boris. "Will you at least have a last glass of Piesporter with me, a toast to the hope of better days? Then you may leave."

"Of course."

Hitler waved a hand without looking at the server, who ducked back behind the wall panel. He reappeared moments later with a silver tray bearing two glasses of wine with the barest hint of yellow. As Boris watched, the man picked up a goblet and started to set it in front of Hitler.

"No, no, you stupid oaf! Serve my guest first!"

"Entschuldigen sie mich, bitte, mein Fuehrer," the man said. He seemed flustered by the sharp rebuke, but after a moment's hesitation, he turned and set the wine in front of Boris. The other glass he placed in front of Hitler.

Hitler picked up his drink and held it over the center of the table. Boris did the same, touching the Fuehrer's wineglass with a ring almost as clear as that of the silver bell.

"To victory, Your Excellency," Boris said.

Hitler looked at him strangely for a moment, then downed the contents of his glass. Boris took a draught of the sweet, light wine, leaving his goblet just less than half full.

Hitler stared at Boris's wine for a moment, then looked at Boris.

"Well, I suppose there's not much more to be said, is there?"

"Not on that matter, I'm afraid, Your Excellency."

"All right then. You're a busy man. You should be on your way."

Boris stood. "Very well, Your Excellency. I wish you all success."

Hitler rose and stalked to the door of the dining room. He pulled it open, motioning Boris through. Without speaking, they passed through the private suite until they came to the doorway to the conference room. When they went outside, Balan and Dimitrov were waiting—thankfully, with the luggage beside them.

"Thank you again, Your Excellency, for hosting us," Boris said, not quite able to meet the Fuehrer's eyes. Hitler gave him a vague wave in return, muttering something that sounded like *"auf Wiedersehen."*

As soon as the Junkers reached cruising altitude, Dobri watched as the king went toward the cockpit. Soon the copilot joined them in the passenger lounge. And then, to everyone's surprise, Captain Bauer came out. He looked at them and spread his hands. "The apprentice wishes to test his wings unaided," he explained.

In a few seconds, Dobri felt himself pressed into his seat as the plane went into a climb. He looked at Bauer, who was staring at the cockpit door like a man trying to decide if he should be worried.

Balan unbuckled and stood. "I'll just check on your pupil, Captain," he said, smiling. But Dobri saw the nervousness in the secretary's eyes as he turned toward the front of the aircraft.

He was gone for several minutes, then came back out and sat beside Dobri.

"We're getting close to the Carpathians," Bauer said, standing. "Scherer, I think our trainee has had enough solo time, don't you?"

The two men went toward the cockpit. Balan leaned toward Dobri.

"When I went in there, he told me he wanted to find out at what altitude his ears would begin ringing. I saw an oxygen line and recommended that he take some, and at first he hesitated, but then took a few breaths."

"He didn't look at all pleased after his lunch with Hitler," Dobri said.

"No, and Hitler wasn't exactly passing out cigars either."

Tsar Boris came back and sat down in the passenger cabin, beaming with pleasure. "Amazing! I must spend more time learning to fly."

Dobri smiled and nodded. But still, he decided he would be happiest when the wheels of this airplane were on the ground at Vrazhdebna Airport.

When they landed, Dobri expected the king to ask to be driven to Vrana, since the tsaritza and the children were there. It was his favorite ritual after returning from a trip: he would go as soon as possible to Princess Maria-Louisa to report his return, and the princess would then announce it to her mother.

But instead, Tsar Boris asked Dobri to drive him directly to the palace. "I must brief the prime minister on this meeting with Hitler," he said. "I'll get out to Vrana a little later."

Dobri swallowed his disappointment. A delay in getting to Vrana meant a delay in seeing Daria. "Yes, Your Majesty."

32

Ｔ he phone rang in Dobri's rooms. He picked up the handset.
"Sergeant Dimitrov, I presume you would be able to drive me to
Vrana in time for lunch?"

At the sound of Tsar Boris's voice, Dobri involuntarily stiffened to attention, even though he wore only his threadbare dressing gown over his under-
wear. "Yes, Your Majesty. When would you like me to pick you up?"

"Eleven o'clock will be fine. At the door near the winter garden, if you
please. I hope to have Captain Bauer with me; I'd like him to meet my
children."

"Yes, Your Majesty."

Dobri hung up the phone. He picked up his watch from the nightstand;
it was not yet nine o'clock. Two hours to fret about what would happen when
he saw Daria.

He thought again about the king's staying at the palace overnight upon
his return rather than rejoining his family. Dobri couldn't escape the feeling
that such a variation from Tsar Boris's customary routine was somehow
related to the unpleasantness that had apparently taken place in Hitler's private dining room.

At three minutes before eleven, Dobri, shaved and in his cleanest uniform, sat
behind the wheel of the king's favorite Packard, idling just outside the door to
the winter garden. He drummed his fingers on the wheel and tried desperately
not to think about the night he had brought Daria home from the Midwinter Ball, through this very door, and what had happened just inside. If her
answer to him wasn't favorable, he would live the rest of his life without the
prospect of finding out what might lie on the other side of such a kiss.

The door opened, and Tsar Boris came out, leading Bauer, who looked
a little embarrassed, probably because he was dressed only in fatigues. Dobri
popped around to the passenger side and opened both doors.

"I tell you, Captain, that you shouldn't be embarrassed at all," Tsar Boris was saying when Dobri got back in. "Queen Giovanna will not be in the least offended by your dress, I assure you, and the crown prince will be positively fascinated by it. You had no warning; this invitation occurred to me only this morning."

"Well, Your Majesty, if you insist."

"I do. Drive on please, Sergeant."

All during the drive from the center of Sofia, southwest on Tsar Osvoboditel and out of the city, Tsar Boris talked with Bauer about flying. It was his new passion, he declared, and as soon as his duties permitted, he would take lessons. Bauer assured him he would be a quick study, if his skill with the Fuehrer's Junkers was any indication.

Dobri turned down the long, tree-lined pavement of Vrana, past the guardhouse, and into the looping drive in front of the royal residence. By the time Dobri had set the parking brake, Crown Prince Simeon and his sister were dashing down the front steps to greet their father.

Tsar Boris scooped them both into a hug, then set them on the ground and introduced Bauer.

"This is the man who flies Herr Hitler's very own private airplane," he said.

Simeon's eyes widened. Even the princess looked impressed.

"Prince Simeon, would you like to escort our guest into the house and introduce him to your mother?"

"Me too!" said Princess Maria-Louisa.

"All right, then, both of you. But go gently. Captain Bauer may not be as accustomed as I am to being pulled along by impatient children."

Dobri parked the Packard in the garage behind the house. He got out and studied himself in the side mirror. As far as he could tell, he looked no worse than usual—maybe a bit better, in fact. He tugged his coattails down, squared his shoulders, and walked toward the house.

He came in at the side nearest the garage, and there she stood, in the entryway, framed by the dark wood of the doorway into the queen's drawing room. He looked at her, trying to read what was behind her dark eyes; she looked at him, and it seemed she was holding herself in check, like someone who was afraid of what she would say or do if she wasn't careful.

"Daria, I…I must know something. I—"

"Where were you?"

His eyes widened at the sharpness of her tone. "Me? I just got back from Germany with His Maj—"

"No, not that! Where were you last Friday? I waited for you all day to come by my rooms, as you were doing every hour on the hour before. And suddenly you just…disappeared! What was I to think?"

The few wits Dobri had left made themselves scarce. He stared at her, feeling like a dog whose master has just given an unfamiliar command. "Friday? I… Well, I was…" And then it came to him. "Friday I was coming to see you, and the devil himself wouldn't let me get there! First, you were out when I came by, off to the park with Her Majesty and the children…"

The set of her jaw loosened slightly at that.

"And then Captain Kalayev sent me on an infernal errand to the Central Police Station, and the dimwit corporal I was with blew out a tire, and we had no spare, and I was filthy, and the next morning I was supposed to leave, and—"

Suddenly she was in his arms, and her hands were on the back of his head. Her face was turned up to him, and their lips were together. Dobri held her and kissed her, and when she finally came up for breath, he said, "Daria, I just want to know one thing…"

"Yes! Yes, Dobri, I'll go anywhere you want to go, live anywhere you want to live. I've done all I can do here, and the queen says sometimes the battle must be fought and sometimes it mustn't. And now I think it mustn't—not until after our wedding anyway, and when do you think we should plan the wedding?"

Again Dobri was stumped for a response. "So…you will?"

"Will what?"

"Will marry me."

"Yes, of course, didn't you hear me?"

"Well, I thought I did, but…"

She pressed her lips to his again but more slowly this time, more softly.

Dobri thought it was better than any wine, any *rakia,* any *slivovitza* he had ever tasted. And when she pulled away, the look in her eyes made his heart leap like a thing gone wild.

"I suppose I must ask Her Majesty's permission," he said in the loudest voice he could manage—barely above a whisper.

"She has already given it."

They wheeled around, and Queen Giovanna was standing in the doorway, smiling like a Madonna in a portrait.

"Your Majesty! I beg your pardon—"

"There is no need, Sergeant Dimitrov. I was coming to find Daria, to tell her to have the staff serve luncheon on the south veranda. And instead, I found two people doing something that has been put off too long already."

Queen Giovanna walked into the main salon, her arms linked to Dobri's on one side and Daria's on the other. Tsar Boris, Captain Bauer, and the children all looked up as they entered. The queen was smiling widely, like someone who knows the world's best secret.

"I believe I will need to consult with Father Antonov about the schedule for the royal chapel," Queen Giovanna said. "It seems we shall need it for a wedding."

Tsar Boris shot to his feet and actually clapped his hands. "Bravo, Sergeant Dimitrov! Bravo!"

"And Mademoiselle Daria had nothing to do with it, I suppose?" the tsaritza said.

"Of course I didn't mean that." Tsar Boris crossed the room and embraced Daria. "I'm so happy for you, my dear," he said. "There aren't that many good men left in the world, I'm afraid. But you've found one of them."

"Yes, I think so," Daria said, and the look she gave Dobri made him want to shout or burst into song or jump up and down. But he did none of those things; he only smiled at her. And, he thought, she knew.

"Well, there's nothing like good news to sharpen the appetite," Tsar Boris said. "Captain Bauer, everyone, I believe luncheon is being prepared on the veranda. For August, it's pleasantly cool today, so dining alfresco seems appropriate, don't you think?"

During the lunch Tsar Boris told his wife that he planned to take Prince Kyril, Colonel Bardarov, and Stanislav Balan on an outing to the Rila Mountains. "Just a few of the boys," he said, winking at Bauer. "I need a little mountain time to clear my head."

"Probably just the thing, Your Majesty," Bauer said.

If you only knew, Dobri thought.

"When will you leave, Father?" Crown Prince Simeon asked.

"In the morning, probably while you are still dreaming," Tsar Boris said. "I don't know, we may even climb Moussala."

"I think the children and I will stay here for a few more days," Tsaritza Giovanna said. "It's so much cooler here than at the palace."

"Good idea. Sergeant Dimitrov, I think you should stay on guard here, at Vrana, until I return. I can't trust my family's safety to just anyone, wouldn't you agree?"

"Very well, Your Majesty." Dobri grinned. Beneath the table, Daria's hand found his.

The following Sunday, Dobri drove the tsaritza, Daria, and the children up to Samokov, on the road to Tsarska-Bistritza and the royal chalet. Tsar Boris met them in his Packard convertible, and together they drove on to Sokoletz, one of the children's favorite places. After a meeting back in Tsarska with War Minister Mihov, the royal entourage took a leisurely walk down to Pessakò, the picturesque town square of the royal resort town of Tcham-Koria. That evening Boris kissed his children and his wife and sent them back to Tsarska-Bistritza.

"I must go back to Sofia tomorrow," he said, "but you and the children—and of course you, Mademoiselle Daria, and your faithful protector—should remain here in the mountain air. I'll call you in a day or two to let you know how things are going."

There was no place in Bulgaria more delightful than Tsarska-Bistritza, especially in August. Monday passed, and Tuesday, and Dobri went about in constant delight. Every move Daria made, every expression of her face, every lift of her eyebrows or curve of her lips—it was as if he were seeing some miraculous thing.

On Tuesday evening he heard the queen wonder out loud why Tsar Boris hadn't called.

"I'm sure he must be very busy, Your Majesty," Daria said. "I don't think you should worry. He'll probably call tomorrow."

On Wednesday morning the phone rang in the chalet, and Queen Giovanna answered. But Dobri and Daria could tell by the expression on her face that she wasn't hearing her husband's voice.

"What do you mean, ill?" she said.

Daria's eyes widened.

"Why was I not told earlier? I'll come down immediately—"

She listened for a long time.

"You're certain?"

Another long silence.

"Very well, but keep me constantly informed, do you hear?"

She hung up. When she looked up at them, her face was pale, her lips pinched. "They say His Majesty is…ill. But they assure me there is no need to worry, that I should stay here with the children, and they will keep me informed." She sat on a nearby divan, her arms crossed in front of her. Dobri could see her weighing the possibilities in her mind…or fighting off dread; he wasn't sure which.

Later that afternoon, when the queen had almost convinced herself to leave for Sofia, a car pulled up in front of the chalet. Dobri recognized the palace doctor, Daskalov, and Inspector Guentchev. The two men wore worried looks as they walked up the front steps. Dobri took them to the drawing room, where the tsaritza sat with Daria and the children.

As soon as Daria saw Daskalov, she gathered up Crown Prince Simeon and Princess Maria-Louisa. "Come, let's do some work on that new puzzle we bought in the marketplace last Sunday," she said, pushing them ahead of her up the stairs.

Dobri turned to leave, but the tsaritza said, "Sergeant Dimitrov, I want you to stay. Please, gentlemen," she said to Daskalov and Guentchev, "why have you come?"

"Your Majesty," Daskalov said, kneading his hat as he held it in front of his chest, "I regret to inform you that your husband's condition has deteriorated." He glanced nervously at Guentchev. "We didn't want to alarm you needlessly, but—"

"Sergeant Dimitrov, get the car," the queen said, standing. "We are leaving for Sofia at once."

"No, no, Your Majesty, there is no need for that," Dr. Daskalov said. "We are going back immediately to monitor His Majesty's condition, and if there is a change, we will call you at once."

Queen Giovanna slowly sat back down, her face a mask of confusion. "I feel as if I should be there with him."

"Please, Your Majesty, don't weary yourself with such a long drive, especially while you're upset. We'll keep you informed."

Dobri saw the two men out and watched them drive away. When he returned to the drawing room, the tsaritza had not moved. He was not even sure she realized Daskalov and Guentchev had left.

At nine o'clock in the evening the telephone rang again. Dobri, Daria, and the queen all looked at each other. Queen Giovanna went into the other room to answer it. She had been gone less than a minute when she came back in. "We must leave at once."

"What's the matter?" the crown prince asked.

"Your father is sick," Queen Giovanna said. "We need to go to him."

"But what about our dinner?" said Princess Maria-Louisa.

"Don't worry, Your Royal Highness," Daria said. "I'll pack your food. We can eat in the car."

It was the longest drive Dobri had ever made. He could feel the tsaritza's fingers gripping the back of the seat at his shoulder; clearly she was willing the car to go faster, always faster down the twisting mountain road. The children, for their part, fell asleep in less than half an hour. Daria sat in the front seat with him, but most of the time she had her arm extended toward the tsaritza, holding her hand.

At 10:30 they arrived at the palace. The queen leaped from the car and half ran toward the door, held open for her by Daskalov and another man.

Dobri switched off the car, then helped Daria carry the sleeping children up to their bedrooms, where she put them in bed without removing anything except their shoes and socks.

After returning the car to the motor pool, Dobri rushed back to the palace. In the foyer of the private wing, he found Balan pacing back and forth.

"Mr. Balan? What's happened to His Majesty?"

"They think it's his heart," Balan said. Dobri felt an icy blade of fear slicing into his breastbone.

"When we were in the mountains, he complained a few times about chest pain. But he wouldn't slow down, not for a minute," Balan said. "It was almost as if he was driving himself, pushing harder and harder."

"He seemed well enough when we were in Bistritza," Dobri said, shaking his head in confusion.

"Yes, but you know how he is: he never wants to worry the tsaritza or the children. You know how strong-willed he can be."

Dobri nodded.

"I'll tell you something, Sergeant. When we climbed Moussala, he did a very strange thing. We were on the way back down from the peak. He had been talking about feeling tired but speaking very little. Suddenly Tsar Boris struck out on a steep path branching off from the main trail. Prince Kyril and I called after him, told him if he felt poorly, he should stay on the main trail, since it was easier. But he just waved at us and told us to go on, that he would rejoin us later.

"Well, I was worried for him, so I left the trail to find him. Sergeant, when I came upon him, Tsar Boris was standing at the edge of a steep cliff, and the look on his face was the strangest thing I have ever seen. I couldn't help remembering his uncle who fell while rock climbing. I called out to him to ask him if he needed any help. He looked up at me, and it was as if I had transgressed some rule. He was cross with me, told me I should have stayed on the trail with the others. I convinced him to rejoin us, but he said very little the rest of the way down the mountain."

"When did he fall ill?"

"Monday night," Balan said. "He was working in Pavel Grouev's office, but Mr. Grouev said that about half past seven Tsar Boris complained of feel-

ing bad and went upstairs. Then Mr. Grouev heard a commotion, and someone told him the king was vomiting violently. Tsar Boris hasn't gotten out of
his bed since. They've even flown in Sajitz, his doctor from Berlin. And I
think they've sent for some other fancy specialist from Vienna."

Berlin... Hitler...the unpleasant meeting...

"Mr. Balan, have you heard anyone speculate about...about the possibility of foul play?"

Balan looked surprised. "No, not at all. His heart is what I've been hearing. God knows he's been under tremendous strain."

Dobri nodded. He turned away from Balan and started up the stairs.

"Oh, by the way, Sergeant Dimitrov?"

Dobri turned back.

"I heard about your engagement to Miss Richetti. Congratulations."

"Oh yes. Thank you."

Dobri went upstairs and found Daria waiting with the queen on a bench
outside the king's bedroom.

"There must be five or six doctors in there with him," Daria whispered.

"Have they told the tsaritza anything?"

Daria shook her head.

Finally the door opened, and Dr. Sajitz came out, with Daskalov following him. Queen Giovanna stood, and Daria stood beside her, an arm around
the queen's shoulders.

"Your Majesty, we're still examining your husband and haven't reached
any final conclusions, but I must tell you that his condition is quite grave. To
us, it appears he's suffered a coronary thrombosis. If he survives, he will likely
be an invalid."

The word *if* struck Dobri almost like a physical blow. For twenty-five
years, Tsar Boris had ruled Bulgaria. Especially during the uncertainties of the
present war, he had come to embody the security of the Bulgarian people. To
imagine the future without Tsar Boris was impossible.

Queen Giovanna was trembling, but she held herself erect and put a few
questions to the doctors. Then she asked to go to her husband's bedside.
Daria started to go with her, but Queen Giovanna held up a hand and shook
her head.

"No, Daria. This is something I must do alone."

She went into the king's bedroom, and Dr. Daskalov quietly closed the door behind her.

Boris felt a cool hand sliding into his. He opened his eyes.

"Giovanna."

"Yes, my darling. I'm here."

"I'm...sorry, *ma chère.*"

She smiled at him, and the beauty and courage of it made Boris wish he were strong enough to weep.

"Don't be silly," she said. "What is there to apologize for?"

He turned his head away from her. "Ah, Giovanna. So many things...so many things."

She was softly stroking his forearm, his cheek. "The doctors say your ticker has played a little prank on you."

He felt the smile trying to form. "Yes. Rather a nasty little prank, I'm afraid."

The weight of his eyelids was too much. He let them close. "How are the children?"

"They're well. Daria is with them constantly."

"Daria...such a lovely girl. I'm happy for her. And her Bailovski champion."

He drew several breaths. His chest felt strange, as if it belonged to someone else.

"Boris, tell me, my dear, what can I do to help you?"

Help? The only help he wanted was rest. But then he realized there was something else after all. He rolled his head to the other side, nearly panting with the effort. He moved his lips but couldn't tell if any sound was coming out.

"What is it, *amore?*" Giovanna said. "What are you trying to say?"

He heard the rustle of her clothing, felt the brush of her hair on his face as she placed her ear near his lips. He gathered himself and forced the air, suddenly as heavy as a sodden blanket in the bottom of a trench, through his vocal cords. The words came out in a hoarse, barely audible whisper.

"Tell Simeon...honor and love. Honor and love."

He had no more strength left. He felt her hand on his cheek, then her lips kissing him.

"Yes, my dearest love. I'll tell him," she said. Then the darkness drifted over him.

The next morning Pavel Grouev found Dobri in the hallway. "Take this to the communications office," he said, handing Dobri a note written in the chancellor's neat hand. "Tell them to send this out to the newspapers and radio stations."

Grouev looked like a man who had had a piece of his lung removed. His eyes looked bruised by lack of sleep.

"Mr. Grouev, are you all right, sir?"

"Thank you, Sergeant, I'll manage. This is just…a very stressful time."

"Yes, sir."

Dobri walked toward the palace telegraph office. As he went, he glanced at the communiqué. It stated very simply that Tsar Boris had fallen seriously ill and for the past three days had been under the care of physicians. When Dobri handed the note to the telegraph operator on duty, the man looked up at him with an expression halfway between fear and incomprehension.

"Chancellor Grouev has asked that you send this to the media," Dobri said.

The operator stared at the note as if it were written in hieroglyphics. "Tsar Boris…ill?"

"Just send it," Dobri said in the gentlest voice he could manage. "The people need to know."

Not long after the initial communiqué went out, Dobri began to hear the murmurs in the hallways of the palace: "…in the prime of health before he went to Germany…" "…wouldn't give Hitler what he wanted…" "…could have been the Communists…"

Dobri didn't like to think that Tsar Boris was the victim of some sort of poisoning. When he heard such talk, he felt a deep sadness, a sense of failure. What good was a bodyguard if he couldn't protect his sovereign?

And yet he knew firsthand how deeply Tsar Boris cared for the fate of his people, how the mounting pressure of balancing both the pro- and anti-German factions of his own government had taxed all the king's powers of diplomacy. Couldn't the strain of such a burden break any man, even one of such mettle as Tsar Boris?

On Saturday, the Feast of the Assumption, Daria sat beside the bed of the crown prince, who was napping fitfully. He had begged her to read to him before he fell asleep—an activity that had ceased at his fifth birthday, over a year ago, by his own request. But in these anxious days, she guessed, even a brave six-year-old needed the soothing rhythm of her voice. She was sitting with her eyes closed, her head leaned back against the chair, when she heard the rustle of clothing. She opened her eyes, and Queen Giovanna stood in the doorway and beckoned her.

In the hallway, the queen said, "The king is resting easier. He has a slight fever, but he seems more settled. Will you go with me to the chapel?"

"Of course, Your Majesty."

Father Antonov was there, and Daria sat quietly as the priest chanted the Roman rite over the queen's bowed head. When he finished, Queen Giovanna told him she wished to remain a while longer to pray. Father Antonov bowed and quietly left the chapel.

Daria watched the queen at her prayers and listened to the silence of the chapel. The walls and ceilings were frescoed with saints and apostles, and the soft glow of the candles made their features softer, more lifelike and forgiving. Daria wondered what words Queen Giovanna was using to beg for the life of her husband She wondered what strength the queen had left and what might still lie before her. Daria watched her lips move silently, watched the furrowing of her brow, and thought about Father Jacob's wrestling with God beside the River Jabbok. He was ever doomed to lose the fall, but he wrung a blessing from his adversary, though it cost him a lifelong limp. What sort of limp might Queen Giovanna carry away from this wrestling match?

She tried to frame words in her mind to aid the cause of her queen and friend but could not. The best she could manage was a sort of silent, inarticulate pleading. Would the God of her fathers hear her prayer in this place?

It was almost noon. Daria heard footsteps approaching from the back of the chapel. She looked up and saw one of the doctors striding quietly but purposefully toward Queen Giovanna, an expression of worried inevitability on his face. Daria felt her heart grow cold.

The doctor bent beside the queen and whispered a few words. Queen Giovanna stood, and the first place her eyes sought was Daria's face. Daria went to her and held her. They followed the doctor out of the chapel and up the stairs to the king's chamber.

A quiet commotion stirred in and around Tsar Boris's bedroom. Doctors went in and out, all wearing worried looks, asking in low, urgent voices for oxygen and various medicines. The queen went into his room. Prince Kyril and Princess Evdokia joined her, kneeling at the head of the king's bed.

He was standing in a mountain meadow beside one of the Rila lakes. A gentle breeze rippled the water, and he could smell the fragrance of the zdravetz blooming along the shoreline. And he knew this was the place; he could finally put down his burden.

He gently laid the soldier on the sweet grass beside the lake. He realized he had been afraid for so long, and now there was no more reason for fear. He could look in the soldier's face, and what he saw would not harm him. He looked down and saw, as all along he had known he would, his own face, composed in the peace of death.

He leaned over and kissed the forehead of the quiet, resting body. He stood and saw a light coming from the center of the lake. He smiled and walked toward it.

Daria watched as Queen Giovanna, braced on either side by the dead king's brother and sister, received the condolences of the prime minister, the doctors, the others who were there. Prime Minister Filov went downstairs and drafted two proclamations, which he read on the radio that evening. The first announced to a stunned nation the death of its beloved king. The second proclaimed the accession of Tsar Simeon II, king of the Bulgarians.

33

Epilogue: Sofia, May 1996

T he crowd finished singing the "Mnogoya Leta" to the accompaniment of the church bells. Strangers hugged each other and said, "He has come back! The king has returned!" It was almost as if they were talking about the second coming of Christ.

But after a while it looked to Dobri as if they didn't quite know what to do with themselves. They hadn't thought beyond the arrival of Simeon in his native land, after all these years. Maybe they thought that as soon as he landed, he would suddenly appear among them like a mystical figure and instantly transform their lives into something better, something barely imagined, something they themselves probably couldn't explain.

Dobri watched and listened and knew it wasn't so simple. There was a distance between where Simeon was now, at Vrazhdebna, and here—a distance that couldn't be measured in kilometers. A distance that could be measured only in years…

When Tsar Boris died, the nation went crazy with grief. It was as if each Bulgarian was mourning his own death in some way. Always Tsar Boris had stood at the helm, they thought. No matter how confusing the times, they could say to themselves, "Tsar Boris will think of something; he will watch out for us." And now their protector was gone—dead, just like any other human.

Tsar Boris's funeral was in the first few days of September, twenty-five years to the month from his accession. Dobri marched in the honor guard with the coffin and the royal family. Prince Kyril, the king's brother, walked beside his widowed sister-in-law. Behind them were Princess Evdokia and Princess Nadejda, the king's sisters. On the other side of Tsaritza Giovanna was her sister, Mafalda. As he marched that day, Dobri kept remembering how, earlier that morning in the palace, Princess Maria-Louisa's face was wet with tears, yet she held herself as tall as she could, imitating her mother. And standing beside her was little Simeon, now crowned with a title far too heavy for the shoulders of any six-year-old, looking more bewildered than anything else. It was his face, above all others, that Dobri remembered from that day.

Behind the royal family walked the members of the cabinet, high government and military officials, diplomats, and foreign dignitaries. Pavel Grouev was there, looking as if each step might be his last.

The long procession wound from Alexander Nevsky Cathedral to the railroad station, where a train waited to carry Tsar Boris's casket to Rila Monastery for burial. And the streets were crammed with weeping, moaning Bulgarians, watching their last hope pass them on a black-draped caisson, his casket swathed in the royal flag of the kingdom of Bulgaria, a kingdom that would soon be no more.

A regency was appointed to govern in Simeon's name: Prince Kyril, Prime Minister Filov, and Minister of War General Mihov. It was the first of three governments that would follow each other in quick succession, each less pro-German than the last, as the Red Army advanced and the Communist insurgency within Bulgaria increased in intensity. Bulgaria's leaders tried frantically to strike some agreement with the Western powers to forestall the certain rise of Communism if the Red Army reached Bulgaria—but to no avail. The Americans and British refused to meet with any Bulgarian delegation unless their allies—the Soviets—were also included. And in the meantime, American and British bombs began to rain down upon Sofia, to the point that the government and military command had to evacuate to Tcham-Koria.

A year after Tsar Boris's death, the Red Army reached the Danube. And although Bulgaria had steadfastly maintained diplomatic relations with the Soviet Union when not a single other German ally did so, Moscow declared war on Bulgaria, and the Red Army entered the country as if invading a hostile nation. Within weeks, the Bulgarian Communist Party, outlawed and severely repressed under Tsar Boris, had taken control of the government and began settling scores.

Tsaritza Giovanna and her children were placed under house arrest in Vrana—though the Communist authorities never used that term. During those days, Dobri remembered, Veltchev, a cook in the palace for at least twenty years, used to sleep on the floor outside the queen's bedroom, in fear that the Communists would try to come at night and abduct her or the children.

When the People's Tribunals began, Queen Giovanna brought Dobri and Daria to her. "Get away from here while you can," she said. "The Bolsheviks will kill everyone associated with my husband's government. Go back to Bailovo or anywhere else you think safe and blend in. That's the secret these days: attract no attention."

But neither Daria nor Dobri could leave the queen and her children. So they stayed at Vrana, wondering each day whether the cars with the red flags would come up the driveway, whether armed men would take Queen Giovanna and the children away to some horrible fate. Dobri, Daria, and the others they would most likely shoot out of hand, since Dobri, at least, was duty bound to resist.

The Jews were sent home from the camps, but their places were soon taken by "enemies of the state." These were the persons lucky enough to avoid outright death sentences. Many officials of the old government simply vanished. Alexander Belev, who had headed the Commissariat for Jewish Questions, was never seen or heard from again. Later, at some of the People's Tribunals, the strange story of Liliana Panitza came out. She was spared because of her secret work on behalf of the Jews. That news brought one of the few smiles to Daria's face that Dobri remembered from those days.

Prince Kyril, Pavel Grouev, Filov, Gabrovski, and more than a dozen other former government officials were taken one night to a corner of the Sofia Central Cemetery, where they were lined up on the edge of a bomb crater and shot. Dobri heard later that Prince Kyril, as he was taking his place in line, removed the gold watch from his wrist and handed it to one of the guards. "I won't be needing this," he said. "You can have it." Pavel Grouev, the king's kindly counselor, apparently died of heart failure while waiting his turn. He was dumped in the mass grave with the others but was spared the shame of being shot by citizens of the country he had served.

The Communists appointed new regents for Tsar Simeon II, though of course the monarchy was a mere fiction by this time, a propaganda device the Communists could use to prove to the world how humane and understanding they were. Fortunately, Todor Pavlov, one of the regents, had had his life spared by Tsar Boris years earlier. He treated the tsaritza and her children with respect.

Finally, at the end of 1946, after a People's Plebiscite, the monarchy was officially abolished. The queen and her children were granted forty-eight hours to get out of the country. Dobri and Daria embraced them for the last time, then watched them get into a car and drive into the night to the train station. After that, finally obeying Queen Giovanna's advice—and with the silent blessing of Todor Pavlov—they left Sofia for Bailovo.

Most of the Jews left Bulgaria for Israel after they were freed from the camps. "Making aliyah," Daria called it—returning to their ancestral homeland. Even the handful of Jews in Bailovo left Bulgaria, never to return. But Daria, true to her promise, stayed.

She and Dobri were married in the Orthodox Church in Bailovo. They invented a different life together, a life that had nothing to do with palaces and guards and the comings and goings of powerful people. Dobri used his savings from the army to buy a few of his oldest brother's sheep, and Daria gave writing lessons to some of the schoolchildren. They lived in a small room at the back of Dobri's brother's house until, after many years, they could afford to move into a cottage with a kitchen, a small sitting room, and a bedroom. They made friends and became a part of the scenery in Bailovo. But it was many more years before Dobri could look at Daria, wearing her homespun clothing and cooking over a wood-burning stove, and not berate himself for bringing to such an estate a woman who had grown up with kings and queens. If Daria ever had similar thoughts, she was too good and kind to voice them. She gave him two sons and a daughter. She died during the winter of 1978. They had been married thirty years. He would never look at another woman.

So many people made pilgrimages to Tsar Boris's grave at Rila that the authorities ordered the remains exhumed from the monastery and transferred to the small chapel at Vrana. This happened while Queen Giovanna and the children were still there, in 1946. After they were forced out of the country, rumors circulated through the country that the Communists robbed the grave, disposed of Tsar Boris's remains, then razed the chapel.

Years passed, then decades, and the world changed. In Moscow, the empire of totalitarianism finally began to crumble and break apart from its own weight. Change was in the air. In Berlin, a wall that had been maintained by force of arms was torn down with hammers, crowbars, and bare hands. In Bailovo, Dobri heard all these things as far-off echoes. With Daria dead and his children grown, his needs had become simpler and simpler until finally he was living in the back room of what had once been his and Daria's house, taking his turn watching his own and other people's sheep. But an event took place that called him out of the half sleep in which he passed his days.

From his Spanish home in exile, Tsar Simeon and his mother had made persistent inquiries through the years about the final disposition of Tsar Boris's remains. Of course, the Communist regime steadfastly ignored them. But when the rising tide of anti-Communism finally toppled the Zhivkov government in 1989, things began to change. The mystique of Tsar Boris had somehow survived the Communist decades, and people were again allowed to visit Vrana. The rumors of the razing of the chapel were confirmed, and the new government promised to make inquiries.

In October 1991 a team of scientists excavated what was presumed to be the site of Tsar Boris's grave and found, two meters underground, the top of a heavy stone tomb. The tomb had apparently survived the demolition of the chapel. With Simeon's consent, the tomb was opened. It was empty.

Then, while the shock of this discovery was still settling in the minds of the scientists, someone found nearby a jar of thick glass. It was filled with a liquid solution and a fully preserved human heart. A smaller vial inside the jar contained a slip of paper.

Back at the offices of the Academy of Science, the jar was carefully opened and the vial retrieved. The slip of paper carried this inscription:

The Heart of H.M. Tsar Boris III
+28. VIII 1943
This heart was placed inside the glass jar by:

Affixed below these words were the signatures of five medical experts, followed by the date: September 4, 1943.

One of the signatories was still alive: Yordanka Kelepova. She confirmed that the team of medical technicians, following the autopsy, had placed Tsar Boris's heart inside the jar and given it to the priests the day before the funeral, to be placed in the casket with the body.

To Dobri, the finding of the heart was like a miracle. How had the glass jar survived the secret exhumation by the Communist authorities bent on erasing Tsar Boris's memory from history?

The heart was taken to Rila Monastery and reinterred in Tsar Boris's original grave. On the fiftieth anniversary of Tsar Boris's death, August 28, 1993, a commemorative requiem Mass was held at Rila. Dobri convinced his older son to borrow a car from one of his friends and drive him to the monastery. With tens of thousands of others crammed into and around the monastery chapel, its courtyard, and the surrounding area, Dobri listened to the solemn chants of the Mass coming over the loudspeakers. He wept openly, like many of those standing around him, but he wondered if any of them could guess how different, how much more intimate, was the source of his tears. Someone told him Queen Giovanna and Princess Maria-Louisa—now grown and married and living in the United States, with children of her own—were inside the chapel, beside Boris's tomb, but Dobri was too old and the crowd too dense for him to even think about trying to get to them.

Two hours after the tolling of the church bells announced his plane's arrival, Tsar Simeon's car turned onto the gold-painted bricks of Alexander Battenberg Square. The cars in the entourage had to crawl along because of the throngs surrounding them. "Tsar Simeon, save us!" they shouted. "Sim-e-on! Sim-e-on!" others chanted.

But the cars didn't stop in front of the National Art and Ethnographic Museum, the former Royal Palace, as many had assumed they would. Instead, they made their way slowly to the building that housed the offices of the mayor of Sofia.

"What is he doing?" Dobri heard people saying. "Why doesn't he go to the balcony of the palace?" The coming of Simeon had reminded Bulgarians—especially the old, like Dobri, but also some of the younger generation—that before the drabness of Communism, there had existed another

Bulgaria. A place where a kind king had ruled a loving populace—not perfectly, but as well as he could, given the opposing forces he had to consider. A place where beauty was encouraged. A place where people trusted their neighbors and even—as in the case of the Jews—risked their lives to protect them.

But Dobri understood. He had seen the men with hidden microphones scattered throughout the crowds. This was Bulgaria; there would always be currents and crosscurrents. Who knew this better than the son of Tsar Boris, who had negotiated with such skill the complicated ways of this little nation in the Balkans? Simeon would not proclaim the reassumption of his crown, not in the volatile atmosphere prevailing today. If he did, there would be no foreseeing the results. There would be no way to measure in advance the mayhem that might be unleashed by the upsurge of popular fervor and its clash with the ugly realities of politics.

Dobri worked his way through the mob, getting as close as he could to the ornate balcony at the corner of the mayor's building. It was a long time before Simeon appeared on the balcony; no doubt, the crowd inside the mayor's building was every bit as thick as that covering the streets and squares outside. But when he appeared, the noise was deafening.

Tsar Simeon had no microphone; no public address system had been erected so he could speak to the nation he had not seen in fifty years. This too failed to surprise Dobri. There were many, he guessed, who had done all they could to keep Simeon from coming back at all. But today, they could look in the streets and see that only so much was within their control. They might erect passive barriers; they dared do little more.

Simeon gripped the railing of the balcony and looked out over the crowd. Even from where Dobri stood, he could see that Simeon was moved to tears by the popular outpouring. He didn't raise his hands, didn't attempt to quiet the crowd. Instead, he simply put his right hand over his heart and patted it. Dobri felt his throat closing with emotion.

Yes, Simeon. There are many times when words cannot hold what we mean.

And then, beyond anything Dobri had dared to hope for, Simeon's eyes met his and held. Though he made no signal or movement, Simeon was studying Dobri; some sort of recognition or understanding was overtaking him. He turned to one of the men beside him and pointed, saying something. The man looked, then turned and left the balcony.

Dobri's heart began pounding. He waited, hemmed in by the crowd, and gripped the foolish staff he had carved with such devotion. Maybe that was all it was; Simeon wanted to know more about the quaint old man with the white hair and beard clutching the ridiculous wooden staff.

The man from the balcony slid sideways through the crowd and reached Dobri. "Come with me," he shouted. "Mr. Saxe-Coburg wants to speak with you."

Mr. Saxe-Coburg. Yes, his family name would be how Simeon would be known to most of the people of his world in exile.

Hardly able to breathe, Dobri followed the man through the maze of the crowd, toward the doors of the mayor's building.

"Who is that?" "He's going in; they're taking that old man in!" "That's one of Simeon's men. Why does he want that old peasant?"

Dobri heard them. Who could blame them? He was asking himself the same questions, though maybe for different reasons.

They reached the doors and went inside. The foyer and staircase of the mayor's offices were, as Dobri suspected, as crowded as every other place in central Sofia. They made their way up the stairs. Dobri held the beech staff like a talisman. They reached a landing on the second story, and the man took Dobri aside, into a room that looked like an office. "Wait here," he said. "Mr. Saxe-Coburg will be with you in a moment."

Dobri sat, holding the staff, and stared around at the room. There was a typewriter, though it looked different from those he had seen during his days in the palace. He supposed the sleek buttoned instrument on the desk was a telephone, but it, too, was very different. And there were machines here he didn't recognize. Maybe there were such things in some of the government offices in Bailovo, but Dobri had avoided such places for so many years that he had no way of knowing.

After about thirty minutes, the door opened, and Tsar Simeon came in. A beautiful woman was with him; Dobri guessed it was his wife, Queen Margarita. Dobri stood and did the best imitation of attention and a salute possible for an old man with a bent back and crooked knees.

"Your Majesty."

Tsar Simeon looked at him, and the expression on his face was like that of someone trying to think of the name of a melody he hasn't heard in many years. "There is something familiar about you, *dyado*," he said, "but I can't quite…"

Dobri realized he didn't at all mind being called grandfather by this man whom he had last seen as a frightened nine-year-old bundled into the back-seat of a car at night.

"Your Majesty, I am Dobri Dimitrov, of your father's Palace Guard. Here, I have brought you this." He thrust the beech staff at Simeon and stood back, half embarrassed, now that the moment had come.

The staff clattered to the floor. "Sergeant Dimitrov?" Tsar Simeon said it in an unbelieving voice. "You are…Sergeant Dimitrov, who married Mademoiselle Richetti?"

Dobri nodded. His throat was closing again, and his voice was useless to him.

Tsar Simeon strode to him and gripped him in a hug. "Sergeant Dimitrov!" he kept saying. "I had no idea… I never thought…"

"It has been many years, Your Majesty," Dobri said in a husky voice. "Much has happened."

Tsar Simeon held him at arm's length and looked at him as if he were seeing a miracle. "Sergeant Dimitrov? But…tell me about Mademoiselle… about Daria."

"She died seventeen years and seven months ago."

Tsar Simeon's hands gripped his arms. "I loved her, Sergeant. I loved her almost as much as I loved my mother."

It was very curious to be called Sergeant again after so many years. It made Dobri smile.

"I'm glad you're back, Your Majesty," he said. "You belong here."

Tsar Simeon gave him a sad smile. "I'm not sure everyone agrees with you."

"But it's true, Your Majesty. Your heart is here, and it always will be. Just like your father's."

Tears glistened at the corners of Tsar Simeon's eyes. "Yes, Sergeant Dimitrov," he said. "Maybe you're right."

LETTER TO THE READER

The first time I heard Jan Beazely begin unfolding some of the story of Boris III of Bulgaria, I had to resist the urge to shout, "Hold it a minute! This story is too incredible to be real; nobody will ever believe these amazing things really happened." And then, as I came to know more and more of the fascinating history surrounding the reign of Boris III and the heroic rescue of the Bulgarian Jews, I realized it was going to be more difficult to decide what to leave out of this novel than what to put in.

Still, because the events and places in this story are so unfamiliar, especially in the United States, it seems appropriate to supply readers with some clues about how to separate historical fact from the novelist's artifice.

During the course of my research, I became almost obsessed with Tsar Boris. Here, it seemed to me, was a man who gathered to himself nearly every heroic trait of all the fairy-tale kings: courage, conviction, kindness, intelligence, a deep love for his subjects, and even a wry sense of humor. But it also became apparent to me that Boris was no plaster saint—no unstained, storybook "good guy." He could also be petulant, harsh, vulgar, and on occasion subject to despondency and despair. Hopefully, this story captures both the light and dark of his character. Naturally, many of the thoughts and much of the dialogue attributed to Tsar Boris in this book are fictionalized accounts that accord in their essentials with the historical evidence. Other events not dealing directly with matters of state are made up from whole cloth, and their only function is to develop the character of Tsar Boris as we conceived it to be for purposes of telling this story. For example, though it is a fact that Simeon and his father enjoyed visiting the Assenov Fortress as shown in the scene in chapter 13, the scene in chapter 28 that takes place at Baldwin's Tower in Turnovo is an invention. We hope it nevertheless encourages the reader to a deeper admiration of Boris's unyielding commitment to his country's best interests as well as setting the stage for Simeon's determination to return to Bulgaria from his exile abroad.

Pavel Grouev, the king's wise and patient counselor, is a historical person.

According to his son, Stephane Groueff, and his daughter, Radka Groueva, he was famously discreet about his conversations with the king and even his own thoughts about those conversations. Still, some of the scenes between Grouev and Boris are hinted at in the historical record, and a few others are based on things Grouev was known to say or opinions he was known to hold.

The actions of Prime Minister Bogdan Filov, Interior Minister Peter Gabrovski, and Commissar for Jewish Questions Alexander Belev are largely known or guessed from public records and the surrounding historical commentary. Their motivations and thoughts are harder to document, but those portrayed in this novel seem consistent with their actions. Lily Panitza was indeed involved in a problematic love affair with Alexander Belev, which made her privy to many secrets of the commissariat. The conflict she must surely have felt between her personal feelings for Belev and her humanitarian instincts is truly one of the most remarkable and puzzling facets of this story. Clearly, her decision to leak important information to the Jewish community was one of the most heroic and tortured undertakings in this narrative. In this case, truth really is stranger than anything Jan and I could have made up.

Metropolitan Stefan is, if anything, painted in this book with muted tones. This larger-than-life crusader for justice quickly fell into disfavor with the Communist regime that took power in 1946 since he was every bit as vocal in his opposition to their excesses as he had been to those of the Fascists. He was demoted from his post as chief cleric of the Bulgarian Orthodox Church and lived out his days in semiexile outside the capital. He died in 1957. Somewhat ironically, he is buried in the churchyard in Plovdiv, next to his frequent rival during life, Plovdiv's Metropolitan Kyril. The stories of Kyril climbing the fence to be with the Jews of Plovdiv and promising to lie across the railroad tracks in front of the deportation trains are taken from historical sources. An interview with a Jewish survivor of Plovdiv brought to light the story of the priest holding the commissariat police at gunpoint, but in her telling, it was Kyril of Plovdiv, not Sofroni of Turnovo, who performed this courageous act.

Daria Richetti is the only absolutely fictional character in this novel. This may disappoint some readers who find themselves captured by the story of her journey toward personal courage, not to mention toward the waiting arms of Dobri Dimitrov. Still, she stands as an important proxy for the plight of the Jewish people and the dilemma this presented to the king: Tsar Boris, while genuinely and painfully aware of their dangerous predicament, had also to think of the fate that awaited his nation if Bulgaria became more directly involved in the war. She is named, by the way, for the lovely Daria Pandurova, the wife of Bozhin "Doc" Pandurov, our guide and fount of historical and cultural knowledge. It was Jan's idea to name our character Daria, a decision to which I assented wholeheartedly.

Dobri Dimitrov is perhaps the most interesting blend of fact and fiction in this story. The real Dobri Dimitrov can be found most Sundays in front of Alexander Nevsky Cathedral in Sofia, soliciting passersby to drop money in a dented old can he holds. Dobri then takes his collection to the church in his home village of Bailovo, where it is distributed to the remodeling efforts of other churches and monasteries. Many of the churches and monasteries of Bulgaria fell into disrepair during the Communist decades, and Dobri has dedicated himself to redressing this neglect. While in Bulgaria, I saw the church in Bailovo, newly refurbished with the aid of the money raised by this nonagenarian. This frail old man, whose principal diet consists of bread and cheese and whose bed is a board covered by a single woolen blanket, has, in effect, rebuilt the churches and monasteries of his country. Dobri was indeed a member of Tsar Boris's bodyguard, and he did await the return of Simeon to Bulgaria, holding a staff he had carved for the occasion. I was privileged to witness the reunion, after a separation of many months, between Dobri and my coauthor, Jan Beazely. To say that these two people love and admire each other is akin to saying that the Pacific Ocean has a lot of water. As far as I know, Dobri's deceased wife was neither a Jew nor a former member of the royal household, but in my mind's eye Dobri will always be young and dashing and brave.

To learn more about WaterBrook Press and view
our catalog of products, log on to our Web site:
www.waterbrookpress.com

WATERBROOK
PRESS